EINSTEIN'S TUNNEL

Other novels by S. P. Perone

The StarSight Project, iUniverse, 2002
Crisis on Flight 101, iUniverse, 2003

EINSTEIN'S TUNNEL

S. P. Perone

iUniverse, Inc.
New York Lincoln Shanghai

Einstein's Tunnel

iUniverse, Inc.

For information address:
iUniverse, Inc.
2021 Pine Lake Road, Suite 100
Lincoln, NE 68512
www.iuniverse.com

This is a work of fiction. Although references to historical characters, events, and settings are included for realism, the overall context is fictional. Technological developments central to the story are fictional, and any connection with existing products is purely coincidental.

ISBN: 0-595-32682-X (pbk)
ISBN: 0-595-66665-5 (cloth)

Printed in the United States of America

To Frank, Celia, Nick, Pearl, Vito, Mary, Martin and Marj…much loved among that Greatest Generation of Americans who persevered through peace and war to share with us their courage, wisdom and inspiration.

CONTENTS

▼

PART III. TIMELESS JOURNEY

EPILOGUE

Acknowledgements

Many thanks to family, friends and colleagues for reviewing the early work and providing invaluable feedback and encouragement. Special thanks to Levi Spade and Jim Birk for checking World War II facts, Nick Parrinello for assistance with Sicilian language segments, and Sammy Perone for provocative discussions of time travel concepts.

.

PROLOGUE

California Coast— August 13, 1944

With his eye pressed to the lenspiece, Captain Kenji Yakimoto hesitated a few moments before lowering the periscope, and admired for one last time the graceful, majestic span of the Golden Gate Bridge. Amazingly, the miniature Japanese submarine, *Kyoto*, had slipped silently past all of the American maritime safeguards. By following closely behind the noisy American destroyer that was returning to the Port of Alameda on San Francisco Bay, Yakimoto now found his tiny vessel only minutes away from cruising undetected beneath the Golden Gate Bridge and into the heart of the Bay.

Of all the Axis submarines poised at this very moment off half-a-dozen American and British seaports, his was the only miniature submarine. Of all the atomic bombs that would be detonated within the next few minutes, only that aboard the *Kyoto* was clearly meant to be part of a suicide mission. The others would be launched from altered doublewide torpedo tubes with 25-kiloton devices housed in specially designed torpedoes with unprecedented range. The Axis crews of these submarines would at least have a chance to turn and speed away before their deadly payloads detonated off the coasts of the American cities of Los Angeles, New York, and Norfolk, and the British seaports of Southampton and Liverpool.

*   *   *   *

This bold *Atomblitzkrieg* was Hitler's desperate but brilliant response to the Allied invasion that had begun on the beaches of Normandy on the sixth of June, and which was presently threatening to break the Nazis' stranglehold on Europe. Fortuitously for the Nazis, their originally misguided program to develop an atomic bomb had been vitalized by the abduction from America of the theoretical physicist, Joseph Rheingold, in July of 1939. Privy to the leading edge of thought regarding nuclear fission that had emerged in the late 1930's within the research labs of Leo Szilard and Enrico Fermi, Rheingold had been aware that the key to producing a feasible atomic bomb was to generate sizable amounts of enriched uranium, U235. More importantly, only Rheingold had postulated a scheme to chemically convert the crude uranium mixtures to volatile compounds that might be separated physically into U235 and U238 components by large-scale partitioning hardware. The German engineers had rapidly transformed this concept into a huge secret facility near Hamburg that had produced many kilos of pure U235 by early 1944.

On April 15, 1944, on the Finnmark plateau near Karasjok, Norway, the first German atomic bomb had been detonated. This 10-kiloton device produced an explosion in the early dawn light that was witnessed by a large group of elated scientists and a small group of keenly observant German military leaders. The device that was exploded ten days later—some 50 kilometers east of the first blast—was observed by many of the same scientists, but was also attended by the *Fuehrer*, Adolf Hitler himself, along with Soviet Premier Joseph Stalin, and Japanese military chief Hideki Tojo.

The Italians were no longer part of the Axis, after their surrender to the Allies in September 1943. Stalin had entered into a non-aggression pact with Japan in April of 1941, but the Russians were engaged at that very moment in a vicious battle with the Germans along the European eastern front. Nevertheless, Stalin had been persuaded by the Japanese military leader that it was urgent, prudent and safe for him to attend the Nazi demonstration of this powerful new weapon.

Stalin observed with awe as the dazzling fireball was transformed into a gigantic mushroom of dirt and debris rising thousands of feet into the still air above the northern plains of Norway, not far from the Russian port of Murmansk. In that instant the Soviet Premier realized that the balance of power had shifted unalterably in the Nazis' favor.

Although the Soviets' conflict with Germany had begun with Hitler unexpectedly opening up an eastern front in June 1941, they had succeeded in defending themselves, finally breaking the back of the German offensive at the battle of Stalingrad in February 1943. The United Nations meeting in Moscow the following October had provided groundwork for a post-war presence of the Soviet Union in Eastern Europe that had inspired a Russian offensive all along the eastern front. Kiev had been recaptured in November, and the Germans were currently retreating, with the very real prospect of a complete collapse when the Allies mounted the long-awaited invasion across the English Channel.

Unexpectedly, on that April morning in Norway, the promise of an Allied victory over Germany and establishment of an Eastern European Soviet empire suddenly appeared as unlikely as returning the energy of the enormous fireball to the minuscule array of split uranium atoms from which it had been unleashed. When Hitler later proposed that Russia join the Axis powers, Stalin hesitated and postured just long enough and skillfully enough to obtain from Germany and Japan a commitment to a substantial Soviet post-war presence on the North American continent. By negotiating a German retreat in Eastern Europe to the borders of Poland, Czechoslovakia, Hungary, and Romania, Stalin insured that Russia would reign from the Ural Mountains to the Baltic countries of Latvia and Lithuania.

At the top-secret meeting in Moscow one month later, Germany's most intrepid General, Field Marshal Erwin Rommel, had outlined Hitler's bold *Atomblitzkrieg* plan to his Russian and Japanese counterparts. Captain Yakimoto and the captains of the five other submarines that would be involved in the initial attack had attended this meeting. The plan had been simple. The German navy had been developing a torpedo capable of carrying a 25-kiloton atomic device and enough propellant to exceed a two-mile range. The goal was to detonate the device underwater within an exposed seaport. Although not nearly as destructive as an above ground detonation, a single blast could destroy the entire port and its navigation channels. The resulting tidal wave would cause enormous damage and loss of life well inland, while the radioactive debris would carry over into densely populated cities. The simultaneous attacks would occur during early morning on the American West Coast; early mid-day on the East Coast; and late afternoon in Britain.

What the original plan had not anticipated was that the Russian-German-Japanese Axis formed in April would have succeeded in launching a successful land-based counter-offensive to the D-day invasion of June 6, 1944. While Russian and Japanese forces invaded Alaska and Western Canada, Russian and German forces utilized Greenland to launch an attack on the Canadian Eastern Maritime Provinces.

The Allies had grossly underestimated the strategic impact of losing the Soviet army's support on the European eastern front. They had not anticipated the brilliant and bold flanking maneuver that would catch the Allies heavily committed both in Europe and in the South Pacific, and unable to stop the massive invasions from the North Atlantic and across the Bering Strait.

By early August, the Axis fronts on either Canadian coast had proceeded far enough inland to establish air bases from which bombers could be launched against the United States. Thus, the submarine-based *Atomblitzkrieg* plan had been expanded to include a wave of nuclear air strikes that would follow within hours as Axis bombers reached Boston, Detroit, Cleveland and Seattle, as well as London.

*   *   *   *

Because of the nature of his unique mission—one from which he had no chance of returning—Captain Yakimoto had been the only submarine commander within the first wave to whom the entire *Atomblitzkrieg* scheme had been divulged. Hideki Tojo himself had described the plan just as Yakimoto prepared to depart from Tokyo on the submarine that would transport the miniature *Kyoto* to within fifty miles of the California coast. It had not been necessary Yakimoto mused. He would have followed his orders no matter what. But Tojo had insisted that this Japanese "hero" know the magnitude of the operation in which he would give his own life.

Now, as he passed under the Golden Gate Bridge, Yakimoto reflected on his gratitude to Supreme Commander Tojo for revealing all to him. As he set the controls to proceed on a course to the south of Alcatraz Island, Yakimoto slid to the floor and squeezed under the partition separating him from the ominous egg-shaped monster that occupied most of the underbelly of the miniature submarine. The detonation scheme was simple: lifting a keyed latch and flipping a large double-poled switch would start a thirty-second timer. When the timer expired, an internal barrier would flip out of the way, allowing the two separated non-critical uranium cylinders to be blown together into one critical mass by conventional explosives. The subsequent atomic fission chain reaction would release 25 kilotons of explosive energy within microseconds—bringing down the Golden Gate and Oakland Bay Bridges, producing a blast and tidal wave that would obliterate all near-shore structures, and dumping radioactive debris over the hills of Oakland and San Francisco.

As the second hand on his wristwatch displayed thirty seconds before seven o'clock in the morning, Captain Kenji Yakimoto turned the key in the latch on the outer skin of the bomb, opened it, and quickly flipped the bipolar switch to start the detonation sequence. Sliding quickly back to the platform above, Yakimoto remained on his knees and brought his head to the ground with his hands outstretched. In the last remaining seconds of his life, Yakimoto prayed for the safety of the Emperor and his country.

Then, just before the blast vaporized his body, Kenji Yakimoto prayed that his sacrifice would not be in vain.

NEW YORK CITY—
OCTOBER 1944

Leaning out the window of her second-story bedroom, sixteen-year-old Esther Goldstein could hear the sounds of the motorized column rolling down Fort Washington Avenue, just a few blocks from her home on West 161st Street. Although some of their neighbors in this predominantly Jewish neighborhood had fled south to Mexico or across the new Soviet border into Florida, most had been unable to leave. Each day they had waited as the Nazi troops expanded their control over every corner of New York City. Today the troops had moved into Washington Heights—and Esther was frightened.

"Come, Esther," her father called from the doorway. "It is time."

Reluctantly pulling her head in through the window, the pretty redhead looked sadly at her father and asked, "Must I do this, Papa?"

"Yes, Esther. It is the only way. Now, please, hurry."

Without another word, Esther moved swiftly past her father, avoiding his grim, sad gaze, and stole quickly down the stairs.

Esther's father, Arnold, was a jeweler. He and his wife, Greta, and their only child, Esther, had escaped Germany in 1935 after Hitler had enacted the Nuremberg Laws that had systematically deprived the Jews of their rights, jobs, and place in German society. Like many other Jewish refugees to New York, they had settled in the Washington Heights section of northwest Manhattan and had begun to reconstruct their lives.

Hitler's *Atomblitzkrieg* had left its mark on New York City. Deliberately avoiding any blockage of New York Harbor, the atomic torpedo had been detonated at the Bayonne inlet. The physical damage had been extensive because of the near-shore chemical and petroleum stockpiles, but upper New York bay had remained navigable—suitable for the impending arrival of German naval vessels. The radioactive debris had been distributed primarily to the east over Lower Manhattan, Brooklyn, Queens and Long Island. Washington Heights had been spared.

Despite the shock and severity of the *Atomblitzkrieg*, President Roosevelt had promised the American people that the United States would continue fighting on the North American, European and Pacific fronts. Although he had known it was a lost cause, Roosevelt's strategy had been to resist the Axis invasion until he could obtain several guarantees. Primary among these was that American Jews and other minorities would be provided humane treatment along with all other Americans in the event of surrender to the Axis forces.

With newly acquired air bases in Canada enhancing his strategic position, Hitler had countered with a threat to send 100 bombers armed with atomic bombs over England and the Eastern United States. Only Field General Rommel, Hitler, and the technicians at the Hamburg nuclear weapons facility had known that the stockpile of atomic weapons had been virtually exhausted with the *Atomblitzkrieg* of August 13. But President Roosevelt and England's Prime Minister Winston Churchill had had no choice but to believe Hitler's threat, and negotiate with the Axis powers for a conditional surrender.

Perhaps because Russia and Japan had wanted to avoid further destruction within the United States, or perhaps because Hitler had known that his threat of further atomic attacks could not be delivered, the Axis powers had agreed to Roosevelt's conditions for surrender. Hitler had even stated publicly that he "had no quarrel with American Jews," as Roosevelt prepared for surrender to the Axis on September 1, 1944.

The week before the surrender, Roosevelt had asked that all gasoline rationing be discontinued and that petroleum and gasoline reserves be released. It was this act that had allowed many of the Goldsteins' neighbors to flee. Unfortunately, the Goldsteins did not have an automobile. Nor were they inclined to run away. Despite all the historical evidence to the contrary, they had preferred to believe that Hitler…this time…was being truthful.

But they had been wrong.

The rumors spread that the *Gestapo*, led by Heinrich Himmler himself, were moving swiftly through the neighborhoods—rounding up Jews, Blacks and other "undesirables." The *Gestapo*, Hitler's secret police organization, was ruthless and powerful. In Europe it had been responsible for the deaths of millions of Jews. Here in the United States it was reported that trains and military transport vehicles were forming a continuous procession headed north to Canadian concentration camps. Officially, the Nazi radio broadcasts had stated that "mass relocations" were underway in order to transport workers where they were needed.

Suddenly fearful, not so much for their lives but for the fate of their attractive teen-aged daughter, the Goldsteins had formulated a plan to hide her from the Nazis. Beneath their home was an earthen cellar that had once been used for winter storage of fruits and vegetables. Covered over with planks and long forgotten, the cellar was currently indistinguishable from the rest of the basement. Mr. Goldstein had stocked the cellar with food, water, canned goods and utensils, and had instructed Esther on a survival strategy. He believed that the Nazis would soon move on to other neighborhoods, allowing Esther to leave her hiding place and contact non-Jewish friends who would get her out of the country. Despite her vigorous protests, the Goldsteins had convinced Esther to follow this plan.

When it was clear that the Nazis were less than an hour away from their street, Esther had been secured in the cellar and her mother and father had returned upstairs to await the Nazis' arrival. Their story was simple: their daughter had been visiting relatives in New Jersey when the atomic bomb had detonated in August. She had been one of many who had died from direct exposure to the blast radiation. The neighbors had agreed to support this story.

The plan had been a good one, except for one thing. The Goldsteins had expected that the *Gestapo* might search the house and basement. They had planned to offer no resistance. But they hadn't expected the Nazis to know they had lied about their daughter's death.

*   *   *   *

The *Gestapo* lieutenant—tall, dark-haired, muscular and handsome—brushed the elder Goldsteins aside and strode defiantly into the center of their front room. Looking slowly around the room and down the hallway, he turned back to the Goldsteins. By this time two other troopers were holding them.

"*Wo ist das mädchen?* Where is the girl?" he asked in German. "Your daughter. We know she is here."

"No. No. She is dead," Goldstein cried. "She died during the atomic attack."

Stepping back towards the fearful husband and wife, the lieutenant lifted his gloved right hand and swept it across Goldstein's face with crushing force. Blood spurted from Goldstein's nose and trickled from the corner of his mouth as he slowly turned his head back to glare at his attacker.

"Tell me where she is now, and I will spare you and your wife any further pain," the Lieutenant decreed.

"She is dead," Goldstein insisted.

As their eyes locked, the lieutenant regarded Goldstein curiously for a few moments. Then he reached out for the wife, grabbing her by the arm, and yanking her roughly out of the grasp of the trooper holding her.

"*Frau* Goldstein, you will walk with me through the house. Please show me where your daughter is hiding."

As he dragged the woman off toward the stairway to the upper floor, neither Goldstein nor his wife said a word or offered any resistance.

After half-an-hour of searching and beatings with no results, the troopers dragged their captives down to the basement. As the torture continued, the Goldsteins' screams echoed off the concrete walls and pierced their daughter's heart. Although the troopers would not have found her hiding place, Esther could not help but cry out for the Nazis to stop. Within minutes she had been extracted and delivered to the lieutenant.

After Esther had been brought to him in the basement, the lieutenant nodded to the other two troopers to take the elder Goldsteins away. Within seconds he was alone with the young girl.

"And why were you hiding from us, my dear?" he asked in English. "You need not be afraid."

Recoiling from the menacing uniformed figure, Esther noticed that he was smiling, but his eyes were cold as ice. He was young, and cruelly handsome, but his eyes were dark and soulless. Despite his quiet demeanor and smile, Esther cringed with fear.

Noticing her apprehension, the lieutenant said, "Let me help you up the stairs. Everything will be all right."

"No. No it won't," Esther cried suddenly. "Where are my parents? Where are you taking us?"

Ignoring her questions, the lieutenant asked, "Your name is Esther, isn't it?"

Realizing the lieutenant would ignore her pleas for information, Esther lowered her eyes and murmured, "Yes."

"Well, Esther, you must pack some things in a suitcase and come with us. You will be sent to a comfortable place in Canada."

"What about my parents?" she asked. "Will they be treated well?"

"Of course," he replied. "Now, let's get your things so we can leave." Grabbing Esther's arm firmly, the lieutenant guided her up the basement stairs.

As they entered the first floor, Esther noticed that the rooms were empty and the front door partly open. Looking back sharply at her captor she asked, "Where are they?"

"They are outside in a transport truck. Everyone is waiting for you. Let's move quickly."

Turning back slowly, Esther moved toward the stairway to her room. Glancing around as she started up the stairs, she said, "Please wait here. I will be just a few minutes."

"Of course, my dear," the lieutenant smiled, as he stopped at the foot of the stairs and watched her climb to the top.

As Esther reached the top of the stairs she glanced behind quickly to see the lieutenant still standing at the foot. Quickly, she darted into her bedroom and ran to the window to look for the truck and her parents. Her eyes opened wide as she searched in vain for the transport truck. Greeting her instead was the vision of a solitary military sedan with a uniformed driver seated behind the wheel, smoking a cigarette.

Whirling around she realized too late that the lieutenant had sneaked up the stairs and was right behind her. As she opened her mouth to scream she felt his hard cold hand covering her mouth and realized with a start that she could make no sound. With blinding speed the lieutenant threw her down on the bed and growled, "Make a sound and you are dead. Do you understand?"

As she nodded her head, the lieutenant removed his hand from her mouth and quickly ripped her blouse to shreds. Lifting up her legs he pulled her skirt over her knees and whipped it away into the corner. Without hesitation he grabbed her loose-fitting cotton panties and slipped them roughly down her legs and tossed them into the corner with her skirt. Standing up and leering down at her with those cold black eyes, the lieutenant quickly unbuckled his belt and slipped down his pants and undershorts. As Esther watched this undressing with horror she gasped as she anticipated the savage attack that was to come. As the lieutenant reached over and pulled her roughly toward the edge of the bed, she clenched her teeth and glared at her captor.

Throughout the prolonged ordeal Esther refused to scream, even when the pain was unbearable. Instead she burned into her memory the vision of this obscenely handsome young face.

Someday she would find that face again.

BERLIN—OCTOBER 1944

Werner Heisenberg, world-renowned theoretical physicist and head of the German atomic bomb project since 1939, was ushered into the *Fuehrer's* office by the young army lieutenant. As they passed through one of the tall hand-carved oak double-doors that extended three-quarters of the way to the thirty-foot ceiling of the outer hall, the lieutenant halted, clicked heels on the marble floor, and extended his right arm stiffly.

"*Mein Fuehrer!*" he exclaimed.

To the lieutenant's side, Heisenberg simply bowed his head and repeated the same salutation. Seated behind an enormous ornate wooden desk in the center of a vast vaulted chamber with ornately draped tall windows, Adolph Hitler acknowledged them with a grunt and an abbreviated flick of his right arm. The world's most powerful man was dwarfed by the enormous red-white-and-black swastika flag that draped the towering wall behind him.

Clicking his heels once again and bowing his head slightly, the young lieutenant whirled around stiffly and strutted back out of the office, closing the heavy door behind.

"*Guten Morgen, Werner!*" the *Fuehrer* exclaimed, rising from his chair and circling around the desk to extend a hand to the visiting scientist.

"Good morning to you sir," Heisenberg replied in German as he gripped the limp hand extended in greeting. He had no idea why the *Fuehrer* wanted to see him. And he was concerned.

He was even more concerned for the scientist who had remained outside Hitler's office, awaiting a later audience.

As Hitler motioned Heisenberg to one of two armchairs in front of the desk, he pulled a silver cigarette case from the side pocket of his military jacket and offered one to his guest. Taking one for himself, and placing it in his mouth, he allowed Heisenberg to pull out a lighter and ignite first Hitler's and then his own cigarette. The two sat down in the armchairs and took a puff of their cigarettes before speaking.

In a casual tone the *Fuehrer* asked, "You have been briefed about the Russian situation, Werner?"

"Yes, *mein Fuehrer*. I understand there are some problems."

"Hah! Those Russian *pigs*! Already that Bolshevik bastard Stalin ignores our agreements. Yesterday they draw a line in Asia to stop the Japanese. Then they protect the American refugees in Mexico. Today they move into Florida. Tomorrow it will be Poland. We have to stop these rotten *ungeziefers*, these deceitful vermin, now!"

"Absolutely, *mein Fuehrer*," Heisenberg agreed, unsure of himself.

Speaking to no one in particular, Hitler growled into space, "If I had had any other choice, I would not have asked that filthy *schwein* to join us."

Heisenberg understood Hitler's frustration. It had been a stroke of genius to put aside his intense hatred for the Soviets and turn them against the Allies. But, with supreme irony, the Soviets had used the past six months to replenish their army, build their navy and air force, and devise a strategy to challenge Germany and Japan for global domination.

Turning calmly to Heisenberg, and changing his tone, the *Fuehrer* asked, "Now, Werner, what is the status of our bomb production?"

Heisenberg knew that the "bomb" Hitler referred to was the atomic weapon his program had developed and that had recently brought the Allies to their knees.

"The status has not changed, sir."

"Only two remain?"

"We must focus on new designs, *mein Fuehrer*. These uranium weapons are—"

"Stop, Werner! Why can't we build more weapons with the old design?"

"The Russians and Japanese have abducted the top American scientists from Los Alamos, Berkeley, and elsewhere. They will have their own atomic weapons soon. We must keep ahead of them."

"*Dummkopf!* We should be bombing Moscow and Tokyo *now*, before they develop their own weapons."

"They have the plutonium produced by the American reactors in New Mexico and Washington. They will be able to produce a weapon ten or a hundred times more powerful than ours…soon. We can not afford to put off our own development."

"When they're digging out from the rubble of our atomic attacks they'll think better of defying us," the *Fuehrer* spat.

"It's not possible, *mein Fuehrer*," Heisenberg insisted, preparing himself for Hitler's wrath. "We used all of our enriched uranium for the *atomblitzkrieg*. It will be many months before we can build up a stockpile like we had."

A vicious scowl appeared on Hitler's face as he threw his cigarette at the large silver pedestal of an ashtray next to his chair and shouted, *"Verdammt!"* He stood up abruptly and began to pace silently for a while behind his desk, in front of the large swastika flag.

Finally, he returned to his seat next to Heisenberg and sat calmly, ostensibly resigned to Heisenberg's troubling facts.

"Werner, you have done a wonderful job," the *Fuehrer* said. "Your atomic bomb has won the war for us. You are a hero of the *Reich*."

Then, after apparently reflecting for a few moments the *Fuehrer* said, "Do as you wish, Werner. Develop the new weapons."

"This is not my wish, *mein Fuehrer*, it is the reality. And I am not a hero, Heisenberg insisted. "We owe everything to the young man who is outside the door, Joseph Rheingold."

With a fury that took Heisenberg's breath away, Hitler whirled around and smashed his fist on the arm of Heisenberg's chair. Jerking his face within inches of Heisenberg's, with straight black hair flying and sweat bristling around his small black moustache, he shouted, "First you tell me there are no more bombs, and now you pass credit to undeserving garbage in your laboratories! I don't want to hear this tripe again! Do you understand?"

Without speaking, nearly paralyzed by the unexpected outburst from the *Fuehrer*, who was usually so composed in private conferences, Heisenberg backed away instinctively and indicated his acquiescence with a slight nod.

"Good," Hitler breathed as he stood up, straightening his hair. "Don't ever give false credit to this *Rheingold* again. Understood?"

Hesitantly, Heisenberg nodded once more.

"And no one must ever know that a *Jew* worked on the atom bomb project," Hitler commanded. "This can not go into the history books, Werner. Do you understand?"

"Of course, *mein Fuehrer*," Heisenberg replied.

"And how many have worked with this Rheingold? What are their names?"

"He worked only with me, *mein Fuehrer*," Heisenberg replied too quickly, sensing danger.

"Humph," Hitler responded with a grunt, gazing sideways at his guest. But he didn't pursue the issue.

Without another word, Hitler walked back behind his desk and sat down in the high-backed black leather swivel chair. He reached for the silver-plated telephone receiver cradled on similarly plated u-hooks extending above a large ornate ebony box. Placing one end of the receiver to his ear he barked into the other end, commanding his lieutenant to bring in the other guest.

＊　　　＊　　　＊　　　＊

Along with two uniformed *Gestapo* officers, Joseph Rheingold had been waiting apprehensively in the vast two-thousand-square-foot marble hall that was the *Fuehrer's* outer office, recalling the first and only other time he had been there. It had been in July 1939. He had flown from America across the Atlantic—accompanied by a Nazi agent—in what would be an exchange that would guarantee his family's safe conduct from Germany. He knew what the Nazis wanted from him.

Rheingold's journey to Berlin had been filled with conflicted emotions: guilt for betraying his American benefactors and anxious relief that he had the power to spare his Jewish parents and siblings from Nazi persecution. Added to this conflict had been the disturbing encounters he had had with two other passengers, Daniel McShane and Diana Sutton, on the overnight Clipper flight from New York. Each of them had undergone strange and inexplicable changes during the flight. To this day their words had haunted him, as they suddenly began speaking about mystifying future events and addressing each other with strange names. He had never forgotten those names: *Andrea* and *Tony*.

"*Herr* Rheingold!" came the harsh call from the lieutenant standing at the doorway to Hitler's office, abruptly jolting Rheingold from his reverie.

Rheingold stood up, tall and proud, and walked determinedly toward the lieutenant. He had worn his baggy dark gray woolen suit, a white shirt and narrow black tie. With his rimless spectacles, frazzled long black hair, high forehead, and large overstuffed briefcase, Rheingold looked like the dedicated scientist that he was. But—despite the shaggy appearance—his lean, rugged physique, bright hazel eyes, dark complexion, and sharp intellect projected an air of authority and confidence. He was ready to do battle with the *Fuehrer*.

*   *   *   *

The *Fuehrer*, from his seated position behind the large desk, glared darkly at Heisenberg as the great scientist re-introduced Rheingold. As he listened to the words of praise, Hitler's patience expired with a loud slap of his hand on the desk as he barked, *"Halt den Mund!* Shut up!"

With a jerk Hitler stood up, sending his chair flying backwards. He walked around the side of his desk to stand over the seated Heisenberg and Rheingold. "Enough, Werner!" he growled. "I don't want to hear any more. *You* are the hero of this war—not this *Jew!"* The *Fuehrer's* last words were accompanied by a scornful jerk of his head toward the stunned Rheingold seated to Heisenberg's side.

Although shocked by Hitler's rage, Rheingold was not dismayed by the *Fuehrer's* insistence that Heisenberg take credit for developing the atomic bomb. Rheingold wanted nothing more to do with it and certainly wanted none of the dubious fame. But Hitler's hateful contempt for him as *the Jew* who had so successfully served the Reich set a sinister tone.

Although the two scientists would have towered over Hitler had they been standing, the *Fuehrer* had shrewdly chosen to confront them while they were both seated. He walked behind them and came around to face Rheingold, glaring down at him with an intensity that would wither most men. But Rheingold returned the gaze without shrinking.

"Do you think, *Herr* Rheingold, that *you* are the 'hero' of the Reich?" Hitler asked disdainfully. "Are you here to collect your reward?"

"I am here because you requested me…" Rheingold responded calmly, adding a testy, "…*mein Fuehrer.*"

With his eyes narrowing and growing darker, Hitler responded by pausing, drawing up to his full height and placing his hands on his hips, while glaring silently down his nose at Rheingold. In his greenish-brown military garb, with the flared tapered trousers tucked into the high black leather boots, Hitler projected a menacing image.

Rheingold gathered his courage and took this moment to speak further. "I am here also to find out about my family. I have not heard from them. I have only the word of the foreign office that they are safely in Mexico. I have upheld my end of the bargain, sir, and I come here to demand proof that you have upheld yours."

Without flinching, Hitler replied darkly, "You want information from me, *Herr* Rheingold? Well, perhaps you can provide me with some information first."

"And what is that?" Rheingold asked.

"Professor Heisenberg has told me of those that worked with you on this atomic bomb project. I need to know their contributions," Hitler commanded.

After glancing briefly over at Heisenberg, who avoided his eyes, Rheingold replied, "Professor Heisenberg knows that I have worked with *no one but him.*"

Smiling thinly, Hitler glanced at Heisenberg briefly before turning and strutting back to the other side of his desk. Taking his seat once again, the *Fuehrer* gazed steadily at Rheingold and said curtly, "You are excused, *Herr* Rheingold. The guards will take you back to your quarters."

Recalling the two *Gestapo* officers standing just outside Hitler's door, Rheingold winced at the tone of the *Fuehrer's* statement. But he was not ready to leave. "What about my family, sir?" he asked. "Will you put me in contact with them now?"

"Of course," Hitler smirked. "The lieutenant has that information for you on his desk. You will be in touch with them today."

While Rheingold and Heisenberg exchanged uneasy glances, Hitler picked up his phone once more and barked instructions to his lieutenant in the outer hall. Within seconds, the two *Gestapo* officers entered the room and strode quickly to Rheingold's chair. Their firm, silent gaze told Rheingold to rise and exit with them. Turning his head briefly before being led out the door, his eyes connected with Heisenberg's. Rheingold was not comforted by the agonizing expression that was returned.

*   *   *   *

Alone once again with Hitler, Heisenberg asked, "His family?"

"Gone," Hitler replied.

Shaking his head, and looking at the floor, Heisenberg muttered, "I didn't know."

Then, lifting his eyes to engage the *Fuehrer* again, Heisenberg asked, "And what will happen to Joseph, *mein Fuehrer?*"

Hitler's icy stare in response caused Heisenberg to wince, and he began to protest. *"Mein Fuehrer—"* he began.

"Stop, Werner!" Hitler commanded. "It is over. Be thankful that you isolated Rheingold from the rest of your staff."

Then he added emphatically, "I don't want this *Jew's* name ever mentioned again. Do you understand? *Werner Heisenberg* will go down in history as the *father of the atomic bomb.*"

Shaking his head slowly, Heisenberg could think of no words in response. He knew that this twisted tyrant, fueled by frustrations vented today, was even now extending the Nazis' genocidal acts to the Americas.

Nothing could express the pain that Heisenberg felt at that moment. A pain that would follow him—regardless of the hollow tributes—all the days of his life.

At that moment, Heisenberg wished fervently that Joseph Rheingold had never reached Berlin in 1939. And, wistfully, he tried to imagine how different the world might have been...

MADISON—NOVEMBER 1944

Throughout the war Professor Garrison Fuller's Memory Research Lab had been the most lavishly funded facility in the Psychology Department. This had been particularly remarkable because practically no one at the University of Wisconsin had known what kind of research was being conducted in the lab.

Fuller's research program had been hammered out at a secret high-level conference held in Washington in the fall of 1939 at the request of Princeton Professor and Nobel Laureate, Albert Einstein. The Department of the Army had sponsored it. The University of Wisconsin had been chosen as the host for the research, and Fuller had been designated as the Principal Investigator. Einstein was a special consultant and visited regularly. The program had become known as the "Einstein Project."

Among individuals participating in the project was Daniel McShane. Daniel had been neither a student nor a professor. Rather, he had been the prized subject of many of the experiments. McShane had been only seventeen when he had introduced himself to Einstein in September 1939—just after the outbreak of the Second World War. He had had an incredible story to tell—a story so bizarre that he had been instructed to reveal it only to Professor Einstein. And it was Einstein who had perceived that Daniel's experience might just provide the key to defeating the Nazi juggernaut that was at that time threatening to quickly overrun all of Europe.

Only someone of Professor Einstein's stature could have persuaded the government to support the project or could have imposed upon a distinguished young professor like Garrison Fuller to undertake the work. Some considered the project pure madness; others simply laughed. It did not help matters that Einstein's own theory of relativity seemed to preclude the feasibility of the project goals.

Nevertheless, Einstein had persisted. And now, with the war over, most would assume that time had run out and the project had failed.

But they would be wrong.

*   *   *   *

Today, as a freezing rain fell outside his second floor office in the Psychology Building, Garrison Fuller was meeting secretly with the two remaining members of the *Einstein Project* team. Stark testimony to the dramatic change in their circumstances after the *Atomblitzkrieg* of August 1944, and the unconditional surrender of the Allies on September 1, was displayed on one wall of Garrison Fuller's office. It was a map of the former United States—where the old state boundaries had been covered up with blank paper on which the new Axis territories had been sketched. A typed legend was tacked beneath the map. Wisconsin was clearly in German territory.

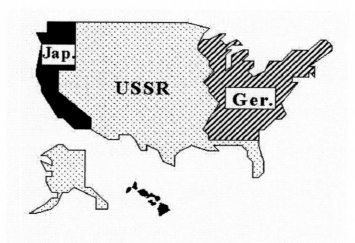

Post-War Occupation of the Former United States, Alaska and Hawaii.
Ger., Germany; Jap., Japan; USSR, Union of Soviet Socialist Republics.

The first of many tumultuous changes that the *Einstein Project* had endured immediately after the end of the war was the sudden disappearance of Professor Einstein. It was rumored that he, along with numerous other Jewish scientists, had sought refuge in neutral Mexico.

The university community had witnessed the loss of most Jewish, Black and Hispanic members at war's end. Along with similar refugees from all of the North American Nazi territory, they had fled to escape the expected ethnic cleansing that had occurred in Europe. Many had fled to Mexico, but larger numbers had fled to Russian and Japanese territories of the former United States. At least for the moment, these refugees were being tolerated by the other Axis powers.

Within the past few days, the university had been overtaken by the Nazi occupation. All administrative positions had been replaced with middle-ranking Nazi officers. All scientific research projects had been cancelled; and students' admissions had come under the purview of the local military commander.

Conceived as a secret program, obviously without Nazi sanction or awareness, Professor Fuller's *Einstein Project* had already lost all of its participants—except the two on which the project had been founded: Daniel McShane and Diana Sutton. Fuller's secret meeting with them today had been brief, dramatic and decisive.

The youthful Fuller, an accomplished full professor in his mid-thirties, and these two vibrant youths in their early twenties, had decided together to defy the Nazi occupation. They would continue the *Einstein Project* as an underground activity. Fuller had managed to purge all university records of their activities during the war, and henceforth all of their experiments would be conducted clandestinely.

Despite the obvious long odds against success, Daniel, Diana, and Fuller were determined to carry on. Living with the threat of Nazi discovery and subsequent swift justice, these three clung steadfastly to Einstein's promise…that their eventual success would salvage the Allied cause.

As contradictory as it sounded, they believed—as had Einstein—that Daniel and Diana would be able to accomplish what their yet unborn descendants had *told* them was possible…*to travel back in time and alter the pivotal events that had led to the Axis victory.*

CHICAGO—OCTOBER 1985

Much had transpired in the three decades since the few remaining participants in the underground *Einstein Project* had sadly concluded that it would be impossible to continue. Diana had returned to her family in New York, while Daniel had moved to Chicago where his older brother, Paddy, and his family had settled during the war. Daniel took on the new family name of "Shane" that Paddy had assumed, and found work with Paddy as an airplane mechanic at the former "Midway" airport, now known formally as *Mittelamerikanische Flughafen*. Although the airport was administered by a pseudo-military staff, where the top positions were held by former Nazi *Luftwaffe* officers, other administrative positions were held by qualified Americans who had joined the National Socialist (Nazi) Party.

And so it was throughout the German-occupied American territories—otherwise known as *Deutsches Reich Amerikanische*, the *DRA*. After the ruthless purge of untold millions of "undesirables" during the late '40's, an uneasy accommodation evolved between the Nazi occupation and the remaining Americans. Rank-and-file workers in all walks of life were the same people who had filled those positions before the war, but top managers were Nazis with ties to the German homeland. American Nazis prospered with the new order, but soon discovered that they were accepted socially neither by the German Nazi ruling minority nor by their former friends, families, or colleagues.

Members of the National Socialist Party filled all law enforcement, military and government offices. The military and high-level law enforcement included only German Nazis, while local law enforcement employed American Nazis for all but the highest positions.

*　　　*　　　*　　　*

Despite the oppressive sociopolitical world in which they lived, much of the Shane clan in Chicago was gathering today to celebrate Tony Shane's twenty-first birthday. Tony's maternal grandmother, as well as his uncle Paddy and aunt Peggy would be there to join his father, Daniel, and his mother, Carmela, for one of Carmela's delicious manicotti and chicken dinners. Paddy's two daughters—Tony's two female cousins—much older than Tony and married to high-ranking American Nazis engaged in the Chicago administrative bureaucracy, would not be welcome, and had not been invited.

An hour before the anticipated arrival of the family guests, Daniel had invited Tony into his den and closed the door. What he had to discuss with Tony had never been revealed to his wife Carmela.

In his early sixties, with thick salt and pepper hair, Daniel was trim and fit. His son was a duplicate of a younger Daniel—tall, with black hair, blue eyes and fair complexion. He was a handsome, fun-loving lad.

"Tony, take a seat," Daniel said after closing the door of the den behind them, "I have something to give you."

"Jeez, Dad, you don't have to—" Tony began to protest.

"It's not what you think, Son," Daniel interrupted. "What I have for you is not a gift. You may not even want it. But it belongs to you, and it's time you received it."

As a puzzled look appeared on Tony's face, Daniel pulled a key from his pocket and unlocked the lower right drawer of his desk. He eased the drawer completely out and placed it on the floor. Then, reaching into the vacancy, he found a narrow gap in the floorboard and used a penknife to lift a rectangular piece of the floor. He pulled out a small, sturdy metal chest and set it on the desk-top. After whirling the combination dial back and forth a few times, the lid of the metal box lifted and Daniel reached in to pull out a single sealed white envelope.

The vintage Pan American Airways logo was clearly visible on the letter's front. It had been stamped by the flight Purser—*July 17, 1939, Foynes, Ireland.*

As Daniel slid the envelope face down across the top of the desk, Tony could read the mysterious statement scrawled across the sealed flap:

For Daniel's son on his 21ˢᵗ birthday—IF Germany wins the war.
Otherwise DESTROY UNOPENED.

"What's this, Dad?" Tony asked as he picked up the envelope, feeling the weight of possibly several sheets of paper inside.

"Tony, this is one of three letters entrusted to me back in 1939, when I was only seventeen. One was for me. One was for Professor Einstein. And one was for my son...for *you*."

"Professor Einstein? Do you mean *Albert* Einstein? The famous scientist?"

"That's right."

"You knew him?"

"No. Not until I tried to deliver his letter. But then I met him at his home in New Jersey."

"Who gave you the letters, Dad? What was in them?" Tony asked.

"I found the letters in my suitcase when I arrived in Ireland for your grandfather's funeral in 1939. I only know what was in the letter addressed to me, Tony."

"How did they get in your suitcase?"

"Apparently, I put them there myself."

"*Apparently?* Don't you know?"

"It's a long story, Tony. Let me tell you about it before you open your letter—"

*　　　*　　　*　　　*

For half-an-hour, Daniel related the story of his bizarre experience in July 1939 when his older brother Paddy had sent him to Ireland on a Pan American Clipper overnight transatlantic flight out of New York to attend their father's funeral. Daniel had arrived in Ireland and been with his sisters and other family for most of a day when, after stumbling and bumping his head, he realized that his last memory was of dinner at Paddy's home the evening before departing on the Pan Am flight, over two days earlier!

It was only after finding and reading the letter addressed to him in his suitcase that Daniel had realized that his memory loss had not been caused by the minor bump on the head. The letter claimed that Daniel had spent the entire flight under the telepathic influence of his yet unborn son from some far distant future time.

Daniel's letter had also revealed that a fellow passenger on the Pan Am flight, Jewish physicist Joseph Rheingold, had been abducted by the Nazis through the efforts of a second telepathic time traveler. Rheingold would be forced to share scientific secrets leading to the development of atomic weapons that would win the war for the Axis powers.

Daniel went on to explain how he had been directed to provide the second letter to Einstein, who had never revealed its contents but had been inspired to act. Before Daniel had left Einstein's study, the esteemed scientist had persuaded Daniel's older brother, Paddy, that Daniel would be needed for a research experiment that could affect the outcome of the war in Europe. By the end of October, Daniel was at the University of Wisconsin, working with scientists engaged in what they called the *Einstein Project*—dedicated to discovering the secrets of telepathic time travel.

Daniel went on to tell Tony about Diana Sutton, who had shown up at the university in June 1942. Although Daniel had no recollection, Diana claimed she had met him on that same fateful Clipper flight in 1939—and that she had also discovered a mysterious letter produced by the telepathic influence of her granddaughter from some distant future time. The letter had instructed her to make contact with Einstein, who had directed her to Fuller's secret project in Wisconsin.

Daniel finished his story by describing how the work had evolved into an underground project after the war, and finally disbanded in the 1950's. By then he and Diana had moved separately to New York and Chicago and moved in different directions with their personal lives.

$$* \qquad * \qquad * \qquad *$$

Tony had remained silent throughout his father's tale. When Daniel had finished, he said simply, "Dad, that's the most incredible story I've ever heard! You've got to be putting me on, Right?"

"It's true, Tony…every word," Daniel responded. Then, handing his son a letter opener, he added, "Perhaps it might help to look at your letter."

With his father looking on, Tony Shane began to read the letter that had been written to him some four-and-a-half decades earlier.

To Daniel's Son,

Hopefully your father will have explained how this letter came into his possession and why you should be confident that this is a genuine message from the future.

The fact that you are reading this letter means that the history of the world as I knew it has changed dramatically. In my lifetime, the United States and its Allies had won the Second World War. In your lifetime, they have not. It is impossible to predict what other historical changes may have occurred.

History of the totalitarian regimes up to 1939 suggests that when they win the war the conquered peoples will not be treated well. If you are willing to help rid the world of what I believe must be an oppressive and barbaric regime, there are several important pieces of information that you will need:

—

—

—

This letter is signed in your father's name, so that you will know it was written by him—but please know that this message is from his son, from yourself, and from a different time line that should have been your destiny.

Daniel

*   *   *   *

After reading and re-reading the seven-page handwritten letter without a word, Tony Shane slowly lowered the letter to his lap and raised his eyes to look into the patiently anxious face of his father. After several moments, Tony said, "I don't know what to say, Dad. This is overwhelming."

"I know, Tony. We can talk about it later if you want."

"No, Dad. Let's talk about it now."

"Can you tell me what was in the letter, Son?" Daniel inquired.

"I don't know if I can, Dad. It's pretty technical, and I'm a little confused. Why didn't you ever say anything about this?"

"Do you believe that the letter is authentic?" Daniel asked.

After a few moments, during which he gazed blankly into the space above his father's head, Tony lowered his eyes and answered tentatively, "Yeah...maybe...I don't know. It's just too fantastic."

Then he added more passionately, "It says I should go back in time and fix it so that the Axis powers lose the war! My God...just saying something like that out loud sounds crazy!"

"It's *not* crazy, Tony. Professor Einstein believed it was possible."

"But, did you ever accomplish anything in the *Einstein Project*?"

"Obviously, we didn't succeed. But we did demonstrate some pretty amazing things."

"Why did you stop?"

"It became too dangerous to continue. We had to break it up, and Diana and I moved away. But, whenever Fuller could arrange it, we would return to Madison. We got bogus travel permits to cross state borders, and got away with it a few times, but we finally had to give up."

"How successful were your experiments?"

"We did it all, Tony. We had telepathic ability. We could communicate emotions and simple commands."

"What about the time travel thing?"

"I believe we did that too. That was our last experiment."

"Did Professor Einstein help to design these experiments?"

"At first, yes. But, after the war ended, we never saw him again. Then, in 1949, Professor Fuller received a secret message. Most of the letter was unintelligible, but we learned that Einstein was safely in Mexico. He said he would send us his latest theoretical work, and that we should be looking at the new technology of digital computers."

"What did he send you?"

"We don't know. We never heard from him again. The only thing I have is a copy of his cryptic 1949 letter."

"Well, how did you demonstrate telepathic time travel?"

"We used Einstein's strategy: memorize computational formulas, compute space-time coordinates on the fly, and mentally generate four-dimensional images of ourselves."

"That sounds impossible!"

"Our mathematicians created simple integer formulas. And the research psychologists developed visualization methods with neural feedback. It wasn't easy, but we demonstrated that it worked."

"What did you do?"

"Fuller designed experiments where the subject arranged a set of markers in a pattern. Then, a few minutes later, the subject was randomly given a blind instruction to communicate telepathically with himself at a minute earlier and rearrange the markers."

"So, what happened?"

"Hard to explain, but the bottom line is that the test subject—Diana or I— *never* executed an action when a later instruction was *not* given. And, 75% of the time, we executed the action *before* the later instruction was given."

"That *is* amazing."

"But we had no idea how to make the leap to time jumps of years or decades. Add to that the risk of being discovered, and you can see why we decided to end the studies."

"What happened to Professor Fuller?"

"He never joined the Nazi party, so he never got promotions like he should have. But, they allowed him to stay on the faculty. He's an Emeritus Professor now, in his seventies, and continues to lecture at the university. He never did any more on the *Einstein Project*, and has apparently survived the Nazi inquisitions."

Because his father remained silent for a few seconds, Tony asked, "Have you told me everything, Dad?"

Hesitating and glancing away briefly, Daniel replied, "There is one more important thing, Tony. But we can talk about it later."

After peering into his father's unrevealing eyes for a second, Tony asked, "Were you disappointed to abandon the project, Dad?"

"Of course we were disappointed—but we believed that someday the *Einstein Project would* be completed," Daniel replied, as he gazed expectantly at his son.

"You mean that *I* should finish the job?" Tony asked with a startled expression. "That's crazy! What could I do?"

"What about the letter, Tony?" Daniel asked tentatively. "Perhaps we just need to pick up the threads."

"I can't do this, Dad! I've got a ticket to graduate school. And I want to teach at the university someday."

Daniel looked at his son and sighed. "I wish you well in school, Son. But you know that university positions are only open to Nazis these days."

"So?" Tony remarked defiantly.

Visibly stunned, Daniel leaned forward and snapped, "Don't even think about it, Tony!"

For a long time Tony simply sat and looked at his father, whose face was flushed, his jaw thrust forward. Finally, he said, "Dad, I'm sorry. I'm sorry for what you and Uncle Paddy and so many others have lost since the war. But I've learned to live with the system, and I think I can be happy with my life."

After sitting immobile for several seconds, glaring at his son, his jaw muscles flexing, Daniel suddenly snapped forward and slapped his hand down hard on the desk. "Don't you realize that what we have is given at the whim of the Nazis. We could lose everything—just like that! Our jobs, our homes, our freedom—with no explanation."

"What do you want me to do, Dad," Tony pleaded, "give up my life for some cockamamie theory that we can change the world? And, even if we could, how do we know we would make it better? We would sure as hell change our own lives. I don't want any part of it!"

Without responding to his son, Daniel calmly removed the metal box from his desktop and returned it to its hiding place. He replaced and locked the lower drawer, and returned the key to his pocket. He then stood up slowly and looked into Tony's eyes. Finally, he said, "What do you want from life, Tony? What will make you happy?"

Without hesitating, Tony replied, "A career at the university."

"Then that's exactly what you should work for, Son," Daniel said with a sigh.

Walking slowly around the desk, Daniel put out his arms. Seeing his father moving toward him, Tony stood up and joined his father in a long, warm embrace.

After several moments, Daniel pulled away. With his arms still on his son's shoulders, he asked, "Do you know the secret to *success*, Tony?"

"I don't know, Dad," he responded with a smile. "But I'll bet you're gonna tell me."

With a slow nod, Daniel said, "A very wise man once told me, 'The secret to success is a modest formula. Simply do what you know you should be doing. An honest man who does this will be successful.'"

"But how do you define 'success,' Dad?"

"Success is not material riches, Tony. Success is measured by self-respect and the respect of your fellow human beings."

"So, that's it? 'Do what you know you should be doing?' Sounds too simple."

"It is Tony. But, trust me, it is the best advice I'll ever give you."

As he stood there at arm's length, regarding his father in a new way, Tony Shane wondered how his twenty-first birthday had become such a solemn affair. In his pocket was a letter from the future asking him to perform a task that would change the world—and end his own; his father was telling him that this was expected of him; and then there was this ambiguous advice that should guide the rest of his life. It was too much!

"Dad," he laughed, "where did you get that advice, from a fortune cookie?"

"No, Tony. I got that advice from *Albert Einstein.*"

As he watched his son's jaw drop, Daniel's eyes crinkled around the edges and his mouth curled into a loving smile. He grabbed his son by the shoulder and whirled him around so that they could leave his den and their heavy discussion behind. It was time to enjoy the family gathering, the delicious Italian dinner, and a celebration of his son's birthday and good fortune.

*   *   *   *

As Daniel and Tony walked into the front room of the house, Tony's mother Carmela cried out from the kitchen, "It's about time you two came out of hiding. Get in here Daniel and help me with the salad!"

As his father shuffled off to the kitchen, and Tony moved toward an easy chair in the front room, the front door bell rang.

"I'll get it," Tony yelled, as he rushed to the door, looking forward to seeing his uncle Paddy, aunt Peggy, and his grandmother. As he opened the door, his smile of greeting turned to a look of surprise. Standing before him were two uniformed secret police officers. The garb of the *Gestapo* enforcers had not changed much in the past fifty years: the shiny black boots, the smart gray-green uniforms with short jackets and flared pants tucked into the boots; the trim cap with leather brim; the shiny leather strap around the waist with holster and Luger sitting ominously on one hip.

"*Ist das die residenz von Herr Daniel Shane?* Is this the home of Daniel Shane?" the taller blonde officer asked in German.

"Wh...Why?" Tony stammered. "What's the matter?"

"Is *Herr* Shane at home now?" the same officer demanded in English, as he shoved Tony out of the way and pushed his way into the hallway. The other, husky brown-haired officer didn't move, but watched Tony for any threatening action. Then he walked through the door also, and shut it behind him.

The taller officer strode into the front room and looked around. Tony watched dumbfounded as the second officer stood next to him, holding his arm. Hearing voices from the kitchen, the officer in the front room quickly stepped through the swinging door and accosted a shocked Daniel and Carmela.

Although he couldn't see the confrontation in the kitchen, Tony could hear the muffled sounds of shouting and a brief struggle. Suddenly, after no more than 10 or 15 seconds, the swinging door burst open and he was shocked to see his father shoved roughly through the doorway, his hands cuffed behind him. The sounds of his mother's protests stung his ears, while the stoic look on his father's face told him that somehow this shocking event had not been unanticipated.

Quickly guiding Daniel through the front room to the hall and doorway where Tony remained frozen in the grip of the shorter officer, the tall, muscular officer seemed oblivious to the pleas and the tugging of Tony's mother. With one hand he brushed her away and sent her reeling back onto the front room floor. In an instant, Tony's father was out the door and being shoved towards an unmarked sedan parked at the street curb. Tony's protests fell on deaf ears as the shorter officer held him firmly in place. But neither officer had observed the brief exchange of glances between father and son, nor had they seen Tony's father mouth the words, *The key...your mother.*

As soon as Tony's father had been secured in the sedan, and the *Gestapo* officer was in the driver's seat with the engine running, the other officer shoved Tony and sent him sprawling on to the floor of the front room. With a harsh command for Tony and his mother to stay put, the officer ran out, slamming the door behind him.

Tony sprang quickly to his feet and ran to the front door. He opened it just in time to see the black sedan speeding away, tires squealing, around the near corner. After standing on the front stoop for a few moments, staring blankly at the empty space where he had last seen the sedan, he turned and returned quickly to his mother who was sitting, stunned, on the edge of an easy chair.

"Mom, are you OK?" he asked anxiously.

"I'm OK, Tony. I'm OK," she cried through her tears, while rubbing the knees that had banged and scraped along the floor. "But what just happened? Why did they take your father?"

"I don't know, Mom. I have no idea. We have to talk to Uncle Paddy. He'll know what to do."

But Tony knew it was hopeless.

People simply did not return when the *Gestapo* took them away.

As Tony replayed the frightening event that had just transpired in their home, he reflected on how calm his father had appeared. Had he expected this arrest? What had he done? Then he remembered the words his father had mouthed to him at the doorway.

"Mom, Dad said something as they took him away. Something about you and a key? Do you know?"

With a blank look on her face, his mother reached down into the wide front pocket of her apron, and pulled out a small key. She looked at it as if she had never seen it before.

"Your father slipped something in my apron while we were struggling with that horrible man in the kitchen. This must be it. Do you know what this is all about, Tony?" she asked, as the tears continued streaming down her cheeks.

Tony reached over and gently removed the key from his mother's hand. *Yes,* he thought, *I know exactly what this is all about.*

There would be no more thoughts of school or university positions. Tony Shane could see clearly now where his life must lead.

PART I.
DAWN OF THE 21ST CENTURY

CHAPTER 1

▼

THE UNEXPECTED

Karl Henson guided his Volkswagen sedan south, moving with the flow of traffic along Lake Shore Drive just north of Chicago. As he had done for the past ten years—each weekday morning since taking the downtown job in 1991—he listened skeptically to the morning news on *der Staatfunk,* the Nazi state radio station. He believed little of the national and economic news, but relied on traffic and weather reports.

Despite the beautiful, crisp September morning and the dark blue waves of Lake Michigan delicately scalloping the sandy beaches to his left, Henson's drive this morning was not relaxed. A spat with his wife of twenty years and a rude encounter with his teen-age daughter had delayed his departure from their modest Glencoe home. He was running late and feeling frustrated.

Reaching the city's edge he could see clearly the upper floors of the 95-story *Landeszentralbank* building, where he worked, on the northern edge of the Downtown Loop. Glancing briefly at the dashboard clock, Henson realized that he would be late for the nine o'clock meeting with his investments task group. At best, he thought, he would be entering the lower level parking area of the building by nine.

Easing toward the left lane, hoping to pass a slow-moving diesel-smoking delivery truck, Henson noticed for the first time in his rear-view mirror the sleek black sedan—with a tiny red-white-and black swastika flag flying from the antenna. Instinctively, he pulled up and swerved gently back behind the smoking truck. Even though he had finally, reluctantly, joined the Nazi party, he still could not breathe easily whenever the *Gestapo* was near. Better, however, the marked cars, he thought. At least you could see them coming. The unmarked *Gestapo* vehicles were the most feared. If one showed up at the door, someone in that household was going to disappear.

As the black sedan moved to the left and quickly sped past him, Henson carefully maintained a steady gaze straight ahead, blankly regarding the billowing smoke ahead. Once the sedan was well down the road, Henson slowly released his breath and glanced quickly to the side and rear to be sure no more Nazi vehicles were around. Then he executed the briefly delayed passing maneuver to get away from the obnoxious truck in his path.

It was ridiculous, he told himself as he felt the tension ease, to have such anxiety. He was a Nazi now. He had been appointed Vice President for Foreign Investments and had held that position for a year. Ironically, he reflected with a sigh, he had clearly been the most qualified for that job for many years before that.

Yes, he was a Nazi—in name, at least, if not in spirit. But he felt his stomach tighten at the thought of submitting once again to a periodic loyalty test administered by the *Gestapo*. Although his inherent political ambivalence had allowed him to pass previous tests, he feared for the day when the cold hard hand of the secret police touched someone in his family, and he might no longer suppress the revulsion he felt for the German occupation.

As Henson turned west off Lake Shore Drive toward the *Landeszentralbank* building several blocks away, he glanced once more at his dashboard to see that it was already nine o'clock. He looked up, gazing over the nearby large rooftop billboard at his distant towering workplace. The billboard was one of many similar structures he had passed during the thirty-mile morning drive. Each contained large color portraits of *Reichskanzler* Heinrich Einsbach and *Vizekanzler* Helmut Freitag on either side of a large red-black-and white swastika symbol. Not that he needed it, but these billboards, strategically placed throughout Chicago—indeed throughout the *DRA*—provided subtle daily reinforcement of oppressive Nazi rule. The *Reichskanzler* in Berlin and the *Vizekanzler* in Washington, together, controlled the daily lives of all Americans in this totalitarian *Obrigkeitstaat* of the twenty-first century.

Although most Americans had learned to avoid conflict with their rulers, such behavior involved forfeiting free speech and other outward signs of disenchantment. One did not dare to protest anything, even the frequent arbitrary changes, from taxes to textbooks, in daily life. To protest was traitorous they had been told, and the *Gestapo* knew how to handle traitors.

As Henson crept to within three blocks of the *Landeszentralbank* building, he reminded himself that not all Americans were capitulating to the Nazis. He thought then of the YLA, the Yankee Liberation Army, that continued to fight for American freedom. Composed mostly of expatriate Americans whose families had fled Nazi genocide in the 1940's, or had been forced out more recently by the *Gestapo's* murderous suppression of political dissent, these valiant men and women continued to disrupt Nazi rule. Although their impact had been minor, and the state news media did not report the many YLA attacks, Henson had followed their activities through the underground newspapers.

As a smile grew across his face, mentally recalling the YLA's recent disruption of the banking computers throughout the *DRA*, Henson was suddenly rocked by a violent vertical shock wave that abruptly kicked his Volkswagen several feet up into the air. With his hands flying off the steering wheel and his body thrust upwards against the loosely buckled shoulder restraint, Henson found himself crashing back to the pavement. While the car bounced wildly, Henson grabbed the steering wheel and struggled for control. Before the bouncing ceased, Henson was struck by a second shock. This time the shock wave traveled horizontally and picked up the car, shoved it backwards, and caused it to begin spinning around.

Realizing that he had lost control of his vehicle, Henson gripped the steering wheel tightly and tried to avoid being tossed around or ejected. His instincts focused on survival, but his mind asked what had happened. He realized just then that the *Landeszentralbank* building appeared shrouded by a vertical column of dust. As the vehicle finally stopped spinning and came to rest, Henson noticed that the vertical column was really a broad cylinder of smoke and debris, rising as if in slow motion into the suddenly dark gray sky above. When Henson was able to look up he saw that the smoke and debris were billowing out horizontally at the upper altitudes. He realized with a start that he was observing what appeared to be a classic atomic mushroom cloud!

Surely it wasn't a nuclear blast, he thought frantically. At this close range there would have to be more damage from the blast…and radiation! But, he thought further, the radiation effects might not be felt immediately. With a sickening lurch in his stomach Henson remembered that radiation sickness might be delayed for hours or days for someone removed from ground zero.

It was then that he noticed damage to buildings closest to the blast. Corners of the closest buildings were blown away, and he could see some of the occupants clinging to exposed beams while others were falling in slow motion to the ground. As a wave of nausea washed over him, Henson looked away and tried to calm himself. *Whatever this is,* he thought, *there are people dying out there. I've got to help.*

Abandoning his car, and running now towards the affected buildings, Henson could see that the *Landeszentralbank* building had literally disappeared. The large billowing cloud overhead cast a dark shadow over the cavernous streets, and Henson could not help but imagine that the enormous mushroom head must contain the vaporized remnants of the 95-story skyscraper and all its occupants. *Incredible!* he thought. *Are we under attack? By whom?*

Turning his attention again to the street ahead, Henson picked his way carefully around deep crevices that had opened up, each belching fire and smoke. About a block from the vacancy that had been the *Landeszentralbank* building he reached the first of many victims lying in the street. The young lady, who had apparently been dressed that morning in a dark gray business suit, was totally nude from the waist up. Severe burns covered the backside of her upper body. Blood was flowing freely from a gash on the head, and one leg had sustained a compound fracture. As Henson knelt by her side, she reached for his hand and turned to look into his eyes. "What happened?" she mumbled while clinging tightly to Henson's hand.

"There was an explosion," Henson replied. "You've been injured, but you'll be OK. Help will be here soon."

Henson had no idea whether the young lady would survive, but he would make her comfortable. After applying his handkerchief to the head wound, he removed his jacket and covered her gently, not knowing if it was the proper thing to do medically. The burns did not seem wet, and he remembered vaguely that victims in shock should be kept warm.

As he mumbled words of comfort to the stricken young lady, Henson looked around for other victims that needed help. He directed other stranded drivers arriving on the scene toward several other victims nearby.

Shortly, Henson realized that numerous occupants of the damaged buildings were screaming for help with injured colleagues who could not escape the perilous structures. Believing that the buildings were in imminent danger of collapsing, the calls for help had become frantic.

Henson called a passerby over to take his place comforting the young lady at his feet and, without further hesitation, took off running through the smoke and debris toward one of the nearby damaged buildings. He heard the sirens of approaching emergency vehicles, but feared they would be too late for many, and too few for all.

As he approached the wide entrance of the building adjacent to the blast that had destroyed the *Landeszentralbank* building, he paused and looked up to determine what direction he would take once inside. What greeted him was a shock. A large portion of the outer skin of the building had disengaged from the twentieth floor and was rapidly descending toward the street where Henson stood. Too late he realized that he could not reach the entrance or back away fast enough to avoid the falling concrete slabs. Raising his arms in a futile attempt to ward off the fatal blow, Henson had just enough time to realize that his wife and daughter would forever remember that he had died on *September 11, 2001*.

CHAPTER 2

▼

EXPATRIATES

Sprawled on his bunk in the cramped crew's quarters of the shrimp boat *Nawlins Sue*, Tony Shane swayed gently as the craft chugged slowly along the Gulf coast about 25 miles west of New Orleans. Shane closed his eyes and tried not to envision the chaos and carnage unleashed all across the *DRA*. The terrorist events that the Yankee Liberation Army had been planning for the past two years were unfolding with horrific and deadly impact at this very moment in New York, Washington, Chicago, and Atlanta. Four dirty 5-kiloton nuclear warheads, which had been moved into place undetected through the underground sewer systems connected to the tallest commercial buildings in each city, would detonate virtually simultaneously with devastating force.

These four landmark structures would be brought down in a spectacular display of YLA determination to topple the entire Nazi regime. Filled with thousands of unsuspecting workers, these mammoth structures would explode spectacularly into a tragedy of immense proportion—one that could not be ignored by the Nazi government as they had the previous feeble YLA attacks. Moreover, it would mark the beginning of a sustained terrorist offensive designed to force the German *Reichskanzler* in Berlin, Imperial Chancellor Heinrich Einsbach, to begin negotiations with the American liberation movement.

Shane squeezed his eyes closed more tightly and clenched his teeth, trying to erase the mental vision of the horrible death and destruction that he and his YLA associates would be causing that day. He had lobbied long and hard to limit their targets to Nazi government installations, but he had been over-ruled by their tru-culent leader, Nathan Carothers. Salomé and Shane had voted for the govern-ment targets; Harry and Carothers had voted for the civilian. As the acknowledged leader of the American rebel organization, Carothers had broken the tie with his vote.

Shane could not help but wonder whether the vote would have gone differ-ently if not for the legacy of barbaric Nazi persecution within the *DRA* of Jews, Blacks, and Hispanics. Harry Churchill and Nathan Carothers were black. Shane had heard the stories of how their parents' families had suffered in the 1940's at the hands of ruthless genocidal Nazi storm troopers. Their parents had narrowly escaped. Harry's had been only children themselves. But, like thousands of other refugees, the parents had infused their offspring with the unquenchable thirst for liberation and retribution. That spirit had become the heart and soul of the YLA movement.

But, on reflection, Shane thought better of Carothers' decision. It had not been personal; it had been strategic. Carothers was determined to assault the civil-ian population and force their voices to join those of the YLA in demanding American independence. The fear of a continuing onslaught of merciless terrorist attacks should accomplish that goal, Carothers believed.

Shane could not argue with Carothers' logic; but he didn't have the stomach for it. He had argued for government targets. Failing that, he had tried to per-suade Carothers that the target date should have been September 1—the anniver-sary of the end of the Second World War. Every year since the war had ended in 1944, Germans all over the world had celebrated on the first day of September. It was a national holiday in the *DRA*, and there would have been very few occu-pants in the towering office buildings that would be brought down. The YLA could have made its point, while sparing civilian lives.

Carothers had argued that the terrorist alert level would be high on September 1, threatening the success of the mission. For this reason he had opted for a target date ten days later—*September 11*—when he believed the terrorist alert level would have subsided to normal. In that respect, Carothers had been correct.

*   *   *   *

Refusing to join his three colleagues huddled in the adjoining communica-tions cabin, awaiting the first reports of the terrorist attacks, Shane remained sprawled on his bunk. Shoving out of his mind the macabre thoughts of the nuclear blasts and their expected tragic aftermath, Shane pondered absently on how he had reached this point in his life.

It had begun in 1985, when his father had been brutally abducted by the *Gestapo* right before his eyes. His uncle Paddy had arrived minutes later, and had persuaded Tony to get out of town as quickly as possible. He urged him to head for the nearest Soviet border, a couple hundred miles east at the Mississippi River. Paddy was certain that his long-time friend from the bootlegging days of the early 1930's, Rico Mironi, would have the connections needed to get Tony across the border.

Within the hour, Tony had been shuttled to a secluded meeting place on the city's south side where Rico Mironi would meet with him personally. Prior to departing his home, however, Tony had used the key his father had left him to retrieve the locked heavy metal box.

Mironi felt it would be better to move Tony south to the Soviet port of New Orleans. Mironi had good connections within the *DRA* railway system and would be able to smuggle Tony safely aboard the *City of New Orleans* express that completed the 1000-mile trek from Chicago to the Crescent City. Tony would have no problem crossing the Soviet border so long as he remained hidden in the crew's quarters. Mironi had used this method to transport numerous fugitives, and he had every border guard along the way on his payroll.

When he had arrived in New Orleans, Tony had been met by a tall, athletic young black by the name of Harry Churchill. The son of refugees from Philadelphia who had fled the black purges of the 40's, Harry had been born and raised in New Orleans. He was part of a network of refugees working with *DRA* citizens like Rico Mironi in a common cause for American liberation.

Tony was stunned to realize the magnitude of the vast YLA underground movement underway within the *DRA*. With the help of Black, Jewish and Hispanic refugees behind the Soviet border, Mironi and his associates—former organized crime figures before and during the war—had been importing guns and other supplies into the *DRA*. So far, the Soviets had looked the other way. Any subversive activities within the *DRA* could only work in their favor.

When he had first reached New Orleans, Tony could think only of freeing his father from the Nazi prison. Keeping in contact with his uncle in Chicago had been facilitated by Mironi's pipeline to New Orleans. But, not even Rico Mironi could arrange for Tony to see or contact his father. His father was probably dead. And, without explanation, Tony had become a wanted man.

It had not been difficult for Harry Churchill to recruit Tony Shane into the Yankee Liberation Army. Before long Shane had been making runs to Mexican ports, picking up guns and other supplies that would be transported to Chicago for distribution to the growing numbers of underground rebels.

At first the rebel activities within the *DRA* had been limited to troop ambushes and assassinations. The rebels would strike with only a handful of freedom fighters, and then quickly scatter into the cover of numerous safe houses networked throughout the *DRA*. Many years of careful organization had gone into preparations for these nuisance attacks; and they had been carried out, at first, without consequence to the rebel organization.

By the 1990's, however, the Nazi secret police had ferreted out informers, and embedded spies within the American underground movement. In December of 1997, a lightning nationwide strike by the *Gestapo* had resulted in massive arrests and executions. Many who had escaped that strike had done so by slipping over the Soviet border. The Soviets had applied token resistance to the influx of the American rebels, and most had been able to disappear through established underground connections. Many had found their way to New Orleans, which was the YLA nerve center for all operations outside of the *DRA*. Most of this influx, however, was shuttled into secluded campsites in the rugged hills of the Mexican Sierra Madre mountains west of Monterrey. Transportation of American rebels by ground through eastern Texas, or by boat through the Gulf of Mexico, attracted very little interference from the Soviet army or navy that controlled both of these routes.

By the turn of the century, many things had changed from the time when Shane had first joined the rebels. Tony's father had either been executed or had passed away in prison; his mother had died of a broken heart. His aunt and uncle were still alive in Chicago, but were in their nineties. Rico Mironi had passed away, but his pivotal role within the *DRA* had been taken over competently by his grandson, Vito Mironi. Harry Churchill and Shane, along with a former New Orleans call girl by the name of Salomé, had risen to positions of authority within the YLA, second only to their charismatic leader, Nathan Carothers.

Carothers, a tall powerfully built black man in his early 50's, had been recruited as a young man for the local New Orleans police force. The Soviets had wisely placed local law enforcement in the hands of the Americans who understood the complex social and cultural mix of New Orleans. Carothers had risen quickly to the rank of detective. During the late 1970's, however, he had been recruited secretly into the YLA organization. For the next two decades, Carothers had continued his successful career within the New Orleans police force, while secretly rising to the top leadership role in the YLA. No longer with the New Orleans police now, Carothers retained many important connections.

Carothers had recruited Salomé to the rebel cause after meeting her during a routine French Quarter murder investigation. Salomé had been a witness to an early morning knifing of a visiting German army officer outside one of the Bourbon Street bars. Because New Orleans was a strategic military outpost, German and Japanese military officers visited the city frequently on official Axis business.

On this particular evening, the German officer had visited an after-hours jazz club alone, but in uniform. When he had left the jazz club around 2 am and proceeded across the street to a noisy strip joint and propositioned one of the female dancers, a flurry of taunts and insults had been his response. When the German officer had slapped the insolent dancer, sending her sprawling and bleeding on to the floor, the bar had become suddenly and strangely quiet. But no one had dared confront the officer.

It was only after he had stormed out the door and proceeded around the corner toward his hotel on Dauphine Street that the officer had been accosted. Out of the side street shadows, it was reported, had come three dark figures who quickly knifed the officer to death and left him lying on the stone walkway with a dark pool of blood flowing into the ancient gutters of the French Quarter.

Salomé had been the only witness, but she had not been able to give any more than vague descriptions of the three shadowy figures that had run away. Salomé had used her mobile phone to call the police, and had remained with the body until they arrived. Strangely, no others had gathered around. Carothers had found only the dead officer, and the solitary figure of Salomé standing over him.

Perhaps it was the fact that Salomé was the only bar patron to have walked out and observe the officer's murder. Perhaps it was the fact that Salomé's firm six-foot frame suggested a hidden strength that even Carothers would be hesitant to test. Perhaps it was the icy cold look in her eyes as she described the vicious murder of the German officer. But, more likely, it was the fact that Carothers' trained eye could tell from the knife wounds that there had been only one attacker. And that had persuaded him that night to invite Salomé to join the YLA cause.

Harry's recruitment had been another matter. Harry's natural athletic ability had attracted the attention of the Soviets who were always looking to bolster their position in international track and field competition. It was Harry's good fortune that there were no Russian athletes that could match his skill and competitiveness in the high jump. So delighted were the Soviets to add Harry to their team that they were willing to provide him with what he wanted most—a university education. And this is what brought him ultimately to Carothers' attention.

With his degree, Harry had obtained a high school teaching position. But his tendency to stray from the Soviet version of American history had been reported to the Russian Governor in New Orleans. The local police had been contacted, and Carothers had been dispatched to issue a stern warning. The Governor never knew that he had been responsible for a prized YLA recruit.

Tony had provided an obvious recruiting opportunity when he had arrived in New Orleans as a fugitive in 1985. Harry had been his first contact, and their friendship had blossomed immediately. Recognizing Tony's rage at the Nazi incarceration of his father, Harry brought him to Carothers. Without hesitation, Tony had joined the YLA.

The *Gestapo* purge of the rebels in 1997 had forced Carothers to make a reluctant and risky change in strategy. Whereas the rebel strategy before had been to amass a large armed underground to support a guerrilla-type insurrection, now, with the guerrilla forces seriously diminished, Carothers turned toward a terrorist strategy. Shane was unhappy with this change, but understood the logic.

For the past two years, they had slowly increased the number and intensity of terrorist attacks within the *DRA*. The most common attacks involved bombings of government buildings, transportation hubs, and bridges. The hijacking of a handful of commercial aircraft had been orchestrated in horribly unsuccessful attempts to free imprisoned rebels. Perhaps their most successful attacks had been conducted by the high-tech associates attached to Tony Shane's division. They had used computer hacking skills to disrupt telephone communications, banking operations, and military computer systems. Even grander schemes were currently on the drawing boards.

But Carothers had become impatient. He wanted to deliver a single, crushing blow that would provide a bold message that could not be ignored. After months of deliberation, the September event had been agreed on. None of Carothers' lieutenants knew how he had somehow negotiated the purchase of ten obsolete nuclear warheads from the Chinese. The warheads had been among hundreds replaced in tactical medium-range missiles. They had been marked for disassembly and recycling of critical materials. But ten of the warheads had been smuggled out of China aboard a tramp steamer headed for the Mexican port of Mazatlan. From there they had found their way to New Orleans and then to the four *DRA* cities where they were at this moment about to detonate.

*   *   *   *

The cabin door banged open as Harry shouted, "Hey, Tony, you gotta come and listen to this! They went off! It's a done deal!"

Raising his head off the pillow and propping himself on one elbow, Shane stared at his friend and said, "You think this is something to celebrate, Harry?"

"Christ, Tony, get over it. It's not personal. This is war, man."

After taking a deep breath, and letting it out slowly, Tony responded, "Yeah, sure, I know, Harry. This is a huge step. Just don't expect me to celebrate. I can't see anything but those poor bastards going down…not even knowing what hit them, or why."

Suppressing his excitement and pasting a somber expression on his face, Harry walked over to the bunk, sat down, and put his hand on Tony's shoulder. "Listen, old buddy, I don't like it either. We just gotta keep the big picture in mind. Freedom doesn't come easy. There's gonna be a price to pay."

"I know, Harry. I understand. Just give me some space right now, OK?"

Standing up, and looking down at Shane, Harry paused a moment and then said, "Sure, Tony." Then he turned and shuffled slowly back to the cabin door. As he started to walk through the open door, he turned his head back and said, "How about let's have a drink when we get back to port, Tony? OK?"

After staring curiously at his friend for a moment, Tony replied, "Yeah. I'd like that, Harry."

CHAPTER 3

▼

CHANGING OF THE GUARD

It was late evening in Washington. The frightful nightmare of September 11, 2001 had unfolded across the *DRA*. But the full meaning of the day's horrible events was not yet understood—certainly not by the uninformed public. And not by those who had witnessed each of the simultaneous massive terrorist attacks at multiple North American sites. Even the leaders of the country were at a loss to explain what had happened. But tonight they were gathered together anxiously within the White House, the seat of power in the Nazi *DRA*.

In the high-ceilinged, brightly-lighted *Lagesitzungszimmer*, the Situation Room, deep underneath the Pennsylvania Avenue landmark, Field Marshal Heinz Koefler simmered darkly, in silence, as he and the others around the large conference table listened to Helmut Freitag, the shell-shocked *DRA Vizekanzler*, speaking with *der Reichskanzler*, the Imperial Chancellor in Berlin. Framed by the huge red, white and black swastika flag that hung from the ceiling behind him, Freitag stood and talked down to the speaker phone. Two tall blonde *Gestapo* officers remained rigid and silent on either side of the swastika flag as the *Vizekanzler* hesitantly addressed the speakerphone in a vain and deeply-flawed attempt to explain the breakdown in security that had allowed the devastating terrorist attacks.

Koefler had warned them, many times, that this could happen. He had pushed hard for a preemptive strike at the heart of the rebel strongholds in Mexico and the Soviet North American territories. Freitag had scoffed at the idea.

"They are like ants at a picnic. A nuisance—nothing more," he had said. "A bombing here, a kidnapping there—a nuisance! Ignore them!"

And Koefler had been unable to argue with the logic. After nearly six decades of occupation, most of the native North Americans within the German-, Japanese- and Soviet-held territories had become resigned to a new way of life. A couple of generations removed from those who had fought valiantly, but vainly, to save the world from the barbaric fascist powers that had raped and pillaged their way through Europe and Asia, Americans below the age of sixty had never experienced *liberty and justice for all*. They had no rights other than those granted by the state. Justice was arbitrary and swift. Americans' allegiance was to rulers in foreign lands.

It had not always been so. For over two decades following the end of the Second World War, underground resistance movements sprang up in various North American territories. These were squashed quickly by overwhelming and cruel military strength. Captured rebels were executed publicly. As were many collaborators—and many more innocents unjustly accused of collaboration.

But, with the decline of insurgency, and the eventual turnover among rulers of the Axis powers, a new age of enlightened government emerged. The autocratic tyranny remained, but Americans who declared loyalty to the foreign regimes that occupied their country were granted certain rights and privileges. Opportunities for the better jobs and higher education were provided. Those who were unwilling to join forces with their occupiers might still hold jobs and be provided basic social services, but they were little more than well-tended slaves to the economic system.

Koefler understood that most North Americans had reached an uneasy accommodation with their foreign rulers. In exchange for a modestly secure existence—and despite the continued lack of personal rights or the threat of severe, arbitrary justice—they abandoned their resistance. As long as they kept a low profile, life was tolerable.

But Koefler had appeared to be the only one recognizing that the threat was not from Americans living within the occupied territories—and that the threat was unique to the German Confederation. The real threat, Koefler had believed, was from the hundreds of thousands of expatriate Americans that had not forgotten that they or their ancestors had been purged from the German-occupied North American territories by a fiercely racist regime. This regime had annihilated untold millions of Jews, Blacks, Hispanics and other "undesirables" unable to seek refuge in Mexico or other territories.

Now, as *Vizekanzler* Freitag completed his fragmented babbling to the *Reichskanzler*, a foreboding silence fell over the room. All eyes were on the speakerphone before Freitag, awaiting anxiously the *Reichskanzler's* response.

As the familiar voice from the speakerphone pierced the silence, Freitag and the others in the room were shocked by the first few firmly spoken words. That is, all were shocked but Field Marshall Koefler. Heinz Koefler had prepared for this moment.

With an almost imperceptible nod toward the swastika behind Freitag, Koefler first locked eyes with one of the *Gestapo* officers, then shifted his gaze briefly to the *Vizekanzler* before connecting once again with the cold blue eyes of the rigid figure. Just as the *Reichskanzler* began to utter the words, "*Vizekanzler Freitag, du bist in Haft,* you're under arrest," the two *Gestapo* guards sprang from their positions and grabbed Freitag from either side. Before the full meaning of the *Reichskanzler's* words had registered with Freitag, he was being dragged briskly toward the nearby side exit. In front of the shocked gazes of all but Koefler, Freitag was whisked through the exit door before he could begin to find words of protest. His muted cries could be heard just as the exit door closed behind two new *Gestapo* officers entering the room, taking up once more the positions on either side of the swastika flag.

*   *   *   *

When the *Reichskanzler* had completed his brief but stern verbal dispatch from Berlin and signed off, the newly appointed *Vizekanzler*, Heinz Koefler, took up his position at the head of the conference table. The stunned members of the previous *Vizekanzler's* national security team nervously awaited his announcements.

Unexpectedly among the group gathered in the Situation Room this evening was *Gestapo* Colonel Manfred Weber from the Western *Gestapo* Headquarters in Chicago. Weber had been one of the few that had shared Koefler's views regarding the terrorist threat from the YLA. Included among the YLA expatriates was the object of Weber's obsession: Tony Shane. Since his disappearance in 1985, when Shane's father Daniel had been thrust in prison for collaborating with that traitorous professor, Garrison Fuller, Weber had pursued Shane. Convinced that Shane had taken up his father's previous mission, and that this mysterious project—attributed to the famous Albert Einstein himself—posed incomparable danger to the Nazi state, Weber had abandoned all other responsibilities. He had focused only on finding Shane and uncovering the true purpose of the *Einstein Project*.

Because of his prescient awareness of YLA activities, Weber had been selected by Koefler to take the lead position in pursuing the upcoming war on the terrorists. Immediately after confirming YLA responsibility for the terrorist nuclear attacks that day, Koefler had ordered Weber flown by military transport to the sprawling Adolph Hitler Airport southwest of Washington so that he could attend the meeting with the security team.

Manfred Weber reflected on the extraordinary change in his circumstances that had occurred this day. Koefler's first official act as *Vizekanzler* would be to promote Weber to the position of Deputy Chief of the Counter-terrorism branch. He would be given broad authority, funding, and resources to track down those responsible for the September 11 attacks. Public execution authority would be reinstated for the *Gestapo*. Although Weber would operate out of the Chicago Western Headquarters, all *Gestapo* resources throughout the German Confederation would be at his disposal.

For the past sixteen of his twenty-five year career, Weber had been regarded as a "lost cause." His solitary obsession with finding Tony Shane and uncovering the *Einstein Project* had isolated him from the mainstream of *Gestapo* activities— the pursuit and punishment of political malcontents and underground activists. Except for his military acquaintance Koefler, none of the Nazi establishment had regarded Weber's concerns seriously. To them, the *Einstein Project* was a fairy tale and the capture of Tony Shane was far less important than that of a thousand other political misfits within the *DRA*.

But now Weber would be vindicated. Shane was most assuredly one of the key members of the YLA responsible for the 9/11 attacks. Now he could track him down…with the assistance of numerous agents.

With the *Gestapo's* unique authority for swift justice and unrestrained torture, Weber would shortly carve out the heart and soul of the YLA and discover the true purpose of the *Einstein Project*.

CHAPTER 4

▼

BEST OF INTENTIONS

"So, you thinking about leaving us, Tony?" Harry asked, when the cocktail waitress had left them alone. Picking up one of the two tall draft beers deposited on the stressed mahogany table, Harry took a long sip and put it back down without hearing any response from his friend. Tucked away in a secluded corner of the Lafitte Lounge off the lobby of New Orleans' St. Charles Hotel, the tall, good-looking black man leaned forward as if trying to pull the words from the shorter, dark-haired white man who had yet to touch his beer.

"What makes you think I want out, Harry?" Tony Shane responded, finally reaching for his beer.

"Look, Tony, anybody can see you're not happy. I gotta tell ya that Carothers is concerned."

"What? He's got a problem with me, Harry?" Shane protested.

"No, No, Tony. That's not it. He's just worried about you."

"Worried! Carothers doesn't 'worry' about people, Harry. He gets rid of them. You know what I mean?"

"Yeah. I know what you mean. But this is different. Carothers can't afford to lose you, *amigo*."

"What are you talking about? I'm no less expendable than Carter or Rosie…and I haven't seen them around lately."

"Christ, Tony, do I have to spell it out for you? You're *untouchable*. You're our connection to the Mironi family inside the *DRA*."

"That wouldn't stop Carothers."

"Come on, he always says you hold the 'key to our future.' He doesn't talk about me like that?"

"That's got nothing to do with Mironi, Harry."

"So? What's he thinking...that you've got *the* plan for the future?"

"Come on, Harry. If Nathan thinks I know the way to go, he sure as hell has a peculiar way of showing it. Look at what we've become these past few years. We're goddam terrorists now, Harry! Savage, cowardly terrorists! Do you know how many innocent people we killed yesterday, Harry? We—"

"Shut up, Tony," Harry commanded in a hushed growl as he leaned over and placed his head close to Shane's. "This isn't the time or place."

Staring intently into Shane's steel blue eyes, Harry slowly relaxed back in his chair as Shane glared silently back.

After continuing to regard Shane with a stern gaze for a few moments, Harry reached for his beer and took a long sip. Replacing it on the table, he looked around carefully to reassure himself that the only others in this secluded room off the main lounge were the two bodyguards that had accompanied them. Manuel Rodriguez was seated next to the large archway to the main bar area, while Johnny Washington was sitting at a table next to the rear exit door.

Leaning forward so they could not be overheard, Harry said, "Look, Tony. This is the deal. We had no choice. The *Gestapo* shut us down in the *DRA* four years ago. What we're doing now gets us the most bang for the buck."

"It's not going to work, Harry," Shane said.

"Why not?"

"Because terrorism never does, not by itself. You need a rebellion that takes on the enemy directly, forces them to engage you militarily. This is especially true with a totalitarian regime like the *DRA*. They don't even have a free press! For Christ's sake, Harry, how are the people going to know what's going on?"

"We got the news yesterday, didn't we?"

"Sure, from our own people with sat-phones. What news do you think most people inside the *DRA* got? It'll take days before the underground newspapers spread the word."

"So, what do you want us to do, Tony?"

"It's the 'key' that Carothers mentioned. He already knows the plan we should follow."

"If it's that clear, why aren't we doing it? What is this plan you're talking about?"

"You don't understand what's involved, Harry. If you did, you would know why Carothers is reluctant."

"Maybe it's time you explained it to me, Tony. Let me decide for myself."

Shane gazed curiously at Harry for a moment. Then, leaning forward, he asked, "How much are you willing to sacrifice to do the 'right thing,' Harry? Your life? Your loved ones? Your friends? Perhaps even an entire race?"

"Whoa, buddy. Hold on there. Are we both drinking the same stuff? What the hell are you talking about?"

"What if I told you we could chop that corrupt Nazi regime off at the knees? Do the same for all the Axis powers? Turn back the clock to the Second World War, and make sure that the allies won that war?"

"I'd say, *go for it.* What the hell are we waiting for?"

"You're not thinking it through, Harry. If we could do that, you and I wouldn't be here talking. We might not even have been born. Are you ready to accept that?"

"Tony, you're not making sense. I *know* what the Nazis did to my people. The Jews and others were carted off to death camps in Canada. But the Blacks were savagely executed wherever they found them. You think I wouldn't change that if I could?"

"Exactly, Harry. That's exactly what I mean. It's the right thing to do. But, it would mean giving up everything we know. Husbands, wives, lovers, friends, whole countries would disappear and be replaced by a whole new world populated by different people. It's a powerful thing this *key* that I hold, Harry. Carothers is understandably reluctant to send us down that path. In fact, I'm not so sure myself."

"Wait a minute, Tony. Up 'til now I've been thinking we're talking *hypothetical.* Are you saying you can *really* do something like this? Change history? That's ridiculous!"

"No, Harry. It's not. It's already been done."

"How's that?"

"The Allies really did win World War II, Harry. Somebody…some misguided soul…was able to go back in time afterwards and make a simple change that tilted the balance towards the Axis. A whole new time line evolved with the Axis winning the war. That is the time line that we are experiencing right now. But there was an alternative time line…a much happier one…where the Allies won the war."

"How the hell do you know that?"

"I was there when it happened."

"What? What the hell are you smoking, Tony?"

"No. It's true, Harry. I was there…well, not me, but my *alter ego*. Myself in the alternate time line. I have a letter to prove it."

Sitting back in his chair, and regarding Shane with a long curious gaze, Harry finally asked, "I'm sure there's got to be a lot more to this story, Tony. But, so far, it sounds like a fairy tale. How much of this have you told Carothers?"

"All of it."

"All of it? And he believes you?"

"Yes. He does, Harry. That's why he's afraid to follow through."

"All right, Tony. What's the rest of the story? Maybe you can scare the hell out of me too?"

*   *   *   *

After listening in awe for half-an-hour as Shane related his strange tale, Harry said, "So, assuming I'm buying all this, Tony, where do we go from here?"

"I'll tell you what we should do, Harry…not that Carothers is going to let us. But, first, let's get some refills on these beers. My throat is pretty dry."

"Yeah. Wonder what happened to the waitress? She hasn't been back for half-an-hour." Then, twisting around in his chair, Harry called back to Manuel, "Hey, Manny. Could you stick your nose into the bar and ask that gal to bring us a couple more beers?"

Turning back to Shane, Harry said, "OK, Tony. What's the plan?"

"Well, first of all, we need to—"

A loud clattering that sounded like glasses breaking on the floor of the bar disrupted their conversation. Harry and Shane whipped around to look toward the archway where Manuel had disappeared. Suddenly, three muscular young white men dressed in black leather boots, tight black slacks, and black tee shirts burst into the room. In their hands were stubby automatic rifles that were easily recognizable as German-made assault weapons. Shane and Harry instantly recognized their attackers as the notorious "Black Shirts"—two generations removed from, but just as cruel and sadistic as, their Nazi "Brown Shirt" Storm Trooper predecessors of the 1930's and '40's.

As Johnny Washington sprang to his feet, his .45 automatic in hand, he was cut down with a vicious burst from the first intruder into the room. The other two trained their weapons on Harry and Tony, shouting at them, first in German, then in English, to get down on the floor with their hands out in front of them.

"*Herunterkommen auf dem boden! Hände Hoche!* Get down on the floor! Hands out!"

Within seconds the intruders had handcuffed both Harry and Shane, dragged them to their feet, and shoved them toward the back door. Before they reached the door, it burst open, revealing two additional black-garbed armed men. Behind them, sitting in the back alley with engine running and side door open, was a long black van. Roughly shoving their captives ahead of them, the three intruders quickly exited through the back door and headed for the van.

Just as first Tony and then Harry were shoved into the van's back seats, a harsh squealing of tires signaled the arrival of two olive drab armored personnel carriers with the instantly recognized markings of the Soviet army. As the two vehicles rolled to a screeching halt on either end of the black van, a dozen Soviet soldiers armed with automatic rifles leapt out into the alley, shouting at the black-garbed young men to put down their arms and step away from the van. The whole incident had happened so quickly that only the unarmed driver was in the van with Shane and Harry.

Realizing that they were outflanked and out-gunned, the Black Shirts quickly surrendered to the Soviets. Without delay they were handcuffed and transferred to the same military vehicles that had brought the Soviet soldiers to the scene. Before these vehicles could back away, a Soviet Captain walked up the alley from his car parked at the end, and leaned into the black van.

"Mr. Churchill? Mr. Shane? I am Captain Vladimir Grutin. Can I ask you to come with me please?"

"Can you get these cuffs off of us?" Harry asked.

Looking around at one of his squad, Grutin barked a command in Russian, and then turned back to the odd couple in the back of the van. "It will only be a moment," he said, as the soldier scurried back to the vehicle where all the kidnappers had been loaded.

Within seconds the soldier returned with a key in hand, and the captives were released from their handcuffs.

"Where are you taking us," Harry asked as they emerged from the van.

"I'm taking you to a safe place, Mr. Churchill. You and your friend here can no longer move around freely in New Orleans."

"What's going on?" Shane asked.

"You may have the answer to that question, Mr. Shane. I don't care to know. I just know that you and your friends have suddenly become the target of a massive Nazi manhunt. Frankly, I don't care one way or the other, but I have my orders."

"And those orders are—?" Harry asked.

"To deliver you to my superior, and then he will see to it that you are reunited with the rest of your colleagues in a safe place."

"Do you know what happened to our men inside the bar?"

"I've been informed they are both dead."

Harry and Shane gave each other a grim look and shook their heads slowly.

Turning back to the Captain, Harry asked, "Did you know about this abduction attempt?"

"We make it our business to know about everything going on in New Orleans, Mr. Churchill. Now, please. Enough questions. Come with me."

*   *   *   *

The stuffy old frame home on Dumaine Street in the French Quarter had been selected by the Soviet Colonel as a temporary safe house where the leaders of the YLA could congregate. With a back-alley accessible courtyard hidden from the street and adjacent homes, they were able to enter unobserved. Like most homes in the French Quarter, the tall narrow front windows were tightly shuttered, preventing any casual scrutiny. The home itself belonged to an attorney, but he and his wife were away on a long trip. They had an understanding with the Colonel that their home could be used as a safe house in their absence. They had no idea who might be there or what might transpire, but they were well paid for their discretion.

It was ten o'clock in the evening before the four leaders had all been transported discreetly to the safe house. Now, by candlelight, in the kitchen at the rear of the house, Carothers, Salomé, Harry, and Shane sat around the kitchen table with a bottle of red wine and four glasses. They had not yet had a chance to discuss the events of the day.

"All right, Nathan, what the hell's going on?" demanded Harry.

"Can't you figure it out, Harry?" Salomé interjected. "Our cover's been blown! The Nazis know who we are and what we're up to, and they're pissed off about the little demonstration we gave them yesterday."

"You mean they figured this all out since yesterday?" Harry exclaimed. "They had to have help."

"You're right, Harry," Carothers spoke up finally. "They must have had help. But, there's much more to it than that."

"What's the story, Nathan?" Shane demanded. "What were they going to do with us?"

"They probably wanted to interrogate you," Carothers replied. "If they had wanted you dead, you would be. But let's take one thing at a time. First of all, let me tell you about the reports I've gotten from the *DRA*. They're not good. We didn't get the kind of reaction we thought we would. Not only are the Nazis pissed off, but we've angered some others...some that we really didn't expect would be upset with us."

"Who are you talking about?" Harry asked.

"Well, the Mironi family for one," Carothers replied. "We may have made a mistake in not warning them in advance about these attacks."

"I don't understand," Harry stated with a puzzled expression. "They've always supported us. They hate the Nazis as much as we do."

"Yes, that's true, Harry. But they draw the line at terrorism."

"Are you saying that the Mironis called for this assault on me and Tony today? I can't buy that. Tony's their man," Harry said.

"I'm not saying that the Mironis did this, Harry," Carothers replied. "What I'm saying is that it's awfully curious that the Nazis didn't know who we were or where we were yesterday, but today they're all over us. Someone had to give them that information. I'm sure it wasn't Mironi himself. But I did hear from him yesterday. He's not happy. Tony, I'm going to have to ask you to meet with him...very soon."

"Nathan, I'm not the guy to talk to Vito Mironi. I've never been sold on this terrorism strategy. And what if someone in Mironi's organization sold us out?"

"That's exactly why it has to be you, Tony."

"Christ, Nathan," Harry interjected, "meeting with Mironi would expose Tony like a deer on a rifle range!"

"Mironi knows that as well as we do. He won't let anything happen," Carothers countered.

"I wish *I* could be as certain about that," Shane remarked.

"You better be, Tony," Carothers countered, "because your meeting with Mironi is crucial to the survival of the whole YLA movement."

"You mean you want me to convince Mironi that he should support more attacks like yesterday's? He'll never go for it," Tony protested.

"No, Tony," Carothers responded, "you need to assure him that we're *not* going to pursue any more terrorist attacks."

"What? I thought you said the terrorism strategy was our only hope. What's going on here?" Harry demanded.

"What's going on is that we've got to buy some time, Harry. The Nazis will install more effective anti-terrorist defenses, and they'll be hot on our butts for a while. As much as the Soviets detest the Nazis, they can't stop every Black Shirt operation inside their territory. We were very lucky today. The bottom line is we won't be able to make another hit like yesterday, Harry…not for a long time. And not *ever* without Mironi's help."

"So, you want me to *lie* to Mironi?" Tony asked. "Tell him that we've given up on terrorism, when we really haven't? I can't do that, Nathan. We have to trust each other. Otherwise it's all over."

"It's not a lie, Tony," Carothers responded calmly. "We won't launch another terrorist attack, if your plan…yes, *your plan*, Tony…is successful."

Shane and Harry just stared at Carothers with their mouths opened in disbelief. Finally, it was Salomé who spoke up. "What Nathan is saying, Tony, is that without Mironi's help, we're stuck, and your plan may be our only choice. Nathan thinks Mironi will help us if he believes we have an alternative to terrorism."

Finally, Shane was able to speak. "What do you know about my plan, Salomé?"

"Nathan explained it to me today, Tony. We talked before you and Harry arrived. Does Harry know about it?"

"Yeah. I know," Harry answered. "Can we talk about it? Together? It's a huge decision. And, it's a goddam long shot like you wouldn't believe."

"Agreed, Harry," Carothers responded, "on both counts. By all means, let's talk about it. But I don't see that we have any other choice. And, frankly, we're running on borrowed time right now. The sooner we send Tony and Salomé off on this mission, the better off we'll be."

"*Salomé?* What's she got to do with this?" Shane demanded.

"Tony, you've got to focus on getting all the missing information, and that's going to take you all over the *DRA*, operating right under the Nazis' noses. You're going to need someone to watch your back, and I can't think of anyone better than Salomé."

"Sounds like you've got this all figured out, Nathan," Shane said with a touch of sarcasm.

Carothers' steady gaze confirmed Shane's remark. Finally, Carothers said, "Look, Tony, we can discuss this decision if you and Harry want, but the bottom line is that Salomé and I have the vote, and we'll end up doing this anyway. So, I recommend that we start planning how we're going to get you together with Mironi, and stop screwing around with this discussion."

As Carothers waited patiently for their reply, Shane and Harry glanced helplessly at each other, and slowly turned to nod their acceptance.

The adventure might begin the following day, Shane thought, but the outcome was as uncertain as anything could ever be.

Part II.
Odyssey

CHAPTER 5

▼

FAMILY TIES

Vito Mironi had been very clear. He could no longer guarantee safe transport by rail across the border from New Orleans. Shane and Salomé had been forced to cross on foot at a remote post that Mironi could control. They had picked up a car on the other side and were driving north toward Chicago.

Although the Germans had installed a superhighway, *Die Zentralautobahn*, between Chicago, New York and Washington that widened to as many as 20 lanes in some parts, most of the remaining highways in the *DRA* had remained virtually unimproved since the end of the war. Existing rail transport had been bolstered and expanded, so that most personal travel within the *DRA* was conducted by rail. Air travel for government or commerce was common. Air travel for personal reasons was closely scrutinized. Shane and Salomé were facing a tedious two-day journey in an older-model Mercedes over mostly two-lane highways.

Shane had been driving for the first hundred miles through Mississippi, while Salomé examined the road maps and plotted out a route that would avoid undue attention from the highway and border patrols. They had false identity and transit papers that would normally withstand all but the most determined examination; but that was before the September 11 bombings and before the Nazis had launched an all-out vendetta against the Yankee Liberation Army. Tony's connection to Mironi had always been his fail-safe cushion; but no one was sure what that might buy him now.

Suddenly, Salomé, who had remained silent for the first couple of hours, put her maps down, turned to Shane and said, "So, you think Mironi's going to welcome us with open arms?"

Glancing to his right briefly before replying to the unexpected query from the passenger seat, Shane shifted his gaze back to the road ahead and said, "He'll be glad to see me. You…I don't know."

Laughing briefly at Shane's curt dismissal, Salomé asked, "What makes you so sure he'll want to see you? I thought he was pissed off at all of us."

"He is. But Vito and I go way back. He doesn't want anything to happen to me."

"Why is that?"

"It's a long story."

"Well…I'm not going anywhere."

Again glancing briefly over at Salomé with a curious look, Shane returned his gaze to the road ahead and remained silent for several seconds. Finally, he said, "The old man, Rico, was very close with my uncle Paddy. They got together in New York back in the 1930's. Bootlegging. Rico was the boss and took my uncle under his wing. After Prohibition ended Rico moved up in the mobs, while my uncle went legit. But they stayed close. When Rico moved his operation to Chicago during the war, Paddy moved too. Rico treated Paddy like a brother, and my father like a son. Rico had only one child, a daughter."

"And the daughter married your father? You're *related* to Mironi?"

"No, no," Shane laughed. "Rico *wanted* my dad to marry his daughter. But dad was Irish, and that wouldn't work. Mironi needed a Sicilian husband for his daughter so their son could take over the family business. He actually arranged the marriage through a Mafia family from Palermo. And, of course, they did have a son—Vito—who took on the Mironi family name."

"So, how does this affect you?"

"I told you it was a long story," Shane replied with a brief chastising glance to the right.

Salomé remained silent as Shane continued: "My dad married an Italian Catholic girl from Chicago. When I was born, he wanted my uncle to be the godfather at my baptism. My mother insisted that they ask Rico Mironi. And my uncle Paddy agreed. So, that's what happened."

"You mean Rico Mironi was your *godfather?*" Salomé asked with arched eyebrows.

"That's right. He was my *padrino*, my godfather, with all that the traditional culture implies," Shane replied with a grin.

"What does that mean?"

"It means that Rico was my benefactor and my protector. Whenever I had a problem I couldn't handle, I could go to him, and, if he thought I deserved it, he'd fix it for me."

"What do you mean—if you deserved it?"

"The godfather-godson thing works both ways. There were certain expectations: Loyalty. Respect. And, rarely, a favor."

After letting these words settle for a few seconds, Shane continued: "The old man, Rico, had moved up in the mobs before World War II. He became even more powerful during the war when he took over the Chicago operations. But he was always planning for after the war, and his strategy was perfect, if not commendable. While some Mafia figures in New York, like Costello and Luciano, volunteered to help the Allies by their influence with organized labor, Mironi kept out of it.

"Somehow Mironi became convinced that the Axis would win the war. So, he cut a deal. He used his influence to cause a rift between Luciano and Costello, and undermined their anti-Nazi efforts. In return, Mironi got exclusive rights to black market and other lucrative activities after the war. The Nazis have allowed the Mironi family to operate in the *DRA* for the past five or six decades. In return, the Mironis have provided generous kickbacks—or at least as much as they've been willing to share. It's been a win-win."

"So, the Mironi family has been in a position to guarantee your safety since you've been with the YLA?"

"That's right—and much more. When I lived in Chicago, it was Rico who got me into college and got me accepted to graduate school. Of course, the graduate school thing didn't work out, but I was on track. And he would've made it possible for me to get a university position also. But, when they took my dad away, those plans fell apart."

"But Rico Mironi is gone now. You're dealing with his grandson Vito. Don't tell me the 'godfather thing' is handed down the line?" Salomé asked skeptically.

"Not exactly, but Vito still respects his grandfather Rico's wishes."

"And will he respect Rico's wishes after what's happened the past few days?"

"I fully expect that he will," Shane replied. Then, after shifting his gaze briefly to see Salomé's curious look, he added: "Vito doesn't really have a choice, you know."

"What?"

"It happened when Rico was in the hospital dying. He called Vito and my uncle Paddy into the room. There was no one else there. Rico looked at Vito and said, 'Vito, you take care of Paddy and my godson Tony as if they were family. If you ever fail them, I swear I'll come back, hunt you down…and cut off your philandering dick!'"

"Now Vito may or may not believe in heaven or hell," Shane continued. "But he does cherish his male member more than just about anything else in this world. And he has no doubt that Rico would come back and shut down his love life in an instant."

After a wicked chuckle, Salomé said, "I think I would have liked Rico…a lot."

After several seconds had passed in silence, Salomé asked "So, what are you going to say to Mironi? Have you got that figured out yet?"

"I'm going to tell him the truth."

"And what's 'the truth,' Tony?"

Glancing again briefly at Salomé with a condescending notch in his brow, Shane replied, "I'm going to tell him that we're backing off from the bombings and we're going to follow a different plan."

"And?"

"And…we need his support."

"Are you going to explain the new plan…what did Carothers call it…*operation rainbow*?"

"No, he'll never go for it."

"Can't you persuade him that it's our only choice?"

"It won't be *his* choice. He likes the world the way it is."

"You may be right. But, will he help us without knowing about this operation?"

"Carothers is counting on me to persuade Vito. We'll be in bad shape if I can't," Shane replied. Then, as another thought struck him, Shane turned toward his passenger and asked, "What about you, Salomé? Can you go through with this plan…this *operation rainbow*?"

"I voted for it didn't I?" she replied flatly.

"Sure, but have you thought it through? It's a suicide mission, you know—for all of us."

"Yeah, I know," she responded solemnly. "That's fine with me."

Taking his eyes off the road again to gaze curiously at his charismatic passenger, Shane took a moment to absorb her physical attributes. The attractive bronze facial features were set off by shoulder-length dark blonde hair with tight natural curls. Her tall, slender frame—attired now in tight jeans, leather boots and a sleeveless blue tee shirt—could have belonged to a fashion model, but instead it concealed the inner strength of a cold-blooded assassin. He realized suddenly that he really knew very little about this person with whom he had been thrown together in perhaps the most important mission of all time.

"Pardon me for being skeptical, Salomé," Shane said finally, "but I can't accept your commitment that easily."

As she turned her head, Salomé met his gaze with a cold silent stare.

"Convince me," Shane commanded.

"You really don't know me, Tony," she responded after a few seconds.

"I know that you and Carothers are an item, and that tells me something about you," Shane remarked.

"Uh oh. I guess we haven't been too discreet, have we? Well…that's not what I'm talking about, Tony. Do you know how I got into the YLA?"

"Sure. I heard the story about Carothers spotting you for hacking up some Nazi officer in the French Quarter."

"That's just the tip of the iceberg, Tony. It's a long story."

"I'm not going anywhere," Shane said with a smirk as he glanced briefly over at Salomé.

With a tight grin that quickly changed to a serious expression, Salomé began her story. "My family lived in New York City during the war. Jewish refugees from Germany. When the war ended, they were unable to leave before the Nazis took over New York. Worse than that, they believed Hitler's promise of humane treatment for American Jews…or perhaps it was just wishful thinking. They should have known better, after all his lies.

"When the *Gestapo* moved through Washington Heights, where this family lived, they tried to hide their only daughter, a teen-aged girl named Esther, so that the Nazis wouldn't find her. But, of course, they did. The Nazi officer, who led the party that invaded their home, beat and tortured the parents, and brutishly raped the daughter. The parents were executed; the daughter was left for dead in the house.

"The young girl, Esther, suffered from a broken arm, a crushed cheekbone, and a concussion. Some Greek immigrant neighbors discovered her a day later, and nursed her back to health. She lost the sight of her left eye, and her broken left arm never healed properly, but she survived.

"That young girl, Tony, was my grandmother. And that depraved Nazi bastard that raped and beat her was my *grandfather*."

As Salomé remained silent for several seconds, Shane glanced over to see that she had turned her head away, apparently staring out the side window.

"What happened to her?" Shane asked.

"The Greek family hid Esther for two years, delivered her baby—a little girl, my mother—and finally arranged to smuggle both of them across the Soviet border. Esther and the baby were cared for by an aunt and uncle in Florida."

"So, your mother grew up in Florida?"

"Yes. In Miami. She married a Jewish boy, and they had me."

"Why do I not think this is the end of the story?"

"It's not. But I'll tell you only the important part…about my grandmother, Esther. She never got over the loss of her parents and her innocence at the hands of the Nazis. She never married, but she worked as a secretary for the Soviet occupation forces. With patience and cunning she eventually discovered the name of the *Gestapo* officer that had raped her. When she learned that he would be visiting New Orleans on business, she arranged to travel there. Without telling anyone else of her plans, she stalked the officer, who was by then a major. One night, when she observed the officer soliciting a prostitute in one of the Bourbon Street bars, she followed them to his room, pretended to be a maid delivering toiletries, and shot the man dead as he opened the door.

"Although she really didn't care whether or not she escaped, she did manage to elude the police and return to Florida. She never told anyone what she had done. That is, not anyone but her granddaughter—*me*. She never told my mother that her father was a Nazi. She made up a story about a Jewish boyfriend in New York who had been taken off and executed by the Nazis."

"And why did she tell *you* the truth?" Shane asked as he glanced sideways.

Returning his gaze for a moment, Salomé replied, "From the day I was old enough to understand, I was deeply disturbed by the stories of the Holocausts—the tens of millions of Jewish lives snuffed out. My grandmother sensed my rage. She believed that someday I might avenge the unspeakable horrors suffered by my people. So, she confided in me this terrible secret of hers. You can't imagine how revolting it was to learn that a filthy Nazi had savagely inserted himself into my ancestry by assaulting a helpless sixteen-year-old girl. That revelation fueled the flames already burning inside of me…that *still* burn."

Then, turning toward Shane and staring until he could not help but turn and return her gaze, Salomé added, "There won't be any release from this fire, Tony—not until the entire Nazi plague is eliminated from this earth. So, you tell me, Tony: do you think I can handle this mission?"

With a subtle shaking of his head, Shane glanced to his right and said, "I don't have any doubt, Salomé."

But, for some elusive reason, he did.

CHAPTER 6

▼

THE WINDY CITY

Chicago had thrived under the Nazi occupation. As the western-most hub for civilian and military matters within the *DRA*, the city had grown in both size and importance. With the Soviet border less than 200 miles west at the Mississippi River, a strong Nazi military presence was demanded. A large air base housing a fleet of supersonic *Luftwaffe* bombers was situated about 80 miles northwest. Another military base about 100 miles southwest was headquarters for the largest armored division of the German army within the *DRA*. The western division of the Secret Police, the *Gestapo*, was housed in a sprawling thousand acre complex thirty miles north of Chicago along Lake Michigan.

Shane and Salomé had decided to take advantage of the heavy afternoon automobile traffic to slip into the city. The car that Mironi had provided for them at the Soviet border was safe, and their personal documents had gotten them past all the back road checkpoints. But now they were in a big city with a heavy Nazi presence. Military vehicles and armed soldiers were everywhere. The recent horrific terrorist strike at the heart of the city had raised the sensitivities of the Nazi authorities and military patrols. Fortunately for Shane and Salomé, the Nazis had not informed the general public that terrorism was involved. And they had not informed local peacekeeping authorities that the terrorist attack had been linked to the YLA. No photos of Shane and the others had been circulated outside of the *Gestapo*.

Carothers' strategy for getting Shane to the meeting with Mironi had anticipated correctly that the Nazis would attempt to cover up the terrorist strike. The
local authorities had no clue that Shane and Salomé were fugitives. In addition,
Carothers had reasoned, a male and female pair traveling together would be less
suspicious than two males. To augment that strategy, their identity and transit
papers identified Shane and Salomé as newlyweds.

At first awkwardly, but then with greater ease, the pair had distracted border
guards with boldly intimate public displays of affection. Although Salomé had
remained aloof when they were alone, Shane was beginning to sense a disturbing
attraction to this female whom he had long considered as a sexless colleague in a
rebel cause. Having experienced a series of casual liaisons with women met in
New Orleans nightspots, Shane had developed no serious interest in any one
young lady. But he sensed that Salomé could be different. Complicating these
fuzzy feelings was the realization that Salomé was Carothers' woman, and Shane
did not want to cross that line.

On the other hand, Shane mused, if *operation rainbow* succeeded, what would
any of these relationships mean?

Shaking his head involuntarily, Shane attempted to refocus his thoughts on
the matter at hand as he maneuvered the old Mercedes through the entrance to
the parking garage of the Mironi office building in Chicago's downtown Loop.
With a sigh, Shane pulled into a parking spot, glanced over at Salomé, and said,
"Alright, Salomé, grab your backpack and our travel papers—we've got a date
with Vito Mironi."

*   *   *   *

As she hustled into the Mironi building alongside Shane, Salomé reviewed
silently her personal agenda…thoughts she had yet to share with her partner. She
was still bristling at Shane's flat rejection of her request to attend the meeting
with Mironi. Shane had insisted that it would have to be private, that Mironi
would not accept an outsider during their personal conversation. She could not
understand Shane's deference to this man. To Salomé, Mironi was like any other
obstacle, something to be removed by whatever means necessary. She would certainly not try to appease Mironi. *Fuck him and his whole mob!* she thought to herself. *Just give me Mironi one-on-one. I'll straighten him out.*

As she followed Shane into the elevator and watched him push the button for
the top floor, Salomé marveled at the relationship that had developed during the
long trip from New Orleans. That Shane respected her had never been in doubt.

That he was physically attracted to her had become obvious, however, despite his attempt to hide it. That the feeling was mutual had not been revealed in any way. Nevertheless, her babbling had provided Shane with an intimate portal to her soul—one that only Carothers had peered into previously. It had been necessary, she knew, to establish rapport...a bond...with Shane, if her mission were to be successful. She had always been rigorously professional in her missions, able to remain aloof and objective. Now, in the most important mission of her life, she reminded herself, she could not allow the complications of personal feelings.

Emerging now from the elevator, and striding with Shane toward the large double-door to Mironi's office suite guarded by two burly guards, Salomé resolved to let Shane handle Mironi in his own way. And she resolved to continue deferring to Shane in her own cynical manner...until the time was right.

*   *   *   *

Although the seeds had been sown by decades of nationalism, even before the Second World War, the German military-industrial complex had grown even stronger after the war. This suited Vito Mironi just fine. A strong post-war economy had fueled his grandfather's illegal black market, gambling, prostitution and drug activities. But the past two or three decades had witnessed the gradual growth of legitimate business. The Mironi mob family was now invested in restaurants, entertainment, construction, casinos and real estate, among others. They did not hesitate to use old-time mob persuasion tactics to tilt the balance sheets in their favor, but the official company books reflected only legitimate enterprise.

Yes, times were good for Vito Mironi. As he absorbed the panoramic view from his office atop the 40-story downtown building his grandfather had built, Mironi reflected on the extent of his influence. Next to the head of the *Gestapo* or *der Vizekanzler* in Washington, that answered only to *der Reichskanzler*, the Imperial Chancellor in Berlin, Vito Mironi could claim to be the most powerful man in the *DRA*. None of the New York mob families had survived the German occupation; and the Mironis had quickly moved into the underworld vacuum.

When the family's leadership had been turned over to Vito, shortly before his grandfather Rico's death nearly a decade earlier, there had been a brief insurgency led by one of Rico's *capos* and supported by the remnants of the New York Costello family. Despite his youth and reputation as a reckless womanizer, Vito had quickly removed any doubt that he carried the same genes and icy resolve of his grandfather. Seeking advice from his grandfather for the first and only time, Vito had learned the name of Rico's most trusted *soldato*, a fiercely loyal family soldier named Pasquale "Patsy" Bruno. Working alone, Vito and Bruno launched a deadly overnight purge of seven conspirators. Although Vito never revealed that he—or Bruno—had been involved in the massacre, from that day forward he had received nothing but unquestioned loyalty and respect from his extended mob family. The torch had been passed clearly and securely from Rico to Vito Mironi.

Today, with large numbers of government employees, from border guards to judges, augmenting their incomes from his unofficial payroll, there were very few obstacles to Vito Mironi's wants and needs. And Vito Mironi had many wants and needs. In his mid-thirties, married, with two children, Mironi placed the needs of his immediate family above everything. This did not deter him, however, from keeping a mistress for Saturday night carousing with his close friends…and their mistresses. Nor did it prevent him from bedding other women during the week, whenever the opportunity arose. But Sundays were reserved for his wife and children. His devotion to nieces, nephews, cousins, aunts and uncles was rock solid. And Tony Shane was included in this close family circle. Although not related by blood, Shane and Mironi had been raised as if they were brothers. There was a bond between them stronger than blood.

But business was business. Mironi's Italian wife knew not to cross that line. And Shane also knew his obligations, for which he had reaped significant benefits. Yet Tony Shane and the YLA had now placed everything in jeopardy. To be reminded of how drastically things had changed, Mironi had only to look a few miles north to the vacant space in the skyline where the 95-story *Landeszentralbank* building had stood just a few days earlier. Fortunately, the YLA nuclear device had been detonated underground, and most of the explosive energy had been directed vertically, affecting almost exclusively the one skyscraper. Although the targeted building had virtually disintegrated with the blast—dispatching some five thousand human occupants into a mushroom cloud of radioactive dust—the surrounding structures had sustained remarkably minor damage. The *Deutsches InformationsBüro, DIB*, had issued a public statement that the fatal explosion had been due to a defective power plant. But the *DIB* had informed Mironi and a handful of others unofficially that it had been a YLA nuclear bomb. They said that it had been a "clean" bomb, with low levels of radiation in the debris, and that the debris had been swept out over Lake Michigan. But Mironi was skeptical. *DIB* statements could not be trusted.

Now, Mironi was facing a dilemma. Mironi's grandfather had gladly supported Shane and his YLA friends because of his personal outrage at the arbitrary incarceration of Shane's father in 1985, and because Shane was his godson. Vito

Mironi had inherited this commitment. But his disenchantment had grown over the past few years, as his own activities became more dependent on the health of the Nazi occupation. Mironi resented the Nazis, but he had long ago decided that it was in his best interest to share their bed.

The nuclear terrorism of September 11 had severely breached Mironi's tolerance for Shane and the YLA. His communication to Carothers had been scathing and unambiguous. Mironi did not condone terrorism, and he would withdraw all support unless this strategy was abandoned. Privately, Mironi was considering dropping all support for the YLA regardless of what future activities they might have in mind. It was no longer in his best interest to undermine the Nazi occupation. He had become too comfortable with the *status quo*.

The real dilemma, though, was what to do about Tony Shane. Not only were they closer than brothers, but Shane had always been there for Mironi when he was needed. Shane's computer expertise had provided Mironi's operation with systems that were shielded from the prying eyes of the Nazi secret police. And Shane's YLA friends had provided useful intelligence regarding Soviet operations.

But things had gone too far. The YLA had to be stopped, and Tony Shane had to be brought under control. Even Mironi could not avoid dealing retribution to a family member for a betrayal that threatened the entire organization. Even though it wrenched out his own heart, the sacred obligation to *La Cosa Nostra* would demand that he take action.

Mironi had not been responsible for sending the Nazis after Shane and the others, but someone in the Mironi family inner circle had leaked crucial information to the *Gestapo*. Mironi did not know whether this had been a capricious act, the misguided action of a loyal aide, or the dirty work of some Nazi infiltrator. Whatever it was, he would get to the bottom of it, and the responsible party would pay a horrible price. Shane might very well be guilty of a treacherous act against the family, but that had not been established. If so, Mironi would deal with it, however reluctantly. But, for now, Mironi was facing the simple fact that Tony Shane was in danger, and he had to be protected. After all, his grandfather Rico…might he rest in peace…would be terribly unhappy if anything happened to Shane. And, Vito Mironi reflected…with a sharp twinge in his groin…so would he.

At that moment there was a sharp rap on the large double door entry to his office, and Mironi whirled around to see the door opening and two figures entering.

"Tony!" Mironi exclaimed, as his secretary, Sharon, escorted into the office a casually dressed figure with a backpack slung over one shoulder. Moving away from his position at the window, and skirting around his large mahogany desk, Mironi moved quickly toward the man who was currently the source of his profound inner conflict. As Mironi approached his visitor, their arms reached out instinctively and they engaged in a long, warm embrace. Then Mironi stepped back, holding Shane at arms length, and said with a grin, "Christ, Tony, you look like shit!"

"You take a thousand mile road trip—without your chauffeur—and see if your pants stay pressed," Shane replied with an equally wide grin.

After patting each other on the shoulder and chuckling, the two men headed to a corner of the office containing a sofa, two easy chairs and a cocktail table. The secretary, Sharon—a tall shapely brunette, dressed in a low-cut black jersey dress—remained at the doorway, waiting for Mironi's instructions.

Mironi asked Tony to take a seat on the sofa and moved over to the wet bar on the opposite side of the room to pour their drinks. On his way across the room, he turned to Sharon and said, "Make sure that Tony's companion is comfortable, Sharon. We'll be in here for a while."

"Sure, Vito," she said, as she turned and slid quietly out of the room, carefully closing the large heavy wooden door behind her.

"Jesus, Vito," Tony exclaimed after Sharon had left, "where did you find this one? Don't tell me she knows how to type too?"

"You'd be surprised at how talented Sharon is, Tony," Mironi replied over his shoulder while shoveling some ice cubes into one of the two cocktail glasses he had grabbed. "How do you want your scotch? Neat? Or on the rocks?"

"Neat," Shane responded, "and make it a double."

After Mironi had walked back towards Shane and placed one of the two drinks in his outstretched hand, he took a seat in one of the easy chairs, lifted his drink and said, "It's good to see you again, Tony. *Salute!*"

Shane raised his drink and responded, "And you, too, Vito. *Salute di Cento Anni!*"

Shane's toast, and Mironi's, had been delivered in the ancient Sicilian language, Sah-*loo*-tay dee chen-*tah*-nee! Good health for a hundred years! The Sicilian they spoke had been inherited from illiterate immigrant ancestors, and had been preserved unchanged by their American descendants. Even today, with Nazi occupation of Sicily, and with "Roman" Italian dialect spoken by the Nazi and Sicilian elite, the old Sicilian language remained firmly entrenched with the working class. Largely unwritten, the language had evolved from centuries of varied conquerors: Greek, Arabic, Latin and Norman-French. Although represented with written Italian words, it was not an Italian dialect but a distinctly different language that varied regionally within Sicily. Because Shane's ancestors were from a small eastern fishing village, while Mironi's were from Palermo, there were numerous differences in pronunciation and vocabulary.

As they sipped their drinks, Mironi mentally compared the two old friends. He, like Shane, was dark-haired and a trim six-feet tall. Both were good-looking and in their mid-thirties. Because Shane's Italian mother had profoundly influenced his ethnic and cultural attributes, Shane had shared many common youthful experiences with Mironi.

But that was where the similarities ended. Mironi's olive complexion, brown eyes and broad nose affirmed his Sicilian heritage, while Shane's steel blue eyes and facial features favored his Irish father. In faded jeans, red sweatshirt and dirty sneakers, Shane's attire contrasted sharply with Mironi's dark, tailored, double-breasted suit. While Shane's long, dark wavy hair was badly in need of a trim, it appeared that Mironi's hair, nails and skin had just been honed by a salon attendant.

After a prolonged awkward period of silence, Mironi placed his drink on the table and said, "Tony, I wish we could chit-chat about old times, but you and I both know why you're here. The sooner we get down to business, the better. OK?"

"I'm with you, Vito. Why don't you start?"

"Alright, Tony. Look, we've got a problem...a *big* problem," Mironi began, as he leaned forward with his hands clasped across his thighs. "And I can't make this one go away. You and your buddies have gone too far this time."

As Mironi paused, with a grimly frozen expression, Shane began to reply, "Vito, I know—"

"You know *shit*, Tony!" Mironi barked. "I had friends who went down in that blast last week. I know their families...their kids. Do you have any idea the grief you've caused?"

"It was necessary, Vito," Shane countered with newfound conviction. "You've gotten too soft. All of you! Look at yourself. You might as well be a goddam Nazi! You—and all the Americans who've accepted Nazi rule—you're keeping them in power. Hell, most of you are even glad they got rid of the Blacks and the Jews."

"So, you hafta kill your own people, you sonofabitch! Is that the only way you get your message across now, Tony?" Mironi shouted, his dark eyes flashing.

"It got your attention, didn't it, Vito? Now you want to do something about it, don't you?"

"You're goddam right I do," Mironi bellowed, his reddened face inching closer to Shane's. "And your YLA buddies are gonna know it!"

"And what if you can't stop us, Vito?" Shane asked, gazing directly into Mironi's menacing eyes.

"I *will* stop you, Tony," Mironi stated flatly, leaning back slightly. It was less a threat than a reluctant statement of fact.

"But what if you *can't*, Vito?" Shane persisted.

Mironi blinked and sat back a little further, deliberately easing the tension a bit. "What're you getting at, Tony? What's your point?"

"My point, Vito, is put yourself in somebody else's shoes. Some American working for some German-owned *DRA* company—someone who doesn't have your power and resources. What's *he* going to think when he realizes the Nazis can't stop us?"

"Who cares?" Mironi growled.

"*He* cares, Vito. He cares because he begins to realize that it's not the YLA that's causing this problem. It's the goddam Nazis—the Nazis, who killed off millions of Americans after the war just because they were Jewish or Black or "undesirable." The Nazis—who have put thousands of Americans in prisons because they were suspected of being "disloyal," who have savagely executed, without trials, thousands suspected of treason or terrorist connections, who prevent American refugees in Mexico from returning home, and who control every aspect of our lives."

"The Nazis didn't set off the atom bombs, Tony" Mironi interjected caustically. "They didn't kill five thousand innocent people in Chicago."

"You're wrong, Vito. They were just as responsible as if they had planted the bombs themselves. And that's what all Americans are going to realize as soon as they think it through."

"All right, Tony," Mironi conceded. "What if your cockamamie theory is true. So what?"

"*So what!* Think about it, Vito. Your average thirty-year-old American doesn't know anything but Nazi rule. They don't have any idea what real freedom is. They only know the world they've been born into. They know it's wrong that the state decides what rights they have, but they live with it. They know about the YLA and the refugees, and they don't care. But, when our bombs begin to take away family and friends—and they realize it's really the Nazis that have brought this down on them—they're going to start making lots of noise. Not just one or two, Vito, but millions of Americans in the *DRA* will begin to put pressure on the Nazis."

Mironi could barely contain himself. "I don't believe my ears! Tell me you don't really believe in this shit, Tony."

For a long time Shane's eyes remained locked with Mironi's. Only the nervous action of his index finger absently circling the lip of his drink suggested that Shane was struggling with some inner demon.

Finally, Shane let out his breath and slowly shook his head. "I'm sorry, Vito. I can't go on giving you this line. You're right. I don't believe in it myself," he revealed. "Don't get me wrong, I still think Carothers is right. I believe it will work," he lied. "But I just don't have the stomach for it. I never wanted these attacks to happen."

"Yeah, I know. Carothers told me you were against it," Mironi admitted, adopting a more conciliatory tone. "But it still happened, Tony. And you didn't even give us a warning. Shame on you."

As his eyes locked with Mironi's, Shane countered, "So, did you send the *Gestapo* after us, Vito?"

Mironi unclasped his hands and sat back, taking a few seconds to return Shane's gaze. His face showed nothing. "Is that what you think, Tony?"

Shane blinked and looked away. "I don't know what to think, Vito." Then silence.

After a few seconds Mironi said, "Look, Tony, I'm disappointed that you might think I passed information to the *Gestapo*. But it wasn't me. And if I find out who it was, there'll be hell to pay. Nobody breaks the trust—no exceptions—and they know it.

"But that doesn't mean I don't understand why they did it. Your YLA buddies are screwed-up terrorists, Tony. I can't condone what you've done. And the take-home message for you today is that I'm cutting you off. I don't even know if I can continue to give you—you, personally—any protection."

Observing Shane's stunned expression, Mironi decided to explain: "Look, Tony, my grandfather decided long ago that our family would watch out for you. That thing that happened in '85 to your dad was a terrible blow to my grandfather. For the first time in his life he wasn't able to pull strings. Your dad died in prison and that broke grandpa's heart. He vowed that the Nazis wouldn't get their hands on you, and he expected me to carry on for him. And I have. But, things have changed."

"So, you don't feel obligated to protect me any longer?" Shane inquired.

"No," Mironi growled. "You're not listening to me, Tony. Do you think I'd let those Nazi bastards get their hands on you? Forget it!"

"I guess I misunderstood, Vito," Shane said. "What's going on?"

"In 1985, this *Gestapo* officer, Manfred Weber, was in charge of the investigation into whatever they suspected your father of doing. After your father was locked up, he was determined to get his hands on you, Tony. I don't know what he suspected. I don't even know why they threw your dad in prison. Your uncle Paddy and my grandfather convinced the *Gestapo* that they didn't know anything.

"I don't have to tell you how well my grandfather and I managed to keep your activities secret. In fact, until the past week, only this investigator Weber, who's a colonel now, was concerned with your whereabouts.

"But that's changed now, Tony. They know you're involved with these terrorists. And this Colonel Weber suddenly has whatever he needs to find you and your buddies. Finding you in New Orleans was only the beginning. You were fortunate that the Soviets didn't take too kindly to the *Gestapo* moving in on their territory. But you're in the *DRA* now, Tony, and you've got a goddam bull's-eye painted on you."

As Mironi paused, Shane said, "Vito, I know it will be hard for you to keep the *Gestapo* off my back now. And I was way off base suggesting you might have informed the Nazis. But, Vito, the YLA needs your help now more than ever."

"I can't do it, Tony," Mironi responded bluntly. "It was OK when you guys were running guns, and messing with government troops and operations. Hell, I got a kick out of watching you screw up their computer systems. But, when you brought nukes into play and killed innocent people, that went way over the line. Your buddies are cut off, Tony. And that's it."

"What if I told you that there won't be any more nuclear strikes? That there won't be any more terrorist activities at all? Would that make a difference, Vito?"

"Carothers already told me that. I don't believe him, Tony. Do you?"

"Yes, I do, Vito. We couldn't pull anything off right now, even if we wanted to. There's too much heat."

Mironi stared at Shane for a few moments and then reached for his drink. Sitting back, he crossed his legs and took a long sip of the scotch, continuing to regard Shane curiously. His brown eyes darkened and narrowed as he lowered the glass and cupped it with both hands in his lap. "All right. Start talking, Tony," he commanded.

As Mironi sat back, sipping his drink and listening attentively, Shane explained slowly: "Vito, there's a way to take down the Nazis without using nuclear terrorism. We have a plan, *operation rainbow*. I can't give you details, and we can't guarantee it will work. But, if it does, this Nazi tyranny will go away…forever. And the Soviets and the Japanese will be taken out too."

With his eyebrows arching ever so slightly at this last revelation, Mironi slowly put down his drink and leaned forward once more. "You think you can bring down all the Axis powers with one shot? You're out of your mind, Tony."

"No, Vito. I'm not crazy. It *can* be done."

"How? I need to hear more," Mironi declared.

"I told you. I can't give you details, Vito."

"Then you're wasting my time, Tony. I mean, look, why should I want you to take down the Nazis? And, even if I did, I can't support some operation you won't describe. And then you tell me you're going to take out the Soviets and the Japanese too? What if *they* get wind of your operation? There's no way I could protect you."

Leaning forward now to match Mironi's pose, Shane found himself looking into Mironi's eyes from a distance of only a couple feet. Solemnly, he said, "Vito, believe me, you do not want to know the details of this operation. But, I will tell you this, they will all come down, and we will have our country back again."

Matching Shane's intent gaze, Mironi replied, "Let's say I believe you. What happens to me? To my family? To my organization?"

"What do you think would have happened to your grandfather Rico if we hadn't been occupied by the Nazis after the war?"

"He would have done fine. Grandpa always covered his bases."

"Exactly, Vito. He would have thrived no matter what. And so will you."

With that, Mironi sat back slowly and took a deep breath, managing not to break eye contact with Shane. "You're very persuasive, *mio fratré*," Mironi said with a slow grin, using the brotherly Sicilian salutation that the two men had reserved for each other since childhood. "But you're not telling me everything, are you?"

"No, I'm not, Vito," Shane responded. "But you know I speak the truth. I wouldn't do anything to hurt you or your family. You can count on that."

"So, you're asking me to support this fucking "rainbow" operation on your *word* alone? Do you think I'm *pazzo*? Even my grandpa Rico wouldn't do it. If he couldn't cover his bases he'd tell you to screw off."

"What if I assured you that everything Rico worked for will survive?"

After staring curiously at Shane for a few moments, Mironi said, "You're toying with me, Tony. I don't like that. It sounds like you're saying one thing, but you really mean something else. Nobody uses that kind of double talk with Vito Mironi."

"Vito, I haven't lied to you. I would never lie to you, and you know that. Yes, my statements have hidden meanings. It has to be that way...for your own good.

I simply can not tell you everything. You will just have to trust me, Vito. This is just between us, *mio fratré*. If you *trust* me, support me on this mission."

"And if I don't?" Mironi persisted.

"I can't guarantee anything, Vito. Carothers has more nukes. He'll use them if he has to…sooner or later."

For a long time Vito Mironi sat and stared while Shane calmly returned his gaze. Then he leaned forward and picked up his drink to take a long sip. With the drink remaining in his hand, he placed his arm on the armrest of the easy chair and continued to regard his "brother." Finally, he said with a sigh, "Tell me what you want me to do, Tony."

With a slight nod, Shane said warmly, "Thanks, Vito," and reached across to grasp Mironi's left shoulder in a brief affectionate grip. Then, sitting back, Shane said, "The first thing you need to do is to get Salomé and me to eastern upstate New York. There's an old friend of my father's who lives there, and she has some very important information for me."

*   *   *   *

Seated in the back seat of the black BMW with darkly tinted windows parked on Dearborn Street, just around the corner from the entrance to the Mironi building, Colonel Manfred Weber quietly puffed on a cigarette. His attention was directed to the conversation emanating from the radio receiver and tape recorder positioned to his left. After nearly two decades of frustration he had finally received *Gestapo* approval to place a surveillance device in Mironi's office. The recently divulged information that Tony Shane had been involved in the terrorist attack had abruptly thrust Colonel Weber into the front line of *Gestapo* activities. For years he had been the solitary investigator following up on the 1985 capture of Professor Garrison Fuller and Tony Shane's father, Daniel. Although the decades of subversive activities that had transpired in Fuller's research labs at the University of Wisconsin had been verified, the precise objective of the studies had never been established. Weber had been convinced that Daniel's son, Tony, was the key to the mystery, but Tony Shane had disappeared before he could be questioned.

After sixteen years of following blind leads, Weber had learned that Shane was in New Orleans and was one of the YLA leaders responsible for the terrorist strikes. Weber smiled at the thought that one of Mironi's trusted inner circle had come to him with the information.

But Weber's smile abruptly disappeared as he realized that the conversation between Mironi and Shane had just ended. And the nature of Shane's *operation rainbow* had not been divulged. With a sharp rap on the glass partition, Weber signaled the driver to get ready to move out. He hadn't learned as much as he had hoped, but he knew that Shane and a companion would be departing soon. And he knew that their destination would be eastern upstate New York.

Vizekanzler Koefler would not be happy to know that he was letting Shane and his companion get away. Weber alone was convinced that the mysterious *operation rainbow* was a greater threat than the nuclear terrorist strikes. Only Weber, it seemed, remembered that Professor Fuller and Shane's father had been willing to die rather than reveal what the objectives of the secret wartime *Einstein Project* had been.

The *Gestapo* investigation had not learned much, but what they had learned had affected Weber profoundly. He still had Fuller's research notebooks that had been found hidden deep underneath the Fuller home in Madison. Despite the secret encoding of experiments and results, Weber had sensed an excitement that could not be contained. Clearly the research had been on the threshold of a spectacular breakthrough. That breakthrough would do no good for the Nazi cause. And Weber was convinced that, after lying dormant for all these years, the *Einstein Project* had been resurrected and embodied in Tony Shane. Weber didn't know where the trail might lead, but he knew he had to follow. At stake was the survival of Nazism. Of that he was certain. And Shane's own words had provided confirmation.

*   *   *   *

Over Shane's protests Vito Mironi insisted on accompanying Shane and Salomé to the parking garage. Along with two burly bodyguards, the three of them descended in Mironi's private elevator to the underground garage level. To Shane's surprise, the elevator doors opened into a large wood-paneled lounge, complete with comfortable sofas, chairs, tables and a wet bar. Waiting for them in the lounge were two large, swarthy gentlemen dressed in dark suits. The two men were seated comfortably in two of the easy chairs reading newspapers. Shane noticed that one of the papers was in German and the other was one of the English underground papers known as *The Voice*. As the elevator door opened, the two men sprang to attention, leaping to their feet and taking a step toward the elevator.

"Paulie…Rocco, relax," Mironi commanded the two suddenly attentive men, as the two elevator bodyguards preceded their party into the room. After a quick scan to be sure there were no surprises awaiting them in any corner of the room, the two bodyguards nodded to Mironi. Turning to his right where Salomé was standing, Mironi put his arm around her waist and motioned with his left hand for her to precede him into the room.

With a sharp glance to her left that would have withered a lesser man, Salomé stepped out of the elevator, followed closely by Mironi. Shane stepped out last, chuckling silently to himself as he envisioned the shock to Mironi's ego that would be delivered by Salomé's castrating response if he were ever foolish enough to make a pass.

"What happened to the parking garage?" Shane asked. "Did we take a wrong turn and end up in the penthouse?"

"What do you think, Tony," Mironi chuckled, "I'm gonna walk out into the garage? You think I got no enemies? Look, Tony, I want you and Salomé to meet Paulie Santini and Rocco Pirrello. They're gonna take you to your next stop in the city."

After acknowledging the two men, Shane turned to Mironi and whispered, "What about our car, Vito? What's going on?"

Mironi grabbed both Shane and Salomé by the arm and guided them over to the bar where they could talk privately. "Forget that old wreck, Tony. Paulie and Rocco will take two cars to your next stop. Then you can take one of the cars on the next leg of your trip."

"You don't have to do that, Vito. We can use the Mercedes. And we don't need drivers to get us out of here."

"Listen to me, Tony," Mironi commanded in a hushed tone as he leaned closer. "These Nazis think I don't know they're watching me, but I know they watch who goes in and out of this building. I'm sure they saw you two. We wanted them to see you. But they're not gonna see you leave."

"You're going to send us out in a different car?" Shane asked.

"Two cars. You go with Paulie; Salomé goes with Rocco. We dress you up differently. Add a wig, and they won't know a thing. But those dumb *Jerries* are out there right now waiting for that old Mercedes to come out. So we have to move quickly. Let's go into the bedroom." With that command, Mironi nodded toward the far wall opposite the bar.

When Shane and Salomé looked over they were surprised to see a large ornate door, partly open, leading into what looked like a bedroom suite. "What do you want us to do?" Shane asked.

"You gotta get these clothes off. We've got doubles for you and Salomé. They're gonna take your car out of here and make those *stunatas*—those crazy boneheads—follow *them*."

Then, brusquely shoving the two towards the bedroom door, Mironi commanded, "Let's go."

As Shane walked into the bedroom suite his first thought was that it had to be at least a thousand square feet. It was lavishly furnished with a king-sized four-poster bed, two satin-covered chairs and a matching lounge, large mirrored dressing table, a massive armoire, a large candelabra fixture in the center of the room, and several ornate lamps adorning the softly painted walls. On one side of the room was an archway into a foyer that appeared to lead to two bathrooms on the left and right, with his and hers walk-in closets in between.

"Alright, Tony...Salomé, you need to give me your clothes, car keys and transit papers. We have new papers for you. You can find something to wear from the two closets on your right. One has my clothes and the other has women's clothing. I know my clothes will fit you, Tony. And, Salomé, you're sure to find something in the other closet."

Momentarily surprised by Mironi's instructions, Shane and Salomé remained motionless for a moment, and Mironi said quickly, "Look, we've got another couple upstairs waiting to get your clothes. So, get moving."

After a quick glance at each other, Shane and Salomé grabbed their backpacks and headed for the closets, realizing that any further discussion would probably be futile. There would be time to work things out later.

$$*\qquad*\qquad*\qquad*$$

The visit with his uncle Paddy and aunt Peggy in Melrose Park had been brief, sweet and selfish. Now, as he guided the large black Lincoln sedan south on Mannheim Road, about ten miles west of Chicago's downtown Loop, leaving Melrose Park behind, Shane wondered if he would regret the act. Paddy had not provided him with any new information—not because of any dementia. His aunt and uncle hadn't seemed to age at all in the past two decades. They were still mentally sharp and modestly active for a couple in their nineties. But Paddy simply had not ever known details of the *Einstein Project* or of any participants but Daniel. The name Diana Sutton meant nothing to him.

When Mironi had provided Shane and Salomé with covert transportation to his uncle's home in the western suburb of Melrose Park, it had become clear that Mironi was taking no chances. They were directed to use the same entrance that

Mironi used whenever he visited Paddy—the same one that Shane had used occasionally during his long exile. After parking in front of a small grocery store one street beyond his uncle's, Shane, Salomé and their two drivers had entered the store. After being guided to the back storage room, they were directed down a stairway hidden under a section of wooden floor. By negotiating through a series of narrow earthen channels cut deep underground, they had found themselves climbing a short flight of concrete steps leading to a door that opened into the basement of his uncle's house. Once inside the basement, the door through which they entered had been covered up by a section of false wall.

Now, as Shane maneuvered the Lincoln through the light evening traffic south of Hinsdale, looking for a suitable cross street to move west, he inadvertently shook his head and marveled at how well Rico and then Vito Mironi had cared for his aunt and uncle.

"What are you shaking your head at, Tony?" came the question from Salomé, abruptly jarring Shane from his thoughts.

"Just thinking about Vito's incredible little empire," Shane responded with a quick glance at his passenger. "I'm sure glad he's on our side."

"Is he?" Salomé asked. "You haven't really told me what came out of your chit-chat."

Glancing again to his right and noting Salomé's skeptical frown, apparent even in the dim glow of the dashboard lights, Shane replied tersely, "Don't worry, he's with us."

"Is that all you're going to say?"

"For now, yeah," Shane replied. "I'll fill you in later when we have more time. Right now, we have to get ready for our next stop."

Before Salomé could respond, Shane turned toward her and placed his index finger to his lips. He was certain that Mironi had the car bugged in some way, and might even have attached a transponder so that they could be tracked.

Immediately understanding Shane's concern, Salomé remained quiet as Shane continued southward on Mannheim Road. He was pretty sure they had not been followed. As he observed the crossroad that he wanted to take west, he deliberately motored through the intersection and pulled into the first service station he encountered. After pulling into a parking spot away from the gasoline pumps, he motioned for Salomé to get out of the car with him.

As the pair moved toward the service station entrance, Shane suddenly grabbed Salomé's arm and pulled to a halt about ten yards from the entrance, away from any traffic. "Salomé, we either have to find the bugs in this car, or we're going to have to get another car. I don't want Mironi to know that we have another stop in Chicago before heading for New York."

"So, what do we do?"

"The last big intersection we passed is where we wanted to turn west. If we can't find the bugs in this car in ten minutes, we'll have to keep heading south and then east until we can find another car."

"OK, so what are we waiting for. Let's start looking."

"You get started. I'm going into the station and ask if we can use their hoist. I think a couple hundred marks might persuade them."

As Salomé headed back and quickly started tearing into the most obvious hiding places, Shane entered the service station and began negotiating with the night manager. The service bays were closed until the next day, Shane was told. But, a hundred marks had persuaded the manager to open the service door, and turn on the compressor that powered the hydraulic hoists.

"Have you found anything?" Shane asked breathlessly after running back to the car and signaling to Salomé to come out.

"Yeah. You were right. There was a bug hidden in the dome light. I can disconnect it, but we need to wait until we find the transponder. We want to get them both at the same time."

"Great! Let's drive into the service bay and get it up on the lift. I'll bet the transponder is attached somewhere under the frame."

With only three or four of the minutes remaining of the ten that Shane had allotted, the Lincoln reached the top level of the hoist, and two unlikely figures hastened underneath with high intensity lights borrowed from the mechanics' work bench. With Shane dressed in one of Vito Mironi's dark suits and Salomé attired in a stunning dark blue dress and high heels, they could not help but draw the amused attention of the station manager. Shane hoped that no one else would notice, and had asked the manager to close the service door once the car was inside.

After several frantic minutes of searching, Shane and Salomé reluctantly agreed that there was no transponder to be found, and quickly decided to lower the hoist, retrieve the car and continue on their way. Without a word they climbed into the car and began backing out of the service area, each realizing that they were now faced with the dilemma of assuming there was no transponder, or stealing a different car. Either course was risky.

As Shane began to maneuver the Lincoln toward the street he abruptly stepped on the brakes, set the emergency, pulled a latch underneath the dashboard, and leapt out of the car. As Salomé rushed outside and he saw the quizzical look on her face, Shane asked her, "Did you look under the hood?"

"Of course," she answered.

"Did you take anything apart?"

"Not enough time, and no tools."

"I saw a tool box in the trunk. Get me a screwdriver, quick."

As he waited for her to return, Shane quickly loosened the wing nut that held the air filter cover. Lifting the cover off and examining its underside he found nothing. Then, after pulling out the air filter, finding nothing underneath, and then replacing it, he handed the cover to Salomé and took the screwdriver she had retrieved. Quickly he began to unscrew the lid covering the bank of electrical fuses.

"Tony. Wait!" he heard Salomé shout. "Look at this."

Turning his head, Shane saw in Salomé's hands the same air filter he had just restored. Just as he opened his mouth to protest, Shane saw what Salomé was pointing at. There, tucked inside one of the hundreds of vertical folds that constituted the efficient air filter, was a flat rectangular plastic package. Mounted vertically and nearly indistinguishable from the similarly constructed filter materials surrounding it, the transponder had only become visible when Shane's tampering dislodged the tiny antenna wires that were now dangling loosely across the top of the adjacent folds of the filter.

With instant recognition of what they had found, Shane motioned to Salomé to give him the transponder and replace the air filter. Then, after motioning that she had cut out the bug in the dome light, Shane took the transponder and walked back toward the service station entrance. As he passed the gasoline pumps, he casually tossed the transponder into the back seat of the unoccupied late model BMW that was being serviced at that time. After grabbing a paper towel from the service rack, he returned to the Lincoln, quickly wiped off the windshield, got in behind the wheel and drove out of the station. But now he headed *north* on Mannheim road, looking for the crossroad to the west that they had passed earlier.

*   *   *   *

It was nearly nine o'clock in the evening when Shane and Salomé pulled into the parking lot of the large low-rise Hotel Excelsior on the outskirts of the vast government research facility located about 25 miles southwest of Chicago's downtown Loop. It was this 1500 acre wooded site that was to have become the home for nuclear research initiated by Enrico Fermi's first nuclear reactor experiment of December 1942 at the University of Chicago. Designated now as the *Heisenberg Institut*, the facility housed some 3000 scientists and engineers engaged in basic research related to German national security. Although most of the workers were American and not German, the top administrative and technical managers were German.

It was at the Hotel Excelsior that night that a large cocktail party was being held in one of the ballrooms that could hold over two hundred guests. Tonight was the opening social event for a three-day conference on cybernetics that had attracted the top researchers in this field from throughout the German Confederation as well as from the Japanese Empire, the Soviet Union, China, the United Arab States, Switzerland, and Mexico. Although diplomatic relations between the German Confederation and most of the other nations were strained, international scientific discourse on non-classified projects was currently tolerated.

Although he had been deprived of a formal post-graduate academic career, Shane's expertise in engineering, electronics and computers had been nurtured with years of study at the University of New Orleans and by practical applications in support of YLA dirty work. Above all, Shane had kept up with the latest developments in computer technology and especially cybernetics—the science of intelligent automated control systems. This was not just idle curiosity. This had been dictated to him by the letter that had been delivered to him by his father in 1985, the letter left by his future self on that airplane flight in 1939.

The papers he had read recently, published by a research team at the *Heisenberg Institut*, might not have aroused more than passing interest among most researchers in cybernetics. But, to Shane, they had suggested that a long-awaited technical threshold had been surpassed. A threshold above which floated the enormous potential of the *Einstein Project*. The key author of these papers would be at this conference. She worked at the *Institut*.

Her name was Sarah Stenstrom. Shane had to meet her tonight, and somehow convince her within the next three days that his mission was her destiny.

CHAPTER 7

▼

SARAH

It was finally happening. The International Conference on Cybernetics that Sarah had worked on so hard for the past year. She had done all the preparation work: setting up and inviting chairs for the special topic sessions; inviting internationally-renowned Soviet cyberscientist, Sergei Chekov, to speak at the plenary session; designing the schedule; editing the abstracts; and overseeing all the minute details required for a successful conference of this magnitude. She was excited. And she was frustrated.

Not yet thirty years old, with a Ph.D. in neural psychology from UCLA, and postdoctoral study in computer science at Stanford, Sarah Stenstrom had been widely recruited for positions in industrial and government research throughout the Japanese Empire. But she soon discovered that the Japanese government labs that supported the research in which she was interested had very few American administrators and no female project leaders. Looking at foreign opportunities, Sarah turned down another postdoctoral position at the University of Zurich before finally accepting a "senior scientist" position at the *Heisenberg Institut* that appeared to offer opportunities for independent research and career growth.

Despite intermittent hostile confrontations between the Japanese Empire and the German Confederation, cordial relations were maintained in scientific circles. Work visas were easily obtained to fill skilled positions, as this benefited both countries. Thus, the traffic in Ph.D.'s flowed readily in both directions, and Sarah had found herself leaving California and moving to Chicago two years earlier. Having known very little outside of the rural wine-producing region of California, where her family operated a large vineyard, before leaving for graduate and postgraduate studies, Sarah remained relatively unsophisticated in worldly realities. This applied to her love life as well as to her understanding of politics and foreign affairs.

At five feet nine inches, with a trim figure and long auburn hair, the attractive green-eyed Sarah caught the attention of many of her young male colleagues. But she had had few romantic episodes. There had been a steady boyfriend for two years in college and a brief affair with her major professor at UCLA There had been no serious love interest in the past three years, despite several ardent suitors.

But Sarah's source of frustration had nothing to do with her love life. She had discovered in the past year, with cruel bluntness, the harsh reality of working within the Nazi government laboratory system. Although there were many successful American and female scientists, even at the highest levels of management or research direction, Sarah had learned belatedly that membership in this community was restricted to Nazi party members. Because Sarah knew that she could never become a Nazi, she also knew just as surely that she would never become an independent project leader. Even the relatively inconsequential responsibility for the current international conference, she reflected bitterly, had not been credited to her. All the programs had identified Dr. Wolfgang Schwarz, the leader of cybernetics research at the *Institut* and Sarah's supervisor, as the conference organizer. Sarah's name on the program was buried within a list that included secretaries and travel consultants.

As she examined herself in her dressing room's full-length mirror, admiring reluctantly the trim lines of the long dark blue gown that she would be wearing to the conference-opening social mixer that evening, Sarah experienced another remorseful episode. How proud her parents would be of her, she thought, if only they could see her. Here she would be tonight, conversing with many of the world's elite scientists—scientists whose names would be recognized even in the remote vineyards of Central California. And her parents would know nothing of it. They had not been allowed to travel to the *DRA*. And Sarah's foreign travel was severely restricted to only those locations dictated by scientific needs. Telephone conversations were infrequent, limited, and monitored. Personal mail was censored. Despite the thrill of working at the cutting edge of cybernetic science, Sarah was devastated emotionally by the virtual loss of her family.

Adding to her frustration was the impact of the Patriot Act, *der Vaterlandsfreund Gesetz*, enacted by the *Reichstag* in response to YLA terrorist activities the past few years. Now Sarah and other government workers were required to submit periodically to "loyalty detector" tests. Using a sophisticated mutation of ancient lie detector technology, these devices were supposed to identify disloyal tendencies of subjects under questioning. Thus far, Sarah had passed her tests, but she lived with the daily threat that the *Gestapo* need only *suspect* someone of disloyal acts to incarcerate them indefinitely.

Do I regret the choice to work at the Heisenberg Institut? Sarah thought to herself as she turned around in front of the mirror, examining skeptically the uncharacteristic low cut gown she had selected. After taking a deep breath, and examining further the carefully applied makeup that provided some color to her pale complexion, she answered herself: *No. Not on a night like tonight. Tonight I'll have fun and meet some interesting people. I won't let myself be sad or frightened tonight.*

With that, Sarah whirled around, picked up her evening bag and light wrap from the sofa bed that was the heart of her efficiency apartment, and headed out the door. Located twenty minutes from the Hotel Excelsior she had just enough time to get there a full hour before the expected arrival of the attendees. German precision dictated that she be there early, and that all preparations be perfectly accomplished before the first guest arrived. Sarah would pay a dear price if anything went wrong.

*   *   *   *

The large Crystal Ballroom at the Hotel Excelsior was filled with nearly three hundred distinguished guests. Scientists from the *Heisenberg Institut* and from around the world, top *Institut* administrators, and a sprinkling of local Nazi brass were distributed in tiny clusters around the room—consuming cocktails, finger food and light conversation. In one corner of the ballroom, beneath one of several huge crystal chandeliers that lighted the room, Sarah Stenstrom was engaged in a technical discussion with her supervisor, Wolfgang Schwarz, and the plenary session speaker, Sergei Chekov. Schwarz and Chekov, in formal black tie attire, provided an interesting visual contrast.

While Schwarz was in his early forties, short, stout and balding, Chekov was sixtyish, tall, slim and handsome. Chekov's dark features and brown eyes were complemented by short steel-gray hair. He switched smoothly between English and German as needed with only slight traces of Russian accent. Because Sarah had long admired Chekov's research and was intimately familiar with his work through journal publications, she expected that she would be in awe of his presence. But she hadn't been prepared for his captivating charm.

Finding herself uncharacteristically flustered, often struggling and stammering in her speech, Sarah asked to be excused as she headed for the open bar to get a refill of her Campari and soda. But, hoping to loosen her tangled tongue, she requested a double-vodka, and took a long sip right at the bar.

As she turned to leave the bar with her drink, a young man in a dark suit who obviously wanted to speak with her approached Sarah.

"Sarah?" he asked. "My God! I haven't seen you since the E.E. convention in New Orleans. How are you?"

Staring blankly for a moment at the good-looking young man in front of her with his black hair and blue eyes, Sarah cursed her poor memory for names. The face was vaguely familiar, but she didn't recall their previous encounter in New Orleans. Nevertheless, she responded, "Well, hello. Good to see you." Then, after a slight pause with a puzzled look, she added, "I'm sorry but I've forgotten your name."

"It's Arthur. Arthur Stone," Tony Shane lied. "We met a year ago at the symposium on cybernetic algorithms in New Orleans. I was there for your talk on the new high-level language you were developing."

"Oh yes," Sarah said with fake recollection. "Of course. Aren't you with the University of New Orleans?" she speculated.

"That's right. I'm on the faculty there. The Electrical Engineering department," Shane replied, knowing that the real Arthur Stone was indeed an E.E. professor there, but had been on leave in South America for two years.

After several minutes of small talk during which Shane continued to take advantage of his knowledge of Sarah Stenstrom's professional work, travel, publications and presentations, the discussion turned toward Shane's work. It was at this point that Shane hoped to command Sarah's attention, not just for the moment, but for the days to follow. To accomplish this he would use, for the first time, technical information that had been provided him in the letter from the future that he had first read back in 1985.

"I'm working in an area that you might find interesting," Shane began. "We're developing methods for implanting microchips in human brains to augment memory functions."

"My goodness," Sarah purred, "I hadn't heard that anyone had gotten that far along. Doesn't that require major surgery?"

"Well, we haven't published anything on this yet," Shane replied. "But, I can tell you this much. We're using an endoscopic procedure involving access through the subject's nasal passage."

"That's amazing! Are you planning to publish this work soon?"

"Actually, I don't think the Soviets will let us publish any of this work right now," Shane replied. "But I'd be happy to talk to you about it—off the record—if you're willing to share with me some of your cybernetic programming tricks."

Sarah paused for several seconds. The alcohol had temporarily enhanced her insight and she felt exceptionally lucid. It was clear and obvious to her at this point that she was being presented with an incredible opportunity. A simple trade of information could benefit her research program enormously. Without further hesitation she responded, "Sounds like a great idea, Arthur. Can we get together tomorrow between the morning and afternoon sessions? I should have about two hours free."

"Sure. Can we get away from the Hotel for lunch? Someplace where we won't see any other conferees?" Shane asked.

Sarah thought for a moment, mentally sizing up this man who had been a total stranger just minutes earlier. Now she was wondering just how far she should go in pursuit of new scientific knowledge. What risks should she take? How trustworthy was this man? She didn't really know the answers to these questions. But, emboldened by the double vodka, she plunged forward. She would agree to meet with Stone. But she would spend some time this evening finding out about him.

"You know what, Arthur. I think we might be able to manage it. Check with me right after the first session tomorrow. I'll be in the Hamburg Room, chairing the session on algorithms."

"Sounds great, Sarah," Shane responded. "I'll be looking forward to it."

*   *   *   *

Trying to make as little noise as possible, Shane inserted the key, grasped the doorknob, and slowly opened the door. Looking into the darkened vacant living area of their suite at the Hotel Excelsior, he noticed a dim light creeping through the partly opened door to the bedroom. Assuming Salomé was either asleep or reading in the bedroom, Shane stepped into the suite. As he turned to close the door, he was shocked to hear the door slammed shut behind him and then to detect peripherally a quick-moving shadowy figure. Before he could gaze into the face of the assailant, he saw a pistol fitted with a long silencer and was grabbed around the neck from behind in a tight grip.

"Tony! You idiot!" came the familiar hushed voice of Salomé in his ear. "You try sneaking in here and you might get yourself killed!"

"Christ! I'm sorry, Salomé. I didn't want to disturb you."

"That's the kind of shit that *does* disturb me," Salomé quipped as she released Shane and shoved him away. "From now on, give a knock so I know it's you at the door."

Reaching up to rub his neck, Shane asked, "Have you been standing behind that door all night?"

"I don't need to park at attention. I heard you coming from way back," Salomé replied as she turned on the light and walked back toward the sitting room.

"Do you think someone knows we're here?" Shane asked as he followed behind.

"It's just a matter of time, Tony," Salomé replied as she flopped into an easy chair, with one long bare leg draped over the arm. It was then that Shane noticed she was wearing only a long shirt and panties.

"Are you pissed because you didn't go to the mixer tonight?" he asked.

"Not for any social reasons. But I shoulda been there to cover your ass. That's why Carothers sent me on this mission. Remember?"

"How the hell are you going to hide a weapon in that skin-tight dress you got from Mironi's place? And how am I going to get close to Sarah if I have a 'wife' on my arm?"

"Oh...it's 'Sarah' now, is it?" she chided. "What base did you get to tonight, Romeo?"

"Don't be foolish," Shane replied. "This is strictly business."

"So, you telling me this bitch is some fat, ugly science geek?" she asked with a sly smile.

"No...not exactly," Shane replied. "She's actually a very attractive young lady."

Shane reached into the small refrigerator, extracted two bottles of carbonated orange drinks, and sauntered into the sitting room. Handing one bottle to Salomé, he sprawled on the opposite sofa, loosened his tie, ripped the cap off his soda, and took a long sip. "Would you like to hear what happened at the mixer?" he asked.

"Not really. You're back safe. That's what counts," she replied. Then, whipping her leg off the arm of the chair and leaning forward, she rapped the orange soda bottle on the cocktail table separating them. "Listen to me, Shane. This operation is too important for you to fuck it up. If someone recognizes you out there, and I'm not around, this whole mission goes down the tubes. You understand that?"

"Getting to Sarah is the key for this mission to succeed, Salomé," Shane replied. "We have to take the risk. And, besides, what the hell could you do if someone did recognize me?"

After taking several seconds to glare at Shane, Salomé responded, "There would be an unfortunate accident."

"Are you threatening me?" Shane asked.

"No, you idiot. But don't tempt me."

A long period of silence—during which Shane simply stared darkly at her—was followed by Salomé's rising to her feet and moving away in the direction of the bedroom.

"Wait!" Shane called out. "We need to talk, Salomé."

Turning around to look over her shoulder, Salomé asked, "Are you gonna keep running around town on your own, Shane? 'Cause if you are, we got nothing more to talk about."

With a sigh, Shane said, "No. I understand. From now on we're joined at the hip. OK?"

With an expression on her face that appeared almost sullen, Salomé returned and resumed her casual pose with one leg over the chair arm, as if to say, *Get to the point, Tony.*

"If you mix with these people as my wife, Salomé, I won't be able to get close to Sarah."

"Some women are *attracted* to married men," Salomé remarked.

"Yeah. But, not this one."

"You know her that well already?"

"That much I can tell."

"OK, I'll give you that. So we'll get me inside some other way."

"You can't pretend to be one of the scientific attendees. They'd spot you in a minute."

"Look, Tony. Don't worry about it. I'll figure something out."

After reflecting a moment on Salomé's many talents, Shane simply nodded his head in acquiescence.

"Alright, let's get down to some important stuff," Salomé resumed. "What do you think Mironi's gonna do when he discovers we tricked him?"

"First he'll be pissed, 'cause he always needs to be in control. And then he'll laugh and give us some respect. But he will tell his guys to find us…or else."

"What does that mean?"

"That means sooner or later, he'll find us."

"Do you think he can find us *here?*"

"In my opinion—no. He thinks we're headed for New York right now. That's where he'll be looking, probably using border guards on his payroll. We're using his transit papers and driving one of his cars. He *will* find us. And that's OK. He'll just have to understand that we have to keep some thing's secret—even from him."

"Does he know the goal of *operation rainbow?*"

"No."

"He's supporting us *blind?*" Salomé asked.

"I guess you'd say that," Shane responded.

After staring at Shane for a few moments, Salomé said, "Bullshit! No way Mironi's gonna do that. What did you tell him, Tony?"

Returning her gaze for a few moments, Shane then looked away briefly, took a deep breath and said, "I told him we were going to take down the Nazis—and the Japs and the Russkies—with one shot. And without any more nukes."

"And he's going for this? Impossible! He's got everything to lose."

"I convinced him that his operations would survive," Shane declared.

"Tony, you're crazy! Mironi will get wiped out just like everything else if *rainbow* works," Salomé cried.

"How do you know, Salomé?"

"What do you mean? Do you know something I don't know?"

"What I mean is nobody really knows what happens if *rainbow* works."

"But you have a theory—right?"

"Well, you might say so," Shane replied as he looked away.

"All right. Give it to me, Shane. What's your theory? And what did you tell Mironi?"

With a sigh, Shane began: "I think that we all exist at this moment on a single time line that extends back to the beginning of the universe. So, if you could go back in time, you could pinpoint a historical event and be there.

"On the other hand, at any given instant—say right now—there are an infinite number of possible future time lines. The one that the universe follows is determined by all of the collective free will choices made by humans from instant to instant, as well as the collective impact of all the presumably chaotic behavior of every other particle in the universe."

"Not that I agree or disagree...or even understand what the hell you're talking about, Tony. But...so what?"

"First of all, mine is only one theory. Harry believes that there is no 'free will'. There is only one possible time line, pre-determined by the 'big bang,' when the universe was formed. Every particle and quantum of energy has a pre-determined destiny governed by the laws of physics and whatever trajectory they were given at the time of the 'big bang'. There is no way we can alter it. And, even if we did, that alteration itself would have been pre-destined to occur."

"Wow! Now you're really losing me, Tony."

"All right, this is the point: I believe that alternative future time lines must be interrelated. That is, if you exist at this moment in this time line, you will exist in practically all of the infinite alternative future time lines."

"So what?" Salomé inquired.

"If we could examine alternative future time lines, we might discover differences in major historical events, but we would find them populated by essentially the same people doing similar things in similar relationships."

"So, get to the point, Tony. What do you think our time line has in common with the time line that would have evolved if the Allies had won the Second World War? That's what this is all about, isn't it?"

"Well," Shane began with a sigh, "I told Mironi that even if the Axis powers were taken down, his operation would survive. And, Salomé, I really believe that."

"Tony," Salomé interrupted, "Mironi doesn't know you're thinking about messing with the time line. He thinks you're talking about some kind of *coup* that will change the leadership today. You've deceived the hell out of him!"

"Semantics," Shane countered. "That's all it is."

"Semantics!" she exclaimed. "You really believe the Mironi mob would survive and thrive under the Allies these past 60 years like it did with the Nazis?"

"Exactly."

"You're out of your mind, Shane! And your theory is all wet. Hitler exterminated tens of millions of Jews. He killed my great grandparents. Don't tell me the same people exist in different time lines!

"And what happens when Mironi learns that *rainbow* will wipe *him* out? You think he'll go for that? He won't be happy that some *alter ego* Vito Mironi is screwing all his broads and drinking all his booze."

For several moments Shane remained silent, looking off into space. Then, with a shrug, he said, "I didn't lie to him, Salomé. That's the important thing. I didn't lie to him."

"You may be right, Tony. But, you'd better pray that Mironi never figures out your version of the truth...at least not *before* we complete *operation rainbow*. Otherwise, even Grandpa Rico's ghost won't save you."

*   *   *   *

"Arthur Stone" had been waiting for Sarah in the back of the Hamburg Room as the last of the morning's speakers had finished answering questions from the audience. The curious mix of German and English dialogue between the international audience and the American speaker was a new experience for Shane. He had attended technical meetings in the North American Soviet territories, but there the universal language had been English only.

As Sarah walked up to him, attired this day in a gray pinstriped suit and high heels, with the skirt just below the knees, Shane thought he noticed a slight hesitancy as they shook hands. The tone in her voice confirmed his misgivings as she said, "Good morning Dr. Stone. Do you still have time for lunch?"

Disappointed by the lukewarm greeting, Shane quickly regained his resolve and said, "I sure do. I'm looking forward to it. Where shall we go?"

Sarah persuaded "Stone" to follow her out a side exit, avoiding the gathering crowd in the hotel lobby, and get into her car parked nearby. She took the driver's seat of her Volkswagen sedan, quickly exited the parking lot, and headed north towards Willowbrook, a few miles away. Maintaining a steady chatter of small talk for the next fifteen minutes, Sarah delivered them to a shopping mall that included a small Italian Trattoria tucked into a far corner.

As they took their seats in a secluded booth, Shane looked around and noted that they were well isolated from the other scattered lunchtime customers. After they each ordered a glass of red wine and began to look over the menus, Shane decided to break the ice.

"Sarah," he began, "am I wrong, or do I sense that you've lost some enthusiasm since we talked last night?"

The prompt delivery of their filled wineglasses gave Sarah a moment to delay her response. When the waiter had left, she said, "I'm sorry, Arthur. It's been a very busy couple of days. And right now I'm just saturated with technical talk. Frankly, I'm looking forward to just enjoying a nice lunch. Perhaps we can talk later about our research programs."

Taking her cue without showing his inner disappointment, Shane simply raised his wineglass to hers and said, "I agree, Sarah. Cheers!"

"Why don't you tell me about yourself, Arthur," she said after finishing her first sip of wine. "Where did you do your graduate work? Where are you from?"

Quickly shuffling through his mental file on Professor Arthur Stone, Shane hesitated ever so slightly before replying, "Miami University, but I'm from New Orleans originally."

"And what about your family? You're married aren't you?"

"Yes. Two kids—boy and a girl," Shane responded, realizing that he would quickly exceed the limits of his mental data base on Arthur Stone if the questions got any more personal. He knew Stone's technical accomplishments very well, but so far that had not been the topic of discussion.

"Now," Shane countered, "why don't you tell me about yourself. Where are you from?"

The personal chatter continued briefly, but subsided as the waiter approached and they took time to decide on lunch orders. After the waiter departed with their selections in hand, Shane decided to force the conversation back to technical matters.

"Last night," Shane began, "you seemed quite interested in our endoscopic implant technology. Can I ask if you've tried anything along these lines at the *Institut?*"

"No. Not really," Sarah responded tersely.

"Do you have encapsulated microcircuitry that might be implantable?" Shane persisted.

"No. Not yet," she replied.

Frustrated, Shane decided to force the issue. "You really don't want to talk about your work, do you?"

This time Sarah took a few moments to look directly into Shane's eyes. "Oh, yes, I would, *Arthur*," she replied with a curious emphasis on the name. "But I don't think that's what this is all about. Is it?"

"What?" Shane asked.

"Let me be blunt, *Arthur*. Why don't you tell me just who the hell you are and what you really want. I know you're *not* Arthur Stone. I checked it out last night. So, what's your game, mister?"

Momentarily stunned, Shane struggled to keep his composure. He had planned to reveal himself eventually—but not until he had gained Sarah's confidence. Her discovery had upset his plans. Quickly, Shane decided there was only one way to deal with it.

"I apologize, Sarah. Yes, you're correct. I am not Arthur Stone. But, please— before you get angry—let me explain."

"You've got about two minutes."

"My name is Tony Shane. I'm involved with the YLA, and I'm a fugitive. The *Gestapo* is breathing down my neck as we speak. They're after me because of the attacks last week."

"What attacks?"

"The *Landeszentralbank* building? Don't you know?"

"You mean the power plant explosion?"

"It was more than that."

"What?"

"I don't want to go into it now. You're not getting the whole story. It was a bombing. There were others—all across the *DRA*. The YLA was responsible."

"Bringing her hand up to her mouth, Sarah exclaimed in a whisper, "You're a *terrorist?*"

"No. No, I'm not. That's what I'm trying to stop. Please—listen to what I have to say."

A wide-eyed Sarah, her hand still up to her face, simply nodded.

"I know you're not a Nazi, and you're no Nazi sympathizer either. You may not be interested in helping our cause, but will you at least try to understand? If you are unwilling to help us, I will walk away and that will be the end of it."

As Shane held his breath, Sarah's gaze seemed to bore right through him. She was not smiling. Finally, she said, "I'm listening."

"There is only one condition I must insist on," Shane began. "You can not reveal any of what I'm about to tell you."

A slight nod signaled her agreement, but she couldn't hide a slight frown.

"What I'm about to tell you may seem fantastic, but it is absolutely true. Have you ever thought about future probabilities? Or alternate time lines?"

With a puzzled expression, Sarah simply shook her head.

"What if I were to tell you that an alternate time line exists where the Second World War was not won by the Axis powers, but by the United States and its allies? That wouldn't be so hard to believe would it?"

With a slight shrug, Sarah replied, "I've heard of this kind of thinking before. It's science fiction. Fantasy."

"Yes, it is. But what if I told you that I have proof that the alternate time line exists. That, I have received communications from that other time line?"

"Now you're really stretching. What kind of 'proof' do you have?"

"It has to do with telepathic time travel."

"You mean telepathic communication across time?" Sarah asked with obvious skepticism.

"That's right. I have proof that it's been accomplished."

Shaking her head, Sarah said, "So what? Even if I believed it was possible, what's the point?"

"The point is that after the Allies won the Second World War, someone many years later was able to use telepathic time travel to go back and alter a pivotal event early in the war so that the Nazis, Soviets and Japanese won the war. That is the time line that we are experiencing now."

Still shaking her head, but with a new curious look in her eyes, Sarah commented, "That's an amazing story. But where are you going with it?"

"Where I'm going is on a mission to undo what was done over sixty years ago. With your help, Sarah, we can go back and fix the original time line."

Suddenly speechless, her mouth open, Sarah's eyes blinked several times before she blurted, "*Me?* You're asking *me* to get involved in this craziness?"

"I hope I can persuade you...yes," Shane replied. "You're our only hope, Sarah."

Gazing intently at Shane, apparently overwhelmed by the unexpected solicitation, Sarah asked, "Where is your proof that this is possible?"

"I will show you. But, before we go on, you need to think about it carefully. You would put yourself right in the same Nazi crosshairs where I find myself. And, if we are successful, the world that we know would no longer exist."

As Sarah remained silent for several seconds, they were interrupted by the arrival of the lunches they had ordered.

As the waiter departed, Shane said, "I know this is a lot to absorb, Sarah. And it's very heavy stuff. Why don't we finish our lunch? Then, maybe we can get together again after the plenary session this evening. That will give you time to digest what I've said. If you think you'd like to go further, I'll show you the proof I've talked about."

Without a word, just a nod and a wan smile, Sarah agreed.

But, as they quietly completed their lunch, Shane studied Sarah's impassive face...wondering silently if he had just gained an ally, or created a formidable opponent.

CHAPTER 8

▼

REVELATIONS

To Sarah had fallen the task of escorting Sergei Chekov around the *Institut* that afternoon. He had been particularly interested in seeing her research labs. Sarah's supervisor, Wolfgang Schwarz, had not objected to the tour, as she could not show Chekov any of the latest work involving human memory function emulation and neuron stimulation. If anything, Sarah would pick Chekov's brain regarding his current work on simulated intelligence using artificial neural networks.

Although the Nazis and the Soviets had both expended many years of research on mind control—extending as far back as the obscene experiments with human subjects under Hitler's rule—they never openly admitted the purpose of their work. Instead they had cloaked it in terms of "artificial intelligence" research. Even Sarah had bought into this euphemism.

But, as excited as she was to have the great Sergei Chekov to herself for a few hours before his plenary address that evening, she could not rid her mind of the disturbing conversation she had had with Tony Shane. If there was any truth to his story, it was mind-blowing. But Shane was a complete stranger, and she wasn't sure how to gauge him.

What does he want from me? she asked herself for the hundredth time. And, once more, she thought: Shane must be disturbed—some perverted scientist obsessed with her, and trying to draw her into his own twisted world.

And yet, his preposterous tale had been related so directly, and he had seemed so credible. *If only I could corroborate anything of what he said*, she thought, when suddenly it struck her. The devastating explosion at the *Landeszentralbank* last week. Shane had claimed it was a terrorist act, and that the YLA was responsible. What if she could corroborate that part of his story? Would that persuade her to consider the credibility of the rest?

Sarah's background thoughts were displaced abruptly as she realized that Chekov was waiting for an answer to a question. "I...I'm sorry," she stammered. "Can you repeat your question?"

With a quick flash of polished white teeth, Chekov laughed and repeated his question. "Did you find Arthur Stone last night?" he asked. "I've been wondering, since you asked me at the mixer if I had seen him. Did you check to see if he was registered?"

"No," she replied more calmly than she expected, "he wasn't registered. I must have misunderstood the person who said he was here."

"Too bad. I would have enjoyed seeing him again."

After a short period of silence, Chekov asked, "And who was that young man you ran into when you left Wolfgang and me to get a drink?"

"I...I really don't know, Dr. Chekov. Just one of the other conferees. He was asking about the morning symposium schedule."

"American chap?"

"Why, yes, I think so."

"Hmmh. Funny he didn't introduce himself. Most young American scientists are eager to get their names known."

"Yes," she nodded, hoping desperately to terminate this discussion.

"I'll bet you must be exhausted from all the arrangements for this conference," Chekov said with an understanding gaze.

"It has been intense," Sarah admitted.

"Look. Why don't you join me for dinner after the plenary session? Consider it a small token of appreciation for all you've done to make my visit so pleasant."

"But there will be refreshments served in the ballroom after your talk. You're expected to make an appearance."

"Yes, I know. I mean after that. Surely we can find a late night supper club."

"I would love to, Dr. Chekov," Sarah replied. "But I am really pretty tired. And I have to give my own talk early tomorrow morning."

The smile never faded from Chekov's face as he responded. "Of course. I understand. Perhaps another time?"

"I would be delighted, Dr. Chekov."

"Wonderful!" he said with enthusiasm. "I'll be visiting the *Institut* for another week or so, and I'll hold you to it, Sarah. And, please, call me Sergei."

*   *   *   *

The hum of conversation in the Crystal Ballroom, following Chekov's talk, was deafening. Sarah had not yet picked Shane out from among the hundreds of conferees distributed in small groups throughout the large hall. But that was good. She had to talk with Wolfgang Schwarz first.

"Dr. Schwarz," she cried out, as she saw him leave a small circle of Nazi administrators about ten feet away. With a broad smile Schwarz acknowledged Sarah, and they moved together.

"Sarah," Schwarz said with enthusiasm, "my congratulations. Everything is going very smoothly."

"Thank you, Dr. Schwarz," Sarah responded. "But I did get some questions that I couldn't handle today. I hoped you might help me out."

"Of course, my dear. What's the problem?"

"Several visitors have asked me about the *Landeszentralbank* explosion last week. Have we caught the YLA terrorists that caused the blast?"

Schwarz looked around quickly, and then leaned closer so that only Sarah might hear his response. "I was just discussing this very matter with the Director of the *DIB*. Unfortunately, those responsible have not been caught. But it is only a matter of time before those bloody *Yanks* are found."

"I hope it will be soon," Sarah lied. "Are there any other assurances I can give people?"

"You can tell them that our nuclear scientists have determined that the radio-active debris was carried out over Lake Michigan. There is no radioactivity danger locally."

Trying desperately to hide the shock of learning that the explosion had really been a *nuclear* blast, Sarah did not risk further comment. She simply shook her head.

Faced with her silence, Schwarz regarded Sarah curiously and asked, "Who inquired about these things?"

Surprised and temporarily thrown off-balance by the question, Sarah hesitated and searched her mind frantically for a response. Finally, she decided to equivocate. "Oh, several visiting speakers."

"Foreigners?" Schwarz asked with a frown.

"Some," Sarah answered.

"Can you name one?"

Scrambling mentally for a lie that might satisfy Schwarz's curiosity, Sarah decided on evasion. "Actually, I didn't know any of the people who raised this question."

With slightly arched eyebrows, Schwarz simply gazed at Sarah for several moments. Finally, he asked, "Dr. Chekov didn't ask about this matter?"

"No. Of course not," Sarah replied.

"Hmmh. That's good," Schwarz muttered, as his gaze drifted away from Sarah briefly. Then, he looked back at her and asked, "Did *any* of our Soviet or Japanese visitors ask about this matter?"

"I believe they were all Americans," Sarah answered, hoping it was what he wanted to hear.

"Hmmh. Please, Sarah, if you have any further inquiries about these matters, refer them to me. OK?"

"Of course, Dr. Schwarz," Sarah responded.

"Good. Now please, Sarah, go on about your business. And continue your good work. Everything is going beautifully."

With a smile, Schwarz patted her shoulder and moved away.

*   *   *   *

As the Crystal Ballroom crowd began to thin out, Sarah searched in vain for some sign of Tony Shane. The thought that he might not show up at all occurred to her. Perhaps he had been apprehended she worried. How ironic, she thought, that her regard for Shane had changed so dramatically that she was now concerned for his safety. His story was not any less fantastic, but at least part of it had been confirmed. And he was certainly a fugitive.

Finally, at ten o'clock, as the hotel attendants began to clean up the ballroom, and the last of the stragglers departed, Sarah resigned herself to the fact that Shane would not show up that evening. She grabbed her wrap and headed out the lobby to the hotel parking lot. As she walked to her Volkswagen she noted that Sergei Chekov was assisting the wife of one of the *Institut's* directors into the front passenger seat of her husband's car, and then following another woman, adorned in a silver evening gown, into the back seat. As Sarah opened the door to her car, Chekov looked over and noticed her. With a slight nod and smile, he disappeared into the car just as Sarah slid into her own.

As she started up the engine and reached for the seat belt, she heard a sound behind her and quickly turned her head. There, with a finger pressed to his lips, was Tony Shane. Momentarily stunned, Sarah could only gasp while Shane whispered, "Don't be afraid. I couldn't take a chance on exposing myself again. Just drive off someplace where we can talk safely."

Without a word, Sarah turned her head forward, put the car in gear and departed the parking lot. As they turned on to the main highway, she said to her back seat passenger, "I'll take you to my place. We should be safe there." In the rear view mirror she saw Shane nod his head.

*   *   *   *

Because of the attendant in the lobby of her apartment building, Sarah first circled around the back and let Shane off near the unmanned loading dock where deliveries were handled during the day. Then she parked her car in the front of the building, entered, and went up to her apartment on the third floor. Instead of entering, however, she went directly to the freight elevator and took it down to the main level. When the door opened, Shane ducked in and they returned to the third floor. After moving quickly down the hall without encountering anyone, Sarah unlocked her apartment door and they slid inside.

"Thanks for agreeing to meet with me, Sarah," Shane said as he placed his backpack on the sofa and removed his black leather jacket, revealing his casual tee shirt and jeans attire.

Noting the contrast with her formal business suit, Sarah's first words were, "I guess you weren't planning on socializing with the brass tonight, were you?" The broad smile on her face was disarming, and Shane laughed. At that moment Sarah realized that the social barrier that had impeded their earlier conversation had receded. Strangely enough the things she had learned that day had drawn her closer to this man whom she still barely knew.

Without further hesitation, Shane sat down and opened his backpack, extracting a manila folder stuffed with papers. Then he stood up and strode over to the round wooden dinette table, laid the folder down, and beckoned to Sarah to join him.

"Why don't you make yourself comfortable, Tony. I need to freshen up. There's beer in the fridge. Or feel free to open a bottle of wine. My 'wine cellar' is behind the pantry door, and you can find an opener and glasses in the kitchen."

"I'd prefer some wine. How about you?" he asked.

"Great. I didn't have a drink at the social, and I could really use one."

As Shane busied himself preparing their drinks, Sarah slipped into the large bathroom/dressing room that was the most attractive feature of her efficiency apartment.

Several minutes later, after slipping out of her suit and into jeans and sweatshirt, she emerged from the dressing room to see Shane spreading papers across the dinette table. Two large glasses of red wine were positioned on either side of the table.

"I opened the Australian Shiraz. I hope that's OK," Shane said as Sarah padded barefoot toward the table.

"Great. My favorite sipping wine," she replied. Then, as she took a seat opposite Shane, she asked, "What's all this, Tony?"

"Some documents you need to see. One is a letter my father gave me in 1985, just before the *Gestapo* took him away. The other is a letter from Albert Einstein to Professor Garrison Fuller at the University of Wisconsin. Einstein sent it from exile in Mexico back in 1949."

"A letter from Einstein! How did you get that? And who is Garrison Fuller?" Sarah asked.

"It's a very long story. I hope you don't have to be at the conference early tomorrow."

Despite her need to put the finishing touches on the talk she would be delivering the next morning, Sarah could not at that moment think of anything more important than listening to Tony Shane's story. "Not a problem, Tony," she said. "Take all the time you need."

*   *   *   *

Tony's story had begun with his "letter from the future" and had ended two hours and one-and-a-half empty wine bottles later with the description of *operation rainbow*. Despite persistent skeptical questioning, Shane had somehow convinced Sarah that his story was valid. For the first time Shane had revealed the entire technical content of the future letter. They then turned to the Einstein letter and Shane's belief that the obscure messages contained secrets needed to implement telepathic time travel.

It was at this point that Sarah could no longer contain herself. "Tony," she blurted, "this letter from Einstein is incredible! Can't you see what he's done?"

Surprised by Sarah's outburst, Shane stared at her expectantly.

"These symbols are characters from the ancient Hebrew language. I don't know what they mean, but I recognize them. Have you had someone look at this letter who knows Hebrew?"

"No. We focused our attention on the English part of the message, but couldn't make any sense of it."

"I have a feeling that someone who knows both Hebrew and English could put the two parts together."

"Is there anyone you can trust who might translate this?" Shane asked.

"Are you kidding? There are no Jews left in the *DRA*. And the Nazis certainly don't include Hebrew in any curriculum. In fact, that's probably why Einstein used the ancient language for this letter in the first place."

"All right," Shane said, "let's put the Einstein letter aside for now. How close are you to putting together the kind of technology described in my 1939 letter?"

"We're very close, Tony, with one big exception. The 'nanotechnology' is not even on the horizon. We have computers on a microchip, but nothing compared to the packing density described in the letter."

"I've read about your work with rats and animals," Shane said. "I know this is touchy, but have you worked with humans?"

"Not in my laboratory!" she exclaimed.

"But in other laboratories?"

"I've only heard rumors."

"Here at the *Institut*?"

"I'm afraid so," she shrugged.

"How much do you know?"

"Nothing!" she protested. "I don't want to know."

"Who would run these experiments?"

"You can probably guess."

"Schwarz?"

"Yes."

"Any idea of where these facilities are?"

Before replying, Sarah took a deep breath. "There's a sub-basement beneath our building. It doesn't show up on the plans or directory. But I've seen technicians disappear from basement labs and reappear mysteriously somewhat later. Access to the sub-basement must be well hidden."

"If you had to guess, what kind of human interface technology might be available?"

Sarah thought about this for several seconds before replying. "Probably an extension of what we've done with animals. Microprobes—microscopic platinum wires—inserted into specific nodes of the brain and connected to computer outputs."

"How many connections can you handle?"

"One thing we've learned is that you don't need a large number of connections to implement sophisticated mental functions."

"What about memory emulation?"

"No way. We simply don't have the conceptual approach, even if we had adequate computer power."

Shane hesitated for several seconds, his brow furrowed. Finally, he said, "The two requirements for telepathic communication with a distant time are to compute four-dimensional coordinates of the target in real-time and augment neural feedback."

"And—?" Sarah asked as Shane paused.

"Do you think you could implement that ability? Do it for a human subject?"

"Maybe. Someday," Sarah mused. "But if you asked me to do it tomorrow. No."

Slowly shaking his head, Shane said, "We have to find a way to do it soon, Sarah. In the next two weeks."

"I don't know," Sarah began. "I could try. But it could get complicated."

"What do you mean?"

"Sergei Chekov. He's going to be at the *Institut* for at least another week. I know he'll be snooping around."

"Doesn't sound like the best situation."

"You don't know the half of it."

"Huh?"

"Chekov asked me out to dinner tonight. I turned him down, but I don't think that will be the end of it."

"Great timing," Shane lamented. "Can you deal with it?"

"What makes you think I want to 'deal with it,' Mr. Shane?" Sarah asked, a coy smile lighting her face.

Shane laughed, and then said, "OK. Let's skip over Chekov for now. Do you have the resources to develop the human interface and programming?"

"Like I said, I don't know. I need to think about it."

"Don't try to figure it out now, Sarah. What is it—two o'clock in the morning? Neither one of us should be talking technical stuff right now," Shane commented as he raised the second empty wine bottle up in the air.

Tossing her head to one side and laughing, Sarah's long auburn hair flipped across her face. As her laughter subsided, she reached up to brush the hair from her eyes, only to find Shane's hand reaching up to accomplish it for her.

"You've got the most infectious laugh," he commented with a smile. "And those lovely green eyes should never be covered up."

Blushing and temporarily flustered, Sarah could only smile and look away.

Standing up abruptly, Shane stretched his hands toward the ceiling and announced, "It really is getting late. I'd better get going."

Standing up herself, Sarah said, "I'll give you a ride back to the hotel."

"Not necessary," Shane remarked as he gathered all the scattered papers into his backpack. "I have a ride waiting for me outside."

"What?"

"Sorry. I didn't want to say anything earlier. It's my partner. The one I mentioned—Salomé. She's paranoid. Followed us here. She's supposed to keep me safe from predators like you."

Sarah laughed and asked, "She's been waiting for you all this time?"

"Yeah."

"Well, I'd better let you get going. You'll have to take the freight elevator again you know."

"I'm getting used to it."

Sarah laughed again, grabbed Shane's leather jacket, thrust it in his arms, and began to shove him towards the door.

"I didn't think you'd be so eager to send me away."

Sarah just smiled and continued her mock ejection of Shane. But, as they neared the door she hesitated before opening it. She had much to say, she realized. It had been the most memorable evening of her life. She didn't know where things were heading, but she knew that Tony Shane would be a very important part of her life over the next few weeks.

"One last thing I have to ask you, Tony," she said with her hand on the doorknob. "Why haven't you asked if I'm going to help you?

"Are you?"

"Honestly, I don't know. This whole idea has just blown me away."

"But you're going to work on the neural augmentation program?"

"Yeah, but I don't know if I can go where you're headed, Tony. I need to think about it."

As Shane regarded her silently, Sarah continued, "One more thing, Tony. How were you so sure that I wasn't a Nazi? That I wouldn't turn you in?"

"That was easy, Sarah. Just look at your publications from the *Institut*. Every one lists that lard-ass Schwarz as the first author. Even I knew he was just the nominal Nazi project leader. Everybody knows you're the real moving force. If you were a Nazi, you would have been the project leader."

"I hadn't thought of that," Sarah admitted, gently shaking her head.

"And look at where they stuck your name on the conference program. You were obviously the organizer, and yet your name was buried in the fine print of the 'thanks for all your help' section."

Still shaking her head, a slight flush crept through her cheeks. Impulsively, she reached up, gently placed a hand on either side of his face, and pulled Shane to her. The kiss was soft, long and sweet, and prompted Shane to drop his backpack and jacket, take Sarah in his arms and pull her close.

As the kiss ended and they found themselves in a tight embrace, Sarah's cheek on Shane's shoulder, Sarah whispered, "I'm sorry, Tony. I didn't want this to happen."

"I know," Shane said. "I'm a little confused myself."

"You understand what I mean, don't you?" she asked.

"Of course," he replied as he gently pulled away to look into her moist green eyes. "What a time to find someone…in the middle of a suicide mission."

*   *   *   *

After speaking with Sarah at the evening's earlier social event, Wolfgang Schwarz had conferred with one of the distinguished Nazi visitors, the local director of the *DIB*. The director had confirmed Schwarz's suspicion regarding Sarah's apparent knowledge of the terrorist strike. None but party members should have had that information, the director had stated emphatically.

There might be a simple explanation, Schwarz hoped. But his instincts told him that something was wrong.

CHAPTER 9

▼

FOREIGN AFFAIRS

Juri Chernovsky loved his job. As First Deputy to the Soviet Foreign Minister, Alexander Topov, he was hardly ever in the public spotlight. Yet, while Topov was involved in countless public appearances and state functions, to Chernovsky had fallen the real responsibilities for foreign affairs. While Topov postured and pontificated about official Soviet foreign policy, it was Chernovsky who negotiated *realpolitik* behind the scenes with countries, armies, rebels and spies around the world.

Today Chernovsky was in Zurich, officially attending the Conference on International Banking and Investment. Delegates from nations around the world were in attendance, most of them legitimately concerned with agendas of currency valuation, electronic fund transfers, and standardized banking practices. Chernovsky was the nominal head of the Soviet delegation, composed mostly of banking experts and economists. However, for Chernovsky and his counterparts representing Japan and China, this conference was an opportunity to discuss unofficially the issue of most vital importance to their respective nations. Along with one other individual, representing the most powerful independent power bloc in the world, these gentlemen would meet to lay the foundation for a pact, both official and unofficial, which would finally resolve intolerable situations that had festered for nearly six decades.

It was ironic, Chernovsky mused, as he walked along the sunny *Bahnhoff-strasse*, that it had taken the efforts of the rag-tag bunch of YLA rebels to finally push this issue to the forefront. Through a series of discreet communications since September 11, each of the interested parties had acknowledged that this was the perfect time to strike. The German *Reichskanzler*, the Nazi military, and particularly the *Gestapo* were focused on finding those responsible for the nuclear terrorist strikes in the *DRA*. In addition, they had re-doubled their counter-terrorism activities throughout the German Confederation. This preoccupation provided the ideal opportunity for the Soviet-led coalition to strike a decisive fatal blow. Finally, they would gain retribution for the heavy-handed Nazi usurpation of the spoils of the Second World War. With one daring stroke, they would eliminate decades of frustrating and ultimately intolerable inequities.

Turning into the lobby of the ancient Edelweiss Hotel on the *Bahnhoffstrasse*, Chernovsky carefully looked around to see if any of the other delegates had arrived. The secret meeting would take place in a suite that had not been disclosed previously. They had arranged to stagger their entries to the hotel. Chernovsky would be the first to arrive at two o'clock in the afternoon. He had reserved the meeting place for the afternoon and evening in the name of a Moscow bank as a hospitality suite for prospective clients. In fact, the bank existed only as a fictitious Soviet paper document, and only the delegates of interest would learn of the meeting place.

Within minutes Chernovsky arrived by elevator at the entrance to the sixth floor suite. As he pushed through the unlocked door, he was met by a handful of hotel stewards putting the final touches on the refreshments laid out for the delegates that would probably be spending several long hours there. In the far corners, on either end of the suite, he recognized the two sturdy plainclothes Soviet security officers that had occupied the suite for the past twenty-four hours. To them had fallen the responsibility to assure that there were no surveillance devices and that all rooms were adequately secure. During the sensitive discussions that afternoon they would be posted outside the entrance to prevent any unexpected intrusions.

Moving into the elegantly furnished main room, Chernovsky noticed immediately that the wall to his left was completely mirrored. He took a moment to examine his own image. He was tall and slender, still handsome and firm despite his sixty years of good living. The hair was still thick and black with heavy bands of gray at the temples. The moustache and goatee were meticulously groomed and died black. His black suit and tie were standard government attire for the foreign ministry, but, Chernovsky noted to himself with a sly smile, he did cut a particularly dashing figure.

Chernovsky moved toward the head of the large conference table of dark polished wood that was surrounded by half-a-dozen leather-covered easy chairs. He seated himself at the head of the table and surveyed the empty spaces that would soon be filled by the figures that, along with himself, were the real international power brokers. With a wry smile Chernovsky noted that there would be no written agenda, and there would be no written record, for the earth-shaking agreements that would be forged that day.

*   *   *   *

"What do the *Yanks* know of these plans?" asked Keido Taguchi in the universally accepted English, as several hours of deliberations neared an end. The Japanese naval undersecretary had long been the designated negotiator for the Japanese Empire's military ruling body, and he had long suspected the secret Soviet—Chinese non-aggression agreement that had been revealed to him that day. Now he wondered what other knowledge had been kept secret from him.

"They know nothing," Juri Chernovsky replied.

"And how can I be certain of that?" Taguchi asked.

"You have my word, Keido. That is all you need," Chernovsky responded.

"And we will not be surprised, as we were today when we learned that our Chinese friends had been invited to join our coalition?" Taguchi inquired.

After gazing benignly at Taguchi for a few moments, Chernovsky replied, "You know better than anyone, Keido, that some negotiations must be kept secret, even from your friends. We have revealed this pact to you at the first opportunity—today. None of the international community outside this room will know of this agreement until after our mission is launched. There could be no more profound indication of our good faith."

With a grudging shrug, Taguchi acknowledged his colleague's logic, but then said, "Perhaps I should have directed my question to the YLA's most generous benefactor." With that, Taguchi turned to face across the table the one member of the conference who did not represent a sovereign nation.

Seated across from Taguchi was Solomon Rothchild, the unofficial leader of the powerful international Jewish community. Although he resided in Miami, Rothchild was one of millions of Jews whose families had fled persecution in Europe and the *DRA* during the twentieth century. With their power base centered in the Florida territory of the North American Soviet State, this hub was linked to large numbers of Jews throughout the world. Although they had no formal governing body or military, their cumulative wealth and fanatical Zionism directed obscene levels of financing to organizations around the globe who might further their cause. The Yankee Liberation Army had been the largest recipient of their lavish funding. These funds had enabled the recent purchase of ten nuclear warheads from the Chinese, four of which had been detonated during the terrorist attacks of September 11.

Rothchild lowered his chin and peered at Taguchi over his wire-rimmed spectacles, a benign smile on his face. He shook his massive bald head ever so slightly as he began to reply, "Keido, you have no reason to fear the YLA. They are our allies in this mission."

"I do not *fear* the *Yanks*, Mr. Rothchild," Taguchi responded. "I fear the proliferation of knowledge."

"Would it quiet your concerns if I were to confirm Juri's statement that the YLA have no knowledge of our coalition or its mission?" Rothchild asked.

"They do not?" Taguchi persisted.

"No, they do not," Rothchild repeated.

Nodding to Rothchild with his thin lips set in a tight line, Taguchi turned finally to the last member of the team seated to his left. With only an arched eyebrow, he directed Tong Liu, the Chinese delegate, to respond to the unasked question.

Tong Liu, the youngest conferee, was in his late forties. His position within the Chinese governing hierarchy was poorly understood, as was most of the secretive totalitarian Communist rule. He was military with the rank of General, but this hardly distinguished him from the rest of the top rulers of the billion plus Chinese people. Because China had had little interaction with the international community until the relatively recent attempts of other nations to exploit China's enormous consumer potential, their foreign service was largely nonexistent. Military personnel handled most aspects of foreign affairs.

But Liu had been the key negotiator with the Soviets to develop the nonagression pact revealed to the group this day. And he had been designated to attend this conference which would commit the Chinese to join with the Soviets, Japanese and virtual Jewish state in an undertaking that would dramatically alter the global political landscape.

After gazing at Taguchi's quizzical expression for several moments, feigning temporary uncertainty at the question being posed, Tong Liu said, "If you are wondering whether the *Yanks* have learned anything from us, please be assured they have not."

"They must wonder why you were willing to sell them the warheads?" Taguchi insisted, waiting for Liu to respond.

With a sigh, Liu replied, "They only know that some 'corrupt' workers in our nuclear re-cycling industry were willing to trade the warheads for enough money to smuggle themselves to Mexico and live comfortably and anonymously for the rest of their lives. What is there to question? Of more concern, I would imagine, would be the interests of their benefactor."

Taguchi took Liu's words as a cue to shift his gaze once again to Solomon Rothchild across the table. Without waiting for Taguchi to form a question, Rothchild laughed and said, "And no one wonders, Keido, about our motivation for aiding the YLA. It is no secret that we crave revenge and retribution for the European and American Holocausts. And it is no secret that we would bring down the Nazi regime if we could."

"On the other hand," Rothchild continued after a few moments, "there is only one *Yank* who knows where the funds came from. And that person is Nathan Carothers."

"There is no one else?" Taguchi asked.

"No," was Rothchild's simple reply.

Several seconds of silence were then broken by Juri Chernovsky. "Although our good friend Keido has not phrased the question, this is what may be of concern, 'Can Carothers, or any other *Yank*, surmise what is our plan? And, must we proceed without the YLA's help? Or should we engage them in our plan?'"

"They have done enough with the recent nuclear terrorist strikes," Taguchi responded. "We risk them learning of our plans if we ask for more."

"Ridiculous!" interjected Rothchild. "We need them to do even more, not only in the *DRA*, but also in Europe."

"I agree," said Tong Liu before Taguchi could respond.

"No! We need nothing more of the YLA so long as we strike quickly," Taguchi insisted. "The Nazis have directed all resources to counter-terrorism. Let them think they have been successful."

Putting up a hand to halt what threatened to become a heated disagreement, Chernovsky said, "Gentlemen, it does not matter what we think. Further action by the YLA is seriously impeded at the moment. The Nazi counter-terrorist measures have been severe within the *DRA*. We will be able to mobilize the Czech and Polish Freedom Fighters in Europe to create further distractions, but we will not see anything from the YLA for a while."

As each of the delegates pondered for a few moments the implications of his statement, Chernovsky found himself reflecting on how it had come to this—this coalition directed against the Nazis. The history of tortured Soviet-German relations over the past six decades was clear in his mind. The German atomic bomb development had pre-empted the Russian offensive of 1944 that would surely have displaced the Nazis completely from Eastern Europe. As compensation, the Soviets had been given all of middle North America, but the Nazis had usurped all the lucrative North Atlantic trade routes. The Soviets had responded by boldly pushing their American eastern border from New Orleans to Florida.

Although Germany had not confronted Stalin regarding Soviet occupation of the Gulf coast, Hitler had countered by declaring territorial rights to all of South America. Neither Germany nor the Soviet Union had challenged Japan's hasty occupation, as the war ended, of Central America. And the Japanese had not objected to Hitler's territorial claims in South America. But Stalin had been furious. He had followed Hitler's claims with his own declaration of Soviet rights to South America. It was only the all-consuming need to enforce their respective occupations of North America that had prevented the outbreak of hostilities. Cooler minds had prevailed, and an agreement had been reached to negotiate a settlement of Central and South American territorial disputes.

The long, bitter diplomatic struggle had resulted in the Pan American Treaty of 1949. South America had been divided between the Soviets and Germans along a north-south boundary that assigned to Germany the regions from Venezuela to Argentina and to Russia those from Columbia to Chile. Japan's rights to Central America had been accepted. Hitler had insisted, however, that the Panama Canal Zone be retained under joint Axis control. Stalin had sided with the Japanese in this dispute, but Hitler had prevailed by agreeing to Mexican neutrality. He also agreed to exclusive Japanese and Soviet interests in specific Southeast Asian territories.

The drawn out evolution of the Pan American Treaty had allowed the emergence of Russia, Japan and then China as nuclear powers and a shift in the balance of power. Over the following decades an international standoff had emerged—with the Soviets and Japanese loosely allied against the Germans. The deaths of Stalin, Hitler and Tojo in the 1950's, and the emergence of more moderate leadership in each Axis country, had been a stabilizing factor. Nevertheless, nuclear stockpiles had continued to grow. Each country continued developing advanced weapons and maintained military presence along many thousands of miles of unnatural political borders.

Officially, the Chinese had remained aloof and independent since World War II, when the Soviets had prevented a Japanese takeover. But, now, with the rising tide of capitalism in China and Russia—and the unquenchable thirst for foreign natural resources—they had become frustrated that the German Confederation had cut them off. Central to this frustration was the Germans' close alliance with the United Arab States, providing military protection in return for nearly exclusive access to petroleum exports.

But this would all change soon Chernovsky mused, as his mind returned to his colleagues' concerns. The issues dividing this new coalition were minor. They were conflicted on whether the YLA should continue their terrorist activities. Chernovsky would assure them that the YLA would not and need not be part of the equation, as this new coalition of superpowers would quickly strike to take down the Nazis once and for all.

But Chernovsky frowned involuntarily as he admitted to himself that he was unsure of the YLA's plans for the critical weeks ahead. Of one thing he was certain: his meeting with Carothers the next day would resolve the issue—one way or the other.

*   *   *   *

As the anti-Nazi coalition was meeting in Zurich to form a rapid plan of action, another meeting, similarly inspired by the recent YLA terrorist strikes, was taking place at the *Gestapo's* eastern headquarters in Chicago. Seated across from Colonel Manfred Weber's desk was a solitary distinguished visitor, engaged in earnest conversation with Weber. The visitor had been on official business in the *DRA* for the United Arab States. His name was Ahmed Sharif, and he was the Director of the Counter-terrorism unit of the UAS's Joint Intelligence Agency.

The JIA was headquartered in Damascus, and had been formed in the 1980's as a coalescence of the fragmented intelligence agencies of the various Middle Eastern countries from Morocco to Pakistan with Arabic and Islamic roots that had come together in the 1960's to form the UAS. With over two-thirds of the world's oil reserves—as well as the Jewish Holy Land—contained within its borders, the UAS sustained its uneasy confederation by the need to preserve itself against powerful outside forces. The Germans, Chinese, Japanese and Soviets thirsted for Arab oil, choosing in some cases to disdain their own reserves. The Jews, having been given a foothold in Palestine by the League of Nations in 1922, had flocked to the Holy Land.

After the end of World War II, the Palestinians and several other Arab countries had quickly allied themselves with the German Confederation. In return for exclusive access to a large fraction of the Arab oil reserves, the Nazis were recruited to sweep the Jews from the Holy Land once again. Although the Nazi military presence had been withdrawn voluntarily in the 1960's with the formation of the UAS, the German-Arab treaty of 1964 assured continued German military support in exchange for most favored access to oil exports.

Sharif's father had been a politically influential and wealthy Palestinian merchant. Despite his family's wealth, Ahmed had joined the military as a young man in the early 60's and had distinguished himself within the intelligence division. By the 1970's he was deputy director of Palestinian Intelligence, and he had quickly moved into the top ranks of the JIA after its formation in the 1980's.

This day, after a decade devoted to perfecting the state of the art of counter-terrorism employed against Jewish infiltrators in the Middle East, Ahmed Sharif found himself in the *DRA* answering questions from various *Gestapo* officials. Obviously ill prepared, but vitally concerned about the recent elevation of terrorist activities to the nuclear level, the *Gestapo* had invited Sharif to meet with their top counter-terrorism people in Berlin, Washington and Chicago.

This mission had thrown Sharif together with Manfred Weber, a long-time colleague, at an exceptionally crucial moment. Weber had just learned that their prime YLA suspect had somehow slipped out from under their tight surveillance. Multiple pursuit vehicles had trailed the car, ostensibly carrying Tony Shane and Salomé, as it sped east from Chicago on the *Zentralautobahn*. It wasn't until it became clear that the YLA car had been abandoned at a rest stop in Ohio that the *Gestapo* realized the duo had somehow escaped. Video surveillance tapes examined later showed that the travelers had shed disguises in the restrooms and slipped away unnoticed. They were not Shane and Salomé.

"Do you know their destination?" Sharif asked after listening to the story of Shane and Salomé's disappearance.

"Eastern upstate New York," Weber replied.

"Do you know the contact?"

"Well...no," Weber replied. "We aren't aware of a YLA cell there. So there must be some other purpose for the trip."

"Upstate New York is a big haystack," Sharif commented, as his body language suggested it was time for him to leave.

"You seem disinterested, Ahmed," Weber remarked.

"Not at all, Manfred," Sharif responded. "Your story is most interesting. But I am running short of time. I was supposed to be in Washington today, but detoured here because of your new position as counter-terrorism Deputy Chief. I should move on."

"Please remain a few minutes more, Ahmed. There is something else you need to hear."

With a sigh, Sharif sat back in his chair, crossed his legs and waited for the rest of the story. Despite his outward show of indifference, he was acutely interested in what Weber might reveal. And he had never intended to leave Chicago this day.

*   *   *   *

After fifteen minutes of uninterrupted disclosure, during which Ahmed Sharif had remained motionless and silent, Colonel Manfred Weber paused and gazed evenly at his colleague with anticipation. He waited for nearly a minute before Sharif made a sound.

"If you are correct," Sharif began, "the next move by the YLA will have a global impact."

"Without a doubt."

"And you want my help?"

"It would be in the best interests of the UAS, don't you think?"

"You have very little evidence of that, Manfred."

"In Shane's own words: they will be 'taking down not only the Nazis but the Soviets and Japanese as well.' I can't imagine anything that would cause greater global chaos."

"Perhaps such an event would *benefit* the UAS," Sharif suggested.

"Perhaps if you knew who was really behind all of this you might not be so glib, Ahmed," Weber stated with a thin smile.

As Sharif responded with an arched eyebrow, Weber continued, "We know that the international Zionist movement provided funds for the nuclear warheads. And the radioactive debris signature was Chinese."

Suddenly alert, Sharif asked, "You're telling me that the Jews paid the Chinese to provide nuclear weapons to the YLA?"

"The conspiracy may extend even deeper my friend."

"What do you mean?"

"We believe the Chinese and Soviets are negotiating something. As you know, the Japanese and the Soviets have contained the Chinese for decades. So we believe the Japanese should not look kindly at a Soviet-Chinese friendship. Yet we have heard nothing from them. We also know that the Japanese are quite agitated over the recent lowering of oil export quotas by the UAS. Now we learn that the Jews may be dealing with the Chinese for the YLA. If you put all these together, what do you get?"

Although the answer sprang immediately to the front of his mind, Ahmed Sharif paused before replying. He did not want to reveal that his own intelligence agency had noted a curious confluence in Zurich that day of the power blocs they were discussing. Weber had just provided the crucial link that might explain the mysterious meeting in Zurich.

Suddenly the magnitude of the problem became clear to Sharif. But this was not the time to expose his concern to Weber and the Nazi hierarchy. He needed time to deal first with the selfish interests of the UAS.

After several moments Sharif equivocated. "I'm not sure what to conclude from your statements, Manfred. Please, go on."

With a huff, Weber sat up straight in his chair and slapped a hand on his desk. "*Verdammt!* Sharif! *Das meinst du doch nicht wirklich!* You can't be serious! Surely you understand the implications. At the very least, you can see that no good can come to the UAS from the Jews working with the Chinese—especially if the Chinese are allied with the Soviets and Japanese."

"Ahh, yes," Sharif sighed, feigning new understanding, "now I see what you are getting at."

"Can you also see that the YLA may be doing the wishes of this powerful alliance?"

"Yes, I do," Sharif answered.

Sitting back once again in his chair, Weber gazed silently at Sharif for a few moments and then said with a grim smile, "Now you can see why we must track the YLA's activity. We need to understand the grand scheme…before it's too late."

"Where do things stand?"

"We have agents all over eastern upstate New York, and surveillance of all border checkpoints. If they show up, we will find them."

"And then what?"

"Then we find out what they are up to."

"You expect them to cooperate?" Sharif chided.

"Not knowingly," Weber replied with a straight face, "but before anything happens, you and I will be on top of it."

"You and I?" Sharif asked as he lowered his chin to peer at Weber over imaginary spectacles.

"Yes, Ahmed," Weber replied. "We will be there."

"You'd better explain yourself, old friend."

"Would you trust this operation to some green lieutenant in the field? You and I, Ahmed, we can get to the heart of this YLA threat."

Leaning forward as if his hearing had been impaired, Sharif asked, "Please tell me you're joking."

"I'm deadly serious, Ahmed. As soon as Shane and his companion are spotted, we can be flown to the location and take over."

"And do what?" Sharif queried.

"Our objective is to learn what they're up to. We'll let them lead us to it."

"And you think we can intervene?"

"More than that, Ahmed," Weber replied with a crooked smile. "We capture these *Yanks* and make an example of them."

"Make an example?" Sharif blurted. "The public doesn't even know they are fugitives. They don't even know about the nuclear bombings."

"Not yet. But they will soon," Weber replied. "The underground papers will have the story within a week or two. Before that, the *DIB* will inform the public about the YLA attacks...as if we had just learned who was responsible. By that time we should have Shane and shut down their mission. We will execute them...*publicly*...over international television."

"What? Executions haven't been public in the German Confederation since Hitler," Sharif protested.

"Our *Reichskanzler* himself, the Imperial Chancellor in Berlin, has given the order," Weber announced proudly. "We will use a firing squad." Then he added with a shrug and a smirk, "I had recommended the *guillotine*."

Even with exceptionally cruel and sadistic overtones, Sharif had no problem with public executions. There was a long history of such activities within his culture. But he was certain that neither Weber nor his superiors, even the Imperial Chancellor, truly understood what the consequences of their actions might be. The international consequences could be disastrous. This thought was enough for Sharif to see clearly what his personal plan of action should be.

After sitting back silently for a time, gazing intently at his fingertips, Sharif looked up at his friend, finally, and said decisively, "You are mistaken, my friend."

"What?"

"We should not wait for Shane to be spotted. We should take on this investigation now."

CHAPTER 10

▼

HIDDEN AGENDAS

As if it had been planned, Ahmed Sharif would be dining that evening at the home of his colleague, Manfred Weber, and his wife Ellen. But it was not the expected company of his tedious *Gestapo* collaborator that excited Sharif at this moment; it was the anticipation of spending the evening with Weber's American wife, Ellen. Over the past fifteen years during which Weber and Sharif had periodically met on business in Chicago and elsewhere, Sharif had suffered these encounters so that he could spend time with Ellen. His infatuation for the tall, blonde and lovely American lady, that Weber had somehow persuaded to be his wife, had now become Sharif's obsession. He believed that Weber was unaware, but he suspected that Ellen knew of his feelings.

Of one thing Sharif *was* certain: Ellen had long been disappointed in Weber as a husband and lover. For many years she had been having an affair with Gerald Moorhouse, a corporate attorney for a San Francisco based import-export company. Ellen, whose influential family operated a large farming conglomerate in the California Central Valley, had been pursued romantically by Weber after he had met her in San Francisco on a visit in 1982. She was in her early twenties, inexperienced with men, and mesmerized by the older, dashing *Gestapo* officer. Although only slightly taller than Ellen, Weber was powerfully built, with rugged features, pale complexion and dark red hair, giving him a wild look that belied his suave demeanor. With the urging of her family, that had anticipated the benefits of connecting with a Nazi official, Ellen had been swept into a hasty marriage and had moved to Chicago with her new husband.

It was not long before the benefits of the marriage were overwhelmed by its defects. Despite the privilege of unfettered travel within the *DRA* and the Japanese West Coast; and despite Ellen's and her family's immunities from oppressive constraints on daily trade and communications, Ellen soon realized that the marriage had been a disastrous mistake. It was when she was in her early thirties, during one of her periodic trips to visit family in California, that she had met and fallen in love with Gerald Moorhouse. Knowing that an American woman could not divorce a German Nazi officer without paying a dear price, Ellen and Gerry had opted for an affair that had thrived over the past dozen years. He visited Chicago often; and Ellen made regular trips to California to visit her family. Sharif made it his business to know about each encounter of the long-distance lovers.

Since his youthful days in Palestine, other men had recognized Ahmed Sharif as an extraordinary human being. From his Arab ancestors he had inherited shrewdness, patience, and wisdom. Physically, he was exceptional. Even now, in his early 60's, his tall, lean frame remained athletic and strong. His skin was dark, and his hair was straight and black, with streaks of gray, and combed straight back. A strong chin, aquiline nose, and piercing dark brown eyes gave him a distinctive air. His family's wealth allowed him to select expensive clothes. Invariably, he would be dressed in a dark suit, with a silk shirt and boldly colored tie. His shoes were hand-made of Italian leather.

Only once, in his twenties, when Sharif had first worked in Palestinian intelligence, had he been seriously involved with any woman. During his travels to North America he had met a young Russian-American woman working for the Soviet consulate in New York. Hopelessly drawn to this attractive young lady, whose physical qualities contrasted so dramatically with those of the Arab women he had known, Sharif courted her shamelessly, but was cruelly rejected.

This experience had taken a strong emotional toll on the sensitive youth. From that day he had avoided any serious relationships. Instead, he took advantage of the sophisticated prostitution services provided throughout the UAS. The trade had been developed by many, but had been perfected by the Saudi Mafia. Using their contacts within the German Confederation they had been able to provide a steady stream of young, virginal, blonde girls taken from Scandinavia and North America. Abducted from homes, schools and street corners while the Nazis looked away, these young teen-agers were treated as runaways despite parents' protests to the police. Because of the state-controlled news media, public awareness of the problem was practically nonexistent. The probability of the return of abducted girls to their families was virtually nil. After years of abuse—beginning as concubines at the highest levels and ending as common harlots in the brothels of Damascus, Baghdad or Cairo—the girls would rather die than reveal their miserable existence to families.

Because of his wealth and position, Sharif was among the privileged that could select from the most desirable of each new sex-slave shipment that reached Damascus. His liaisons were infrequent, but they were intense. He was demanding and cruel, and he refused to be with the same young lady more than once. But he knew that when he finished with each one that they would probably remember that experience as the *least* degrading of their wretched lives.

Sharif had had no room in his soul for love or affection…at least not until he had met Ellen. Now, although his sexual appetite had not diminished, he was less inclined to take advantage of the temptations offered in Damascus. Instead, he found himself consumed by obsession for a woman who was not only married to his colleague, but also had been involved in a passionate affair with the true love of her life. This obsession might never bear fruit, Sharif had thought sadly, as he would not intrude on the only happiness in Ellen's life.

The profound irony of this impossible situation had not been lost on Sharif.

*   *   *   *

"And what brings you to Chicago this time, Ahmed?" Ellen asked, as she delivered the vodka martini he had requested. Dressed in a long, clinging black dress that accented her trim figure and long blonde hair, Ellen moved closer to Sharif as she awaited his reply.

As Sharif inhaled the intoxicating blend of scents both natural and synthetic given off by the tall, lovely lady who had drawn within his uncharted circle of intimacy, he sensed an unusual vulnerability this evening. Momentarily, with a furtive smile, Sharif responded, "Can't you guess, Ellen?"

Ignoring his hidden meaning, Ellen replied, "Of course. You must be here because of these awful bombings. I hope you can help us find the cowards responsible for this terrible tragedy, Ahmed." With these last words, she reached out and placed one hand on Sharif's arm. Although welcoming her touch, Sharif sensed a slight tremor.

Before Sharif could respond, Weber called out from the bar across the room, "Careful, Ellen. You don't want to tempt Ahmed to give away state secrets." He followed this with a short laugh, and strode quickly to join the pair with a gin and tonic for Ellen and a Campari for himself.

"I don't want any state secrets, Manfred," Ellen countered. "But I would like to know that you and Ahmed are working hard to find those bastards."

"What do you know about these attacks, Ellen?" Sharif asked. "Surely you haven't learned anything from the state television channels." He followed this comment with a mocking look at Weber.

"Hah! You've caught me, Ahmed," Weber said as he held up a hand in surrender. "I've spilled the beans at home. It's impossible, you know, to keep secrets from my seductive wife." He punctuated this last statement with a wink to Sharif.

As a slight flush bloomed on her cheeks, Ellen said, "I'm sorry, Manfred, if I spoke out of turn."

These hasty words of contrition only served as a troubling reminder to Sharif of what he had long suspected: that Weber was abusing this lovely woman both physically and mentally.

"No. No. Please don't apologize, Ellen," Sharif insisted, in an attempt to sweep the issue away. "I would have brought it up myself if you hadn't said something. It should be common knowledge within your circles that the YLA was responsible for the nuclear explosions."

Momentarily miffed by Sharif's intrusion, Weber added: "That's true, Ellen. We can speak freely tonight."

Bolstered by their support, Ellen asked, "Can either of you explain to me why anyone would want to take so many innocent lives? Did you know, Ahmed, that we lost many friends when the *Landeszentralbank* building was destroyed? I just don't understand."

"Clearly, the YLA are a bunch of thugs," Weber interjected. "They have no hope of taking on the German Confederation militarily. So, in desperation, they resort to these meaningless and cowardly acts of destruction."

"But what do they hope to gain?" Ellen asked.

"They want us to treat them as the rightful representatives for their people," Weber replied. "But that will never happen. We don't negotiate with terrorists."

"But won't that just cause them to carry out more attacks?" Ellen asked.

"Not if we find them first. And we will," Weber responded as he brought his drink to his lips.

Although Sharif had been quietly sipping his drink during this exchange, he took advantage of the pause to turn to Weber and ask: "Do you think it's that simple, Manfred?"

"To find them? Of course it's not simple. But we will do it."

"No. That's not what I meant," Sharif persisted. "Can we simply regard these terrorists as pests that should be exterminated?"

"Absolutely. What else should we do? Surely, you don't believe we should negotiate with them!"

Shaking his head, Sharif sighed and said, "Manfred, we've dealt with terrorists for decades in the UAS. The Jews have a dozen different terrorist groups dedicated to one cause or another. They have taken many Arab lives. And we have taken ten times as many Jewish lives. Do you now where that has gotten us?"

"I think you're going to tell me, aren't you, Ahmed," Weber replied with a smirk.

"It isn't funny, Manfred. It's a disgrace. The cycle of violence will never end. Meeting terror with terror does not work. We will never win this conflict with the Jews. And you will never win the conflict with the YLA...if we both continue the policy of meeting wanton violence with wanton violence."

"As I said before, what would you have us do, Ahmed?" Weber asked with a new edge to his voice.

"We need to listen. What is the message? Why do they persist in a futile, suicidal exercise?"

"We already know the answer, Ahmed," Weber growled. "They want their country back. Well, they can't have it. They lost the war. It's over. They need to move on."

"Are you sure the message is that simple, Manfred," Ellen interjected unexpectedly.

"What do you know?" Weber snapped as he turned angrily to his wife. "This is none of your business."

"You forget, Manfred," Ellen persisted, "my family is American. I know how much has changed because of the war. There are strong feelings that you do not understand."

Sharif saw that Ellen's face was flushed and her eyes were misty. He knew what was coming and why.

As Manfred remained speechless, absorbing his wife's outburst and deliberating how severely he should chastise her, Ellen disarmed him.

"I am so sorry, Manfred," she murmured. "I had no right to criticize. You are right. These attacks must be met with force." Then, as her voice diminished to a whisper, and she looked away, she added hoarsely, "It's just that there were so many innocent people...how can they be so heartless...I don't understand...they're Americans just like those they killed...so many innocent victims..." Finally, as her words became barely audible, and the tears were flowing freely, Ellen turned and fled to the bedroom, dropping her drink on the dining room table along the way.

As Weber excused himself to be with his wife, Sharif nodded reluctantly but feared the worst. That the man was confused and angered at his wife's behavior was obvious. That Weber remained oblivious to the real cause of his wife's distress was also clear to Sharif.

Someone without Sharif's keen senses would not have heard the prolonged muffled scream. To Sharif it was like a sharp knife had pierced his own heart. Mercifully, the sound subsided, and Sharif was thankful that he was there to require Weber's prompt return.

Sharif longed to act. But this was not the time.

For Ellen's sake, Sharif hoped Weber would never discover the source of her discontent. He hoped that Weber would never learn that Ellen's lover, Gerald Moorhouse, had been among the victims of the September 11 attack on the *Landeszentralbank* building.

But Sharif knew. He knew that Ellen had been waiting in her lover's bed at his hotel, waiting for his return from the early morning meeting. In an instant the terrorist strike that morning had stripped Ellen of the love of her life…and had destroyed thousands of other innocent lives as well. No wonder she felt their pain. No wonder she wanted answers.

Sharif understood. He understood that the answers were more important than the retribution that Weber would pursue. This belief had been burned into his soul through too many years of Middle Eastern carnage.

Someday, Sharif vowed, he would share his soul with this woman that he loved. And someday soon Weber would reap the bitter fruit of his twisted life.

*   *   *   *

Nathan Carothers hated Miami. It was neither hotter nor more humid than New Orleans, but it was utterly devoid of the essence that defined New Orleans' charm and seductiveness. But he had selected Miami to meet with Juri Chernovsky of the Soviet foreign ministry for a very good reason. His YLA colleagues could not know about this meeting…or about any association with the Soviets and their secret coalition.

While Harry and the others believed that Carothers was meeting with Solomon Rothchild—presumably to obtain the additional funding their newly acquired fugitive status required—Carothers was engaged in an earnest conversation with Chernovsky. The setting was a neutral suite in the Fontainbleu Hotel. Carothers had not come to this meeting willingly.

"Nathan," Chernovsky was saying, "our coalition is divided on whether we need further action by the YLA inside the *DRA*. To give us time to resolve the issue, I've assured them that there will be no more terrorist acts for the near future."

"You know that we're hamstrung right now, Juri. We can't do a thing."

"Let me *tell* you what I know, Nathan. I know that you have two top agents in the *DRA* right now. They're on some kind of mission, and I want to know what it is."

"Even if what you say is true, Juri, why should I reveal anything to you?"

"Do I have to remind you who arranged for the Chinese to provide the nuclear devices?" Chernovsky countered.

"And you haven't benefited from our strikes in the *DRA*?" Carothers replied sarcastically.

Chernovsky sat back in his chair and stared at the huge black man seated across from him for several moments. Before speaking again he took a sip from his glass of chilled vodka. "Nathan, old friend, this is getting us nowhere," he said calmly. "Let me lay my cards on the table. We need each other. We can't ignore that. Now I broke a trust when I revealed to you what our coalition was engaged in. All I am asking is that you tell me what your agents are up to. Then we can talk."

This time it was Carothers' turn to sample his drink. He sat back, sipped his scotch and deliberated. Finally, he said, "They're planning to steal the Nazi mind control technology."

"And?"

"And what?"

"Where? How? Who? Give me more, Nathan. We can't take a chance that your agents' actions will interfere with our own."

"I hardly see how that's possible."

"Let me make that decision, Nathan. Now, please, give me the rest of the story."

"On one condition, Juri. You can not intervene. We need to finish this mission. It will in no way interfere with yours."

"If that is true, then you will have nothing to fear from us."

After a deep breath, Carothers exhaled and said, "It's Tony Shane and Salomé, two of my three captains. They're infiltrating the mind control lab at the *Heisenberg Institut* in Chicago. We expect the mission to be completed within the week."

"What will you do with this technology, Nathan?"

"We're more concerned with what the Nazis planned to do with it."

"How advanced is this?"

"Pretty damned scary. They're close to implanting micro-controllers in human brains," Carothers lied.

It wasn't his first lie, nor would it be his last. He had revealed just enough of the truth to satisfy Chernovsky's prying. But if Chernovsky ever learned the whole truth, Carothers could expect nothing less than speedy elimination of his captains and their leader.

Ironically, Carothers reflected, Tony Shane could not learn his secrets either.

After a long contemplative interval, during which he continued to tap his fingers noiselessly on the arm of his chair, Chernovsky said finally, "Let them finish their mission, Nathan. We will not interfere. But we will need to see this technology when you get it. Agreed?"

"Agreed," Nathan lied.

CHAPTER 11

▼

ON THE ROAD AGAIN

As she accelerated through the interchange with the *Zentralautobahn* on South Cicero Avenue, about twenty miles south of Chicago's Loop, Salomé adroitly avoided the early morning rush of autos entering and exiting the ten-lane super-highway. She glanced briefly at her passenger. Tony Shane was busy studying the crude map Vito Mironi had given them, laying out the safest route from Chicago to New York. Salomé knew only that they would pick up old route 30 south of Tinley Park and head east. The rest of the agenda was still in Shane's head, to her chagrin.

Finally, as the traffic thinned out she said, "Alright, Shane. Congratulations. You've got Sarah Stenstrom on board. Now where are we going? And what the hell are we gonna do when we get there?"

"You know where we're headed, Salomé. Up-state New York. We'll get more specific as we get closer," Shane replied tersely.

"Oh no we won't. You're gonna level with me right now, Tony."

"What's your problem?"

"I'm working in the dark here, Tony. I can't protect you and this operation when I know less than the opposition. You understand?"

"What opposition?" Shane asked.

"Christ, Shane," Salomé snapped, "half the world! Did you forget that the *Gestapo* almost put you and Harry away? And what about Mironi? If he finds out what you're *really* up to...well, forget about Grandpa Rico's blessings. And if the

Soviets or the Japanese get wind of our operation—and I think they will—there won't be any place we'll be able to hide."

"Well you're full of doom and gloom today," Shane remarked as he glared back at his driver and partner. After remaining silent for several seconds, his jaw muscles working, Shane added with a sigh, "OK. You're right, Salomé. It's time to let you in on the whole plan."

"'Bout time, asshole," she responded with a quick sideways glance.

Ignoring Salomé's rudeness, Shane began: "Bringing Sarah on board is key to the technical part of the operation. Now we have to figure out how to use that technology the way Einstein envisioned and devise our mission to 1939."

"You've got to be kidding!" Salomé exclaimed. "You don't even have a scheme?"

"I only know we have to prevent Joseph Rheingold from joining Heisenberg's atomic research team in Berlin in 1939."

"So, you *do* know what needs to be done?"

"Not exactly. According to my father, Professor Einstein decided we couldn't simply undo what had been done before. He had a better idea."

"And what the hell was that?"

"My father didn't know. That's what we hope to find out in New York."

"You can't get it from Einstein. He's been dead for decades."

"He confided his plan to one person, Diana Sutton, the other telepathic receptor with my dad on that 1939 flight when Rheingold was abducted. That's who we're going to see in New York. She lives near Lake George, in Fernville I think."

"You *think?*" Salomé asked with a sharp glance at her passenger.

"I know how my father and Professor Fuller used to contact her. But that was over fifteen years ago. She would be over eighty now, if she's still alive."

"You haven't tried contacting her in all these years?"

"Just one time—to let her know that my dad was in prison and to warn her about the *Gestapo*. There's been no reason to contact her since then. And I didn't want to give the Nazis a clue to where she was."

Driver and passenger remained silent for several minutes as they neared the route 30 turnoff and the early morning traffic picked up again. Finally, after negotiating the intersection and turning east, Salomé asked, "Did I hear you say that you don't know how Einstein planned to use this computer technology?"

"Yeah. That's right. Digital computers were just a fantasy until the late 40's. Einstein could only imagine what technology might evolve, but he did develop a technical plan."

"Don't tell me—we don't know his technical plan either. Right?" Salomé remarked sarcastically.

"Well, yes and no. A lot of the technical stuff was included in my letter. But, what we're missing is Einstein's theoretical perspective—what he worked on while in exile in Mexico."

"How are we going to get that?"

"Good question. It's not in any of his published work. If he put any of this on paper, it's hidden someplace where the Axis scientists won't ever find it."

"And of course you know where it is," Salomé sneered.

"No, but my dad had some clues. When they took him away, I was left with a small strongbox filled with useful documents, including a photo of Diana Sutton, her contact information, one of Professor Fuller's research notebooks, and a smuggled letter from Professor Einstein in Mexico."

"A letter from Einstein? That must be interesting."

"You bet, if I could just understand it," Shane responded. "Half of it is filled with unintelligible symbols. The rest is English narrative, but makes no sense at all."

"Can I take a look at it?"

"Can you read Hebrew?"

"The letter's written in Hebrew?"

"According to Sarah. Would you be able to translate?"

Shaking her head, Salomé replied, "No…I'm sorry. I rejected everything Jewish when I was growing up. That was part of my rage…my bitterness."

Slowly nodding as he gazed at Salomé, Shane said, "Well, I still want you to take a look. Harry thinks the gobbledygook is really an elaborate 'treasure map'. He took a copy of the letter, and he's in Monterrey now poring through Einstein's old records."

"Did your father tell you anything about Einstein's letter or his research notes?"

"No. He had just begun to tell me about this whole affair the day they took him away," Shane replied as he gazed absently out the side window. "And I never saw him again."

"Perhaps he could have given you the key, Tony. But," Salomé added as she glanced sympathetically over at Shane, "I'm sure there were many things you would love to have talked to him about."

CHAPTER 12

▼

NEW OLD FRIENDS

The stately white Victorian home facing north on Washington Street was surrounded by numerous structures of similar vintage and charm in this old, established Fernville neighborhood. Situated on a grassy acre lined with tall stately elm trees, the three-story home appeared to step out of a nineteenth century picture book. A low white picket fence in good repair enclosed the front yard, with a gate adjacent to the front sidewalk. A long stone walkway led to the front porch which was set back about fifty feet. The area immediately behind the home was screened from the view of passersby with a thick hedge of tall lilac bushes. Two large maple trees graced the front lawn, partly screening the upper floors of the home from view. The large front porch continued around the west side, while the large front room on the northeast side of the home extended forward beyond the front porch. A large rounded extension of the front room rose up three floors like a tower, each level graced with a set of four narrow windows. The front windows were very tall, suggesting 12- or 14-foot ceilings for the main floor front room.

Fernville was situated in the Adirondack foothills about twenty miles from the Lake George resort hotel where Shane and Salomé had found a room. It was a small community with Quaker roots reaching back to the eighteenth century. In the early twentieth century it had become a summer haven for the wealthy families that had brought congestion to the counties directly north of New York City. For Diana Sutton, it had eventually become her full time residence.

As Shane and Salomé ascended the porch steps and approached the ornately designed front door, they were surprised to see the door open and a pretty young blonde woman dressed in bluejeans and gray sweatshirt step out to greet them. If Shane hadn't known better, he would have thought it was Diana Sutton herself. She looked exactly like the picture of Diana in her twenties that he had found in his father's strongbox.

"Hi," the young lady said with a bright toothy smile, "can I help you?"

"Good morning," Shane replied while brandishing his most charming smile, "we're here to see the lady of the house—Diana Sutton. Is she home?"

As the young lady's smile faded slightly, she replied, "She's not seeing visitors today. Can I ask who you are and what your business is with her?"

"Please," Shane said, "could you just tell her that it's the son of an old friend of hers, Daniel Shane—who she might have known as Daniel *McShane*."

As her brow furrowed, the young lady appeared to examine Shane's face closely for a moment. Then, suddenly, she cried, "You're Daniel's son? Oh, my God! Please come in. My grandmother will be so happy to see you!"

Shocked by the sudden reversal and unexpected revelation that they had just met Diana Sutton's granddaughter, Shane and Salomé stumbled through the doorway. After identifying himself as Tony Shane and introducing Salomé, Shane learned that the granddaughter's name was Andrea Martin. Then Andrea confirmed that her grandmother was indeed Diana Sutton Kreutzwil.

Asking Shane and Salomé to remain in the large foyer, Andrea excused herself so that she could announce their arrival to her grandmother.

After disappearing into the interior of the main floor for several minutes, Andrea returned for them. Shane and Salomé were then escorted toward the back of the main floor and directed into a large solarium exposed to a back courtyard adorned with colorful plants, shrubs and trees. In the center of the solarium, seated in a large white-painted wooden rocking chair sat a fragile-looking gray-haired lady in a long dark green velveteen gown. A small beige blanket covered her lap and extended over her knees.

"Grandma," Andrea said as the trio moved closer to the rocking chair, "This is Tony Shane and his companion Salomé."

"Come here and let me take a look at you," the old lady commanded with a firm voice that belied her fragile appearance. Her piercing blue eyes gazed directly at Tony Shane as she held out her hand.

Shane took a hesitant step forward and reached for her hand. As he felt her gaze inspecting every facial crevice, he marveled at the surprising firmness of her grip. Pulling him down so that his face came close to hers, she said, "Can't believe it. I thought it was Danny himself walking into this room. You've got his eyes and mouth. Same hair too. No wonder Andrea let you in."

Stunned speechless by the bold reception, Shane pulled himself up straight and simply smiled for several moments. Finally, he said, "I'm so pleased to finally meet you. And I want you to meet my friend, Salomé."

"Salomé?" Diana asked with raised eyebrows. "What's your last name, young lady?"

"It's just 'Salomé,' ma'am," she responded. "No last name."

"My, my," Diana commented while shaking her head. Then, turning to Shane, she said, "Your father said you would come here some day, Tony. But after he was taken away by the *Gestapo*, I was afraid it would never happen." Then, as her eyes moistened, she added, "I can't tell you how happy I am to finally meet you."

"Diana—may I call you Diana?" Shane began. "You probably know why I'm here."

"Of course you can call me Diana," she responded. "And, yes, I suspect I do know why you're here. We have much to talk about. But, first, make yourselves comfortable. Let Andrea bring us some tea and biscuits. I'm sure you've come a long way."

*   *   *   *

While enjoying the refreshments, Shane and Salomé listened as Diana quickly summarized several decades of personal history. She had lived with her parents in Westchester county after returning from England in 1941. And she had later married Harri Kreutzwil, a Jewish physicist from Columbia University. But Kreutzwil had gone to work for the Manhattan Project in Los Alamos, and Diana had traveled to Madison to participate in the *Einstein Project* with Daniel and Professor Fuller. After the war her husband had been taken off by the Soviets. Her parents had looked after her daughter, Mary, throughout Diana's long absences during and after the war.

Her daughter had married and given birth to Diana's granddaughter, Andrea, some twenty-seven years ago. Diana, Mary and Andrea were direct descendants of Jason Foxwood, eighteenth century land baron of upstate New York. It was Foxwood family property here in Fernville that Diana had decided to occupy some twenty years ago, and which was now shared with her granddaughter. Mary and her husband remained in Westchester county.

By some miracle, Diana had escaped the 1985 *Gestapo* purge that had taken away both Professor Fuller and Tony's father because of their earlier work on the *Einstein Project* at Wisconsin. Apparently, Professor Fuller had successfully concealed records of her work on the project. Over the years, she had slowly become more comfortable, no longer regarding herself as a fugitive.

But the arrival of Shane and Salomé that day had resurrected old anxieties. When Shane had asked Andrea why she had let them in, despite her suspicions, she had not answered immediately. Instead, she had asked to be excused for a few minutes. When she returned, she was carrying a sturdy metal strongbox, much like the one Shane's father had used. After unlocking the box, she reached in and pulled out an old black & white photograph and showed it to Shane. "My God," Shane exclaimed, "that's a picture of me!"

Diana explained that the picture was of Shane's father Daniel taken when he was in his twenties. It had not taken long for Andrea to make the mental connection to the old photograph once Tony had identified himself at the door.

*   *   *   *

As the last of the teacups and plates were whisked away by Andrea and Salomé, and Shane found himself alone with Diana, he asked, "Do you know why I'm here?"

"Of course, Tony," Diana replied. "You're here to finish up what we began sixty years ago. The *Einstein Project*."

"That's true, Diana. But there's more. You know about the terrorist attacks? The atomic bomb set off in New York?"

"What!" she exclaimed. "I don't know anything about that."

"I was afraid of that," Shane remarked.

Quickly, Shane related recent events that the Nazis had kept out of the news. He described his involvement with the Yankee Liberation Army after his father had been imprisoned, and how the YLA had finally resorted to nuclear terrorism. He pointed out that he and Salomé were fugitives, and they were placing Diana and her granddaughter in danger by being there. He and Salomé had both been opposed to nuclear terrorism, he said. It was because they wanted no more of these monstrous attacks that they were on a mission to fulfill the *Einstein Project*. And that had brought them to Diana.

"And what do you want from me, Tony?" Diana asked.

"First of all, how much does Andrea know?" he replied.

"Everything. You can speak freely in front of her."

As if on cue, Andrea and Salomé returned to the solarium. As they took their seats, Diana said, "You're just in time. Tony has something to tell us."

Looking directly at Andrea, Shane began: "Your grandmother tells me that you know all about the *Einstein Project*, so I'll get right to the point. I believe it is possible now to complete the work that Professor Einstein began back in 1939. Computer technology exists that may support telepathic time travel to the distant past. We haven't tried it yet, but Professor Fuller's results back in the 1940's are reason for optimism."

"Excuse me," Andrea interrupted, "but I don't see how you can be so confident. At the very least you would have to do a number of preliminary experiments. The programming alone would require major development."

As Shane shifted his gaze to Andrea, regarding her with new respect, Diana interjected, "I forgot to mention, Tony, that Andrea has completed her master's degree in computer science. She teaches at the college in Warrensburg."

As a broad smile grew across his face, Shane nodded and continued, "You're absolutely right, Andrea. It's not trivial. Fortunately, we have the world's foremost expert on neural computing working with us. But that won't be enough. We need to learn the two things that Professor Einstein tried to provide before he died—the missing theory for telepathic time travel, and a feasible plan for altering the World War II time line."

Then, turning to Diana, Shane said, "Diana, my father said that you received a letter from the future just like he did. And I received a letter as well. We need to get what clues we can from these letters."

"I can tell you what was in my letter," Diana volunteered. "It said that it was from my granddaughter from a different future time line. It explained the strange memory loss during part of the flight to England. It said that my granddaughter had been forced to take over my mind telepathically on a mission from the future involving Nazis and Joseph Rheingold. I knew that Rheingold had disappeared from our flight. The letter directed me to contact one of Rheingold's colleagues at Columbia University when I returned from England, and find out if Rheingold was working for the Nazis. If so, I was told to contact Professor Einstein at Princeton University, and he would tell me what to do."

"There was nothing else?" Shane inquired.

"Just two things. One was that a second world war would begin with the German invasion of Poland at the beginning of September."

"And the other thing?" Shane asked.

"I'll tell you that later," Diana replied.

"And what did you do after reading the letter?" Shane persisted

"I destroyed it. I thought it was some kind of elaborate joke, and I suspected your father had planted the letter in my suitcase. But, of course, when the war in Europe broke out as predicted I started to believe that the letter was authentic. So, when I returned to New York in 1941, I contacted one of Rheingold's colleagues at Columbia and found out that Rheingold was indeed in Berlin working for the Nazis. That was when I contacted Einstein, and by 1942 I was in Wisconsin working with Professor Fuller and your father."

"What took you so long to follow through? My father was working with Professor Fuller by the end of 1939 or early 1940."

"Two things happened. One was my marriage to Harri Kreutzwil—the colleague of Rheingold's that I had met at Columbia. The other was giving birth to my only child Mary. But not actually in that order."

Noting the puzzled expression on Shane's face, Diana smiled and nodded to her granddaughter. It was Andrea who explained: "What my grandmother is trying to say, Tony, is that Harri Kreutzwil became her husband; but he was *not* my grandfather. My grandfather was *Daniel*—your father."

As Shane's jaw dropped and his face went blank, Diana said, "That's right, Tony. I'm afraid I was pretty naughty. I took advantage of Daniel on that overnight flight in 1939. He had no idea he had fathered my daughter. But I finally had to tell him before the *Einstein Project* broke up."

"Why didn't you tell him right away?" Shane asked.

"I didn't want Daniel to feel obligated. We were very young."

"But then why did you tell him later?" Shane asked with a frown.

"Your father began to think that he and I were supposed to be together. So, I finally had to tell him about my daughter and husband—and about the other thing that was in the letter."

"What was that?"

"The letter said that I was pregnant with Daniel's child, but that he was supposed to marry someone else. Of course, when I first read it I was certain this was part of the elaborate joke Daniel was playing on me. But it didn't take long before I realized the part about being pregnant was true.

"When I explained to Daniel that we couldn't marry, I had to tell him about our daughter too. He was wonderful about it. Until the *Gestapo* took him, he never failed to keep up with what Mary was doing."

"I...I don't know what to say," Shane stammered. "This must be what my father was going to tell me just before they took him away. But I never suspected—"

Shifting his gaze to Andrea, Shane's eyes suddenly widened as he said, "I guess that means that your mother is my…my *sister*. And, Andrea, you must be…my *niece*."

"Please don't make me call you *Uncle Tony*," Andrea said with a laugh that mercifully provided some comic relief.

As Shane shook his head and smiled, Salomé chose this moment to break her silence. "Look," she said with a sigh, "this is all wonderful warm and fuzzy news. But, you know what, folks, we've got the *Gestapo* on our tail and we need to figure out what we're going to do next. So, Tony, why don't we ask Diana if she can help us figure out Einstein's strategy for the time travel mission."

Jerking to attention, Shane responded by nodding his agreement with Salomé. Then he turned to Diana and asked, "Is it true that Professor Einstein told you the strategy he had for dealing with that 1939 event that tipped the war to the Axis powers?"

"We all talked about the fact that we couldn't just go back and save Rheingold from the Nazis," Diana replied.

"Why not?" asked Salomé. "That seems the most obvious approach."

"That's precisely why we can't do it," interjected Andrea. "Let me explain, if you don't mind, Grandma."

"Go ahead, child. You know it as well as I do," Diana smiled.

"It's like this. Einstein believed that time travel would never be the exclusive tool of the good guys. If we could do it, so could the bad guys. So, he tried to come up with some fool-proof intervention in the time line—something that couldn't be undone by a subsequent time traveler."

"So what did he propose?" Salomé asked impatiently.

"I don't know," Andrea replied.

"You don't know!" Salomé exclaimed. Then, glaring at Diana, she asked gruffly, "Haven't you told Andrea about this?"

"I'm afraid there's nothing to tell," Diana responded.

Throwing up her arms, Salomé threw a look of disgust at Shane as if to say, *We're wasting time here, Tony.*

Reaching out to gently touch Salomé's arm, indicating he would take over, Shane looked at Diana and said, "Did Einstein have a plan or didn't he?"

"He did," Diana replied. "But he didn't reveal it to me. He believed it would be too risky for me to have that knowledge."

"Then how are we supposed to get the plan?" Shane asked with an edge to his voice, beginning now to share Salomé's frustration.

"I'm sorry, Tony," Diana began. "This must sound confusing to you. Try to understand that I have been burdened with this troubling knowledge for nearly sixty years. I have revealed this particular fact to no one—not even Andrea."

As the other three occupants of the room suddenly became alert and still, Diana hesitated for a few seconds, and then began to speak as if narrating a fairy tale to a group of schoolchildren.

"It was October 1942," she began. "Professor Einstein was visiting Professor Fuller's lab in Wisconsin. The four of us—Danny, Professor Einstein, Professor Fuller, and I—were meeting in Fuller's office at the university. I'll never forget it. I was in such awe of Dr. Einstein. He was someone we had seen in newsreels at the movies. And yet he was not intimidating in the least. He sat there smoking his pipe and listening most of the time. Occasionally he would ask a question—the simplest question—that would bring the conversation to a halt. Invariably it was a question that no one had posed before, and that no one could answer. He would just leave the question hanging and tell us to move on. Then, later, he would put his pipe down and answer his own question, usually by describing one of those simple thought experiments for which he was so famous.

"Of all the fascinating aspects of Dr. Einstein, though, one in particular stands out in my mind. He didn't believe in time travel to the past. Not only was it inconsistent with his theory, he would say, but it also created impossible situations, like the classic paradox of the son going back in time to kill his father before the son was conceived.

"And yet he believed in what we were doing. I never understood that. And one time I worked up the nerve to ask him how he could support something he didn't think was possible. He said that he couldn't discount the credible encounters that Danny and I had had in 1939 with time travelers from the future. Then he said something I'll never forget. He said, 'All the great advances in science were considered impossible before they were accomplished.'

"At this particular meeting in Madison, Dr. Einstein posed one hypothetical question that he did *not* answer. That question was, 'How can a time traveler to the past make a change that can not be undone by a subsequent time traveler?'

"We all took stabs at answering but could never come up with anything satisfying. Dr. Einstein just remained quiet, smoking his pipe, smiling at us with the creases around those large soulful eyes.

"It was after this session that Dr. Einstein pulled me aside and asked to speak to me in private. When we spoke, he told me that he knew exactly what our time travel mission should be, but could not reveal it to anyone. Then he said something that sent chills up my spine. He said, 'Don't ever forget this conversation, Diana. Someday you will understand this plan.'

"That was all he said," Diana concluded.

Silence.

No one spoke for a long time. Then, finally, Shane took a deep breath and sighed, "There's more to this story, isn't there, Diana?"

As a smile slowly formed on her face, the gray-haired woman, who had not yet emerged from the nostalgic mental excursion to her youth, slowly nodded.

"Yes, Tony. There is one more thing," she said. "Professor Einstein speaking those words to me was the last thing that I remembered until I found myself in my bed about an hour later."

"You had a memory loss!" Shane exclaimed as a wide grin appeared on his face.

Shaking her head, Salomé asked, "So what?"

Still grinning, Shane glanced at Salomé and then returned his attention to Diana. "Perhaps Diana could explain it to us," he said.

*   *   *   *

Although they had come to New York seeking information, Shane and Salomé were leaving with much more—another passenger. On the previous day Shane had not known of Andrea's existence, while now he regarded her as the key to *rainbow's* success. Diana had held this secret key close for so many years. *Did my father know?* Shane wondered silently as he guided the Lincoln sedan down route 17. Fernville, and Diana, were far behind them. Soon they would be at the Pennsylvania border, near the western edge of New York.

As Andrea slept peacefully in the back seat, Shane and Salomé spoke quietly in the front of the car. Shane was driving and it was the middle of the night. The border checkpoint was less than an hour away.

"You know what you have to do, Tony," Salomé was saying. "And time's running out."

"King's Crossing," Shane responded.

"What's that?"

"About ten minutes down the road. Check the map. From there we can take any of three minor roads to the border."

"Will you call Mironi then?"

"No! God, no. He's probably in bed with his secretary. Not to be disturbed. I've got a local number to call."

"For what?"

"To get Andrea through any one of the three border posts."

"What's the point? If Mironi wants to stop us, we won't get past *any* check-point."

"It's not Mironi I'm worried about."

"The *Gestapo?* That's what Mironi is supposed to handle."

"Yeah. I know."

"So—?"

"Have you noticed we haven't heard from Nathan?"

"What're you getting at, Tony? You talked to him on the sat-phone just after we left Fernville."

"He was supposed to call back, Salomé."

"So? He's late. No big deal."

"Carothers is never late. Something's wrong. I know it."

"What are you thinking?"

"I don't know. Maybe the Nazis found him? Or, maybe the Soviets figured out what we're doing?"

"Not likely, Tony."

"All right. Let me tell you what's really bothering me."

"What's that?"

"Andrea."

"Huh?"

"She's a new factor. Carothers didn't know about her until we called. Now, suddenly, we're not hearing from him. Coincidence? I don't think so."

"Tony, you're imagining things. You can't suspect Carothers of anything."

"Why not? *Operation rainbow* was never his first choice. Maybe now he sees that we might actually have a chance to succeed."

Salomé just stared at Shane for a long time. Finally, she shook her head and said, "Sorry, Tony. You and I must be thinking of two different people. Nathan's a straight shooter. You're just strung out. Get a grip. He'll call soon."

As if on cue, the sat-phone chirped, and Salomé grabbed it. It was Carothers.

"Nathan, you're late," she barked.

For several minutes she maintained the securely encrypted connection, listening most of the time. Then she disconnected and turned to Shane.

"I got the story," she said. "They've been discreetly checking out Andrea—trying to find out if she's on the *Gestapo's* watch list. The same kind of check they did for Diana before we contacted her. They got a big zero. Andrea's not on anybody's radar screen. Anyway, that's what took the extra time. So—fuck off, Tony. You're going paranoid on me."

Shane remained silent for a long time, focusing on the road ahead. As they passed a sign indicating that King's Crossing was a mile ahead, he finally spoke. "I'm still getting clearance for three check points."

CHAPTER 13

▼

CONSPIRACY THEORY

They had made it through the New York-Pennsylvania checkpoint near Bradford without incident. Shane had not told Mironi's Pennsylvania contact about the additional passenger. He had asked only that the car not be searched. Andrea had hidden in the trunk. They had pulled over fifteen minutes past the checkpoint at an isolated service station to allow Andrea's return to the back seat, and for Salomé to take over the driving.

With the Ohio border less than an hour away, and the knowledge that they had successfully negotiated one checkpoint, Shane decided to use the same ploy. He used a payphone near Edinburg, just a few minutes from the border, to call the same Pennsylvania contact. Again he requested that the car not be searched. And again they made it through the checkpoint without incident.

But they had not gone unnoticed.

Salomé had turned off route 224, selecting a county road that would take them north to pick up a state highway headed for Perrysburg about twenty-five miles west. They had stopped briefly along a desolate stretch to release Andrea from the trunk and return to the road. After several minutes, Salomé had unexpectedly turned west on a crossroad and accelerated to seventy-five miles per hour.

"We've got a tail," she announced. "Hang on."

She turned left onto the next crossroad and accelerated to ninety. Shane's quick glance out the rear window confirmed a pair of headlights apparently following their same course at high speed.

As they approached route 224 once more, Salomé was forced to slow down as a T-intersection and stop sign loomed ahead. Despite the early hour, the truck traffic was considerable. Knowing that the tail was quickly closing the gap, Salomé made a snap decision. She gunned the engine and cruised through the stop sign, negotiating a sharp left turn on to route 224, and barely squeezing between two large semi-trailer trucks headed in opposite directions. The loud blare of horns greeted her rudely, but no one suffered a scratch. And Salomé quickly put as much space between the Lincoln and their delayed pursuers as she could. Before they could re-establish pursuit, Salomé had pulled into one of several residential roadways and was quickly heading south through a housing tract southeast of Akron that she hoped had another access road running parallel to route 224.

Within minutes Salomé had found the access road she was looking for. And within ten minutes they were safely tucked inside moderate state road traffic headed west. They had lost the tail. But they were shaken.

"Good job," Shane told Salomé, before turning around to behold the pale-faced Andrea. "Relax," he commanded. "We're OK now." He was rewarded with a tentative smile that slowly broke into a broad grin as he continued to engage Andrea with his eyes.

After nodding to Andrea, Shane turned his attention back to Salomé. "We've got to stop somewhere so I can call Mironi. He needs to know about this...or explain it to us."

"You think Mironi set the tail on us?"

"Who else? The Pennsylvania contact probably had orders to get hold of him. And they had time after our New York border crossing to set up something in Ohio. There weren't that many checkpoints to cover."

"Is Mironi trying to stop us?"

"No. I don't think so. He just doesn't like mysteries. When they told him we didn't want the border guards to get nosy, all of his alarm bells went off."

"So, now what?"

"I don't know. This may be good news. It probably means that Mironi doesn't know where we've been. He only knows we were traveling to upstate New York. The Pennsylvania crossings were the first where we had to notify them in advance. Before that we just had to use our transit papers."

"I'll bet he's really pissed that we shook the tail."

"You bet he is. But not with us. Those guys in the tail car will have to answer to Vito. But I've got to talk to him before this gets out of hand."

"What are you going to tell him?"

"I'll tell him what's going on. That's the only thing that will satisfy him now. And I'll ask him to get us bogus transit papers for Andrea."

"You think he's gonna be OK with all this?"

"Yeah. Vito's just upset that he's not in control—and that his goons have screwed up. He'll be OK as long as I call him now. So pull over at the first pay phone."

*   *   *   *

"What's this, Tony?" Mironi asked with mock anger, "You break off contact with me, and then you call in the middle of the night! What kind of respect is that?"

"I'm sorry, Vito," Shane responded. "There were some people I had to see. They didn't know I was coming. I just couldn't tell you about them until I knew they were with us."

"You took care of that business?"

"Yes, Vito. I did."

"So, tell me now what's going on," Mironi said. It was not a request.

"Can we talk?" Shane asked.

"Yeah. We're secure," Mironi replied.

Quickly, Shane began to relate the events of the past few days. Without giving specifics, he revealed that he had made a contact at the *Heisenberg Institut* that would help him carry out *operation rainbow*, and that they were returning to the *Institut.* He then revealed that they had picked up a passenger in New York who would be involved. They needed transit papers for this passenger, and Shane gave Mironi her description—but no more.

"You're pushing me, Tony," Mironi said when Shane had finished.

"I know that, Vito. I know you want all the facts. But I can't do that right now. I promise to give you everything you want to know…as soon as we complete this mission."

"That's not good enough, Tony. You want transit papers, you've got to tell me what's going on."

It was a flat statement, and Shane knew better than to test Mironi further.

"Alright, Vito. I'll make a deal. You meet with me when we get back to Chicago and I'll give you the whole story."

"Not good enough, Tony. I need something now."

"Look, Vito. I'll tell you now about the other people involved. Then I'll give you the rest of the story in Chicago."

Mironi remained silent for several moments, and then said, "Tell me about the other people."

After receiving Mironi's assurance that he would not take any action on the information, Shane told Mironi about Sarah Stenstrom and Andrea Martin.

"Who are these broads?" Mironi asked rudely.

"Sarah's a scientist. She's agreed to share some new technology with us."

"What about this Andrea?"

"Andrea's my niece," Shane replied. "And don't ask how. I'll tell you later. The important thing is she can help us."

After a few crude comments designed to dispel the tension between them, Mironi instructed Shane on how to pick up the transit papers for Andrea. Then they set up a meeting in Chicago upon Shane's return.

"Thanks, Vito," Shane said as they prepared to disconnect. "Oh, and by the way, you can call off your goons now—the ones that tried to tail us at the Ohio border."

"What? What are you talking about, Tony? I don't know anything about any tail."

"You're not messing with me, are you Vito?" Shane asked.

"I swear, Tony. We haven't put a tail on you. Sure, we've been checking on your border crossings—but that's it."

"Well, *somebody's* tried to track us down. You got any ideas?"

"Do you want me to find out?"

Shane hesitated for a moment and then said, "No. Let me think about it."

They hung up, but Shane stood there in the phone booth for a long time. He needed to clear his mind. And, he needed to talk to someone else. He needed to talk to Harry.

CHAPTER 14

▼

OTHER POINTS OF VIEW

Ahmed Sharif was livid. He was working with a fool!

But it was not the time to act—not yet. There were too many unknowns.

For no good reason, Weber had brought Shane's car into view. The micro-transponder they had planted on the Lincoln sedan the previous evening, in Fernville, had allowed instantaneous GPS satellite tracking. Because of Weber's bungling, the fugitives knew they were being followed. Hopefully they wouldn't find the hidden tracking device, but they had been alerted.

As Sharif glared to his left at Manfred Weber, he noted that the driver was staring fixedly at the road ahead, deliberately avoiding eye contact or communications with his passenger.

"Look, Manfred," Sharif said, "It's done. Let's not remain angry with one another. It's time to consider our next move."

Averting his gaze from the road briefly, Weber nodded toward Sharif and said, "I agree, Ahmed. What do you think?"

"They appear to be headed west, not south. I suspect they're returning to Chicago."

"For what purpose?"

"That's what we must find out," Sharif declared. "What have you learned from your sources?"

"We know that they picked up a female passenger from the Fernville home," Weber replied. "A young woman by the name of Andrea Martin lived there with her grandmother. She's a computer science instructor at the local college. There's no previous record of these people coming to our attention."

"If they're part of the YLA, they've done a good job of keeping it secret."

"There's something else going on here," Weber insisted. "And it might have something to do with the grandmother. I've asked my office to dig up her background."

"How much do you know?"

"Her name is Diana Sutton. Early eighties. Lived in Fernville for about twenty years. She was married in 1941, to a Jew. We believe he was taken to Canada after the war. Deceased now. Her daughter was born before the marriage. The father is unknown, but was not a Jew."

"Is that all you know?" Sharif asked as Weber paused.

"So far."

After a few moments of thought, Sharif turned sharply toward Weber and said, "Make sure your people do a thorough check on the old lady's husband. He may be the key. What was he doing in 1941? How did they meet?"

Slapping his palm to his forehead, Weber uttered a German expletive, and exclaimed, "Of course! This isn't a YLA plot. This old lady is from the same generation as Shane's father. This is Shane following up on the Fuller work. I'll bet that if we dig deep enough we'll find a connection between Diana Sutton, Shane's father and the *Einstein Project!*"

"You may be right, Manfred," Sharif said. "But those connections have been long buried."

Sharif paused for a few moments and then remarked, "The old lady may be the best source of that information."

*   *   *   *

After a detour to Toledo where they had picked up Andrea's transit papers, Shane and Salomé had taken turns driving through the rest of Ohio and half of Indiana. Following old route 52, they had decided to spend the night at the Rhinelander Motel on the outskirts of Lafayette. They had taken two rooms for the first time during their trip. They agreed that Salomé should spend the night in Shane's room, however, sustaining the pretense that they were traveling as man and wife.

Prior to their arrival in Chicago the following day, Shane needed to make contact with Sarah and Mironi. But, more importantly, he needed to talk to Harry. That was why he found himself wandering around a large grassy field adjacent to the motel at midnight, the sat-phone pressed to his ear. His closest friend, Harry Churchill, was on the other end, talking to him from another securely encrypted sat-phone in Monterrey, Mexico.

Fortunately, the YLA had been able to remain a step ahead of the Nazis in sat-phone technology. Not only were messages solidly encrypted, but the communication method was unique. Each YLA sat-phone was designed to piggyback on the nearest television station's satellite communication channel. The sat-phone messages were randomly dispersed among the billions of digital packets of information. On a television screen it appeared as random noise. But each YLA sat-phone had an identical random-number generator. Each message began with a numeric code, setting the initiation point of the random-number generator so that the receiver phone could extract all the relevant message bits. To protect their technology, each YLA sat-phone was lined with high explosive to allow self-destruction.

After telling Harry about the meeting with Diana Sutton and her granddaughter Andrea, Shane briefly described their plan to bring Andrea back with them to Chicago. He explained to Harry why Andrea was the key to developing a successful final strategy for *operation rainbow*. Then he related the alarming incident that occurred after crossing into Ohio, and his suspicion that Carothers might be trying to undermine their mission.

"Andrea is a new factor," Shane was saying. "She gives us an edge we didn't have before, and I think Carothers is afraid this project might really work."

"Doesn't make sense, Tony," Harry responded. "Even if Carothers has reservations, he wouldn't have someone following you. You're contacting him regularly—aren't you?"

"Well…yes," Shane replied.

"Have you been straight with him?"

"Absolutely."

"So why would he be following you, Tony?"

"Perhaps he doesn't trust us."

"Forget that, old buddy. Why do you think Salomé came with you? Even if he didn't trust you—which he does—he knows Salomé is solid."

"So, how do you explain the tail?"

"What about Mironi?"

"Already talked to him. He knows we can't go anywhere without his help. He's not wasting time tailing us."

The connection at Harry's end remained silent for several seconds. Then he said, "It's got to be the *Gestapo*. They picked you up somehow."

"Why wouldn't they just stop us at a checkpoint?"

"Maybe they just want to know where you're going," Harry suggested.

This time the connection remained silent on Shane's end for a while. Finally, Shane said, "Maybe the new transit papers we got in Ohio threw them off."

"No way. Once the *Gestapo* gets a sniff, new transit papers won't help. I am really concerned, Tony. Did you hear what happened in New York City yesterday?"

"What?"

"The *Gestapo* picked up three of our people there, part of the crew that nuked the Manhattan skyscraper. They executed them—flat out—publicly."

"It wasn't on the news. What happened?"

"Those Nazi bastards didn't even explain. Just called them YLA terrorists and set up the firing squad. It was televised locally."

The connection went silent for several seconds as Shane decided to change the subject, "Look, Harry, we already know the *Gestapo* is out there. But is there any chance the Soviets or Japanese have gotten wind of *operation rainbow*?"

"Funny you should ask, Tony. Carothers took a quick trip to Miami a few days back. And you know who he talks to when he goes there."

"Rothchild?"

"Probably."

"What's that got to do with the Soviets or the Japanese?"

"Just call it suspicion, Tony. But if your tail turns out to speak Russian or Japanese, we've got a big problem."

"What are you getting at, Harry?"

"Just thinking ahead, Tony. What if Carothers really did snooker us with *operation rainbow*? What if he just sent us all away to buy time to carry out his real plan—whatever that is. Who would he find as an ally? Think about it. We're not the only ones who want to take down the Nazis."

"Christ, Harry. You're really scaring me. If there's any truth to this, *operation rainbow* won't be a secret for very long. And we're all at risk."

"It's just speculation, Tony. Even Carothers' trip to Miami is not suspicious by itself. But, if there's a chance we're being set up, you will be a very visible target in Chicago, and you won't know where it's coming from."

After a few moments of reflection, Shane said, "You're right, Harry. I'll have to re-think our Chicago rendezvous plans. But there's another issue right now. Have you found anything in Einstein's papers in Monterrey?"

"Not much. Einstein's quarters here have become a national museum. To get a look at anything interesting I've gotten access to the archives. None of the technical stuff mentions time travel. So, I'm focusing on personal correspondence. I haven't found anything to or from Fuller. Do you have any idea what else I should be looking for?"

"We learned something from Diana Sutton. Einstein apparently suggested to her back in 1942 that she would someday learn about his strategy for a time line intervention. We think that means that he would only reveal this information to a time traveler from the future."

"Sounds promising. But you need the time travel theory first, before you can go back."

"Right on, Harry. I always said you weren't as dumb as you looked."

"Don't be a smart-ass, Shane. What's your point?"

"My point is if Einstein wasn't willing to reveal his intervention strategy, then maybe he's carefully hidden the time travel theory as well."

"So?"

"He gave Diana a clue about how he would reveal the intervention strategy, didn't he? So, perhaps we should look for a clue to where we might find the time travel theory."

"You're saying I should be looking for some kind of treasure map?"

"Well, maybe not a treasure map. But something ambiguous. Something that doesn't belong or doesn't make sense."

"Thanks a lot, pal. You're giving me a lot to go on."

"Wish I could tell you what to look for, Harry. But, you're good at figuring out mysteries. You'll know it when you see it."

"You may be right, old buddy," Harry said with a yawn. "I'll get on it right after I catch some sleep—which will happen soon as I get rid of this paranoid nut that's been keeping me on the phone all night."

"Good night, Harry," Shane crooned.

"Catch ya later, Tony."

Part III.
Timeless Journey

CHAPTER 15

▼

TODAY

Could affairs be any more chaotic? Shane wondered as he and Salomé departed the YLA safe house in Hinsdale, about five miles northeast of the *Heisenberg Institut*. After meeting with Mironi at the Melrose Park rendezvous that afternoon, and learning that the *Gestapo* had been tracking them, Shane had decided they could no longer lodge in commercial hotels. Although Mironi had grilled Shane and extracted nearly all the strategic details of the *rainbow* mission, Shane had succeeded in keeping from him the heart of the operation. Shane implied that the objective was to obtain "mind control" technology...and allowed Mironi to jump to obvious, but wrong, conclusions.

From Sarah he had learned that Schwarz had made a "loyalty testing" appointment for her on Monday—two months ahead of schedule. He had claimed it was a "routine" *Gestapo* response to "recent terrorist activities." Sarah was certain she was being targeted, and she was afraid she would fail the test.

Sarah had spotted the secluded access to Schwarz's sub-basement research facility, but had not yet been bold enough to explore. She had, however, observed enough to note that no workers appeared to occupy the facility overnight. Complicating her efforts was Chekov's ubiquitous presence in her lab and insistence on seeing Sarah socially.

Harry had found a videotape record of a television interview with Einstein done in 1955. He believed it contained the clue that Shane was looking for regarding telepathic time travel theory. Shane would get the full story by sat-phone that evening.

Carothers had called to alert them that the Soviets and Japanese were growing suspicious of the YLA activities inside the *DRA* post-9/11, and might be tracking Shane's progress. He didn't think they knew about *operation rainbow*, Carothers had said. But Shane had little faith in that statement. If Carothers said he wasn't sure whether they knew, that meant the secret was out.

Andrea had been left behind at the safe house to work on the time travel programming required for the very first journey—her own. At least the safe house in Hinsdale was located near the *Institut*, and Shane would be able to rendezvous with Sarah shortly. They had agreed to meet at nine that evening near the Italian Trattoria in Willowbrook where Sarah and Tony had lunched previously. Mironi had provided them with a different car, picked up clandestinely in Melrose Park. They had ditched the Lincoln and picked up a new black Packard sedan—probably bugged—but Shane didn't care.

Within minutes, Shane had guided the Packard to the Willowbrook shopping mall where he and Salomé would meet with Sarah. Silently, he cursed Mironi's obsession with large, expensive American luxury cars—and the Germans' post-war decision to retain American production facilities for Lincolns, Cadillacs, Packards and Chryslers, while converting other facilities to German models. He was thankful that they would all be switching to Sarah's less-conspicuous Volkswagen for the trip to the *Institut*.

Salomé was certain they had not been followed from Melrose Park. At least that was comforting.

*   *   *   *

"Goddamit!" Weber exclaimed as he terminated his connection with the last of the three *Gestapo* surveillance vehicles that had joined him in following Shane's Lincoln into the Melrose Park neighborhood. The Lincoln's three passengers had disappeared into the Italian deli and not reappeared. After an hour, two obvious Mironi goons had exited the deli and taken off in the Lincoln. Weber had just been informed by phone that the deli was devoid of customers and that no one had been seen leaving the immediate vicinity.

"Perhaps we should go inside and check it out," Sharif suggested.

"Absolutely not!" Weber responded. "We can't let them know we're looking for them."

"So, what do we do next?" Sharif asked, although he had already conceived a plan.

"We take what clues we have and figure out what they're doing here in Chicago," Weber replied. "Then we catch up with them."

"What clues do we have?"

"Ahmed, old friend," Weber replied with a smirk, "you're an old hand at this. Perhaps you should tell me?"

After gazing steadily at Weber for several seconds, Sharif decided to test his friend. He responded by raising his hand to stick out a thumb. "First of all," he began, "we know that the young lady from New York is a computer scientist." Raising a second finger, he added, "Secondly, we know that Shane is trained in electronics and computer technology. And, third," as he raised another finger, "it appears that something in Chicago is necessary for *operation rainbow*." Sequentially raising the remaining fingers of his hand, Sharif added, "Fourth, it appears this operation is computer-related; and fifth, Vito Mironi is helping them."

As Sharif paused, Weber said, "Very good, Ahmed. But you could also add that Shane is not leveling with Mironi. Mironi wouldn't support a mission to disrupt the *DRA*. He has too much to lose."

"Can you be certain of that, Manfred?" Sharif asked. "Perhaps *operation rainbow* will leave Mironi in an even more powerful position than he holds now."

"I don't see how."

"That's exactly why we need to understand better what Shane is up to. What did we learn from the old lady in New York?"

"Nothing. She used a fast-acting poison. But, we found some interesting items in her home. And we dug up information on her Jew husband as you suggested. I have the entire file sitting on my desk."

"Are there any other clues we're overlooking?" Sharif persisted.

"Like what?"

"What's going on in Chicago right now that might have drawn them here? And what about the biggest clue of all—the one we're overlooking?"

"What's that?"

"What was Shane doing those two days before they left Chicago for New York?"

"We don't know."

"Precisely. That's what we need to find out. Perhaps it was something that could only have been done then," Sharif suggested.

"Hmmh. There was one high security event during that period when we lost Shane. A large number of foreign visitors—scientists—were in Chicago to attend a conference at the *Heisenberg Institut.*"

"Do you know the topic of the conference?"

Scratching his head, Weber replied, "Cybernetics? I think that was the topic. I can verify it."

"That may be it, Manfred. Shane's expertise is in computers. And he went to New York to pick up yet another computer expert. He may be connected to someone who attended that cybernetics conference."

"That's a long shot, Ahmed."

"Perhaps. But, humor me. Let's check it out," Sharif insisted.

Suddenly, Weber snapped his fingers. "Ahmed, there is something that might be related. A Dr. Schwarz called today from the *Institut* to schedule a loyalty test for one of his colleagues on Monday. We test all *Institut* workers periodically, but this test would be months ahead of schedule. Schwarz is obviously suspicious of this employee."

"You give 'loyalty' tests to all government workers—even Nazi members?"

"Of course. All government employees must renew their *eidesstattliche Aussage*, the loyalty oath, annually. And they must submit to testing with the new *Koehler-Chekov Treuedetektor* on demand. This machine uses dozens of biosensors and computer analysis. It's virtually one hundred percent accurate. In fact, coincidentally, the co-inventor of the detector, Sergei Chekov, was at the cybernetics conference last week."

"How long have you been doing these loyalty tests?" Sharif inquired.

"Since *der Vaterlandsfreund Gesetz,* the Patriot Act, that was passed three years ago by the *Reichstag* in response to escalating terrorism."

Sharif shook his head. "Manfred, you can't believe that this is the answer to preventing terrorism?"

"We must be sure our employees are loyal to the *Reich*. That is the first step in preventing terrorism."

"When governments require loyalty tests and loyalty oaths they are in serious trouble. If you are suspicious of all, you have faith in none. Such tests are evidence that force, not consent, sustains the will of the government."

"What would you have us do? Hire terrorists in our government labs?"

"You should think about *why* anyone—citizen or alien—might feel so strongly as to cause indiscriminate carnage, without regard for their own lives. When you put as much effort into answering that question, Manfred, as you do your 'loyalty tests' you will resolve the problem."

"Again you're wasting our time with your speeches, Ahmed," Weber growled. "Let's get back to my office where we can put all of our clues together. I have a feeling we may be visiting the *Institut* soon."

Sharif hid his frown. This barbaric and unenlightened Nazi approach to terrorism was disconcerting. But, perhaps, with Sharif's prompting, Weber could at least do the competent investigative work needed to find Shane and his colleagues.

*   *   *   *

After introducing Sarah to Salomé, Shane had asked Sarah to drive them to the *Institut.* Thanks to Vito Mironi, each of the interlopers was now in possession of identity badges that provided them access to the *Heisenberg Institut* and to Sarah's laboratory. The badges were duplicates of those of real workers at the *Institut,* and they were accompanied by matching identity papers. These papers, plus a sizable bribe to the swing-shift security guard at the North Gate, had gotten them inside this night.

Now, deep within the sub-basement's *Neuralones Forschungslaboratorium,* the Neural Research Lab, Shane pored through hundreds of programming files at the main console, while Sarah studied carefully the human interface hardware. Salomé remained distant but vigilant, stationed at the main entrance to the underground facility. Any technician who might decide to check up on anything during that night would receive a rude and fatal reception.

"What do you think?" Shane wondered aloud as he focused on deciding which, if any, of the existing programs would be helpful to them.

"These bastards have done no more than take my work with chimps and adapt the connections to the human brain. There's nothing new here."

"Is that good or bad?"

"The good news is I don't have to change any of the interfacing; the bad news is the connections are too primitive for our purposes."

"Doesn't that depend on the programming?"

"What do you have in mind, Dr. Frankenstein?" Sarah asked, "You want to teach somebody to dance?"

"I want to know if the four-dimensional images created by the computer can generate electrical impulses to stimulate the telepathic region of the brain."

"Sure, if you can show me where that is."

"Don't you know?"

"Never thought about it. Did you get any insight from your letter?" Sarah asked.

"Don't you remember? I told you they used some sort of imaging device with telepathic subjects before inserting the microchips," Shane replied. As hard as he tried to suppress his anxiety, he felt himself getting impatient and irritable.

"We can use the P.E.T. imaging machine."

"What's a 'P.E.T.' machine?"

"Positron Emission Tomography. It measures positron emissions from biological systems, with 3-D mapping. Identifies localized brain activity. I've used it with chimps. Perhaps we can image you and Andrea under telepathic conditions and pinpoint hot spots."

"How do you feel about positioning the probes with human subjects?"

"I've done it many times with chimps. We use the nasal passages and endoscopic techniques."

"In case you haven't been paying attention, I'm not a chimp."

"I had a pretty thorough anatomy course in graduate school. I've poked and probed human brains before."

"Not any that could poke back I'll bet."

"You starting to have some doubts, Shane?" Sarah asked.

"That's all I have, Sarah. *Doubts*." Then, shaking his head, Shane commented to no one in particular, "We must be crazy to think we can get this jury-rigged contraption to work."

"My end will work, Tony. You just concentrate on getting your stuff together," Sarah insisted.

"Yeah. I will…but not here tonight. I've found everything I can use, and I see what high-level programming will be compatible. I'll have to translate most of the code Andrea and I have generated."

"I agree. We shouldn't spend any more time here than necessary," Sarah responded. "We can work on the programming back at my apartment. I've got a computer system at home with the same compiler that we use here."

Nodding his head and closing down the console work station, Shane picked up his notebook and motioned for Sarah to join him as he headed quickly out of the Neural Lab to join Salomé. It was after midnight and they still had a full day's work to do before trying test runs the following night.

Shane knew that they could not afford any delays. It would be impossible to keep their activities secret—from the *Gestapo* or Mironi—for very long.

*   *   *   *

Salomé had reluctantly agreed to return to the safe house, while Shane and Sarah headed for Sarah's apartment. They would work through the night. Because it was a Friday night, Sarah would not have to show up for her job at the *Institut* in the morning. They would have about eighteen hours to work on the programming before returning to the Neural Lab the following evening. They had agreed on a rendezvous with Salomé and Andrea around noon Saturday to bring Andrea to Sarah's place and bring her up to speed. Shane and Sarah were reluctant to admit it, but they also had to slip in several hours of sleep if they were to be effective the following evening.

Alone now inside Sarah's apartment, Shane and Sarah were each actively engaged in the daunting task of translating their crude concepts for telepathic time travel into a language understood by the *Institut* computer systems. Sarah was seated at the computer workstation, while Shane was conversing with Harry Churchill on the sat-phone. It was Shane's desperate hope that Harry had found the key to interpreting Einstein's enigmatic letter to Garrison Fuller regarding time travel theory.

"I'm telling you, Tony," Harry was saying, "Einstein was a genius."

"I know that, Harry. Everybody knows that," Shane pointed out. "Now tell me what he did that you're so excited about."

"Shortly before he died he gave an interview. All the papers, radio, TV picked it up. I saw the tape. I tell ya, It was a stroke of genius, Tony."

"What did he do?"

"Nothing."

"Nothing? What the hell are you talking about?" Shane yelled, his patience waning.

"Tell me, Tony. Did Einstein believe in time travel, or not?"

"Yes and no. His General Theory of Relativity predicted that travel into the future is possible at speeds close to the speed of light. But he never suggested that travel into the past was possible."

"Well, guess what? In his last interview he said two things, and I'm paraphrasing. First, when the interviewer asked him if time travel to both future and past were possible, he said that past, present, and future all exist simultaneously. Humans create the illusion of time in their heads. Therefore, he said, travel to either past or future doesn't involve 'time travel' at all. One just stands still and looks in the right direction."

"Hadn't he said things like that before?"

"Sure. But it's the second thing he said that caught my attention. When the interviewer asked him to explain how he might travel into the past, Einstein said, 'Even if I knew, I would never put it down on paper. It would be too dangerous.'"

"I agree with him. What's your point?" Shane asked with thinly-veiled impatience.

"Tony. Listen. He said he *would never put it down on paper!* He didn't say he would 'never reveal it' or 'never tell anybody.' But, no, he said he wouldn't put it down on paper."

"I'm sorry, Harry. I don't get your point."

"Christ, Tony. He was talking directly to us! That was a message for us. He was saying *don't pay attention to that letter to Fuller* because he would never have put the theory down on paper. That letter is just a big fat red herring. Just rely on the information in your letter from the future."

After remaining silent for several seconds, Shane said, "Hmmh. You may have something, Harry. I hope you're right. We haven't been successful in translating the letter."

Shane's tone was conciliatory, hoping to atone for the rude impatience he had just exhibited to his dear friend.

"You don't need to translate it, Tony," Harry insisted. "This is just another example of Einstein's obsession with secrecy."

"Yeah…like not telling us his intervention plan."

"You don't have a plan yet!" Harry exclaimed.

"That *is* the plan, Harry. Another touch of genius perhaps. Einstein set things up so that no one will ever find out how we alter the 1939 time line."

"So, how will you get the job done, Tony?"

"I wish I knew, big guy. I wish I knew."

*   *   *   *

For a long time after his sat-phone conversation with Harry, Shane reclined on the sofa with his forearm covering his eyes. Too many things were happening too fast, and the sheer physical demands of the past week had finally caught up with him. Harry's insistence that there was no magic bullet in Einstein's letter to Fuller had been the last straw. With no clear intervention plan, no theoretical guidance, and an untested apparatus with inadequate programming, Shane was experiencing uncharacteristic despair. Unrelentingly optimistic for so long, he felt himself literally crashing to earth.

It was the softness of her hair as it brushed against his cheek that first alerted his senses. The kiss that arrived tenderly was returned with unexpected fervor that stirred up from a tortured depth. Suddenly, Shane found himself pulling Sarah to him in a long passionate embrace. As she pulled away Shane reached out to pull her back, but Sarah pushed his hands away and began to unbutton his shirt.

Within seconds they had slipped onto the plush rug and were frantically removing their clothing. Stripped to their underwear, Shane and Sarah clung to each other tightly as they enjoyed a long passionate kiss. Then Sarah moved over Shane and sat up as she straddled him. For a moment their eyes locked and communicated an unspoken message. Their breathless passion could not be denied; yet, they understood in that moment that a threshold would soon be passed that would complicate their lives in a way that no previous lovers had ever experienced.

As the moment passed, Shane drew Sarah to him, kissed her and reached behind to unfasten her bra. As they rolled over, Sarah reached down to slip off her panties and Shane removed his shorts. Once again their eyes met in a silent communication as they joined together and writhed on the floor. More slowly and passionately than they had ever before experienced, they climbed to a climaxing peak of wild abandon, and then collapsed tightly into each others arms.

After absorbing each other in this position for several minutes, Sarah raised up on one elbow and looked down at Shane, her long auburn hair falling forward and surrounding his face. With a sly smile she said, "I hope you don't think this is the way I behave every Friday night."

"I hope you don't think I'm doing this because it's our *only* Friday night," Shane responded in a misguided attempt at humor.

Momentarily cooled by Shane's dark remark, Sarah could not hide a momentary flash of pain.

"I'm sorry," Shane added. "That wasn't funny. I'm not very good at this, Sarah."

"Who is?" she responded with a forced smile. Then, after a few moments of silence, she added, "I don't know whether I wish we had met sooner...or never met at all, Tony. But I feel something I've never felt before."

"Yeah," Shane responded slowly. "Me too."

"What are we going to do, Tony?"

Reaching up to caress her cheek and run his fingers through her hair, Shane took a moment to respond. Then he said softly, "My dad once told me that I should always do what I knew I *should* be doing. I think he must have known that something like this would come along." Then, after a moment, Shane added slowly, "I think we both know what we have to do, Sarah."

"Doesn't make it any easier, does it?" Sarah acknowledged.

"No," Shane responded as he pulled her to him once again, "but I have a strong feeling about us, Sarah."

Holding her close, then, he murmured softly in her ear: "I don't believe something this good can ever go away."

But Shane knew in his heart that this amazing, but unexpected, relationship with Sarah was destined to add yet another formidable obstacle to the success of the *Einstein project*.

*   *   *   *

It was well after midnight, and the lights burned brightly in Manfred Weber's office at *Gestapo* headquarters. Throughout the evening and early morning hours he and Ahmed Sharif had pored over the paltry information gathered from Diana Sutton Kreutzwil's home and the surprisingly voluminous report on Harri Kreutzwil that had been received late in the evening. Sharif's insistence on pursuing Kreutzwil had paid enormous dividends.

Although Diana had written off her husband as long since deceased in a Canadian concentration camp, Kreutzwil had been located—very much alive. Immediately after the war he had been abducted from Los Alamos by the Soviet occupying forces, and delivered to a nuclear research facility on the outskirts of Leningrad. He had worked for the Soviets for several decades in their nuclear weapons program. None of his letters to Diana had ever reached their destination.

Following Weber's bulletin to the Nazi foreign intelligence agency, *Der Nachrichtendienst*, earlier that week, Kreutzwil's extensive file had been discovered in Leningrad, and had been copied covertly by a Nazi operative there. The file had arrived in Chicago that evening. Among the many items in the file were several references to the relationship with his wife. It was that part of the file that Weber and Sharif were discussing.

"According to this, Kreutzwil met Miss Sutton in 1941 when she showed up in his lab at Columbia looking for his friend, Joseph Rheingold."

"Is that the same Rheingold, the Jew who was responsible for the first German atomic bomb?" Sharif asked.

"Astonishing coincidence, don't you think?" Weber responded.

"What was Rheingold doing at Columbia?"

"He wasn't there. He was already working with Heisenberg in Hamburg on the German atom bomb project."

"How did a Jew get involved in that?" Sharif asked.

"I guess you've never heard that story, Ahmed. Heisenberg convinced Hitler that we should persuade Rheingold to work for us. Hitler agreed, but the fact that a Jew was responsible for the success of the program was a well kept secret until after Hitler's death in '56."

"What was Sutton's connection to Rheingold?"

"According to Kreutzwil, she had met Rheingold on the same Clipper flight to Europe where he was abducted. She looked him up when she returned from England and learned that Rheingold was working in Germany."

"Was Rheingold Sutton's lover? What was her concern?" Sharif asked.

"Good question. They only met on that flight, according to Kreutzwil. But it's what happened later on that gets really interesting."

"What's that?"

"Kreutzwil and Sutton had a whirlwind courtship and married in '41. They had a daughter, but the daughter was not his. The daughter was born in England in 1940—and get this—nine months after the flight where Sutton met Rheingold."

"You think the daughter was Rheingold's? They slept together on that overnight flight?"

"Not according to Miss Sutton. She always claimed the daughter was fathered by a Brit, not a Jew."

"Fascinating," Sharif murmured. "What else?"

"Kreutzwil and Sutton had a strange relationship. He went to Los Alamos to work on the Manhattan Project, while his wife went to Wisconsin and worked with Professor Garrison Fuller. He lost track of her after the war."

"Fuller is the same one that you tracked all those years, Manfred?"

"The same. And that means that Miss Sutton was working with Tony Shane's father, Daniel, on the *Einstein Project*."

"So, there's the connection with Shane! That must be why he traveled to New York to see her," Sharif exclaimd.

"This is very significant, Ahmed. It means that Shane has resurrected the *Einstein Project*—just as I feared."

"But we don't know what the *Einstein Project* is about," Sharif lamented.

"Ahh, but we now have a hint," Weber stated with a broad grin.

"Did Kreutzwil know?"

"No, but Diana Sutton did—and she left us a clue."

As Sharif regarded Weber with arched eyebrows, Weber reached into the box of materials retrieved from Diana's home in New York. The item he retrieved was a worn paperback entitled, *Einstein Simplified: Theory and Practice.* "Here. Take a look at page 149," he urged Sharif.

Sharif opened the book to page 149 and examined the contents. He noted that there were a number of pencil markings, underlined passages, and margin notes. Flipping back a few pages, Sharif discovered that the topic of the section was "General Relativity Theory and Time Travel." Returning to page 149 he noted the underlined sentences and read the scribbled margin notes.

Without commenting, Sharif shifted his gaze to Weber who was waiting expectantly for his reaction. Shaking his head, he said, "Manfred, I know you've been obsessed with this *Einstein Project* for years. But, surely you're not thinking that it has to do with—"

"Time travel!" Weber exclaimed. "That's it. That's what Fuller was experimenting with."

"Ridiculous! That's the realm of physics, not psychology. Fuller was a psychologist, wasn't he?"

"True. But Einstein himself guided this project. There was no need for another physicist."

"So what was Fuller doing?"

"Look at Sutton's margin notes."

"Which ones?"

"Here," Weber said as he rotated the open paperback on the desktop so that they could both read the text. "What does it say here?" he asked as he pointed to one of the underlined passages:

> *Future time travel is consistent with relativity theory. But travel to the past is not. Einstein has said that—unless some phenomenon exists which defies the laws of physics—travel to the past is not possible.*

"Now, what is written in the margin?"

"I think it says, 'telepathy an exception,'" Sharif replied.

"That's right. Telepathy. Mental communication. That's why a psychologist was the project leader," Weber exclaimed.

Sharif regarded Weber with a cocked eye for a moment, and then said, "Neither of us is qualified to judge what this means, Manfred. We need a physicist and a psychologist. Do you have either at *Gestapo* headquarters?"

Weber thought about it and shook his head. "Not here. Perhaps in Washington." Then suddenly his face brightened. "Dr. Schwarz from the *Institut!* He identified himself as a physicist when he called me yesterday. We could talk to him. He has a high security clearance."

"Good. Get him on the phone," Sharif commanded.

"It's the middle of the night!" Weber protested.

"If you're right about Shane's mission, Manfred. We don't want to waste a minute."

"What? When did you change your mind, Ahmed?"

"It just occurred to me what the objective of the *Einstein Project* is."

"What?"

"Connect the dots, Manfred. Rheingold...atomic bomb...Sutton there when Rheingold abducted...and Sutton's statement about telepathy and time travel. What do you get?"

Weber remained silent for several seconds as he contemplated Sharif's deductions. Finally, he reached for another sheet of paper from the Kreutzwil file. Placing the paper in front of Sharif, he pointed to a statement that Kreutzwil had made back in 1944.

Sharif read the statement, and looked up at Weber, a thin smile forming.

"Yes, that's right. Daniel McShane—Tony Shane's father—was on that same 1939 flight!" Weber announced.

$$* \qquad * \qquad * \qquad *$$

Wolfgang Schwarz grumbled to himself as the guard escorted him to Weber's office deep within *Gestapo* headquarters. A phone call had come in the middle of the night. And Colonel Weber had insisted that Schwarz drive as soon as possible from his Hinsdale residence on the southwest side all the way to the *Gestapo* complex many miles north of Chicago. Even arriving there by six in the morning probably would not satisfy the colonel. Schwarz was in a foul mood. The reason for this urgent meeting had better be good.

Admitted to Weber's office, Schwarz stuck out his hand in greeting and then noticed the dark, well-groomed foreigner sitting on one end of a sofa against the wall. "Good morning, Dr. Schwarz," Weber crooned, "thank you for getting here so quickly."

Schwarz simply nodded and grunted. After the introduction of Sharif, Weber informed Schwarz that their conversation would be top secret and could not be revealed to anyone. Schwarz simply nodded, and sat down to listen.

"Dr. Schwarz, what do you know of Einstein's theory of relativity?" Weber began.

"I'm familiar with it. Studied it extensively during my doctoral work. I've taught a course on the topic at the *Institut.*"

"Fine. Wonderful," Weber commented, "that's just what we needed to hear. Now, tell us, have you ever considered whether time travel is allowed by Einstein's theory?"

"Einstein didn't believe time travel to the past was possible. Travel to the future—yes. But one could never return. He believed that travel to the past was fraught with impossible paradoxes."

"Is that it?" Sharif asked. "Cut and dry?"

"The theory has changed a lot since the 1950's, gentlemen. Modern physicists believe there are many exceptions and refinements to Einstein's theory of relativity."

"For example?" Sharif asked.

"Well, for one thing, black holes have been discovered in space. We know that the enormous gravitational fields of these objects can distort the space-time continuum. If you can imagine space-time folding over on itself, you can conceive of a physical trip to the future—or past—that might involve infinitesimally small amounts of energy. Contrast that with Einstein's belief that travel to the future required achieving speeds close to the speed of light."

"So, modern physics supports the idea of time travel—and with much less difficulty than Einstein had imagined," Sharif summarized.

"It is only speculation. There are other theoretical concepts of space-time that would deny the possibility of time travel."

"Like what?" Weber asked.

"Difficult to explain in layman's terms. One theory, for example, states that the universe is completely self-contained, but still has no discernible boundaries. Hard to imagine, but it can be described mathematically. This concept explains certain astronomical observations, but it absolutely precludes the possibility of time travel."

Sharif and Weber nodded their heads absently, trying to absorb the unfamiliar concepts. Finally, Weber asked, "Are you familiar with mental telepathy, Dr. Schwarz? I realize it's not your field."

"Surprisingly enough, I am familiar with telepathy. My doctorate is in physics, but my postdoctoral studies were in a neural psychology department. What is your question?"

"This is indeed fortuitous," Weber observed. "Perhaps you can tell us if there is a theoretical understanding of the phenomenon?"

"No. Not really. We can make measurements. But we don't begin to understand the phenomenon."

"Have you ever heard of any research involving both telepathy and time travel?" Sharif asked.

Schwarz frowned and shook his head slowly. "No. Never heard of anything like that. Frankly, it sounds preposterous."

As Sharif and Weber again nodded their heads and stared ahead blankly, Schwarz asked, "Can you tell me what this is all about, Colonel Weber?"

Weber snapped out of his reflections and smiled politely as he said, "I'm sorry, Dr. Schwarz. I can not. I'm sure you understand."

"Of course," Schwarz responded. "Do you have any other questions?"

"I don't think so. You've been very helpful," Weber replied. "The guard outside the door can escort you out."

With that, Schwarz whirled and slipped out of the office to join the guard and depart *Gestapo* headquarters. A thin smile formed on his face.

* * * *

As Wolfgang Schwarz left the office, Manfred Weber turned to Ahmed Sharif and slowly shook his head. "It appears our theory has just gone up in smoke," he said.

"Perhaps, Manfred. Perhaps," Sharif responded. "But, I think we should keep it on the table. Time travel may not be the purpose of this conspiracy, but there is no doubt that Tony Shane is up to no good. And these ties we've discovered to Rheingold and the German atomic bomb project during World War II can not be coincidental. Something big is afoot. It is tied to the original *Einstein Project*. And it will come to a head very soon."

Nodding his head slowly, Weber murmured, "It looks like there are more sleepless nights in our future, Ahmed."

* * * *

The all-night meeting at *Gestapo* headquarters had been very productive. But it had not gone unnoticed. Because one of the night security guards was also on Vito Mironi's secret payroll, the guard had made a point of eavesdropping on the conversation before and after Schwarz's arrival. Although he had understood little of what transpired, the message he delivered to Mironi had enraged the man.

Someone was in very deep trouble.

*   *   *   *

The return drive to Hinsdale had flown by for Wolfgang Schwarz. His mind was working furiously to try and sort out the meaning of the incredible conversation that had just transpired at *Gestapo* headquarters. One thing was certain. Schwarz had received much more information than he had given. The glazed eyes of Weber and Sharif confirmed their lack of understanding of the concepts he had discussed. They were no closer now to solving whatever mystery they were addressing.

But Schwarz had experienced an epiphany. Why had he not thought of it before? It was obvious now. Telepathic subjects should be the objective of future experiments in the Neural Research Lab.

And he knew the most qualified person to conduct those studies.

As he decided spontaneously to drive directly to the *Institut* and begin preparations for the new studies he envisioned, he prayed silently that Sarah Stenstrom would pass the loyalty test.

*   *   *   *

Their newly found intimacy had resolved the sticky problem of how Shane and Sarah would get any sleep on Saturday. After several hours of intense work—with Shane producing the appropriate space-time computational functions and Sarah translating these into computer code—they opened up the sofa bed and dropped instantly into exhausted sleep. The alarm was set for three hours, as they were expecting Salomé and Andrea to join them in four.

Well before the alarm went off, the pair was awakened by an inner restlessness evoked by anxiety regarding their unfinished work. Still exhausted, they could not drag themselves from the bed.

It was Sarah who broke the silence. "Tony, I have so many questions. We have so much more to learn about each other. I want to know what foods you like, what books you read…everything about you, Tony." Then, as she turned on her side to look at him, and she felt her eyes filling up, she said, "There just isn't enough time."

Shane turned on his side to look at her, and reached out to brush away a tear. "Don't put yourself through this, Sarah. Let's just be thankful for what we have right now."

With a brave smile, Sarah asked, "Can you at least tell me about your work with the YLA, Tony? What's your relationship with Salomé? Carothers? Harry? And what about Vito Mironi?"

"The answers to those questions are not simple, Sarah. It could take hours."

"It's not a random question, Tony. My life these past few days has been turned topsy-turvy. I feel like I've been caught up in a tornado. I believe in what we're doing, but, if I am completely honest with myself, I'm in this because I believe in you. Because I trust you. Now I'm wondering how you feel about your colleagues. Do you trust them?"

"I understand, Sarah. Let me try to answer. First, Harry. He's my best friend. I trust him with my life. No…I trust him with my soul. I feel lost without him at my side right now."

"I'm sure he feels the same."

"If Harry could change the color of his skin, he would be here in an instant," Shane murmured.

"What about Carothers?"

"I know Carothers wants to be here too. But, he's the biggest, most-menacing black man you'll ever see. He wouldn't last ten seconds in Nazi territory."

"How do you feel about Carothers?"

Shane took a deep breath and exhaled. "Carothers is not my friend. He's my leader. I respect him to hell. But I don't trust him. If it's him or me, I know who he chooses."

"What about Salomé?"

"She's a mystery to me. Or, at least, she was. This mission is the first time we've been thrown together. I've learned a lot about her. She's Jewish, you know. And she's more committed than any of us to carrying out this mission. With her it's personal."

"Do you trust her?" Sarah asked.

Again, Shane took a deep breath and exhaled. Shaking his head he said, "I guess I don't know. Our relationship just doesn't run that deep. I'm sure you've noticed that she's the 'enforcer' among us. She's tough, physically and mentally. She can kill in an instant, without remorse. Yet, I see love and compassion there. She's just very good at covering it up."

"Do you trust her, Tony?" Sarah persisted.

"To carry out this mission…absolutely. Beyond that…I just don't know."

"How about Mironi?"

"You know that story—Vito's family commitment to me. But, if he ever thought I was disloyal, he wouldn't hesitate to take me out himself."

"I thought you two were like brothers?" Sarah asked in disbelief.

"There's a strict code, Sarah. And it's much more serious and unforgivable if a family member breaks the code."

"Don't you think it's kind of scary, Tony? Three of your four closest colleagues...who hold your life in their hands every day...you're not sure about?"

"Not quite right, Sarah. I'm absolutely sure about Mironi. I know exactly where he stands. But, with my YLA colleagues, uncertainty is the nature of the business. Rebels, terrorists, guerillas...they don't survive if they trust anybody. Ultimately, you learn you can only count on yourself. Harry and I are fortunate. We know we can trust each other. That just doesn't happen in our business."

After gazing into Shane's earnest eyes for a few moments, Sarah reached out and pulled her body as close to him as she could. Then she murmured in his ear, "There's one more person in your life now, Tony. And you can trust her with your life...and with your soul."

Under other circumstances, Shane thought, he would have cherished these words of commitment from Sarah. And, yes, he did so even now. But, despite the warm glow of their embrace, Shane could not help but be troubled by the specter of devastating future choices that they would have to make.

CHAPTER 16

▼

TOMORROW

They had arrived at the *Institut* at ten o'clock that evening, confident that they would not be disturbed. There was much work to do. Somehow they had to complete preparations for a test run before daylight.

The previous afternoon at Sarah's apartment had been occupied with the application of simple telepathic tests. As they expected, Shane and Andrea had exhibited rudimentary telepathic abilities. The surprise had been that Salomé had also. Sarah, unfortunately, had not.

Working feverishly that evening within the Neural Research Lab, Sarah had subjected each of the other three to P.E.T. scans, confirming and locating the telepathic centers of their brains. In each case she had confirmed that the spots were accessible endoscopically.

Now, after Salomé had left them in the lab to resume her post near the solitary entrance to the sub-basement, Andrea was completing the transfer of compiled programs to the computer control console. Shane was setting up the electronic interfacing; and Sarah was preparing the microprobes that soon would be inserted endoscopically into Andrea's brain.

"I think we'll have enough resolution for the test run," Sarah was saying. "You told me we needed eight separate outputs and four inputs. But, won't we require more outputs for the longer time jumps? Aren't the calculations much more complicated?"

"We'll need at least sixteen outputs if we want to transmit the space-time computations for a jump to 1939," Shane replied.

"How do you figure that, Tony? I'm not sure I can squeeze that many microprobes in."

"It's complicated, Sarah. I've thought about it for a long time, using the crude descriptions I found in the letter from the future, and what I've read about Einstein's space-time computations. Perhaps if I were a physicist or a mathematician I could do it more efficiently. I had hoped that Einstein's letter to Fuller would tell us specifically how to do it, but that's been a bust."

"All right, Tony. I'll see what I can do to squeeze in more probes. Are you sure it'll be OK to use analog inputs? Are you concerned about the precision?"

"You tell me, Sarah. How sensitive is the brain to variations in voltage? That's what limits the precision, not the computer."

"The brain is basically a digital device, Tony. But the brain also controls analog functions. What we're trying to do here is make contact with those analog controllers. It's like adjusting the magnitude and force of the motion of your finger after your brain has computed that you're lifting a teacup. Here, we're using our supercomputer to do the computations that the brain is incapable of handling, then transferring the outputs for telepathic communications."

"So, you still haven't answered my question. How precise are the brain's control functions?" Shane persisted.

"Well, it's like this. An athlete's brain must control its body to within incredibly narrow tolerances. When a pitcher throws a curve ball that crosses the plate at the waist, just catching the last quarter inch of the outside corner at a speed of 95 miles per hour—and he does this over and over again—how many muscles and tendons and ligaments are controlled with what precision? You do the calculations, Tony. I don't know, but I'll bet you that the corresponding digital precision has got to be greater than 32 bits."

Shaking his head and smiling benignly, Shane said, "Wow! I guess you answered my question all right. But how did you come up with that baseball analogy? That was great."

"Five years on a girls' softball team back in my home town. And too many years of listening to my dad cheering for the Seals on the radio," Sarah smiled.

*   *   *   *

The wall clock in the Neural Research Lab indicated nearly three o'clock in the morning as Sarah completed attaching the multiple microprobes endoscopically to a supine Andrea. Except for the nasal area, where an improbably thin teflon-coated cable was inserted, Andrea's head was nearly completely enclosed by the helmet probe of the P.E.T. machine. On the monitor facing Sarah was a three-dimensional image of the area of Andrea's brain being accessed endoscopically. Superimposed on the current image was the previously scanned image taken during a preliminary telepathic experiment.

The programming had been completed and checked out. The space-time computations were set for a telepathic journey forward in time of only three days. The location was identical to where they were at the moment—except for the space-time dislocation that would occur over the next three days. The target receptor was the future Andrea herself.

"Are you ready, Andrea?" Shane asked.

"Yes," came the firm reply. The local anesthetic did nothing to impair her mental or vocal responses.

"I'll go over this again," Shane continued. "You focus on communicating with yourself at the future place and time we've programmed. If this works, you will apparently lose consciousness here, but you will be experiencing everything your future self is experiencing at that time and place. All of this will be taking place in your brain, and you will remember it. But the future Andrea will not remember the experience. She will suffer a memory loss corresponding to the entire time that you are in telepathic control. But you will have access to all of her memories.

"You may suffer some disorientation. Don't panic. Just proceed as if you are the future Andrea, physically and mentally. When you are ready to return to current time, just make that mental decision and focus on communicating again with yourself in this time and place. That event will tell the computer to change its outputs to the current space-time coordinates. And, *voila*, you'll be back with us."

"OK, Tony. I understand," Andrea murmured. "Let's do it."

"With less confidence than he had just expressed, Shane nodded to Sarah to initiate the computer's output sequence. Within seconds, Andrea would lapse into unconsciousness, and they would all hold their breaths until she re-emerged from the telepathic journey. At least, that was what they hoped for.

Shane reached for the hand of this incredibly brave young lady, and squeezed it. "We love you, Andrea. Good luck," he said.

*   *   *   *

Andrea's peaceful state of unconsciousness had not relieved Shane's anxiety. Ten minutes had passed, and he could see that Sarah was concerned at the utter lack of sophisticated measurements of Andrea's physical state beyond blood pressure and pulse. Here they were, she had said, performing delicate pseudo-surgical procedures on a human being without proper medical support, praying that nothing might go wrong—and not even sure what to look for if it did. Although the endoscopic procedure was minimally invasive, and Sarah had performed it many times with chimps, the leap to human subjects should have been taken in stages. But they had had no choice, he told himself. And, at least, the P.E.T. machine could monitor brain activity. They didn't know what to look for, but anything catastrophic would be obvious.

At the moment, the P.E.T. was indicating that the telepathic brain centers were very active, and that was reassuring. Noting the time that had passed, Sarah turned to Shane and asked, "Shouldn't she be returning now? We asked her not to keep this up for too long."

"How long do you think the *next* trip will take?" Shane countered. "Andrea knows she'll need at least an hour next time, based on Diana's recollection of her meeting with Einstein back in 1942. She's going to push this test as far as she can."

Shaking her head slowly, Sarah murmured, "Poor girl. She still doesn't know about her grandmother, does she?"

"I didn't have the heart to tell her what Mironi found out. What a gutsy lady. She took her own life—knowing that those Nazi bastards would have squeezed the *Einstein project* out of her somehow."

"Are you going to tell her?" Sarah asked, nodding toward the unconscious Andrea.

"I don't know," Shane responded.

"Maybe you won't ever get a chance, Tony," came the unexpected comment from a familiar deep and threatening male voice in the direction of the entrance to the lab.

As both Sarah and Tony turned their heads in shock, the formidable nattily-dressed figure of Vito Mironi stepped through the darkened doorway into the bright light of the Neural Research Lab. Menacingly, Mironi held in his hand a large black .45 caliber automatic. Behind him, firmly grasping a gagged Salomé were the familiar figures of Paulie Santini and Rocco Pirrello.

"Vito!" Shane exclaimed. "What the hell are you doing here?"

"Precisely my question to you, Tony," Mironi responded evenly. "And you've got two minutes to answer before I put a slug into the brain of that pretty young lady lying there in front of you."

Because Shane's immediate response was to stall for time, he turned first to Sarah and said, "Sarah, please meet my good friend, Vito Mironi. You've heard me talk about him. I guess he's here to give us a hand."

"Don't make wisecracks, Tony," Mironi growled, as he glanced at his watch. "You've got a minute forty-five." With that Mironi walked toward them and pointed the .45 directly at Andrea's forehead.

"All right, Vito. Back off, and I'll tell you what's going on here," Shane said more calmly than he felt.

Without moving, Mironi barked, "Talk!"

"This is it, Vito. This is what I told you about—the mind control technology. We're running a test on this young lady."

"Bullshit!" Mironi growled. "I know what's going on here, Tony, and it's not fucking mind control. Now I'm giving you one last chance to level with me before your *test subject* gets blown away. Thirty seconds. Talk!"

Glancing at Sarah's panic-stricken face and then back at Mironi's grimly set jaw and dark scowl, Shane hesitated for only a few moments before beginning to speak. "You're wrong, Vito. This is the mind control technology I told you about. What I didn't tell you—and hoped I never would—is what we're using it for. What we're trying to do is use it for telepathic time travel. That's it, Vito. So help me, that's the truth."

"Ten seconds, Tony," Mironi said evenly as he cocked the hammer on the .45. "I want the whole story. Now!"

"Vito, please, I'm begging you. Leave the girl alone. I'll give you the whole story, but It will take more than ten seconds."

"Start talking. I'm listening," Mironi commanded without backing off.

"We're trying to use time travel to go back to the past and take down the Nazi regime," Shane said hastily. "That's it in a nutshell, Vito. I swear."

Holding his menacing position for several long seconds as Sarah and Shane held their breath, Mironi suddenly lifted the weapon, carefully released the hammer, and looked over at Shane. "Tell me the rest of the story, Tony," he said. "It's beginning to get interesting."

Releasing his breath, Shane said, "Thanks, Vito. I'll give you the whole story. But I can't leave Andrea right now. If anything happens, my first obligation is to take care of her. OK?"

"Fine. Just talk, Tony," Mironi said in a more civil tone.

"This all began with my father back in 1939..." Tony began. For the next several minutes he quickly described the *Einstein Project*, how they had conceived *operation rainbow*; Andrea's identity; Sarah and her involvement; and what was the real objective of their mission. As he finished, Mironi remained silent for a long time before flashing a big toothy grin.

"Thanks, Tony," Mironi said, still grinning. "I'm glad you finally told me the truth."

"I've never lied to you, Vito," Shane protested.

"Sure, Sure. I know, Tony. You just misled me," Mironi countered as his grin switched abruptly to a glare. "People don't play those games with Vito Mironi. *Capisci?*"

"You wouldn't have liked the truth, Vito," Shane countered.

"What makes you think I like it now?" Mironi growled. "Your crazy plan will get rid of the Nazis—and everything else! You ever hear the one about throwing out the baby with the dirty water? You think I can let you do this stupid thing? Forget about it."

"It's the right thing to do, Vito," Shane persisted.

"For who? Not for me," Mironi snarled.

"Can't you think of anything but yourself, Vito? Think of millions of Jews that were exterminated. Think about my father who was dragged off to prison to die without any formal charges. Think of that abomination multiplied by tens of millions of other victims. Shouldn't we undo that if we can?"

"Sure. Take out the Nazis. Have your revolution. I'll support that. But, you're trying to do something that takes out me and my family too. I can't allow that, and you know it."

"It won't take you out, Vito. You will still exist. You'll be part of a different time line—a better universe. One without the Nazis, or the Axis. One without concentration camps or persecution. It'll be a better world, Vito. And you and your family will be a part of it."

"How do I know that will happen? And what good is it if I don't experience it myself?"

"Think about it this way, Vito. You won't ever know your great-great grandson. But, you know he'll be here someday. He'll carry your genes, and he'll carry on your legacy. You want that. You're proud of it. And you want it to happen."

"What's your point, Tony?"

"The point is you don't have to personally experience something to know that it is the right thing and to want it to happen. That's what we're doing here.

Sarah, Andrea, Salomé, myself—we've all decided that it's better for the world to be free, even if we won't experience it ourselves. And I'm convinced that each of us will be part of that new world—that alternate universe—even though our present selves will not be conscious of it."

"Not only will we not be conscious of it, Tony," Mironi interjected, "but we won't even continue to exist. Isn't that right?"

Slowly nodding his head, Shane responded, "That's what we think will happen, Vito. If our mission is successful, this present universe should simply disappear...like it never was."

As Mironi took a deep breath and exhaled, prepared to comment on Shane's last statement, a new sound disturbed the silence.

"Tony? Sarah?" came the feeble sounds from Andrea's mouth. Although her eyes were wide open, it appeared she could not see them.

Suddenly, all eyes in the room focused on the young lady who had been lying motionless in their midst for the past tension-filled minutes. "Andrea," Shane said sharply, "I'm right here. Can you see me?"

Blinking her eyes several times, and then focusing apparently on Shane's face before her, Andrea broke into a grin and said, "Yes. Yes, I can see you now. Am I back?"

"Yes, you are. We need you to just remain still for a while. Sarah needs to remove the probes and other monitors before you can sit up."

"Tony," Andrea continued anxiously, "I've got a lot to tell you. It's important."

Glancing tentatively at Mironi, Shane returned his attention to Andrea and said, "It can wait, Andrea. Just relax. We need to make sure you're OK."

*   *   *   *

As Sarah worked carefully to disengage Andrea from the probes and insure to the best of her ability that there would be no bleeding or risk of infection, Shane took Mironi aside for a conversation. Salomé, although still restrained by Mironi's men, glared at Mironi and aroused Shane's fears that she might initiate some spectacular rescue attempt. He knew she was capable, given the right opportunity. This prompted his first words to Mironi.

"Vito, I don't know how you got past Salomé. You must have taken her by surprise—"

"Did you forget the North Gate guard is my guy?" Mironi interrupted. "He told us about your visiting schedule last night. We've been here a while."

"Well, you need to restrain Salomé better. Those two goons are not going to keep her down if she wants to get nasty."

Mironi's quick glance at Salomé's determined stance persuaded him to take action. Within seconds Salomé was handcuffed to a load-bearing pillar near the lab entrance; but her gag had been removed. Then Mironi spoke to her directly. "I apologize for the restraints, Salomé. I know you are angry and frustrated. But Tony and I have some important matters to discuss and we can't afford any disruption. You'll be set free as soon as we reach an agreement."

Moving into a small office adjoining the lab, Shane and Mironi sat down to talk. Shane began by asking, "Why didn't you just kill Andrea, Vito—if you're so opposed to our mission?"

"Because I knew you were just running a test," Mironi smirked.

"How did you know that?"

"We were listening to you and Sarah for quite a while before you knew we were here. Frankly, I was curious about how the test would turn out."

Shaking his head, Shane asked, "How did you know about our grand plan, Vito? Where did you get your information?"

"You don't need to know that, Tony."

"We haven't told anybody about this. Only Carothers and Harry knew about it. Did you get this from either of them?"

Mironi laughed out loud. "Tony, you're crazy. Funny crazy. You think I don't have other sources? You think other people haven't figured out what you're doing?"

"Listen, Vito. If the wrong people find out about this, we're dead meat."

Again Mironi laughed. "You don't think I'm enough of a threat? You kill me, Tony."

"I guess I'm hoping you took what I said to heart, Vito. I'm hoping you'll let us finish this mission."

"Not a chance," Mironi declared. "I'm sorry, Tony. Nobody will get hurt...this time. But you guys try anything like this again, and we'll wipe out every YLA member in the *DRA*. And don't think we can't do it."

Shaking his head and beginning to feel the full weight of this tragic turn of events, Shane could find no words to respond.

"Don't feel bad, Tony," Mironi continued. "You made a great speech back there. Almost had me convinced that I should join this goddam suicide plot. But I can't."

As Shane opened his mouth to respond, he heard Sarah calling him sharply from the lab.

"Tony," she cried, "you better get here quick."

As Shane and Mironi rushed into the lab, they found Andrea seated in a chair with Sarah standing beside her. Still in her hospital gown, Andrea's long blonde hair had been brushed, and packing had been applied to her nasal passages. Dark circles under her eyes were testament to her recent ordeal.

"Tony," Sarah exclaimed, "you have to hear what Andrea has been telling me."

"Tony," Andrea began, her voice shaky and tentative, "I did link up with myself three days into the future. We were all right here in the lab."

"Did you find out if your next mission—tomorrow—will be successful?" Shane asked.

"No. There was no recollection of the mission. But there was a recollection of Mr. Mironi stopping us from doing any further work after this test."

Shane threw Mironi a nasty look before returning his attention to Andrea.

"But that's not the worst of it, Tony. We weren't down here running experiments. We were down here to avoid the radiation."

"What radiation?" Sarah asked.

"From the nuclear explosions."

"What?" Sarah and Shane exclaimed together.

"It was horrible. Chicago was gone. Wiped from the face of the earth. We were able to survive because we were in this sub-basement."

"What happened?" boomed the next question, from Mironi.

"As near as anyone could tell, it was a surprise attack early Tuesday morning. Apparently the Soviets were joined by the Japanese and the Chinese, and attacked the German Confederation all over the world. All the major cities have been bombed."

"How did you learn that?" Shane asked.

"There's a radio. Over there," she pointed to the far wall. "We could get a few stations that were outside of Chicago and still on the air."

"Oh shit!" Mironi exclaimed. "Everybody's gone? My wife, my kids?"

"Did the Germans retaliate?" Shane asked, ignoring Mironi's wailing.

"According to the radio, yes. The Germans claim they were able to get off a couple dozen ICBM's targeting Moscow, Tokyo, Beijing, L.A., Miami and a few other major cities. But who knows whether those reports are true. The only thing I know for sure is that Chicago was wiped out."

As Mironi continued to mutter to himself, Shane paused and looked around at everyone in the room. Noting the pale faces and startled expressions, he stood up and addressed them all.

"Listen," he barked, "all of you. What Andrea is telling us doesn't have to happen. Listen to what I have to say."

Then, taking a step back toward the center of the room so all could see and hear him, Shane began, "What Andrea has seen is very disturbing. But it's not the last word. We have it in our power to change the outcome of the next few days. Let's keep calm, and think about what we can do."

Turning and staring directly at Mironi, Shane waited until their eyes locked. Then he said firmly, "Vito, everything is up to you now. If you let us proceed, we may be able to head off this disaster. If not—" Shane let the thought dangle.

Rapidly regaining his composure, Mironi said, "Look, Tony. What if we just warn the Nazis about this impending attack? They can be prepared."

"Sure, Vito. And what will that accomplish? They'll just be better prepared to insure that the entire world gets wiped out in a global nuclear holocaust. Would that make you feel any better?"

Mironi glared darkly at Shane for a long time, his jaw muscles working. Finally, he lowered his eyes and said, "OK, Tony. What do you want to do?"

"Thanks, Vito," Shane replied warmly. "First thing you can do is turn Salomé loose so she can help." Then, turning to Sarah and Andrea he said, "We have to look again at Einstein's letter to Fuller. If I'm not mistaken, it will tell us whether or not we can believe what we see when we look into the future."

*   *   *   *

With Mironi and his men hovering, Shane, Salomé, Andrea and Sarah retreated to one of the small conference rooms in the Neural Research Lab and began to deliberate on the hidden meanings in Einstein's letter from 1949. While each of the others had taken a turn at interpreting the letter, this was the first that Andrea had heard of it. After examining her copy for a few seconds, Andrea exclaimed, "I've seen this letter before. My grandmother had a copy."

"Did she understand it?" Shane asked.

"I'm sure she didn't, but she knew it was some kind of message," Andrea replied.

"Could she read the Hebrew part?" Shane asked.

"Sure. Her husband was Jewish. She took Hebrew lessons. And, besides, she said that Professor Einstein advised her to do it."

"My God," Sarah exclaimed. "Do you think he really intended for us to understand this letter? Tony, you were so certain that it was just a big hoax. 'A red herring' you called it."

"Yeah. But that was before Andrea's trip to the future. Now I'm not so sure. On the video tape interview that Harry saw, Einstein said that he would never reveal how to travel into the past—or more specifically, that he would never put it down on paper. I've been focusing on the second part of the clue, and completely missed the first part. He was revealing to us that he *would* tell us about *future* time travel. I'm sure of it."

Then, looking directly at Andrea, Shane continued, "I'll bet that's what we'll find when we figure out how to decipher his message. Damn! I wish I had asked Diana about this letter when we were there!"

"Why don't we just call and ask her about it?" Andrea asked.

Suddenly the room became very silent, as Shane, Sarah, and Salomé exchanged glances. Finally, Shane turned to Andrea and said, "I'm sorry, Andrea. We haven't told you, but your grandmother is gone. She died a few days ago."

"Wh…What? What happened?" Andrea cried, as she raised a hand to her face in astonishment.

"I didn't want to tell you this, Andrea. She took her own life. The *Gestapo* got to her somehow after we left. She apparently took poison before they could extract any information from her. I'm really sorry."

As both Sarah and Salomé moved to her side, Andrea buried her face in her hands and sobbed. After a while she regained her composure and used a tissue to wipe the tears from her face. Looking at Shane through bloodshot eyes she said, "She always said that we could never reveal what we knew about the *Einstein Project*. I thought she might do something like this, but I never took it seriously. I don't know if I would have had the courage. She was one tough lady."

Shane remained silent, but reached out and placed a hand on hers. Then, after a few moments, Andrea shook her head to clear away the melancholy thoughts and said briskly, "All right, let's take a look at that letter. I'm sure grandma wants us to get this right."

As each of them returned to their places, Shane asked, "Do you understand Hebrew? Do you recognize these symbols?'

"Of course. My grandmother made sure that I knew whatever I needed for the *Einstein Project*. Let me see if I can make some sense out of this."

While Shane recited the items he believed they already understood, Andrea spent several minutes examining the ostensibly mathematical part of the letter with its ancient symbols. Then she grabbed a pad of paper and a pencil and began to make notes. Looking over her shoulder now, Shane could see that she was writing out a series of six equations containing a total of six different conventional alpha symbols, **A** through **F**. Then she turned the sheet around so that all could see.

"What does it mean?" Sarah asked.

"Nothing, by itself," Andrea replied. "This is the code that will allow us to make sense out of the English part of the message."

"What kind of code?" Shane asked.

"I remember my grandmother telling me that this was a kind of game that Professor Einstein played with the mathematicians in Fuller's research group at Wisconsin. He would put together a cryptogram that no one could figure out. Then he would give them a clue. But the clue was always contained in a set of simultaneous equations. If you solved the equations for each of the unknown variables, that provided the key to interpreting the cryptogram. So, here's the set of equations I've extracted from the Hebrew text. There are six variables. If we can solve these six equations we can then figure out how to apply the six constants to the cryptogram."

"No wonder I couldn't make sense of it," Salomé interjected. "I don't know math. I was looking for a text message."

"And I didn't help any," Shane added. "But, let's not worry about spilt milk. Let's get working on these equations. Sarah, do you have a program in the computer that solves simultaneous equations? These do not look very straightforward."

"We've got it, Tony. Let me go feed them in," Sarah responded.

*   *   *   *

The computer had taken a few seconds to solve the equations. But, in 1949, Shane mused, they would have had to be solved by hand. And that would have taken perhaps a week. After extracting the six constants, however, the daunting task of applying them to the English cryptogram was now consuming each of them. Even Salomé, without any mathematical skills, attempted to find the key for unlocking the cryptogram.

After about an hour of trial and error, Shane looked at the time and said, "It's four a.m. We should think about leaving soon."

"Tony," Sarah responded, "This is Sunday morning. Nobody's going to come in today."

"And besides," Salomé added, "if Andrea's report is correct, we've only got until Tuesday morning to get this job done. By my count that gives us only two more nights, and we've got two more missions planned. We don't have time to waste."

"Maybe we can do the next mission yet this morning," Andrea volunteered. "I'm ready to go."

"Oh no you're not," Sarah countered. "If we don't wait at least twenty-four hours before re-inserting these probes, we're running the chance of infection, inflammation or hemorrhaging."

"Sarah," Andrea said evenly, "think about it. Will it make any difference either way? I'd rather take my chances with the probes than the nukes."

Momentarily stunned by the stark logic of Andrea's message, Sarah simply remained silent and flushed as she nodded her head slowly.

Just then, Salomé interrupted with a shriek. "I think I've got it. Take a look. See if this makes any sense."

She flipped her notebook around so that all could see. She had transposed about thirty words from the English text. They said:

> *Theoretical Considerations for Future Time Travel. General relativity allows that an object (or individual) can travel into the future by moving for a time at a speed approaching the speed of light.....*

Without reading the rest of it, Shane exclaimed, "You've got it, Salomé. What did you do?"

"I couldn't get a large number of different words from this limited text, until I realized that the code was directed at syllables, not words. Then, I used some of the constants as spacers, and some for repetition. There are twenty-one different combinations of two different constants. So, you scan through the text twenty-one times and extract different words and syllables each time. If you use the order of constants from lowest to highest as the sequence for extraction, this is what I've gotten so far."

With each taking a different portion of the decoding, they generated a script translation that included Einstein's punctuation and emphasis:

> ***Theoretical*** *Considerations for **Future** Time Travel.*
>
> *Deductions from general relativity allow that an object (or individual) can travel into the future by moving for a time at a speed approaching the speed of light. The time traveler is not instantly transported to some future date. Instead, when an object moves at nearly the speed of light, the perception from the point of view of someone remaining stationary is that time has slowed down for that object. Then, when the motion of that object returns to zero, the object would have experienced a*

shorter increment of time than its stationary counterparts. If the traveler were a living person, that person would have aged less than his counterparts who remained stationary. Thus, to the traveler, it would appear that time on the stationary world had moved forward to a future exceeding the time interval experienced by the traveler. Unfortunately, no similar journey can be undertaken into the past, nor could the traveler into the future return to where he started.

*None of this denotes time travel as commonly perceived. The phenomenon of instantaneous transport to a future time is not consistent with the general theory of relativity. However, some theorists consider the possibility that space-time can be impacted by large gravitational fields so severely that it curves back on itself. I believe this is possible, although not yet demonstrated. If this curve in space-time occurred, there might be a mechanism for **tunneling** directly to a future time without having to experience a journey of finite duration. The reverse path would be prohibited, however, just as it would be for the example involving finite travel times given above.*

*Also consider that past, present, and future exist simultaneously. Consider that superimposed on future space-time is a bell-shaped probability distribution of an infinite number of possible future time lines. Therefore, If travel is accomplished by instantaneous tunneling to a future time, there are an infinite number of possible future time lines. The one that will be accessed should be the **most probable future** based on conditions at the time of travel.*

A. Einstein

After examining the translated letter from Einstein for several minutes, Sarah asked, "How is this relevant, Tony?"

Shane had noted four important points, but would mention only three.

The fourth was subtle, but perhaps the most significant. That he would keep to himself.

Scratching his head, Shane replied to Sarah's question. "There are three things: first, Einstein insists that travel to the past is not possible, second, he applies the laws of probability to future travel, and third, he alludes to a 'tunneling' mechanism for instantaneous connection to a future time line."

"The first item is somewhat disturbing," Shane added.

"Not," Andrea interrupted, "if you remember to whom this letter was addressed. He sent the letter to Professor Fuller, who knew that Einstein believed in telepathic time travel to the past. After all, that's what the whole *Einstein Project* was about. So, Einstein knew Fuller would ignore that part of the message. That part was meant to throw off anyone who wasn't supposed to see this letter."

"Of course," Shane exclaimed as he slapped his forehead, "that's exactly the point. We need to look at this in the way that Fuller would have. He would have focused on two things—the probability factor regarding travel to the future, and Einstein's curious allusion to 'tunneling.' That's a term that wasn't widely understood in 1949. Einstein must have been telling Fuller that he believed telepathic time travel involved a 'tunneling' mechanism."

"What's that?" Salomé interrupted.

"It's nature's way to avoid energy barriers," Shane replied, "like the way enzymes facilitate chemical reactions so our body doesn't need to heat nutrients to five hundred degrees. Or the way charges pass through metal-semiconductor barriers."

"What's that got to do with time travel?" Salomé persisted.

"Well," Shane began, "think about two cities, both at sea level, separated by a 5000-foot high mountain. For a train to travel from one city to the other takes an enormous amount of energy getting over the hill. Now, if a tunnel is blasted through the mountain, the train can travel between the two cities with very little energy. Einstein's comment suggests that instantaneous time travel requires a low energy "tunnel" between different points on a time line."

"But he also said you could only travel one direction, to the future," Salomé pointed out.

"Again," Andrea interjected smoothly, "Einstein only *appeared* to reject travel to the past in this letter. He must have known that Fuller would ignore that...and recognize Einstein's suggestion that telepathic communications create that low-energy tunnel through time."

"That's right," Shane interrupted. "Back in 1949 this letter told Professor Fuller that Einstein had reconciled telepathic time travel with his own theory of relativity. That must have been a monumental leap for Einstein at that time. That was before quantum tunneling was well understood. This letter must have given Fuller the conviction he needed to continue his dangerous work on the *Einstein Project*."

As Shane's statement hung in the air for a moment, Sarah interjected, "I agree, Tony. That clue must have meant a lot to Professor Fuller...and perhaps to us too. But isn't there another hidden message? About conditions in the present determining the most probable future? Doesn't this imply that we can change the present *by travel to the past?* This is something that Einstein never uttered publicly. In fact, if I'm not mistaken, he was quoted as stating just the opposite."

"So what?" Salomé grumbled. "What does that do for us?"

"Well, for one thing," Shane replied, "it tells us that Andrea's vision of the immediate future could very well be inaccurate. She observed the most probable future for conditions existing now. Those conditions could change tomorrow, and the nuclear holocaust might not occur."

"Or it might occur sooner," Salomé asserted.

"Or we might eliminate the possibility altogether by an appropriate intervention in the past," Shane offered.

"All right!" roared Vito Mironi from the conference room door. "Forget all this technical crap. Give me the *bottom line*, Tony."

"Bottom line, Vito, is that there's a chance that the nuclear devastation that Andrea reported from the future won't actually happen," Shane replied.

"What chance? Give me the odds," Vito demanded.

"Nobody can tell you that, Mr. Mironi," Sarah answered. "We only know that it's the most probable future—if we do nothing."

"What the hell does that mean?" Mironi rejoined. "And call me 'Vito,' kid."

"It means get your ass in a bomb shelter, Mironi," Salomé exclaimed.

Smiling wanly to head off Mironi's angry retort, Shane said, "She's right, Vito. It would be like betting against the favorite at even odds in a horse race when the next closest nag is going out at 50 to 1. *Capisci?*"

Clearly appreciating the analogy, Mironi just nodded his head glumly. "OK," he said finally. "What are you going to do about it?"

"We're going to work like hell to accomplish our mission, Vito. We've got forty-eight hours."

"You mean you all are willing to throw your lives away? Even if this nuclear attack never comes?" Mironi asked with a puzzled look.

"Vito," Shane replied slowly, "we were willing to do that even before we heard from Andrea. The only thing that's changed is that now we know we must get the job done in *less than two days*. So, are you with us—or against us?"

Mironi stood in the doorway for several seconds, a scowl on his face, the black .45 automatic still in the hand that hung loosely at his side. His jaw muscles worked furiously and he glared at Shane. Finally, he returned the .45 to his shoulder holster and growled, "Get moving, Tony. We'll hang around and watch."

*   *   *   *

Andrea insisted upon initiating the next task immediately. This would direct her to link telepathically with her grandmother, Diana, in 1942. They needed to know what Einstein had revealed to her regarding his intervention plan for the 1939 time line.

Despite her misgivings, Sarah had re-inserted the microprobes, thankfully without incident. Shane had re-programmed the computer controller to generate the necessary space-time coordinates for the much longer journey to the past. Again, he had asked Sarah if she could increase the number of output probes, and received a negative response.

"I just don't think we can transfer enough information with just eight probes, Sarah," he said. "We need at least twelve, maybe sixteen."

"It's just not possible with the probe technology we have now, Tony. Is there any other way? Can we transmit the information serially instead of in parallel?" she asked.

"You mean like multiplex the outputs?" Shane asked. "Hmmh. I don't know. It might work."

Then, after thinking about it for a few seconds, Shane said, "No. I don't think so. Multiplexing would just be confusing, I'm afraid. The brain wouldn't know how to put the information together."

"Look, Tony," Sarah said, "let's just go ahead and try. What do we have to lose? What's the worst that could happen? She doesn't make contact, or she connects with a different part of space-time. Either way we learn the deficiencies and make adjustments."

"All right," Shane sighed, "let's go ahead."

$$*   *   *   *$$

Fifteen minutes had passed with Andrea lying unconscious and motionless on the examining table. Shane, Andrea and Salomé hovered anxiously, hoping that no alarms would sound. Their collective prayer was that Andrea would be all right, and that she would awaken soon with a vivid memory of perhaps the most consequential conversation of all time.

As Sarah scanned the P.E.T. monitor screen for the hundredth time, she thought she saw a slight brightening of the spot that represented the center of telepathic activity in Andrea's brain. "Tony, look at this," she said. "Something's going on. There's been a change in telepathic activity. It's increasing."

"What does that mean?" Shane asked with concern.

"It may mean she's trying to come back," Sarah responded.

"Shouldn't that trigger the computer to generate the return coordinates?"

"Yes. But it's not," Sarah replied with alarm.

"Should we start the return sequence with manual over-ride?" Shane asked.

"I don't think so. Maybe she's still trying to link up with Diana. I think we should just stand pat."

As Shane nodded his head, he observed an abrupt change on the computer's display screen.

"Look," he said, "It's switched to the return coordinates. She's trying to come back."

"Tony," came the feeble sound. "Tony...Sarah," Andrea muttered.

"It's OK, Andrea," Sarah cooed as she grasped Andrea's hand. "We're right here, sweetie."

After about twenty minutes of medical attention and careful removal of the attached microprobes, Andrea was coherent and ready to report on her journey.

"I'm not sure what happened," she began. "I felt like I was floating in space. I could hear Diana's thoughts, but I didn't see anything. And the thoughts were fragmentary...disjointed. It was like I was listening to bits and pieces of several different unrelated conversations. I tried to concentrate harder and that helped. I think I heard several complete sentences. But these were thoughts, not spoken words. It was like she was thinking about what someone else was saying."

"Could you tell who she might have been conversing with?" Shane asked.

"I'm sure it was a man. Maybe a teacher delivering a lecture or something. That's what it seemed like."

"When did you decide to return?" Sarah inquired.

"I got tired. It was too hard to concentrate. I just felt like I should get back."

*   *   *   *

After Andrea's failed attempt, all of them, including Sarah, returned to the YLA safe house in Hinsdale. Mironi went off to spend the Sunday with his family, while Paulie and Rocco were left behind with the *rainbow* team at the safe house. Mironi assured Shane that he would be present for further activities at the *Institut* that evening.

Shane and Sarah were alone in the kitchen, talking in hushed tones across the table. "Do you think Andrea's attempt would have succeeded with greater resolution at the outputs?" Sarah asked.

"I'm certain that's the problem," Shane responded. "If Einstein's 'tunneling' concept is valid, the secret to communicating with the distant past must depend on how precisely we match the brain wave patterns and space-time coordinates of the target. Selecting the time traveler to be a telepathic descendant satisfies part of that equation. It's up to the computer to deliver the other part to the traveler's brain—"

Suddenly, Shane seemed to think of something. He sat back and stared blankly at the ceiling for several moments. Then, turning to look at Sarah with eyes wide, he said, "Now I understand why those crude time travel experiments my dad did in the '40's were successful, even thought they used really crude space-time computations. They succeeded because they were communicating with themselves at a different time. The brain wave patterns were identical, so there was no telepathic energy barrier to tunneling."

"How crude were the computations?"

"They used integer formulas, committed to memory and executed mentally. These formulas were in the materials left by my dad. When I was younger I memorized them, and tried to repeat their experiments."

"Did it work?"

"I don't know. I thought so, but there was no independent observer. And I didn't know how to set up a legitimate experiment."

"So how does this relate to our problem?"

"It suggests that we can compensate for poor accuracy in one tunneling requirement by higher accuracy with the other."

"You've lost me, Tony."

"Andrea was able to communicate with herself in the future, but not with Diana in the past. Perhaps there was some mismatch with Diana's brain patterns. I think that more precise space-time computations compensate for that mismatch."

"And you think the precision is limited by the number of implanted probes?"

"Exactly! Are you sure there's no way to increase the number of probes, Sarah?"

"Not with the technology we have available, Tony. I'm sorry. We need a whole new design. And there's an upper limit to the number of accessible nodes."

"Hmmh. That gives me an idea," Shane said as he scratched his chin. "What if we use the computer to reduce the dimensionality of the output—without reducing the information content? Then we could transmit the same information with fewer probes."

"Of course!" Sarah responded excitedly. "I should have thought of that. We've done that with artificial neural networks."

"Do you have that capability on your portable computer?"

"Sure. It's a standard package."

"You've got the space-time programs copied to this system too?"

"Are you thinking of working on the dimensionality reduction here today?"

Without answering, Shane jumped up and retrieved Sarah's briefcase-sized portable computer system from the next room. He placed it on the table between them and opened it up. "All right," he said, "show me how to access the neural network package."

*   *   *   *

After half-an-hour of effort, during which Shane was completely absorbed by work at the keyboard, he was startled by a gentle tap on the shoulder.

"Tony," Sarah said softly.

Shane paused and reached up to grasp the hand that had touched his shoulder, but he remained focused on the script displayed on the computer screen.

"Tony, I'm worried about this loyalty test scheduled for tomorrow. I don't think I can pass it."

Whirling around to gaze into Sarah's troubled face, Shane said, "I'm so sorry, Sarah. I totally forgot about that. What can we do? Can you postpone it?"

"No way. These tests are always given with short notice, and there's no excuse accepted for missing an appointment."

"You don't think you can fool the machine?"

"Nobody has yet," she replied, taking the seat next to Shane's.

A heavy silence persisted for several moments until Sarah volunteered, "There is one possibility that's been in the back of my mind, Tony, but I hesitated to bring it up. It's a real long-shot."

"For God's sake, Sarah, don't hold back. What is it?" Shane insisted.

"You've heard of the loyalty test machine that they use—the *Koehler-Chekov Treuedetektor?* The co-inventor is right here in Chicago. Sergei Chekov."

"You mean that Russian guy who's been trying to get into your pants?"

"The Russian *gentleman* who would like to take me to dinner," Sarah corrected.

"What are you thinking, Sarah?" Shane asked with a frown.

"I'm thinking he's asked me to dinner tonight, and I haven't had a chance to reply with my usual 'no thank you.' Maybe this time I ought to go out with him. Maybe I can learn something. What if this machine has an *Achilles' heel?*"

Moving his chair closer, Shane reached for both of Sarah's hands, leaned forward, and looked into her eyes. "Do you think you're some kind of *Mata Hari*, Sarah?" he asked. "This guy is not likely to spill any state secrets. And what will he expect in return if he does?"

"I know what you mean, Tony," Sarah replied. "But, I haven't come up with a better plan. Have you?"

"No…but I sure don't like *your* plan. What if he figures out what you're trying to do?"

"What motivation would he have to report me to Schwarz? There's no love lost between the Soviets and the Germans."

Shane, struck by Sarah's logic, responded with an admiring grin. "You've been thinking about this, haven't you?"

"Guilty, as charged, your honor," Sarah smiled. "It's been on my mind since Schwarz told me about the loyalty test."

"I don't like it, Sarah. But, I have to agree. It may be the only way." Then, after thinking for a few moments, he added, "Do you have any idea what to ask him?"

"I understand the general principles of the *Treuedetektor*. Chekov and I are in the same field. He even discussed the device in his talk last week. It would be natural to bring it up over dinner."

"Yeah, sure," Shane scoffed, "except that this guy's gonna be thinking about something else *after* dinner."

"Why, Tony Shane," Sarah said with a coy smile, "you're not jealous, are you?"

Without replying, Shane stared into her eyes for a moment, and then drew her close and kissed her gently on the mouth. "I think I love you, Sarah," he murmured.

As she gazed back into Shane's steel blue eyes, Sarah whispered, "Me too— *you*."

* * * *

Shane's implicit approval of Sarah's evening adventure with Chekov was not given without serious mental reservations. Sarah saw Chekov as a charming scientific colleague; Shane saw Chekov as a high-ranking Soviet citizen…one that must be well connected to the Soviet leadership. Shane could not help but wonder why such a valuable Soviet asset like Chekov would be here in the *DRA* on the eve of a nuclear attack.

He didn't know what Chekov's real agenda might be, but he was sure it wasn't what it appeared. And he wasn't pleased that Sarah might soon find herself in the middle of high stakes intrigue for which she was woefully unprepared.

CHAPTER 17

▼

THE CHEKOV FACTOR

Sarah lingered over her coffee while Sergei Chekov enjoyed a glass of 15-year old port. Chekov's dark brown eyes absorbed each detail of the lovely creature seated next to him. The candlelit antique dining table, framed by lace-curtained windows, with darkly painted walls and rich wooden trim, provided a perfect setting for the lithe young lady with the long auburn hair. Attired in a knee-length dark-green evening dress, revealing creamy smooth shoulders above a modest bosom, Sarah's lovely classic features appeared perfectly in tune with the elegant surroundings of *The Golden Rooster* restaurant-farmhouse located a few miles north of the *Institut.*

The evening had been delightful for him...and also for Sarah he thought. They had talked of many things...their families, their interests in music and the arts, Chekov's world travels, and Sarah's passion for cooking and fine wines that had been part of her family's California heritage. And, most importantly, they had not talked of science, politics, world affairs or the German hosts for his trip to the *Heisenberg Institut.* He had sensed Sarah's resentment for her supervisor Schwarz. And he had not wanted to spoil the evening with any references to that part of her life.

Chekov had no illusions. Sarah was half his age. Probably involved with some fine young man, and not likely to engage in a casual sexual encounter. But Chekov approached these affairs scientifically. Successful fornication was a matter of probabilities: one in four, by his count. And the others...well...he had always enjoyed the company of accomplished and beautiful young women, regardless of whether they shared his bed at the end of the evening. Whether or not Sarah might be inclined toward a more intimate relationship had yet to be seen. On more than one occasion a reserved dinner companion had transformed surprisingly into an aggressive lover before dawn's early light.

But, Chekov reminded himself, this evening with Sarah was about more…much more…than a possible sexual conquest.

*   *   *   *

Chekov sighed as he cleared his mind and gazed across the table at Sarah. It was time, he thought, to find out where things might be going. Leaning forward to signal a more intimate tone he asked, "Is there a young man in your life, Sarah?"

Taking a moment to sip her coffee first before reacting to the abrupt personal shift in conversation, Sarah replied, "I don't know. Maybe."

"Surely you would know whether you are sleeping alone, my dear?" Chekov asked with a disarming smile.

Warming to the exchange, Sarah laughed and sidestepped. "Yes, I certainly would," she replied. "But how about you? Aren't these long trips away from home pretty *difficult?*" She emphasized the last word with a sly understanding glance.

"If you're asking whether *I* am sleeping alone, I will at least be forthright with *you* and admit that I am…unfortunately." Chekov punctuated the remark with a penetrating gaze.

Sarah chose to remain silent and return his gaze with a smile.

"I see we've reached an awkward moment," Chekov remarked as he drained his glass of port and placed it on the table. "Perhaps we could retire to the lounge at the Hotel Excelsior for a drink before I take you home? They have a blues group that plays delightful music until some ungodly morning hour."

"That would be nice," Sarah replied with a demure smile. "I'm taking the morning off tomorrow."

*   *   *   *

The music had been delightful. And the late hour drinks had eased the conversation to even more intimate disclosures. Despite his growing desire for this lovely creature, Chekov had forced himself to focus on technical matters, avoiding for the moment the intimacy he would pursue later.

When he had exhausted the technical topics, and Sarah had finished a second strong cocktail, Chekov had decided to engage more aggressively in the physical familiarity he desired. And the invitation to dance to one of the slowly sensual rhythms had finally brought Sarah's and Chekov's bodies together for a prolonged intimate encounter.

*   *   *   *

With eyes closed, Sarah clung to Chekov and swayed to the alluring tendrils of sound. She knew she had consumed too much drink, and she could feel Chekov's passion rising. She wasn't certain how she would deal with that, but she hoped somehow to turn his fervor to her advantage. She wanted information from Chekov; and she knew what he wanted from her. She just didn't know how the bargaining would play out in the end.

As she had anticipated, Chekov decided to take the next step.

"Would you care to finish our drinks in my room?" he whispered in her ear as their bodies moved together slowly to the captivating musical beat.

Sarah pushed away so that she could look into his eyes and say, "Perhaps it would be a quieter place to *talk*."

"Of course," Chekov responded with an understanding smirk. "Shall we go?"

*   *   *   *

After Chekov had poured two glasses of vodka that had been chilled in the refrigerator of his suite, he delivered one to Sarah, and took a seat on the sofa, leaving a comfortable distance between them. Raising his glass to hers, he toasted, "*Das vidanya.*"

As Sarah clinked her chilled glass with Chekov's, her mind continued to work furiously as it had since they had left the cocktail lounge. "*Das vidanya,*" she repeated before taking a tiny sip from her glass. As the cool liquid slowly lit a fire in her chest, Sarah steeled herself for the mental and physical jousting that would soon follow.

But she could wait no longer, she decided.

"I want to thank you for a delightful evening, Sergei," she began. "It has been a very trying weekend for me."

With a concerned frown, Chekov asked, "What is it?"

"Oh," Sarah demurred, "it's nothing. Please ignore me."

"Please," Chekov persisted, "if something's wrong, I would like to know. Perhaps I can help."

"I'm sorry I said anything, Sergei. It's just something that came up, and I have to deal with it tomorrow. That's why I'm taking the morning off."

"What is it?" Chekov asked again.

"Oh, it's one of those loyalty tests. Dr. Schwarz has scheduled one for me tomorrow afternoon."

"Is that something to be concerned about?"

"Not normally. But, for some reason, he has scheduled the test a couple months early. That does concern me."

Chekov took a sip of his drink and set it down on the cocktail table. He gazed into Sarah's eyes for a few moments and then reached over to extract the drink from her hand and place it on the table next to his. Then he wrapped both of her hands with his and asked, "Sarah, is there a problem?"

Sarah knew what he was asking—was she afraid that she might not pass the test. Her reply would have to be carefully phrased.

"I don't know, Sergei. I've never joined the Nazi party, and that automatically makes me suspect. I don't approve of their behavior, and I've not kept that a secret. But I know better than to be blatantly anti-Nazi. Those foolish people generally disappear."

"But you've passed these tests before?"

"Of course. I wouldn't be here if I hadn't."

"Has something changed?" Chekov inquired with a sideways glance.

"I don't know. Perhaps," Sarah replied.

Taking on a fatherly tone, Chekov proclaimed: "You shouldn't feel like a criminal, Sarah, just because you don't agree with all of the state policies. The Nazis can't incarcerate everyone."

"Then why, Sergei, am I so frightened about the loyalty test tomorrow?" Sarah cried with genuine emotion. "Why is there even such a test?"

Chekov removed one hand from Sarah's and brought out a handkerchief to dab a small tear from beside her eye. Then he placed the handkerchief in her free hand and took the other between his once again. He gazed at her for a long time before taking a deep breath and saying, "You are right, Sarah. It is difficult to live in this society. The Nazis are smug and cruel and autocratic. Much has changed since Hitler's time, yet the fact remains that yours has been an occupied country for over fifty years."

"I lived in Japanese California for most of my life, Sergei. They were not oppressive."

"That wasn't always the case, Sarah. With the Soviet Union, it was Stalin's death in the 50's that opened up our society. Today we are pseudo-democratic."

"We don't get much news, Sergei, except for the underground newspapers. Do the Axis powers continue to fight over political boundaries?"

"No, my dear," Chekov responded with a chuckle. "Now we fight about who will get the biggest piece of the China market."

"You see, Sergei," she began, "I am so ignorant of world affairs. The Nazis allow very little to get out.

"Sarah," Chekov began solicitously, "you don't belong here. I would love to have you join my laboratory at the University of Moscow. Your work would complement mine beautifully." With these words, Chekov raised a hand and wrapped it gently around Sarah's bare shoulder.

As Sarah smiled back with her wide green eyes, Chekov suddenly reached for her other shoulder, pulled her close and kissed her gently on the lips. Caught by surprise, Sarah responded to the kiss and put her hands on Chekov's sides. Chekov responded by wrapping his arms around her and delivering a long passionate kiss.

Sarah knew where this was leading. Pushing Chekov away gently, she looked into his face that was now flushed with passion and said, "Sergei, please, I'm not ready for this."

Taking a breath, and quickly regaining his composure, Chekov smiled, pushed back voluntarily, and said, "I apologize, Sarah. That was presumptuous of me." Then, taking one of her hands with both of his, he asked, "Can I assume from your words that you might be ready for this another time?"

"I…I don't know, Sergei. I like you very much. And I am flattered that you might want me to join your laboratory. But, this is all too much for me to handle right now. I think I may be in trouble with the authorities—and that would interfere with any plans I might make."

"You needn't worry about the loyalty test tomorrow, Sarah," Chekov said with a knowing smile. "I can tell you how to avoid failing."

"What?" Sarah asked with surprise.

"Do you think I'm a fool, Sarah? I've known about the loyalty test for a couple days. Did you think that Schwarz would not use this opportunity to ingratiate himself to the inventor of the damned equipment? He told me he would be testing you. And he told me why."

Pulling her hands away from Chekov and bringing them up to cover the embarrassed flush of her face, Sarah could utter only, "I'm sorry, Sergei."

"Don't be sorry, Sarah. You thought you might persuade me to help you. Well, I'm ashamed to say that I was going to let you do your best."

"I...I don't know what to say," Sarah murmured as she lowered her eyes.

Chekov placed a finger under Sarah's chin and lifted her face so that their eyes could meet once again. "You don't have to say anything. I dislike those Nazi bastards as much as you do. And I dislike what they've done with my work. That pig, Koehler, took my invention and adapted it for the *Gestapo*. This perverse *Koehler-Chekov Treuedetektor* was never what I envisioned for my research."

"I had no idea," Sarah said with genuine surprise.

"Look, Sarah," Chekov said firmly, "I am serious about the invitation for you to join my laboratory. I have admired your work for some time. And I am also quite attracted to you. You are a delightful young lady whose company I have enjoyed very much. I will help you."

Taking a moment to reach out and take Chekov's hand, Sarah said, "I feel the same way, Sergei...truly. I have enjoyed your company very much...much more than I had envisioned. But, honestly, there is someone else in my life. I've only recently met him, but I think I am truly in love for the first time. I hope you can understand. Perhaps if we had met at a different time—." She let the words trail off.

"Enough said, my dear. We each have other commitments. Now, let me tell you what you need to do tomorrow to pass that absurd loyalty test."

*   *   *   *

The clock on the BMW's dashboard indicated just past midnight when Chekov delivered Sarah to her apartment building. They both knew that he would not be coming up to her apartment. But Sarah lingered before departing.

"I thank you, Sergei," Sarah said as she turned to look at her driver. She reached out to put a hand on his and added, "I am grateful for your help; but I am also grateful for your friendship."

"And I too," Chekov said with a slight bow and a smile.

"I know that you have acted on faith in helping me. Your faith is not misplaced. You know why Schwarz suspects me and understand why I misled you, but I haven't told you what is going on. And I thank you for not asking. I am going to tell you one thing, however, that you must keep to yourself. And you must act on it, Sergei...for yourself and for your family."

A puzzled look was Chekov's only response.

"Do not wait until Tuesday evening to return to Moscow, Sergei. Do whatever you can to get a flight out of Chicago...out of the *DRA today*."

"But why?" Chekov asked with a furrowed brow.

"I can not tell you. Please, find some excuse, and leave the country as quickly as you can."

With these last words, Sarah leaned across and kissed Chekov on the cheek and squeezed his hand. Then she turned and bolted from the car.

*   *   *   *

As she entered her apartment, and headed for the telephone, Sarah acknowledged wearily that there would be little time to sleep this night. She was supposed to join up with the *rainbow* team at the *Institut* within two hours. Yet, she could not do that without first placing a secure call to Shane. She was certain that Shane would not rest until he had heard from her...that she was all right, and that she needn't fear the loyalty test that afternoon.

*   *   *   *

Long after Sarah had run into her building, Sergei Chekov sat alone in his car smoking a cigarette. Foolish girl, he thought sadly...foolish, beautiful creature. Sarah would soon be talking with her lover...telling him how she had enticed the great Sergei Chekov to save her from the Nazi inquisition, without succumbing to Chekov's lustful advances.

Yet, although Sarah had divulged a compassionate warning—perhaps to compensate for the sensual pleasures she had denied him—she had unwittingly provided Chekov with a more precious gift. Sadly, Chekov thought, the evening's events would ultimately turn Sarah's future in an unfortunate direction

CHAPTER 18

▼

YESTERDAY

Sarah's eventful late dinner engagement had delayed the arrival of the *rainbow* team at the *Institut's* Neural Research Lab until two o'clock Monday morning. Fortunately, Shane had completed all of the re-programming of the space-time computations through the artificial neural network algorithms, producing a dimensionality reduction to eight outputs. They had only to be transferred to the computer control console in the Neural Research Lab.

Andrea was mentally prepared for her next telepathic journey—this time to 1942—and all the microprobe connections had been made by Sarah. Mironi and his men were scattered throughout the lab, and Salomé had taken a position near the sub-basement entry.

As Shane completed his last-minute instructions to Andrea, he nodded to Sarah to initiate the computer program that would begin transmitting outputs from the highly refined space-time computations to Andrea's brain. The P.E.T. display screen indicated that the telepathic brain centers were becoming quite active. Within several seconds Andrea appeared to lapse into unconsciousness. Shane noted the time: 3:14 am, Monday morning.

✳   ✳   ✳   ✳

The surroundings were surprisingly dark. Only the solitary incandescent light of a gooseneck lamp illuminated the small office. Seated behind the desk, across from her, was the instantly recognizable figure of Albert Einstein. His long gray hair was tousled, and he puffed slowly on a large briarwood pipe. As Andrea blinked with surprise at the abrupt change in her surroundings, she felt her hand rise instinctively to her face in an expression of astonishment. Then she realized that it was not *her* hand. And then she became aware that this body was not *her* body. The clothing was unfamiliar as was the feel of her extremities; the curve of her spine; the padding of her buttocks on the hard chair; the ample bosom.

It was then that she realized she was no longer Andrea Martin. At that moment Andrea was experiencing the body and mind of her grandmother, Diana Sutton. This was Diana at twenty-three years. And this was the meeting with Professor Einstein at the University of Wisconsin that Andrea had hoped to link with. A sudden surge of excitement filled her, and she blurted in a strange voice, "Professor Einstein!"

Removing the pipe for a moment, Einstein smiled beneath his heavy gray moustache, and his eyes crinkled as he said, "Diana, I think we have a visitor."

Diana's face remained expressionless as Andrea's mind sought its bearings. For several seconds Andrea searched through Diana's memories, recalling quickly the conversation with Einstein that had just transpired. He had been telling Diana that she would someday learn of his intervention plan—the intervention in 1939 that would de-rail the Nazi's atomic bomb program.

"Professor Einstein, you're right," the young lady announced. "It's Diana's granddaughter—Andrea Martin. It appears we've been successful."

"This is indeed curious," the great man said, as he took a few moments to regard more closely the pretty young lady before him.

"I've wondered how we would meet," he continued after a while, "but I was certain that we would. Please, tell me about yourself...Andrea. Should I call you 'Andrea'?"

"Please do, Professor Einstein," she replied. "I'm Diana's granddaughter. I live in the year 2001. We've achieved telepathic time travel, just as you envisioned back in 1939."

Einstein puffed on his pipe for a few moments, continuing to regard Diana with obvious glee. "And why did you join me today, Andrea?" he asked as he slipped the pipe from his mouth. The sparkle in his eye erased any hint of intimidation.

"My grandmother—Diana—told us the story of her meeting with you on this date—October 13, 1942. She said you had a strategy for intervening in the 1939 time line. She said you wanted to do something that couldn't be undone by some other time traveler."

"And you are here to learn that strategy?" Einstein asked.

"Yes. You were just discussing this topic with Diana. Isn't that right?"

The large head of tousled gray hair wagged for a few moments, as Einstein chuckled. He removed his pipe and set it down in a pipe stand and swiveled in his chair to face Diana and cross his legs. "You're absolutely right young lady. I am so impressed. This can't be your first telepathic time excursion?"

"No, it's my second. The first was a test of the equipment—a short jump into the future. Would you like to know how we've done this?"

Shaking his head vigorously, Einstein replied, "No. No. I am so very curious, I admit. But I don't think it would be good for me to know too much about the future. It is enough that I learned about the previous interference of time travelers in 1939. I know that we are following a time line that was not supposed to be— and that we hope to change. I don't want to know much more—with one exception. Is it true that the Nazis will win the war with the atomic bomb? And will the world suffer horribly with Nazi domination?"

"Yes, Professor Einstein. I'm sorry to say that is true. And it's not just the Nazis—"

"Please. No more," Einstein commanded as he put up a hand, palm forward. "That is all I want to know."

"I have so many questions for you, Professor Einstein, but I don't know how long I can sustain telepathic control. Can you...please...tell me about your plan?"

Indicating no apparent feeling of urgency, Einstein reached for his pipe, removed it from the holder and returned it to his mouth. He shifted his gaze back to the young lady while puffing for several seconds. Finally he said, without removing the pipe, "I'm afraid I'm going to disappoint you, my dear." Then he removed the pipe from his mouth and said, "I can't tell you the plan."

"What?" Andrea exclaimed. "You promised us!"

"Don't be alarmed, Diana...Andrea," he countered. "There is a plan. And it will be revealed to you. But not now. I can only tell you now how to discover the plan."

"*Discover?*" Andrea asked with concern. "Is this another riddle like your letter to Professor Fuller?"

"What letter?" Einstein asked as both bushy eyebrows raised.

"Ummh. I'm sorry," Andrea stammered as she caught the mistake. "It's a letter you will write to him in the future, Professor Einstein. I shouldn't have mentioned it."

"Well, I don't know what you're referring to, but this is not a riddle. The fact is I have a definite intervention plan. It will prevent the Nazis from obtaining the atomic bomb. And it will be virtually impossible to undo by some other time traveler."

"And why can't you tell me your plan now?"

"Part of the plan is that it will never be transmitted to the future. It will forever remain in the past," Einstein stated flatly. He returned the pipe to his mouth and puffed slowly with smiling eyes revealing a sly satisfaction.

With mouth partly open, Andrea murmured, "I don't understand."

"I assume, Andrea, that you are working in the future with colleagues—perhaps with Daniel McShane's son?"

Nodding several times, Andrea finally uttered a few jumbled phrases: "Yes. Tony. But it's 'Shane' now, I mean then, I mean in the future. And with some others. Sarah and...."

"Please," Einstein interrupted. "No more details. What I'm asking is do you have a mission planned to travel back to 1939? To carry out the intervention in the Rheingold abduction?"

"Yes," Andrea responded. "But we needed to learn your intervention strategy first."

"Of course. I understand. So this is the message you will bring back to your colleagues. The intervention plan will become obvious when you visit Joseph Rheingold's laboratory on July 3, 1939. I was there at Columbia University for a meeting with Professor Leo Szilard, Rheingold's supervisor. He had called me there to discuss notifying President Roosevelt regarding the urgency of beginning to develop an atomic weapon. At ten o'clock that morning, in the third-floor conference room of the Physics Building, I met with Szilard and his research group, including Joseph Rheingold. Later that summer, Szilard drafted a letter for me to send to President Roosevelt. But there were other incidents that summer. When you travel to that time, it will become obvious what you should do."

"Professor Einstein," Andrea protested, "why can't you just reveal the plan to me now? What difference does it make if we learn it now or later?"

"It's very simple, Andrea," Einstein replied as he removed his pipe and set it down once more in its holder. "If you learn it now, you take it back to the future with you, and it is no longer a secret. If you learn the plan on a trip to the past where the plan is then executed, the plan remains in the past forever."

"How can that be?" Andrea asked with a bewildered expression.

"Once the plan is executed—or once the plan is set in motion so that nothing will interfere with its execution—the time line will switch instantly to the most probable outcome of the intervention. Simply stated, the time line that we are all following now will disappear, to be replaced by one where the Nazis do not win the Second World War. That means that the travelers to 1939 will not return to their future. They won't return at all. That future will not exist any longer. Our conversation today will never happen. The *Einstein Project* will never be needed. And so on."

"What will happen?" Andrea inquired.

"What I expect is that the world will experience the original time line that existed before the Rheingold abduction of July 1939 changed the outcome of the war. That is, the Allies will win the war and the future will proceed as it was supposed to."

"Couldn't some future time traveler in that other time line go back and carry out the Rheingold abduction again?"

Smiling now, with his eyes crinkling, Einstein picked up his pipe once more and took several puffs before responding. "I'm not going to answer that question, Andrea. Your next trip—to 1939—will answer it for you."

*　　*　　*　　*

Before finishing her conversation with Einstein, Andrea learned several other facts surrounding the meeting with Szilard in July 1939. These facts would be essential to a successful telepathic mission.

After leaving Einstein's office in the Psychology Building, Andrea headed across the Wisconsin campus toward University Avenue. Crossing the busy street, she walked two more blocks into the residential area near campus before coming to Professor Garrison Fuller's home. It was a large brown frame bungalow surrounded by large elm trees and snuggled among other similar structures belonging to Wisconsin faculty. With three upstairs bedrooms and a basement, the structure provided a comfortable home for Fuller and his wife, while allowing temporary lodging for Diana Sutton and Daniel McShane.

It was early evening when Andrea arrived at the empty house. Andrea knew that she should abandon her telepathic communion with Diana, but she couldn't do it. She wanted more time. She didn't want to encounter anyone other than Professor Einstein, as there would be no accounting for the possible consequences. She knew from Diana's memories that she could expect to be alone at the house that evening. She wanted to spend more time exploring Diana's memories—enjoying and admiring the brazenly independent Bohemian life that her grandmother had pursued in a time before Nazi oppression. Somehow she felt it would be a fitting tribute to the wonderful bond she had had with her grand-mother.

After climbing the creaky winding wooden staircase to the second floor, Andrea entered Diana's small bedroom and locked the door behind her. She flicked on the small wall light with the circular floral shade that cast an irregular glow across the patterned wallpaper. Then she walked to the far side of the bed and flicked on the floor lamp with a pull chain hanging down below the large beige linen shade. She reached across the chest next to the bed and turned on the large wooden Zenith table radio. She watched as the tiny reddish front dial lit up and the glow of heating vacuum tubes emerged from behind the set. After about half-a-minute, when sounds began to emerge from the large speaker encased above the dial, she twisted the small knob set in the middle. Carefully, she attempted to line up the small pointer on the knob to around 700 kilocycles where she would listen to a favorite program, the Bob Hope Show. With a little dithering she managed to coax the maximum clearest sound from the radio and confirmed that she had indeed found the correct station.

After removing her heavy cardigan sweater and placing it on the chair next to the bed, Andrea sat on the edge of the bed to untie and remove her black and white saddle shoes. Without removing her white cotton socks, navy blue wool skirt or white blouse, she lifted her legs up on to the bed and lay back on the pillow. Andrea took the time to simply absorb Diana's surroundings. The subdued lighting of the room; the wallpaper with subtle floral pattern; the lace curtains enclosing wood-framed windows, with exterior storm windows already installed for the long winter; the simple maple furniture.

Then she became aware of the opening sounds of the Bob Hope program. Tonight's show, Hope announced, would include the actress, Bette Davis as a guest star and Frances Langford as the featured singer. It was the first radio show being broadcast from the famous Hollywood Canteen. As Andrea listened, she learned that the actress Bette Davis was president of this unique USO facility that catered to enlisted men of the armed services stationed in Los Angeles. It was a wartime commitment of scores of Hollywood personalities to provide entertainment and support. A bevy of young actresses volunteered their time as hostesses and dance partners for the nightly hordes of young servicemen that flocked to the facility. As Bob Hope recited the names of several female celebrities that had worked there recently—Hedy Lamarr, Lana Turner, Dorothy Lamour, Betty Grable, Marlene Dietrich and others—Andrea wondered if there were any young male celebrities to service the WACS and WAVES.

Andrea couldn't help but be distracted by the humor of the Hope show. She marveled at how her mind generated a vibrant mental image of each of the participants and their imaginary surroundings. From Diana's memories she realized that actors reading their lines in front of large microphones delivered the radio skits, but the visual images they projected were fascinating. For someone who had been born well after the golden age of radio, Andrea was mesmerized by the subtle charm and imagination of this lost art.

As she listened to the closing appeals for the purchase of War Bonds, and Hope's trademark closing lyrics, which were always some take off on "thanks for the memories," Andrea let her mind relax with Diana's memories. She focused on the memory of the night Diana had shared with Daniel McShane—Andrea's grandfather and Tony's father—during the historic transatlantic flight to England. Although Andrea deceived herself that this mental journey was for the benefit of *operation rainbow*, she enjoyed re-living with Diana those tender moments shared with Daniel. She marveled at Diana's uninhibited sexual prowess. But most of all she enjoyed the exhilarating sense of freedom that was all but unknown for a young lady living in the twenty-first century.

Andrea continued her nostalgic mental journey for some time before reluctantly concluding that she must return to her colleagues anxiously awaiting the result of her visit to 1942. With a sigh, she closed her eyes and concentrated on returning.

*   *   *   *

It was shortly after five o'clock Monday morning when Andrea regained consciousness in the *Institut's* Neural Research Lab. This time there was no disorientation. She was immediately alert and ready to talk. "Tony," she exclaimed, "it was wonderful! I met Einstein. He gave me a message for you."

"Andrea," Sarah said, "take it easy. We have to get these probes off and check you out. Just relax, honey, and you can tell us all about it."

For fifteen minutes Sarah worked with Andrea, performing the delicate endoscopic removal procedure and packing her nose. Then, with a warm terrycloth robe wrapped around her, Andrea was assisted into the small conference room where she could meet with Shane, Salomé and Sarah. Paulie and Rocco maintained surveillance, while Mironi attempted to convince Shane that he should be included in Andrea's debriefing.

"Vito," Shane was saying, "you really don't want to know this part of the plan."

"I get to know everything, Tony. That's the way it has to be. Understand? *Capisci?*" Mironi declared.

Simply nodding his head, Shane put on a thin smile and motioned for Mironi to squeeze into the small conference room.

"All right, Andrea," Shane said. "What happened?"

"It was wonderful," Andrea breathed. "He was the most beautiful person— with the kindest, gentlest eyes. He was expecting me, he said. And he didn't want to know anything about the future." Then, after a brief pause, she added: "Well, he did want to know one thing. He wanted to know if the Nazis won the war and continued their nasty ways. I told him, and would have added much more, but he stopped me."

"What about his plan?" Shane asked with barely subdued impatience.

"He didn't tell me."

"What?" Shane and Sarah shouted together.

"Wait! "Andrea interrupted. "Please listen to the whole story."

As the others regarded her with fascination, Andrea recounted her entire conversation with Einstein. When she finished, no one spoke for several seconds. It was Mironi who broke the silence.

"What a crafty old sonofabitch!" he exclaimed. "If he had been in charge of the Genovese family, they'd still be running New York."

Shane just shook his head, and said, "Sure, it's a great idea. But what the hell are we supposed to do? We've got just one shot at this thing. Tonight, that's it. What if we can't figure this thing out?"

"You'll figure it out, Tony. Einstein was sure of that," Andrea remarked calmly. "I believed him."

CHAPTER 19

▼

MIRONI'S DILEMMA

It was already late afternoon on Monday, and Vito Mironi had resolved nothing. His first inclination early that morning, after leaving the *Institut* and Tony Shane's mission behind, was to head for his secret hideaway in the Mironi Building. He knew that his mistress/secretary Sharon would be there, asleep, anticipating his customary nocturnal visit and attendant vigorous sexual coupling.

And he had given in to that urge.

While most men would be distracted by such an encounter, Mironi instead derived a focused coolness and clarity of mind that enabled him to resolve thorny business issues. On more than one occasion the course of his next financial move, selection of a new *capo*, or the identity of the infrequent traitor in his organization had become crystal clear after half-an-hour of sexual abandon.

But that had not happened this morning. Vito was just as perplexed at the end of this day as he had been at its beginning.

The question Mironi faced was that with which he had struggled since Tony Shane had finally revealed to him the true purpose of his mission. Mironi had been ready to shoot it all down, until Andrea had delivered the stunning prediction of impending nuclear devastation—now only a day away. He had done the right thing then by letting Shane's plan proceed.

But where would it all lead? And at what cost? Shane had tried to convince Mironi that their personal sacrifice was inconsequential. Mironi knew that wasn't true. Perhaps Shane and the others had nothing to lose, but Vito and his grandfather Rico before him had built a powerful personal empire. Mironi had much to lose. And Mironi alone had the power to shut down the *Einstein Project*. The fact that he had not done so yet surprised and disturbed him.

Bringing his considerable capabilities for focus and logic to bear on this dilemma, Mironi had reached only one conclusion. A nuclear holocaust might cause unparalleled devastation across the planet, but Mironi would survive and so would his organization.

He had already made contingency plans. Without giving anything away, he had ordered two dozen of his top men in Chicago to take their families and travel to a sprawling 500-acre ranch retreat that Mironi maintained for his organization in Southern Illinois. Although bogus, the meeting scheduled for tomorrow was not unusual. Mironi did this once a year…without advance notice. But this retreat would place his key people and their families out of harm's way. And Mironi had called for similar retreats for his people in New York and Atlanta.

Sunday had been spent with his wife and kids. Today the family had been sent to be with his wife's parents in northern Wisconsin. His wife had asked no questions. They had gone through similar drills before, whenever times were dangerous for Mironi and anyone around him.

But his wife had known that this crisis was different. Mironi had made love to her as he had not done in years…with passion and tenderness. And when he had put his family on the train today, there was a look exchanged, like when a loved one goes off to a battle from which there will be no return.

Yet, Mironi had not despaired. As in every crisis he had faced, Mironi could always see clearly the way out, the best road, the correct solution. This time, however, he was faced with perhaps the greatest dilemma of all. Torn between the shrewd passion for self-preservation that had served him well all these years and devotion to his 'brother' Tony Shane, Mironi faced an impossible choice. Complicating that choice was Mironi's own inherent sense of justice and fair play, but at what price? Surely, Shane's cause was just…but with unfathomable sacrifice.

Restless and irritable, Mironi had retreated to his personal hideaway late in the day. Despite their protests, he had kicked out his bodyguards and ordered Sharon off to her sister's home in Peoria. He sat in the large, darkened, wood-paneled room all alone, a double scotch in hand.

For the first time since he had taken over control of his grandfather Rico's organization, Vito felt the need for guidance. *What would you do, Rico?* he asked. But no one answered.

Vito Mironi sipped his drink and thought dark thoughts. Once more he reached the same impasse. He alone had the power to choose which of two paths the world would take after today. Which would it be? A world battered by global devastation, but with Vito Mironi thriving—or an unknown alternative universe of hope and promise, but one that this Vito Mironi would never see?

For a long time Mironi sat and sipped his drink, staring blankly into the darkness. Frustrated at his indecision, he began to reminisce. He thought of his youth and the crazy things he and Tony had done. The girls, the cars, the family gatherings. And then his thoughts turned to Shane's father, Daniel, and to the strong bond he shared with Vito's grandfather, Rico. Finally, he reflected on Tony's dedication to his father Daniel's legacy: the *Einstein Project*. But he also remembered that Daniel had given Tony much more than that.

It was then that Mironi realized with a start that the solution to his dilemma had been right there for him to see all this time.

As he swallowed the last of his drink, Vito Mironi slowly shook his head and allowed a thin smile to grow. Then, suddenly, he threw his head back and laughed, hearing his voice echo around the empty room.

CHAPTER 20

▼

TODAY AGAIN

The urgent ringing of Sarah's phone on Monday morning had awakened them both well before the alarm clock had gone off at noon. Struggling to shake the troubled dreams from her head, and peering through fog-shrouded eyes, she picked up the phone and tried to sound awake and cheerful. "This is Sarah," she said.

"Sarah," came the familiar voice of Wolfgang Schwarz, "I hope I haven't disturbed you. I need to see you today. Can we get together in my office after your appointment this afternoon?" Schwarz refrained from referring to the loyalty test, but they both knew which appointment he referred to.

Shrugging her shoulders at Shane to signify her surprise at the call, she replied to Schwarz. "Of course, Wolfgang. Shall we say three thirty?"

"Fine, Sarah. I'll see you then," Schwarz responded, and hung up.

"I wonder why he wants to see me?" Sarah mused. "You think he's expecting to fire me?"

"He'll be disappointed. You're going to pass that test with flying colors—thanks to your friend Chekov."

"Tony, you're not upset with me about Chekov, are you?"

"Hell no!" Shane exclaimed. "You played that game about as well as anyone could. And you got what you needed. What's to be upset about?"

Unconvinced by his words, Sarah climbed back into the bed, snuggled close to Shane, and asked, "Can we talk, Tony?"

Shane pulled her close and replied, "Sure, Sarah. But can we get business out of the way first?"

A slight nod of her head against Shane's chest signified her assent.

"I'll go over the plans in detail with Salomé and Andrea this afternoon, but I need to know if you understand what we're going to do," Shane inquired.

"It will be you and Salomé. I'll have you hooked up to two separate outputs on the computer. You'll be able to function independently, but you'll travel back to the same space-time coordinates. You will go back to Szilard's lab at Columbia University on July 3, 1939 like Einstein advised. According to my research there were three postdoctoral associates working with Szilard: Joseph Rheingold, Harry Kreutzwil, and Margo Hoffman. You'll link up with Kreutzwil, and Salomé will link up with Margo Hoffman. After that you'll be on your own."

"That's basically it," Shane confirmed.

"Tony, why is Salomé going on this mission?"

"Andrea can't do it. She's exhausted. And you said she couldn't survive another hook-up to the microprobes right now."

"Why don't you go alone?" Sarah asked.

"Redundancy," Shane replied. "If one of us can't complete the mission, the other will."

"But aren't you concerned? Neither one of you has gone on a mission before. And you're attempting to link with minds that are not related to you. What if you can't do it?"

"We have to try. My letter from the future said that they learned it wasn't a requirement that the target be related. It helps, but it's not required. It said that there was a linkup like that during the 1939 Clipper flight. It didn't last very long, but it worked."

"What if it *doesn't* work?"

"We can always send Andrea. It might not be healthy for her, but not doing it would be even less healthy."

"I know," Sarah murmured as she reflected on the imminent nuclear disaster.

"What do you think will happen?" Sarah persisted.

"If we're successful, Sarah, it will mean the end of the world as we know it," Shane responded. "As Einstein explained to Andrea, we just won't come back...and nothing here will survive. Life will continue on a whole different time line. A better one."

"We won't see each other again, Tony?" she asked in a tiny voice.

"I don't believe that, Sarah. I believe that in that alternative universe, we've already met. Under different circumstances, certainly, but I'm sure that we meet, no matter which time line survives. We're destined to be together, Sarah. I'm sure of that."

"What about the others? Andrea? Salomé? Your father? Mironi? Your friend Harry? Do you think they'll all be a part of our lives in that alternative universe?"

"Yeah. I do," Shane replied. "I really do."

*   *   *   *

The facility where the loyalty test would be applied to Sarah was located in the Bio-Medical Building adjacent to the Cybernetics Center where she worked. Within the comfortably large testing room was a large computer system and medical examining table. A physician and nurse were responsible for attaching the numerous intrusive probes and biosensors. These were connected to a large electronic console adjacent to the examining table. A trained *Gestapo* official was required to operate the *Treuedetektor* machine and interpret the computer outputs from behind a partition with one-way reflective glass.

For today's testing, Wolfgang Schwarz had requested someone from Manfred Weber's office—a routine procedure. He was surprised, however, when Colonel Weber himself arrived to conduct the test personally. Even more surprising was the presence of Ahmed Sharif. Surely, Schwarz wondered to himself, these two gentlemen had much greater responsibilities during this critical time following the nuclear strikes at the heart of Chicago and other *DRA* cities. Their unusual interest in this test—or in Sarah Stenstrom—was most fascinating.

For her part, Sarah was totally oblivious to the presence of these two powerful figures. She appeared calm and ready for the testing as she walked into the room dressed in a tan khaki skirt, lightweight green sweater, and dark brown flat shoes with nylon stockings.

Because Weber and Sharif were separated from the examining/testing room by the enclosure with one-way reflective glass, Sarah was unable to perceive their presence. But they would be able to observe all of her reactions when the attending physician administered the unique set of loyalty test questions. By design they would also be able to observe when she was alone in the room.

Before the doctor and nurse entered the room, Sarah followed previous instructions and began to remove her clothing and slip into the hospital gown. Weber and Sharif observed this operation with more than professional regard.

Fortunately for Sarah, Chekov had prepared her for this covert surveillance, and she made the most of it. She performed her unofficial strip tease slowly and deliberately, revealing herself seductively to the spellbound observers. As they gaped at her provocative motions, Sarah surreptitiously stirred a portion of 50-micron-sized polystyrene beads into the blue jar of clear gel next to the examining table. This gel would be used shortly to make contact with numerous optical sensors designed to detect through her skin any subtle chemical changes in her blood.

If Chekov had been truthful, these apparently transparent beads would cause scattering of the laser light probes. The resultant interference would foil the multivariate analysis program of the *Treuedetektor*. The raw data would appear acceptable to the operator, but the hidden noise would deceive the interpretive program, and the output would render a passing decision.

Only a skilled computer analyst would be able to determine that the machine had erred, and why. But this analysis would take precious time to conduct—assuming any suspicions were raised in the first place. By then, Sarah prayed, *operation rainbow* would have run its course.

*   *   *   *

Manfred Weber's frustration was reflected by the appearance of a dark scowl. He had been prepared to confront the attractive, but duplicitous, young lady in the examining room with the results of the *Treuedetektor* test and extract from her the information that would most assuredly lead to the fugitive, Tony Shane. But he had not been prepared for Sarah Stenstrom to *pass* the loyalty test!

After their middle-of-the-night questioning of Schwarz, they had become suspicious of his all-too-smooth dismissal of their time-travel hypothesis. Since then they had dug more deeply into Schwarz's background and activities at the *Institut*. What they had learned about his studies—and also those of Sarah Stenstrom—had convinced them that the Cybernetics Research Center might very well have been the target of Shane's temporary disappearance before his trip to New York that past week.

The *Treuedetektor's* tacit declaration of Sarah's innocence had burst that bubble with depressing force. Weber was almost inconsolable. They had placed all their eggs in this basket. And it had just fallen apart. It was Sharif who said finally, "Manfred, don't beat yourself up. There is more to this, old friend. I'm certain of that."

"Hah! Don't toy with me, Ahmed. This is a bust. We're back to square one, and we've lost precious time in our pursuit of Tony Shane," Weber wailed.

Sarah had dressed and departed while Weber and Sharif had checked and re-checked the machine's outputs. Repeatedly, the instruments returned the same response. The subject had passed the loyalty test.

"Tell me, Manfred," Sharif persisted, "are we not among the best in our field? Have there not been very few that escaped our pursuit? We do not make mistakes, you and I. Do we?"

"Are you trying to cheer me up, Ahmed? Save your breath."

"I'm not trying to cheer you up. I'm trying to tell you to have more faith in your instincts...and in mine. We both concluded that Miss Stenstrom had to be involved with Shane and the *Einstein Project*. I don't think we were wrong."

"But the test, Ahmed—" Weber protested.

"Forget about the test. With enough time one of our technicians will find out how the machine was misled. In the mean time, let's not forget about Miss Stenstrom. We should look even more closely at her. And, don't forget, we now have an advantage we didn't have before."

After taking a deep breath and exhaling, Weber's countenance slowly transformed from its dark frown to a pale smile. "Ah, yes, Ahmed. Perhaps we will get something out of this yet."

*   *   *   *

When the secure phone of the safe house chirped, Shane raced to pick it up. He was delighted to hear Sarah's voice. She had called from a pay phone to tell him excitedly of her successful bout with the *Treuedetektor* machine. She would be meeting with Schwarz shortly, she had said, and she asked for Shane to meet with her at her apartment after dark, using the clandestine entry arrangements they had worked out. She would call if anything changed.

After speaking with Sarah, Shane relayed the good news and announced his intention to join Sarah later, realizing that either Paulie or Rocco would have to transport him.

Then Shane retreated to the privacy of one of the bathrooms, and initiated the first of two sat-phone calls that had to be made. The friendly male voice that answered indicated that the call had been expected.

"Tony, you asshole!" cried Harry Churchill in mock derision. "Where have you been? What's going on? Talk to me, old buddy."

"Everything's falling in place, big guy," Shane began. "Let me bring you up to date." Shane then took several minutes to review the events of the past couple days while they had been out of touch. Shane finished by stating that the team's final mission would be that evening. He did not provide any details.

"I know you can't give me the whole picture, Tony," Harry remarked, "but can you give me the odds for success?"

"Wish I knew, Harry. We'll be flying blind most of the way. The thing is, you better be prepared for what happens if we fail."

"You mean the *big bang* tomorrow morning? Where I am now is so far away from civilization we'd have to send up a satellite to see any action," Harry responded, explaining that he had retreated to the YLA rebel quarters in the rugged Sierra Madre mountains. "But you're not gonna fail, Tony."

"Yeah. I feel confident too. But, Harry, remember when we talked about this whole intervention plan? We never did decide how we would know that it worked. Have you thought about it?"

"Sure. It's pretty simple. When the deed is done, all of us just disappear—and we're replaced by a whole different—and better—world. We'll know it when it happens. It'll make me happier than shit! I'll just say good riddance!"

"You make it sound too easy, Harry," Shane laughed. "But, seriously, Andrea told us something Einstein said that really intrigues me. He said that whenever everything is in place for the intervention to occur without fail, that's when the crossover to the new time line will happen."

"So?"

"So...why hasn't the crossover happened yet? Does that mean we're destined to fail?"

"Jesus Christ, Shane. You are the biggest worrywart in the world. Look, even I can figure this one out. You haven't given me the intervention details, but I gather there are still some loose ends to be worked out. Right?"

"Well...yeah, I guess so."

"So...when you work out those loose ends, and there are no more obstacles, it'll happen. *Poof!* It's all over."

"It's kind of weird to think we can change the world just by concocting a plan to do so."

"It all has to do with those multiple probable futures, Tony, that you extracted from the Einstein letter. As soon as you fix things so that a different one becomes more probable, it takes its place at the bottom of the energy well. Then, anything that is a consequence of that also has to happen."

"This is really scary. Where did you pick up all this scientific talk?"

"I been listening to your crap for a long time, Shane."

Shane chuckled for a moment and then switched to a heavier topic.

"Seriously, Harry, before this all goes down tonight, do you have anyone you need to talk to?"

"Naw, just you, old buddy."

There was an awkward silence for a few moments as two grown men struggled for composure. Then Shane blurted, "I've found someone, Harry."

"Don't tell me you and Salomé got it on? I knew Carothers made a mistake sending that chick out on the road with you," Harry chortled.

"Come on. You know better than that. It's someone else. It's Sarah, the one I've been talking about."

"Christ, you just met her, Tony. You're just not that smooth, pal. What did you drug her with?"

"I'm serious, Harry. She's the one. And she feels the same way."

"Jeez, Tony. That's really scary. How are you two going to handle this job tonight?"

"We'll do it, Harry. There's no doubt. We know it's the right thing—especially now that we know what's coming tomorrow."

"Doesn't matter, kid. It's gonna be rough. Wish I could be there."

"Yeah. Me too."

After a few moments of silence, Harry said, "Look, Tony. Get your butt moving now. You got the most important thing to do anyone ever did. Don't think about anything but that. And…remember what we talked about before…we'll be together after all this, Tony…in a better world."

*   *   *   *

The call to Nathan Carothers was easier, in a sense, than that to Harry. Shane respected Carothers, but there was no strong bond between them. Nevertheless, Shane felt he needed closure with Carothers. And, in any event, Carothers would have called if he hadn't heard from Shane.

After providing an up-date on activities like that he had given Harry, Shane finished by saying, "I hope you'll be in a safe place tomorrow morning, Nathan— just in case our mission doesn't succeed tonight. New Orleans is bound to be a target for retaliation."

"Don't worry, Tony. I'll be in the hills with Harry," Carothers responded.

Shane paused a moment, unsure that he should pursue the question foremost in his mind. Then he said, "I have a question for you, Nathan. You don't have to answer, but I need to ask it. Did you know about this planned surprise attack?

And this secret alliance with the Chinese? Has the YLA been involved in this somehow?"

"That's *three* questions, Tony," Carothers responded with mock reproach. "But I'll answer them—on one condition. You don't share this information with anybody. OK?"

"Does Salomé have this information?" Shane persisted.

"Not from me," Carothers answered.

"I'm sorry for bringing it up, Nathan. I know that you and Salomé have been close. But I need to know where we stand. Salomé is a key player in *operation rainbow*. I can't afford to have any doubts about her."

"Don't worry, Tony," Carothers responded. "You can count on Salomé. She'll be a rock for you."

Shane's silence prompted Carothers to continue.

"Did I know about this new alliance, you asked?" Carothers began. "Yes. I learned of it this past week. Did I know they were planning a surprise attack? I learned that too. Did the YLA play a part in this conspiracy? In a small way, yes."

"Why didn't you say something to us, Nathan?" Shane asked angrily.

"Would it have made a difference?" Carothers replied. "I couldn't have told you when this alliance would strike. I wasn't given that information."

"What did the YLA do to help them?"

"We provided the distraction. Since our nuclear strikes, the entire German Confederation has been mobilized to find terrorists. They're looking for trouble in all the wrong places. The alliance will strike with ICBM's from every direction…including China. The Nazis won't know what hit them."

"You approved of this, Nathan?" Shane roared. "They'll be massacring our own people in the *DRA*!"

"It wasn't my call, Tony."

"Did you know they were using us?" Shane persisted.

"No, I did not, Tony. Of course I knew they were willing to finance our terrorist strikes. Rothchild paid the Chinese a huge sum for the nuclear devices, and we were willing to accept their help. But I was shocked to learn about this planned all-out attack on the German Confederation. That was when I learned that we had just been pawns in this deadly game."

"I can't tell you how disappointed I am, Nathan. We should have known about this."

"That's irrelevant now, Tony. You need to focus only on completing your mission. Now you know how urgent it is."

"What if we hadn't learned of the planned attack from Andrea's trip to the future? We wouldn't know about the urgency. That's a truly scary thought."

"Listen, Tony. Quit over-analyzing this. Let me give you the bottom line. You learned something that even I did not know—the timing for the surprise attack. Now you have a timetable for completion of your mission that I could not have given you."

"Are you kidding? If we would have—" Shane began.

"Stop it, Tony!" Carothers interrupted. "Let's stop this *bullshit*. Now get this straight. *You were never meant to succeed with your mission.* It was a diversion. I needed you out of the way so we could set up the next round of nuclear strikes. Did you want me to get rid of you some other way, Tony?"

Shane's stunned silence was the only response for several seconds. Then Shane cried, "You sonofabitch! I never thought you were sincere about *operation rainbow*. I convinced myself that I was wrong, but I guess I wasn't. Christ, Nathan, don't you know how to be straight with anybody?"

"Listen, Tony. That was then. This is now. Now it's clear that your mission *has to succeed*—not just for the original purpose, but also because we're on the brink of a global disaster. I want you to succeed, Tony. That's the truth."

"The truth!" Shane snarled. "You don't know the meaning of the word, Nathan."

The moments of silence that followed underscored the intense alienation the two men felt. Then, with a hostile tone, Shane asked, "I assume Salomé was supposed to sabotage the mission if we got close to succeeding? Was that the plan, Nathan?"

"Yes, it was, Tony. But not like you think. She would have simply delivered my orders to terminate the mission. Nobody would have been harmed. And don't fault Salomé for duplicity. Those were my instructions. And I had a hard time convincing her. She wants to see *rainbow* succeed more than any of us. And, now, she will do her best to see that it happens."

After taking a deep breath to calm his emotions, Shane said, "Alright, Nathan. Let's say I understand your motives. You did what you had to do. Salomé followed orders. What about Harry?"

"I never considered trying to flip Harry. He's been playing this game straight, Tony. Harry would never deceive you."

"Thanks, Nathan," Shane said with a sigh.

"Whether you believe it or not, Tony, we're *all* with you. We can't always be on the same page every day, but in the end we're all working for the same thing.

We want our country back. And, by God, Tony, it looks like it's come down to *you* now to make that happen."

After taking a few seconds to digest Carothers' words, Shane responded solemnly, "You're right, Nathan. It's on my shoulders now."

*   *   *   *

After disconnecting from Shane, Carothers remained motionless for a long time. He had disclosed more than he had planned, and yet he had been far from truthful. He would not be with Harry tomorrow. Nor would he be in New Orleans. And there were other discrepancies that would affect Shane profoundly. No matter what the outcome, Carothers feared, tomorrow would bring the ultimate moment of truth for Tony Shane.

*   *   *   *

For a long time Harry Churchill continued to turn over in his mind the last conversation with Tony Shane...filled with remorse that so many of his words had been lies. Knowing that Shane would struggle with debilitating conflict if he had learned the truth, Harry had chosen to mislead his dear friend. Harry was not in the Sierra Madre mountains as he had claimed. He was in Monterrey...hiding from the Nazi Black Shirts that had tracked him there, and who would be reaching him any minute. Carothers knew Harry's situation, but had promised not to tell Shane. There was nothing either could do. As Harry checked the firing clip on his Soviet-made assault rifle, and peeked out the window of the tar paper ghetto shack, he saw the first of a half-dozen heavily-armed Black Shirts sneaking down the alley behind the cover of an advancing pickup truck. As he waited for a closer shot, Harry smiled grimly, recalling his final words to Shane: *we'll be together after all this, Tony...in a better world.*

*   *   *   *

It was after dark when Shane reached Sarah's apartment. As soon as she closed the door behind him, Sarah reached for Shane and drew him close. Barefoot, and dressed only in a soft yellow cotton duster that reached to her knees, Sarah wrapped her arms around Shane and buried her head in his shoulder.

"I'm so glad to see you," she whispered.

"You're trembling, Sarah," Shane observed as he held her close. "What's wrong?"

"It's been an ugly day, Tony. I'm so glad it's over."

Leaning back, Shane looked into her eyes and realized she had been crying. "I'm sorry, Sarah. I wish I could have been there," he murmured as he bowed his head forward to kiss her throat and squeeze her close once again. "Do you want to talk about it?" he asked gently.

Without letting go, Sarah wagged her head and murmured, "Unh Uh. Just hold me for a minute, Tony. I'll be OK."

They embraced in silence by the door for a long time, with Sarah remaining motionless and Shane softly stroking her hair. Then Sarah slowly pulled away, took Shane's hand, and dragged him over to the sofa. They sat down facing each other, with two filled glasses of red wine already on the cocktail table.

After removing his shoes and light jacket, Shane sat back on the sofa, bringing one leg up so that he could sit sideways to face Sarah. Casually dressed in jeans and tee shirt, Shane looked and sounded much more relaxed than he was. After taking a long sip of the wine, he placed one arm on the back of the sofa and nodded towards Sarah.

"What was worse," Shane asked, "your loyalty test or the meeting with Schwarz?"

"They were both bad, Tony. But the worst part of the day was knowing that tonight would be our last."

Shane's silent gaze prompted Sarah to add quickly, "But I don't want to spoil it by talking about it, Tony." Then she picked up her wineglass, turned to Shane and asked brightly, "Would you like to hear about my bizarre meeting with Schwarz?"

"I would, indeed," Shane replied, eager for the change of subject.

"You'll never guess what that fat Nazi wants me to do," she teased. "He wants me to work with him in the Neural Research Lab!"

"What? Did you tell him you already took over the Lab?" Shane chuckled.

"He would have croaked if he thought I'd ever *seen* the Lab. He thinks it's a big dark secret."

"Did he tell you what they've been doing down there?" Shane asked. "Did he mention their mind control experiments? With human subjects?"

"That's the scary part, Tony," Sarah replied. "He skipped right over that part. He just jumped right into *telepathic time travel!*"

"Where did he get that idea?" Shane exclaimed.

"That's what I'm concerned about, Tony," Sarah replied. "During our entire conversation I had the idea he was just toying with me. Like he really knew all along what we've been up to, and he was just trying to trap me."

Shane thought for several seconds and then said, "No. He doesn't know. If he did we wouldn't be here. He probably got the time travel idea somewhere else, totally independently.

"If he did," Shane wondered out loud, "then he would want the best person around to help him with it, wouldn't he?"

"Of course," Sarah responded. "I see where you're going."

"But the big question is who put the time travel bee in Schwarz's bonnet?" Shane asked.

"You can see why I've been so worried. Schwarz hasn't had an original idea since I met him. Somebody must have pulsed him with this concept."

"I can see one possible explanation," Shane remarked. "Maybe the *Gestapo* tumbled to the purpose of *operation rainbow*. Perhaps they got something from Diana. Maybe we've been under surveillance. In any event, who would they contact for expert opinion on the feasibility of telepathic time travel? Schwarz is an obvious choice. He's a physicist. He's a Nazi. And he can be trusted."

"But what does it mean for us?"

"It means," Shane sighed, "we'd better pray that they haven't figured out how close we are to succeeding."

The prolonged heavy silence that followed was interrupted only when each took a sip of wine.

"Would you like to tell me about your loyalty test?" Shane asked, changing the subject.

"I was about as nervous as a horse in a glue factory," Sarah joked. "I thought for sure I would spill those polystyrene beads all over the floor."

"Did they leave you alone in the examination room?"

"Yes, but the operator was behind a one-way mirror."

"So, how did you slip the beads into the optical gel?"

"I distracted the operator."

"And how did you do that?" Shane asked with an arched eyebrow.

"Would you like a demonstration?" Sarah purred as she reached up and began to untie the lacing at the neck of her duster.

Reaching out to halt her fake strip tease, Shane chuckled, "All right. I get the idea. Save the demonstration for later."

"Seriously, Tony," Sarah continued, "I was scared to death. I never thought they would let me out of that room. Then, when I did leave, I thought for sure Schwarz was going to tell me I was fired—or arrested."

"Obviously, Chekov's strategy worked for you," Shane commented.

"Yes," Sarah responded, lowering her eyes.

"And Chekov gave you this free ticket out of the goodness of his heart?" Shane asked with a disarming smile.

"We went over this last night, Tony," Sarah responded. "Chekov didn't get into my pants."

"What about your pretty head? Did he get in there?" Shane asked still smiling.

"He asked me some technical questions, if that's what you mean."

"What kind of questions?"

"I don't remember too well, Tony. I was drinking. And Chekov was just making shop talk until I was tipsy enough to take advantage."

Shane's skeptical gaze prompted Sarah to add, "Besides, what good would any technical secrets do him now?"

Shane's shrug acknowledged Sarah's logic, yet his skeptical gaze persisted.

"I do have a confession, though, Tony. There's something I haven't mentioned."

"What is it?" Shane asked. "Did you run into Chekov again today?"

"That's just it, Tony. Chekov flew back to Moscow today."

"So? Are you telling me you miss him?" Shane teased.

"No. I'm telling you he wasn't supposed to leave until tomorrow."

"I don't understand," Shane said with a puzzled look.

With a sigh, Sarah blurted, "I told him to leave *today*, Tony. I'm sorry. I just couldn't let him stay here. He should be with his family. They have a country home far from Moscow."

The significance of what Sarah had done suddenly hit him, and the realization showed on his face.

"You're not angry with me, are you?" Sarah asked.

Shaking his head, a concerned look on his face, Shane asked, "What did you tell him?"

"Nothing, Tony. I swear."

"You persuaded the man to change his flight and leave a day early—with no explanation? That's hard to believe."

"It's not hard to believe, Tony. Chekov saved my life—and much more than that. Why would he not believe that I would try to do the same for him?"

Shaking his head, Shane managed a thin smile. Then he grinned and said, "Sarah. You're amazing. The more I learn about you, the more fascinated I am."

"Then you're not angry?" she said. "I couldn't bear it, Tony. Not tonight."

Reaching out to cover Sarah's hand that rested on her thigh, Shane said, "Of course I'm not angry, Sarah. I'm glad you did that for Chekov. In fact," he added as he pulled her closer, "it stirs up something in me I can't even explain." Then as he leaned over to kiss her, he murmured, "I think I'm in love with an angel."

As they moved together, Shane became instantly aroused physically as one hand slid down her back over her buttock and across her thigh, sensitive fingers confirming Sarah's nude form underneath the light duster. Unexpectedly, Sarah pushed him away, and turned her head to avoid his lips.

"What's wrong, Sarah?" Shane asked, suppressing the passion he felt rising in his loins.

"It...it's something that's bothered me all day, Tony," she responded, not looking at Shane.

Shane pulled back, reached out to tilt her face toward him and said, "Talk to me, Sarah."

Gazing at Shane through tear-filled eyes, Sarah murmured, "How can we go through with it, Tony? How can we throw this all away?"

"Do you mean *us?*" he asked.

"Us...Chekov...Mironi...Andrea...everyone. How can we do it?"

"How can we *not* do it, Sarah?" Shane countered. "The world's going to blow up anyway."

"But we could survive, Tony," Sarah pleaded. "Isn't that important to you?"

"Survive? In what kind of world?"

"Would it matter...as long as we were together?"

Shane regarded her uncertainly for several seconds before replying, "Yes...it would matter, Sarah. In your heart you know that."

Shaking her head slowly, Sarah turned away and said, "I'm sorry, Tony." Then, after a moment, she turned back and declared, "I've just discovered the most wonderful thing a human being could ever want...a soul mate...someone I want to know better, deeper, fuller...and enjoy every moment with...for the next fifty years. And you're asking me to just throw that away. Well, I don't think I can, Tony. Can you?"

Shane remained quiet for a long time, peering into Sarah's green, tearful, distraught eyes.

"Sarah, I don't know if these words will come out right...so please bear with me. I've never felt this way about anyone. I can't put it any better than what you just said—about wanting a future that revolves around *us*. I *do* want that…so very much that it hurts.

"But this thing we're in is bigger than *us*, Sarah. We have the opportunity…no, we have the obligation…to prevent the suffering, the atrocities, the ethnic cleansing that's gone on for the past six decades. How can we *not* do this?"

Shane paused for a moment to search futilely for some spark of agreement in Sarah's eyes. But, before she could respond, Shane continued in a softer tone. "And still, it's more than that with me, Sarah. I've never told anyone but Harry about this."

For the first time since she had pulled away from him, a glint of concern and curiosity displaced the despair in her eyes.

"My father dedicated his life to this mission," Shane began. "Just before the *Gestapo* took him away he had been begging me to carry on for him…and I turned him down. I turned him down, Sarah…like the selfish sonofabitch that I was!

"When I realized that he was really gone…*forever*…that he had given his life so that we might someday prevent millions from dying at the hands of Hitler and his butchers…that was when I vowed to do whatever it took to fulfill his dream. To resurrect the *Einstein Project*.

"I joined the YLA and learned firsthand about the Jews and the Blacks and the others whose families had lost everything after the war. Parents, grandparents, aunts, uncles had been abused and executed because they couldn't escape quickly…or trusted Hitler's lies. I took on their passion, their cause, as my own…not just for myself…but for my father.

"I've followed Carothers for over fifteen years now. I was even willing to be part of some horrible things, because I knew that someday the time would be right to finish the *Einstein Project*.

"Well, Sarah, this is it! I can't stop now. My personal wants or needs…my love for you…just don't amount to a piss ant's booty at this point. What we have to do is bigger than both of us…more important than my friendship with Harry or Vito…or anything else.

"I've got to do this, Sarah…no matter what. So…are you with me, or not?"

For a long time, Sarah kept her distance from Shane on the sofa, gazing uncertainly into his passionate eyes. Finally, she took his hand in both of hers and raised it up to press tightly against her bosom. She was no longer looking at Shane with despair. Now her eyes reflected something that came from the depth of her soul—the love, passion, and commitment that she truly felt.

"I *am* with you, Tony," she whispered. "You're absolutely right. Nothing else really matters now."

Holding his hand to her breast, Sarah reached out with her other hand to draw Shane close to her and bring his lips to hers in a tender message of surrender.

The tender kiss became long and passionate, and Shane's soulful connection with Sarah quickly turned physical as he began to caress her warm, yielding body. Sarah's hands explored Shane's body in return, adding to his arousal. She paused briefly to gaze into his eyes, and Shane could see the desperate craving that reflected his own rising passion.

But, suddenly and unexpectedly, he pulled back and held Sarah's arms. Their eyes remained locked, and Shane could see a combination of yearning and surprise in her expression. Her lips were parted, and he wanted so badly to crush them with his...but he could not.

"Sarah," he murmured. "I'm...I'm sorry. We can't do this...can we?" But he didn't move away. Instead, he pulled her close and hugged her tightly. "You understand what I mean, don't you?"

Taking a breath, Sarah nodded her head slowly against Shane's shoulder. "Yeah. I know, Tony. How do you make love...for the last time?" She asked, as her eyes filled.

Nodding vigorously to tell Sarah she had captured his exact thought, Shane could not speak. The words choked in his throat.

*　　*　　*　　*

They remained locked together for a long time...silent and close, absorbing one another, inhaling each other's being, lost in an ecstasy that superseded any need to communicate with words.

When finally they pulled apart, it seemed that a century had passed. They arose silently, a somber acknowledgement that they must return to the profound task waiting for them at the *Institut*.

But Shane was certain that Sarah now shared what he was feeling...the warm glow that sprang from a kind of spiritual symbiosis that had joined them together in a way that no earthly physical encounter ever could. There was no further need for anything but a touch...or a glance...from either to fulfill the other.

With a profound sense of relief, Shane observed that Sarah was at peace, finally, with the dreadful mission into which he had selfishly drawn her.

For the moment, at least, she remained blissfully unaware of the ubiquitous dark forces he sensed that were about to strike from unexpected directions.

CHAPTER 21

▼

FRIEND OF FOE?

Mironi was waiting for them when the *rainbow* team showed up at the Neural Research Lab just before midnight Monday evening. He was alone, standing just inside the lab, when Paulie and Rocco escorted the team in.

But he had a gun in his hand.

"Let's you and me go into the conference room, Tony," Mironi commanded with a wave of the gun. "The rest of you give us some space."

They walked into the small room, Tony first, and Mironi closed the door behind them.

"What's going on, Vito?" Shane demanded as he whirled around and faced Mironi. "You change your mind?"

"I never said I was gonna let you go through with this *pazzo* plan, Tony," Mironi replied, the .45 automatic in his hand pointed precariously at his lifelong friend.

"So, you're going to stop us now? Are you crazy? You'd rather be vaporized by a bomb?"

"Forget it, Tony. You think I'm gonna stay around for the fireworks? I've already got my family and my guys out of town. We'll survive just fine. You said it yourself, we Mironis always land on our feet."

Shaking his head angrily, Shane blurted, "You bastard, Vito! I should have listened to Salomé. She said you'd be too fucking self-centered to ever let us go through with this."

- 231 -

Laughing at Shane's heated remarks, Mironi said, "You should listen to that bitch, Tony. She's got street smarts that you'll never understand."

"All right, Vito. I guess it's your call now," Shane conceded, "what are you planning to do with us?"

At this question, Mironi arched his eyebrows and remained silent for a few moments.

Shane's words did not reflect what was really on his mind. He was frantically calculating the odds that he and Salomé might overtake Mironi, Paulie and Rocco. Hoping that Mironi would not notice, Shane glanced briefly beyond the glass partitions of the conference room, at Salomé. He could see that she was glaring at Mironi and knew she was also thinking of taking action. She had surely been relieved of her weapon by Paulie or Rocco; and Shane had none. So they would have to use all of the chicanery in their arsenal.

"Do you want to tell the rest of them about your decision?" Shane asked, nodding towards the lab.

Mironi didn't flinch, and his gaze never wavered. He continued to look directly at Shane, holding the gun steady.

"What should I tell them, Tony?" he asked with a twisted grin. "And don't try to distract me, pal. It won't work."

"Tell them you're going to rot in Hell just like Hitler and Himmler and the rest of those Nazi bastards!" Shane snapped in frustration.

Shaking his head slowly, Mironi remarked, "That's ancient history, Tony. Get over it. We all need to move on."

"Into Hell? Are you out of your mind, Vito?"

"Look, Tony. I didn't come here to argue with you."

"Then what the hell do you want from me, Vito? Just 'whack' us...or do whatever it is you do to anyone that gets in your way. Get it over with," Shane growled. "But first I want to hear you tell Andrea that her grandmother gave her life for nothing. Tell Salomé that she'll never avenge her family's deaths. And tell me I can't finish the job my father began and died for...that your grandfather supported until he died. Tell us all, Vito. And tell me that Rico would do the same thing."

Shane watched as Mironi's face turned crimson and a vicious scowl appeared like nothing he had seen before. He hoped his words would unbalance Mironi just enough to give Shane an edge. If Mironi faltered at any point, Shane would go for the gun. And he knew Salomé would follow his lead. Paulie and Rocco would be no match for her if she were given the tiniest opening.

After several seconds of stewing at Shane's words, Mironi said, "Tony, I told you I didn't come here to argue. And, if you'll shut up for a minute, I'll tell you what it is you want to hear."

Shane's intense glare was his only response.

"Here's the deal, Tony," Mironi began. "I'm not here to stop you."

Shane's stunned expression brought a brief smile to Mironi. But, before Shane could speak, Mironi continued.

"I'm here to tell you that Vito Mironi is in charge of this show. I can stop it anytime I want, and you need to know that."

"But what's your point, Vito?" Shane asked, a wrinkled brow revealing his confusion.

"My point is that I've got a lot to lose here, Tony, and I'm trying to cover all my bases. I've already taken steps to survive a nuclear attack on the *DRA*...if it comes to that. Now I need to cover myself to survive your crazy plan."

"What the hell are you talking about, Vito?" Shane cried. "We already talked about this. This time line that we're on right now will end...*tonight*...if we're successful."

"Right, Tony. But what if you're not? What if you screw things up so badly that things get even worse? Can you predict anything once you start fooling around with past events?"

"What are you saying, Vito? You want some written guarantee?"

"You're damn right, I do!" Mironi exclaimed. "I've thought about this a lot, Tony. Yeah, I'm willing to give up everything I have, and do whatever I can, to see the *Einstein Project* succeed."

Mironi paused and smiled, as Shane was stunned once again.

"That's right, Tony," he continued. "I've thought about it. I thought about what Rico would do in my position. I thought about what you needed to do for your dad. And, most of all, I thought about *us*, Tony. You and me. Since we were kids, we've disagreed and fought about many things, but we've always supported each other. You never passed judgement, and you've always been there for me...and I for you. I don't want to see that end.

"I have to tell you that I still don't grasp this idea that we can change history and make all the bad stuff go away. I meant it when I said we should all just get over it and move on.

"But, if there's any chance that you're right...that you can pull this off...then I can't stop you, Tony. As self-centered as I am...and that's not a bad thing, by the way...I *won't* stop you. I won't stop you because I know deep down in my gut that you're doing the right thing...and I do believe that the Mironi family will thrive in that alternate time line you're gonna create.

"But, if there's any chance that this mission will *not* work, Tony, I am here to tell you that I will kill it cold, *right now*," Mironi added with an air of finality that could not be ignored.

Shane took a few moments to absorb what he had just heard, staring blankly at Mironi's earnest face. Then he asked, "What do you want me to do, Vito?"

"I want you to tell me what you're going to do on this mission tonight. I want to know how we can tell if it's successful. And I want to know exactly what will happen if the mission succeeds.

"But that's not all, Tony. I need to know how we can tell if something goes wrong, and what we can do about it."

"Jesus, Vito," Shane responded, "you're asking for stuff I can't give you."

"Look, Tony, it's this simple. I've struggled to come up with the decision to let your mission go on. I've gotten beyond that now. But, I swear to you, it will not go if you don't satisfy my questions.

"Now, let's not waste any more time. Give me some answers," Mironi commanded.

Shane shook his head and collected his thoughts for a few seconds. Then he said, "Vito, you're right. We don't know what the hell we're doing. We don't even know what the strategy is going to be, if and when we link up with the targets in 1939. And we can't guarantee that our intervention will produce the time line change that we want."

The dark expression on Mironi's face reflected his displeasure with Shane's remarks, yet he said nothing, waiting for Shane to go on.

"I can tell you this, though. Sarah and Andrea will be in charge of the mission. They will be able to monitor the status of telepathic linkages. It will be possible to return voluntarily if things go wrong. And Sarah will have the option of aborting the mission if she sees something going wrong."

After taking a deep breath to absorb Shane's remarks, Mironi said, "None of this is very reassuring. And how do I know you're leveling with me?"

"Look, Vito," Shane pleaded, "if you'll let Sarah join us now, you can ask her about the protocol she'll follow while I'm doing the time jump. She'll tell you the same thing."

"OK, let's say I believe you. This is what we're gonna do. You get Sarah in here and you tell her that when you do your time travel thing, I'm in charge. At the first hint of any problem, I'm gonna tell her to jerk your chain. *Capisci?* And I'm gonna want to know what the back up plan is. I get to decide if and when we use it. And, finally, we set a time limit on this whole operation. If it ain't gonna work, I want to know it and I want to get out of town, pronto.

"Do you understand what I'm saying here, Tony?"

As Shane glanced once more into the lab to catch Salomé's anxious gaze, he realized that it was now or never. Either he had to make a move on Mironi, or he had to agree to his demands.

Reluctantly, Shane concluded that he had but one choice.

"All right, Vito," Shane said, "we'll do it your way. Let's get Sarah in here and go over the details. But, we've got to be quick. We've already wasted precious time."

For the first time, Mironi's look softened and his brown eyes connected with Shane. "Look...Tony..." he stammered.

"Stow it, Vito," Shane interrupted. "Let's just do it."

"No, Tony," Mironi persisted, "I have only one more thing to say. Right now you're pissed at me. But when you have a chance to think about it, you'll realize I'm doing the right thing...for all of us. You've been so caught up in the ideology of this project that you haven't thought about other consequences. Christ, doesn't it bother you that you dragged Sarah into all of this? She never asked to be part of some suicide mission. She doesn't have any scores to settle. She's so goddam starry-eyed over you she'll do anything you ask. Don't you feel just a little twinge of guilt or responsibility?"

Shane knew that the pained look on his face revealed to Mironi that he had struck Shane's most vulnerable spot. But, he said nothing.

"And what if things don't work out? You've been so busy figuring out how to make this thing work you haven't even thought about a contingency plan.

"That's why I had to step in, Tony. That's what I do. I make tough cold-blooded decisions about life and death and justice. Most people can't or won't make decisions when these three things are involved. I can and I do. That's why the Mironis have survived and will survive.

"Tonight I'm just trying to make sure that my 'brother' survives too," Mironi concluded with a warm gaze at his friend.

Then Mironi surprised Shane by returning the .45 to his shoulder holster and sticking out his hand in conciliation.

Taken aback momentarily by Mironi's gesture, and still absorbing the chilling logic and yet compassionate tone of his statement, Shane hesitated just long enough for Mironi to withdraw his hand.

But then Shane recovered and said, "I'm sorry, Vito. I should be grateful that you're thinking logically about all this. I guess I forgot how you cut through all the bullshit and get right to the heart of things. You're absolutely right, *mio fratré*...as usual." Then Shane took a step forward and added, "Goddamit, Vito, come over here and give me a hug!"

CHAPTER 22

▼

THE DAY BEFORE
YESTERDAY

The final strategy enjoyed the curse of all grand plans: it was a compromise. From the very beginnings of the *Einstein Project,* it had been expected that Daniel's son and Diana's granddaughter—at some unknown future date—would link telepathically with Daniel and Diana to undo the Nazi abduction of Joseph Rheingold during that pivotal transatlantic Clipper flight in mid-July of 1939. But now it was clear that Einstein himself had not enjoyed the same vision. Andrea's telepathic meeting with the great man had changed the focus of the *rainbow* team to a meeting between Einstein and Leo Szilard at Columbia University in early July of 1939.

A great debate among the *rainbow* team had followed. Central to that debate was Sarah's fear that Andrea's brain tissue could not withstand yet another invasive microprobe installation without more recovery time. But, before the burden of the final telepathic mission could fall on Shane alone, Salomé had volunteered to join him. Reminding the team that her great-grandmother, Greta Goldstein, had resided in the Washington Heights section of Manhattan in 1939, Salomé believed she could link telepathically with that ancestor. Greta could then meet up with Daniel, both controlled telepathically by their descendants, to visit Columbia University at the time Einstein had pinpointed.

Although this was a good plan, there were several flaws. Both Daniel and Greta would have to escape their respective family commitments and travel to the university. Even if that could be done without delay, precious time would be lost. Then, upon arrival at the university, they would have to find a way to interact with the key principals—Szilard, Einstein and others—to discover an intervention strategy.

With the clock ticking down to a nuclear holocaust in present time, the telepathic mission had to be completed quickly. If not, *operation rainbow* would not only fail to spare the world from six decades of Nazi tyranny and atrocities, it would allow the current time line to plunge forward into Armageddon. This recognition forced the team to adopt an alternative strategy—more efficient, but disturbingly uncertain.

The strategy adopted was for Shane and Salomé to link telepathically with two known members of Szilard's research group at Columbia: Harri Kreutzwil and Margo Hoffman. Both were Jewish-German refugees, physicists like Joseph Rheingold and roughly the same age—early thirties. They would certainly be included in the meeting with Einstein on the target date. Although telepathic linkage with someone other than one's self or a blood relative was a virtually unknown quantity, Shane's letter from the future had said that it had been demonstrated briefly during that pivotal 1939 Clipper flight. The factor that had sealed the decision was that Einstein had provided them with the precise location and timing for the telepathic linkage. The space-time computations could focus very tightly, compensating for the fact that the telepathic targets were less compatible. Hopefully, this strategy would access successfully Einstein's "tunnel" to the past.

In any event, Vito Mironi was now in charge. In his hands would rest the decision to go or abort, based on whatever wisps of information Sarah might gather in present time.

*   *   *   *

At forty-five minutes past midnight on that fateful Tuesday morning, Shane and Salomé lay side by side on two separate examining tables in the secluded Neural Research Lab. The endoscopic insertion of the microprobes had been completed and each was connected independently to the computer that would shortly begin transmitting the space-time computations. Helmets connected to the P.E.T. machine shielded much of their heads, and Sarah anxiously examined the visual 3-D displays. She would have the crucial task of interpreting these displays to determine if telepathic linkages were successful. Her observations would dictate Mironi's decision to terminate the mission or switch to the backup plan—attempting to link Shane and Salomé, or possibly Andrea, with their direct ancestors.

While Sarah busied herself with last minute operations at the computer console and the P.E.T. displays, Vito Mironi and Andrea approached Shane and Salomé. After paying their respects to Salomé, they turned to Shane. Andrea bent down, kissed the small portion of one cheek that was still exposed and said, "Take care, *Uncle* Tony."

"I told you not to call me that, *brat!*" Shane said with mock reproach. Then, in a serious tone he added, "Thanks, sweetie, for making all this possible."

As Andrea moved away, Mironi slid close to Shane. "Well, *stunata*," he said—turning the Sicilian descriptor for an insane person into a term of endearment, "I guess this is it. This is what your father hoped you would do." Then, taking Shane's hand he said, "None of us knows how this is gonna turn out. But you do what you gotta do, Tony. I'll be right here for you."

"Thanks, old friend," Shane responded slowly. Then, as he gripped Mironi's hand, he murmured, "*Arrivederci, Vito!*"

As the moment arrived to initiate the procedure, Sarah became the last to speak with Salomé and Shane. First, she touched Salomé's arm and said, "This is a brave thing you're doing, Salomé. I'll do my best to make sure everything works. Good luck."

Then moving to Shane's side, she leaned over to kiss him on the mouth. Despite the array of electronic cables and hardware surrounding his head, the kiss was delivered warmly and tenderly. Shane reached for her arm and grasped it, preventing her from leaving. While still leaning over him, Sarah whispered, "No 'good byes' tonight, Tony. We will meet again, my love."

Before releasing his grasp on Sarah's arm, Shane whispered in her ear, "You can count on it, sweetheart. I'm not letting you get away!"

Determined not to become emotional, Sarah straightened up and moved quickly to the computer console. Hoping no one would notice, she brushed a tiny tear away from her cheek.

"All right," she said, "concentrate on your targets. Imagine the time, place and circumstances." She examined the P.E.T. displays as the telepathic brain centers for both subjects slowly began to change to first a dull red and then an orange hue. She hoped the desired yellowish color would soon emerge when she initiated the space-time computational outputs. Without another word, not wanting to disturb their concentration, Sarah executed the sequence of keystrokes that would hopefully propel Shane and Salomé to their 1939 rendezvous.

*   *   *   *

Shane felt as though he was floating in a space devoid of light and substance. There was no awareness of his physical self, but he was keenly aware of his mental faculties. His mind focused on the mysterious Harri Kreutzwil and the time and place of the targeted event in 1939. The peculiar disembodied state of being, rather than distracting or disturbing Shane, actually provided the most favorable conditions for focused mental energy that he had ever experienced.

The duration of this disembodied experience was immeasurable. Shane could have been floating for seconds or hours. He could not tell. But, suddenly, it was over and he found himself abruptly transformed to a living, breathing human form once again—except that now he was looking at a number of different faces scattered around a rectangular wooden table. They were in a conference room illuminated by bright sunlight filtering through venetian blinds. As Shane struggled to maintain composure, he did a quick inventory of his own physical sensations: the feel of the hard wooden chair against his back and buttocks, confirming a lean, tall frame; a well-manicured right hand curled around a pencil, poised over a pad of paper filled with scribbled notes; a plaid cotton shirt and heavy cotton slacks with sturdy low-cut oxford shoes. He peered at the rest of the world over a pair of rimless spectacles, obviously required for reading but not for distance.

Scanning the memory of the creature whose body had suddenly become his, Shane was delighted to realize that he had indeed connected with Harri Kreutzwil. Most importantly, Shane extracted from Kreutzwil's memory details of recent moments, recalling the content of the conversations within the conference room. Then he scanned more carefully the faces around the table. Seated directly across from him, Shane recognized immediately the presence of Albert Einstein. Smoking his pipe, he was dressed casually, with an oversized long-sleeved green linen shirt, unbuttoned at the collar, and heavy dark brown linen slacks. Einstein's feet were not visible, but Shane suspected the man would be, characteristically, without socks.

Seated to Shane's right, at the head of the table, was a distinguished-looking gentleman with black hair combed straight back. Dressed in a trim black suit and tie, he was obviously in charge of the meeting. From the piercing dark eyes and handsome face, the famous physicist and molecular biologist, Leo Szilard, was instantly recognizable to Shane. Shane's research had revealed that this Hungarian scientist—who had held a post at the University of Berlin before fleeing in

1933 to escape Nazi persecution—had collaborated with Einstein in the 1920's. He had also filed patents in Germany on the cyclotron in 1929 and on the electron microscope in 1931. After fleeing to England, Szilard had became one of the first to recognize the feasibility of atomic energy, attempting unsuccessfully in 1936 to convince his colleagues, Niels Bohr and Enrico Fermi, that research in this field should be controlled. Presently, at Columbia University, he was engaged in the cutting edge of research on atomic fission, being among the first to recognize that uranium could sustain a chain reaction.

The purpose of the meeting with Einstein this day was to convince him of the feasibility of developing an atomic bomb, and the urgency for the United States to undertake such a program before the Germans. Szilard had volunteered to write a letter to President Roosevelt for Einstein to deliver, with all the weight of his 1922 Nobel Prize in Physics and international renown.

Seated to Einstein's right was an unfamiliar young man, probably late twenties or early thirties, with frazzled long black hair, high forehead, and rimless spectacles similar to those worn by Kreutzwil. He appeared lean and tall, with bright hazel eyes, dark complexion, narrow hooked nose, and firm chin. In contrast to Kreutzwil's casual dress, this man was attired in a baggy brown suit, white shirt, and plain dark tie. From all that he had researched, Shane was certain that this had to be the infamous Joseph Rheingold.

To Shane's left, at the other end of the table, was the remaining occupant of the conference room. This was a handsome young lady, probably late twenties. She was wearing a white peasant blouse and a brown leather vest laced up the front. Shane could not see her skirt or legs, but she appeared to be short—well under five-and-a-half feet—and stocky. With raven shoulder-length straight hair, dark complexion, and blazing brown eyes, the young lady radiated an air of vitality and determination that projected her securely into this male-dominated world of physics. Without a doubt, Shane thought, this was Rheingold's friend and colleague, Margo Hoffman. And, he hoped, this was now the vehicle for Salomé to join the fray.

Shane knew that the meeting this day would result in a letter from Einstein being sent to President Roosevelt on August 2, 1939. And he knew that the Manhattan Project to develop a U.S. atomic bomb would result. But he also knew that Joseph Rheingold would be lured to Berlin in July by a false Nazi promise that he would secure the safety of his family remaining there.

Shane still did not know how to intervene in Rheingold's abduction. Einstein would know, but not until later. And Einstein would demand that the task be carried out in such a way that it could not be undone...and such that the strategy was not known in the future. Einstein had assured Andrea during her trip to 1942 that the plan would be obvious.

So far, Shane could see no obvious plan. But, as he glanced toward Margo Hoffman, he thought he saw a glimmer of recognition. Her dark eyes regarded him intensely, and a thin smile flashed. Salomé was with him.

*   *   *   *

Salomé was rapidly becoming acclimated to the body and mind of Margo Hoffman…and she liked it. Not only was Margo bright and aggressive, she was also physically fit and strong-willed. Although the young lady's shorter stature and stocky build were unfamiliar to Salomé, she felt very comfortable with the physical prowess and determined outlook that Margo possessed.

After completing a survey of the others seated at the table Salomé's gaze rested on the young man to her right. From Margo's thoughts and memory she recognized this man as Harri Kreutzwil, but there was something odd about his appearance. Then, after glancing briefly to her left and right several times, a thin smile slowly appeared. Finally, she peered intensely at the figure to her right, receiving a glance in return that assured her that Tony Shane was indeed with her. It was clear that he had not yet seen what she had. She knew now what Einstein had planned. It was too perfect!

*   *   *   *

It was clear from the conversation at the table that the meeting was winding down. Szilard announced shortly that he, Einstein and Joseph Rheingold would remain in the conference room for some private discussion, while the remaining occupants would be dismissed.

As Margo and Kreutzwil picked up their things and began to depart the conference room, Shane heard Joseph Rheingold call out that he would meet with them later. But Rheingold had said they would meet in "Jacob's office."

Puzzled by the specification of an unfamiliar name and place, Shane searched Kreutzwil's memory for a connection to Rheingold's reference. Lost in thought, Shane stopped in his tracks before following Margo through the conference room doorway. He glanced back briefly at Rheingold with a puzzled look, and then stumbled into the hallway to join Margo.

"Salomé?" he asked in a hushed whisper as he caught up with Margo. A quick nod and smile confirmed his suspicion.

"Tony?" she asked in return, and he responded with a nod.

"Can we go to Margo's office?" Shane asked. "You know where it's at?"

Hesitating only briefly, Salomé responded with, "Sure, it's one floor down. Let's go."

After hustling down the corner stairway in silence, Shane and Salomé hurried down the broad hallway until reaching a door with a frosted glass window that opened into a large bare office. The office contained a small wooden desk and chair, two visitors' chairs, and a large blackboard. A clothes tree stood in one corner. A wooden filing cabinet occupied the far corner, behind the desk and chair. There was no window. A single incandescent light fixture hanging from the center ceiling illuminated the room, while a metal gooseneck lamp provided lighting for the desktop. The small mirror that adorned the wall to the left of the desk chair provided tribute to a woman's vanity.

Salomé flipped on the ceiling light as they entered the office, closing the door behind them. She motioned to Shane that he should take the seat behind the desk while she remained standing near the blackboard. Waiting for Shane to speak—to learn whether Einstein's vision had been revealed to him as it had to Salomé—she picked up a piece of chalk as if to write something on the board.

"Where are we supposed to meet with Rheingold? Where is 'Jacob's office'?" Shane asked.

"You don't see it, do you, Tony?" Salomé asked.

"See what?" Shane replied.

"Kreutzwil's memory doesn't tell you who 'Jacob' is?" Salomé asked with a grin.

Shane then recalled what he had retrieved from Kreutzwil's memory. "Jacob! That's what Rheingold calls Kreutzwil sometimes. Of course. He wants to meet in Kreutzwil's office."

"Don't you know why he calls Kreutzwil 'Jacob' sometimes?" Salomé persisted. "Turn around and look in the mirror, Tony."

After rotating around in the swiveling desk chair, Shane carefully examined Kreutzwil's reflection in the wall mirror. Within seconds it all became clear: the logic behind Einstein's intervention strategy, and the reason for Rheingold's mysterious reference to "Jacob." The face peering back at him in the mirror could have been that of Joseph Rheingold himself. Harri Kreutzwil could have been Rheingold's twin! Except for Kreutzwil's hair and complexion being slightly lighter, and a small moustache, he and Rheingold had the same face.

This stunning observation prompted other facts from Kreutzwil's memory for Shane to absorb. Rheingold and Kreutzwil were so alike in facial features, physical build, education, and family background that they readily passed for twins. In fact, Joseph had christened Kreutzwil with the fictitious name of "Jacob," his "twin brother."

As Shane turned back to face Salomé, the broad grin indicated his understanding. "This is it, Salomé!" he exclaimed. "This is what Einstein had in mind. We persuade Rheingold to let Kreutzwil take his place on that flight to Europe. The Nazis will bring someone back they think is Joseph Rheingold—embracing the secret pathway to an atomic bomb—but they really get Harry Kreutzwil, competent physicist but not the man who can deliver the goods."

"Great idea, but will Kreutzwil do it?"

For several seconds, Shane searched the man's memories and emotions. Finally, he responded, "Absolutely. Rheingold and Kreutzwil are like brothers. They've been close friends since their teens. Completed their university degrees at the same school and were separated only during their doctoral dissertation work. They fled Germany together in 1935 and both ended up at Columbia working with Szilard. Kreutzwil is working on moderating materials for sustainable chain reactions, but he doesn't know what Joseph has achieved on the production of enriched uranium. Apparently Szilard is so paranoid about the Nazis learning our atomic secrets that he has forbidden members of his research group to share progress reports with each other."

"You're sure he'll do it then?" Salomé persisted.

"I'm certain," Shane replied.

"How do you see this playing out, Tony?" Salomé asked. "Let's go through it step by step."

"First," Shane began, "we know that Einstein is inviting Rheingold to return with him to Princeton. We persuade Rheingold that Kreutzwil has to take his place. My understanding is that the Nazi agents will accost him before he returns here, and they persuade him to fly back to Berlin to work with Heisenberg."

"Won't somebody realize the switch has been made?"

"Not Einstein. He just met both of them today. As for the others, they still have trouble telling the two apart. That's why Kreutzwil wears a moustache and they dress differently every day. In fact, before the moustache they sometimes switched places just for fun. Of course, Margo and Szilard aren't supposed to know that," Shane chuckled.

"What if Rheingold refuses to go along?" Salomé inquired. "We can't force him."

"We have to tell him the truth. We tell him that there is no way he can save his family. They're already gone. And then we explain what the Nazis will do with his knowledge. The balance of power teeters on the knife edge that he holds in his hand."

"But the war hasn't begun yet in Europe. How can we explain the urgency?" Salomé asked. "Do we reveal who we are? That we know the future?"

"We'll have to. Margo and Kreutzwil won't remember any of this after we break off. Rheingold will have to persuade Kreutzwil of our plan and explain how it was revealed to him. But he will be persuasive. Kreutzwil understands the Nazi threat. He saw the brutality of the Storm Troopers and the *Gestapo* first hand. Germany has already swallowed Austria and Czechoslovakia. Now they're looking at Poland. He knows it's just a matter of time before the global conflict breaks out."

Pursing her lips and fiddling with the laces of her vest, Salomé took several seconds to digest Shane's words. Finally, she said, "I think you're right, Tony. This plan will work. And the Nazis will never understand why their plan for Rheingold will fail. Einstein is right. They won't be able to go back and fix the problem because they won't know they've abducted the wrong man."

"There's just one thing that bothers me," Shane interrupted. "If this is the perfect plan, and everything is set to fall in place, according to Einstein's theory, the new more probable time line should exist *now*. If that were the case, the Tony Shane and Salomé in that future telepathic laboratory in Chicago shouldn't exist any more, and we shouldn't be here right now telepathically in the form of Margo Hoffman and Harri Kreutzwil."

"I don't understand," Salomé said.

"There must be another obstacle to the success of this plan," Shane declared. "There's something we've missed, Salomé."

After several seconds, Salomé spoke out. "We've overlooked one thing Tony. Someone will inform the Nazis about Rheingold's work. And it must be someone from Szilard's research group. I'm sure Kreutzwil won't do it. Perhaps it will be Margo."

"Hmmh. Hadn't thought of that. Can you extract anything from her memories?"

"No, it's probably in the future. But we might find something in her correspondence."

"Do we need proof?" Shane asked.

"If she's the one that betrays Rheingold, that is a crucial link to the abduction plot. What if Einstein's plan requires that we uncover or prevent her duplicity?"

"Hmmh. I don't see it. The substitution strategy we've uncovered is surely what Einstein had in mind. If Margo is destined to betray Rheingold, then so be it. She won't remember that we set up Kreutzwil's substitution, and Rheingold will still be safe."

"Humor me, Tony. Let me take a look in Margo's correspondence files."

"Sure. But be quick about it. I have to meet up with Rheingold in Kreutzwil's office pretty quickly."

"All right, I'm going to squeeze behind you and get into the filing cabinet," Salomé said as she moved behind Kreutzwil's chair and began digging through file drawers.

The chair slid forward slightly as Shane made room for Salomé. For a few moments he closed his eyes. Shane's thoughts were racing as he tried to assure himself they were on the right track. The consequences of failure were enormous and frightening. He was so certain. But why hadn't the time line switched? What was wrong? What obstacles remained?

He became aware that Salomé's file searching behind him had grown silent. He began to turn around, when he sensed rapid movement behind him, and something flashed before his eyes. Suddenly he felt a tightness around his neck, and he reached up with both hands instinctively to discover a narrow leather cord digging into his throat.

"Salomé!" he cried hoarsely. "What—?"

"Shut up, Shane," she growled. "Don't make this any more difficult for either of us."

As he strained to get his fingers underneath the cord cutting into his throat, Shane sputtered, "Please...don't..."

"I'm sorry, Shane," she said with a strained voice, using all of her strength to hold him in his chair. "This has to be done. I can't let you go through with this."

"Wh...why?" came the hoarse cry.

"Because I want to see the Nazis blasted off the face of the earth. I don't want some alternative universe. I want those bastards to pay a horrible price—with their own blood. *And I want to see it happen.*"

"Bu...but..." Shane croaked as the dark cloud of unconsciousness began to numb his senses and his brain. At some level he knew that it was Kreutzwil, not he, that was dying. But it didn't matter. Kreutzwil's death would foil the intervention just as surely as would his own. He struggled to hang on—to avoid the return to the future that would seal the mission's failure. As the sense of impending death closed in, fleeting thoughts of family and colleagues whom he had failed filled his mind. Sarah's face came close. But his last thoughts were of Carothers and Salomé. Had this been the strategy all along—for Salomé to discover and thwart Einstein's intervention plan? How could Salomé...the least expected...have been *the final obstacle?*

*   *   *   *

Sarah, Andrea and Mironi had been riveted to the P.E.T. displays for the past half-hour, ever since Shane and Salomé had lapsed into unconsciousness in the heart of the Neural Research Lab. The glowing telepathic portions of both images had remained at a comforting bright yellow hue during that entire time.

But Sarah was anxious. The telepathic connections were tenuous. Surely they could not hold on much longer. "Andrea," Sarah exclaimed abruptly as she shifted her gaze to the young lady next to her, "we should be thinking about our backup plan. Let's give it another ten minutes, and then I'll hook you up. OK?"

"I'm ready to go," Andrea replied quickly.

"She's right," Mironi interrupted, quickly taking charge. "Let's get her set up now."

"Please, don't waste your time," commanded the unfamiliar voice with the distinctive German accent. As the three whirled around they were shocked to see Wolfgang Schwarz, wearing a white lab coat, walking into the room. At his side were two tall gentlemen in dark overcoats, with large black pistols equipped with silencers in their hands. One of them was instantly recognizable to Mironi. It was Colonel Manfred Weber of the *Gestapo*. The other was a dark foreigner. They fanned out from Schwarz's side, keeping their weapons trained on Mironi.

Sarah was the first to respond. "Dr. Schwarz, what are you doing here?" she cried with surprise. "And who are these men with you?" she asked with as much indignation as she could muster.

"They're *Gestapo*," Mironi declared, as he raised his hands. "Don't do anything foolish, Sarah."

"Ahh, good advice, Mr. Mironi," Schwarz said with a perverse smile. "And, Sarah, your outrage is surely misplaced. It is *I* who should be asking why *you* are here. But, of course, I know what you're doing. And it is time to put a stop to it. So, please, step aside—all of you—while I get at the console. We'll put a stop to this nonsense once and for all."

"Please do as he says," Weber threatened. "We will not hesitate to eliminate anyone who interferes." Then, gazing directly at Mironi, Weber added, "Please remove the weapon from your shoulder holster with two fingers, place it on the floor, and kick it over to me. And don't think your two gunmen will be able to help you, Mironi. They're both dead."

"How—" Mironi began as he responded to Weber's command, wondering what had happened to Paulie and Rocco.

"Did you think there was only one entrance to this facility?" Schwarz interrupted. "That would be a fire hazard," he added with a crooked smile. "Your men never saw us coming."

Refusing to move away from the console, Sarah pleaded, "Dr. Schwarz, we're doing nothing wrong here. Please let us continue."

Following a wicked snicker, Schwarz replied by spreading his arms to either side and asking, "Do you know who these gentlemen are, Sarah? This gentleman to my right is Colonel Manfred Weber of the Secret Police. He has been pursuing Tony Shane for many years. To my left is Mr. Ahmed Sharif, Director of Counter-terrorism for the United Arab States. He has been working with Colonel Weber ever since the 9/11 attacks. They know all about *operation rainbow*. They've asked me to come down here and put a stop to this sorry mission."

"What do they know?" Sarah asked indignantly.

It was Sharif's turn to speak. "Did you think you could keep such a miserable plan secret from us? We know about your telepathic time travel nonsense. About the *Einstein Project*. We're here to make sure it doesn't happen."

Desperate now to stall for time, Sarah glanced at the P.E.T. monitors to be sure Shane and Salomé were still telepathically active before responding to Sharif. With some alarm she noticed that Shane's telepathic image center had faded somewhat to an orange-yellow hue. "How did you find this out?" she asked Sharif.

"Enough stalling, Sarah," Schwarz interrupted. "Move away from that console and let me in." Without waiting, Schwarz moved ahead and roughly shoved both Sarah and Andrea aside. As he took his seat at the computer console, Sarah and Andrea stood to the side, observing with alarm the vacillating coloring of the telepathic center of Shane's P.E.T. image.

As Schwarz began to pull up relevant displays on the console screen, preparing to shut down the experiment underway, Sharif chose to respond to Sarah's question. "There were many clues that allowed us to figure out what you were doing here, Sarah," he began. "But the final step was when we supervised your loyalty testing today. We congratulate you for foiling the test. I assure you we will find out how. But, that is irrelevant. The significant fact is that one of the olfactory biosensors attached to your scalp was tucked beneath the skin under local anesthesia. It's still there, but not for vapor sensing. It is a microtransmitter. We've been monitoring your conversations since the afternoon. It was all we needed to pin down the final details."

Instinctively, Sarah reached up to feel the top of her head where one of the biosensors had been attached. Lifting up the hair, she was able to detect the slightest bump. She wagged her head at Sharif and blurted, "You bastards!"

Suddenly, Andrea cried, "Sarah, look! Tony's P.E.T.! It's going crazy!"

All eyes focused on Shane's P.E.T. display. The glowing telepathic portion of the image was gyrating between bright yellow and dull red.

"What does that mean?" growled Schwarz from the console.

"Nuh...nothing," stammered Sarah, as she wondered secretly if it meant that Shane's mission had been accomplished. That he was attempting to return.

"Can you shut this down *now?*" Sharif asked Schwarz with an implied command.

"I'm not sure," Schwarz responded with anxiety. "They've changed all the controls. I'm working in the dark."

"Well, I know how to fix it," Sharif asserted as he stepped toward the two examining tables in the center of the room. He took aim at Shane's forehead and nodded to Weber to do the same with Salomé.

While Sarah screamed, the scene seemed to play out in slow motion. Sharif hesitated for a moment as Weber moved swiftly to Salomé's side, raised his weapon and squeezed the trigger. As Weber's silenced projectile shattered Salomé's brain, Sharif unexpectedly tilted his weapon away from Shane.

Sarah remained frozen as she saw the gun swing in Weber's direction, and she thought she heard Sharif mutter, *This is for Ellen, you bastard.*

A piercing *phfft* accompanied the discharge that struck Weber squarely in the temple, and he pitched sideways, crumpling to the floor.

Quickly tilting his weapon back, Sharif prepared to dispatch Shane just as Salomé and Weber before him. But he had wasted a valuable and fateful second.

As he began to squeeze the trigger, Sarah shrieked and threw herself at Sharif's weapon. The noxious *phfft* of another silenced shot pierced the air as the missile from Sharif's weapon punctured Sarah's chest. Sarah's momentum knocked Sharif away from Shane, and they toppled on to the floor.

The sudden diversion allowed Mironi to reach down undetected, and to remove the small 9mm Beretta concealed in an ankle holster. Bringing the weapon up and releasing the safety, Mironi moved quickly to stand directly over the fallen Sharif. Sarah's dead weight had immobilized his weapon arm, and Sharif stared up helplessly at Vito Mironi's menacing Beretta.

A strange calm seemed to come over Sharif as he stared at the man who would promptly take his life. He appeared unafraid, even curiously at peace.

Without hesitation, Mironi squeezed the trigger and directed a slug into the center of Sharif's forehead, bringing instant death to the man that had so recently held Shane's life in his hands.

As the loud discharge from Mironi's weapon echoed off the walls and violent death unfolded all around her, Andrea suddenly summoned the courage to move. She jumped on Schwarz's back and tried to tear him from the console. But he was too strong and easily shoved her aside. As she crashed into the examining table containing the lifeless body of Salomé, she looked backwards to see Vito Mironi whirling away from Sharif's motionless body and taking aim at the back of Wolfgang Schwarz. Once more a loud bang filled the room as Schwarz's head exploded and he slumped over the console.

Mironi rushed to help Andrea to her feet, and she turned immediately to the P.E.T. display screens. Salomé's display was understandably blank, while Shane's now glowed with a reassuring bright yellow telepathic center. Heartened by this observation, Mironi and Andrea rushed to the fallen Sarah and turned her over on her back. The large blood stain across her chest and the pale color of her skin were enough to tell them she was mortally wounded. But she was conscious and smiling faintly.

Mironi raised her head slightly so that she could see the P.E.T. display, while Andrea held her hand. "You did it, Sarah," Andrea said softly. "Tony is still alive and still engaged. He'll pull it off. You'll see."

"Can you..." Sarah began faintly, "can you take me...to him?" she murmured.

Without hesitation, Vito Mironi reached underneath, picked her up and gently placed Sarah on the wide examining table next to the unconscious body of Tony Shane. Then Andrea helped her take Shane's hand in hers.

Mironi turned to Andrea and asked, "Can you operate the console for Tony's return?"

Shaking her head slowly, Andrea replied, "It doesn't matter, Vito. Tony won't even try to return. He knows that he must succeed. And, if he does, there won't be anything here to return to..."

As Sarah listened to Andrea's last words she struggled to turn her head slightly so that she could gaze at Tony's serene face next to hers. She opened her mouth to speak, but no words would come. As her surroundings slowly dimmed to a black void, she became aware only of her thoughts. But those too quickly faded away.

*   *   *   *

"Harri...Harri!" Margo cried excitedly. "Are you OK?"

It was Shane's turn to be disoriented. Looking into the anxious face of Margo Hoffman he struggled to retrieve his memory. Slowly he realized that Margo was looking at him as Harri Kreutzwil. She had called him "Harri." As he struggled to respond, he gazed carefully into Margo's dark brown eyes. Salomé wasn't there. He was sure of it.

"Margo?" he croaked softly, barely able to speak. "Tell me what happened." He reached up to rub his tender throat as he listened.

"I don't know, Harri. The last thing I remember we were all in the conference room. Next thing I know, I'm in back of you with a chord wrapped around your throat. I don't understand."

"That's OK," Shane said comfortingly, regaining his voice. "You didn't do this to me. But we need to talk. What time is it?"

Margo looked at her wristwatch and gave the time. Shane quickly calculated that over half-an-hour had passed since they had left the conference room.

"I need to see Joseph right away," he said, suddenly feeling an adrenaline rush. "Help me up. We're meeting at my office."

"Do you want me to come with you?" Margo asked.

"No. I have personal matters to discuss with Joseph. Just sit tight. This injury was not your fault, Margo. I'll explain later."

As Margo helped him to his feet, Shane considered her actions carefully. If Salomé was no longer in contact—if Margo Hoffman was acting independently—then perhaps Salomé had been unable to sustain the telepathic connection.

Then it struck him.

If Salomé had returned to the future, she had taken with her the secret of the intervention plan!

Shooting out the door, heading in the direction of Kreutzwil's office, Shane's thoughts turned frantically to the necessity of dumping his simple plan. It had to be modified.

But how?

As he rounded the corner, he saw Rheingold standing not fifty feet away, waiting for him at the office door. At the sight of the man whose appearance was so strikingly similar to Kreutzwil's, his hand instinctively went to his throat to feel the bruises that would surely distinguish them. Thinking absently about how the bruises might be addressed with makeup, the answer to his burning question struck him like a flatiron.

With a wide grin suddenly spreading across his face, Shane sped towards Rheingold. The modified plan quickly unfolded in Shane's mind...along with the other message that he would relate to Rheingold. The message that he had not shared with anyone...not even Salomé. The message that Einstein had produced in 1949, and that only Shane had understood.

*   *   *   *

Rheingold seemed dumbfounded as he watched and listened to his friend Harri Kreutzwil relate a fantastic story that was purportedly coming from "Tony Shane," from the future. He had listened politely, but appeared to have believed not a word. Nevertheless, Shane continued pacing before the seated Rheingold and finished his story by describing the identity-switching plan to deceive the Nazis.

Suddenly, Rheingold pushed out the palm of his hand and said, "Harri, please don't go any further. I don't know where you got this outrageous story, but I don't want to hear any more."

As Rheingold began to rise to his feet, Shane stopped pacing and asked calmly, "What will it take to convince you that I'm telling the truth, Joseph?"

Rheingold sat down, shook his head, and said, "I can't think of anything, Harri."

"Haven't you wondered how I knew you would be traveling to Princeton with Professor Einstein? And other details of your meeting with him?"

Rheingold shook his head slowly and said, "Harri...or Tony...or whatever I should call you, can't you see how utterly fantastic your story sounds? How in the world could you travel through time?"

"I'll explain that later," Shane lied. "But, first, let's go over how you will carry out the identity switch."

Reluctantly, Rheingold listened as Shane detailed the modified plan he had devised. Instead of switching places with Kreutzwil immediately, Rheingold would travel to Princeton with Einstein. Then, just before Rheingold's planned return to Columbia, precisely before the Nazi abduction, Kreutzwil should travel to Princeton and switch places with him. This would give time for Kreutzwil's neck bruises to heal, and time for grooming changes to facilitate the identity switch.

"Now here's the second part of the message," Shane continued. "When Professor Einstein comes up with this plan, he realizes that even this strategy is not foolproof. Some future time traveler might find yet another way to manipulate the outcome of the global war.

"Einstein realized that the real problem is telepathic time travel itself. So, the second part of his plan is for you to prevent its development."

"Did he tell you this?" Rheingold asked sarcastically. "And did he tell you how I might accomplish this?"

Ignoring Rheingold's disdain, Shane continued, "Einstein will record his thoughts in an ambiguous letter that he will write in 1949. Buried within that letter is a hint on how we might defeat telepathic time travel."

"What kind of hint?" Rheingold asked, prompted by scientific curiosity.

"Einstein used oversized capital letters for the first letter of each of three paragraphs in his letter—like the medieval monks did when making copies of the Bible. I didn't think anything of it until I strung together all three oversized letters. They spelled: D—N—A"

"What does that mean?" Rheingold asked.

"It's an abbreviation for deoxyribonucleic acid—probably the most important molecule in human biology. In 1949, when Einstein writes his letter, DNA is just beginning to be looked at regarding genetic characteristics. Einstein must certainly be aware of this work in 1949, and he tries to tell us that the secret to telepathic time travel will be found in the molecular biology of genetic materials."

"I'm afraid this is out of my field, and way over my head," Rheingold protested.

"Yes, but it will not always be so," Shane countered. "Your mentor, Leo Szilard, has expertise in molecular biology. He can tell you what is already known about DNA. If Einstein's intuition is correct—that telepathic ability is hereditary—then the secret to controlling it will require genetic engineering. This is something not even dreamed about today, but which will evolve rapidly in the future."

"I'm sorry, Harri, but this conversation is getting out of hand," Rheingold said as he began to rise as if to leave.

Shane put a hand on Rheingold's shoulder and gently pushed him back into the chair.

"Joseph, please, will you let me finish?" he asked. "This is more important than you can imagine."

As Rheingold remained seated stiffly, Shane continued, "You *must* avoid the Nazis, Joseph. You are destined to work with the Americans to develop an atomic bomb. Beyond that, you must use your unique scientific position after the war to discover the genetic requirements for telepathy."

Shaking his head slowly, Rheingold remarked, "You're asking a lot of me, Harri."

"It's not Harri that's asking. It's a whole future generation…many who will suffer and die if you do not follow through."

"But what do *you* say, Harri? Talk to me as my friend," Rheingold pleaded.

"Harri can't speak to you now. He will when I let go of my control," Shane responded. "But he won't remember any of this. His last memory will be of your meeting with Szilard and Einstein."

"What?"

"And then you will have to persuade him to help you."

"Persuade *him*? Persuade *you*, Harri? I don't even believe this myself."

Shane felt like the wind had left his sails. He had failed miserably to convince Rheingold of anything.

With a sigh Shane came before the seated Rheingold on one knee and put his hands on the arms of the chair. "Joseph, there is only one thing that will convince you that my story is true…when the Nazis abduct you. But then it will be too late. Please, let Harri take your place as I explained.

"What have you got to lose, Joseph?" Shane pleaded.

As Rheingold sat silently for several moments, Shane rose and sat back on Kreutzwil's desktop, moving aside the large world globe.

Finally, Rheingold spoke.

"All right, Harri…or Tony…you finally make some sense. I'll discuss this with you…with Harri…whenever you're back to yourself. In the meantime," Rheingold continued, as he rose from his seat and stepped toward the office door, "I'm going back to my office to think about it."

Exhausted, Shane simply nodded his head. But then he remembered one last crucial instruction for Rheingold.

"One last thing, Joseph. You and Harri can never tell anyone about this incident today or your identity-switch plan. Never! Not anyone…except for the granddaughter I mentioned in my story."

Shaking his head in silence, Rheingold opened the door to leave.

"Don't forget," Shane warned again.

"I won't," Rheingold sighed as he shut the door behind him.

*   *   *   *

Shane arose and paced for several minutes, sorting through numerous questions. Was his job done? Clearly, Rheingold was unconvinced. Yet, if Rheingold followed through with the identity switch, as it appeared he was willing to do, everything should work out.

But, if that were so, why was Shane still here? If Rheingold truly planned to follow through, the time line that Tony Shane had come from should no longer exist.

And yet he was still here.

That could only mean that the time line had not shifted to a favorable outcome of the war.

There must be another obstacle! Shane told himself. *But what could it be?*

*   *   *   *

Shane's troubling thoughts persisted until they were interrupted by the sound of Kreutzwil's office door opening. Glancing up, Shane was surprised to see Rheingold standing just inside the doorway once again.

But this time there was a gun in his hand!

"What—?" Shane cried.

"Surely you're not surprised, Shane," said Rheingold, "that another time traveler would show up."

"Who are you?" Shane asked.

"It's Nathan Carothers," was the response.

"Nathan? How did you—?" Shane began.

"It's a long story, Shane."

"Are you here to help? Or is that gun pointed at me for a reason, Nathan?"

"I'm not here to help, Shane."

"What the hell are you doing, Nathan?"

"Obviously, I have a different agenda."

"And getting rid of Kreutzwil is part of it?"

"Exactly."

"Where did you get the gun?"

"I did my research. One of your fellow faculty members here belongs to the Downtown Gun Club. I borrowed it from his office."

His mind racing frantically to cope with this entirely unexpected confrontation, Shane realized he desperately needed more information…and time.

"How did you get to Chicago? Did you take Salomé's place in the setup at the *Institut*?"

Laughing harshly, Carothers replied, "You are so naïve, Shane. It's incredible! You have no idea what's going on in your own world."

"All right, Nathan. So, I'm an idiot. Humor me. Tell me what's going on."

After hesitating a few moments, Carothers sighed and said, "I guess you have a right to know, Shane…you won't be able to do anything about it."

Pulling a chair over, Carothers sat and motioned for Shane to do the same. The gun remained pointed steadily at him as Shane sat down on the edge of the desk, next to the large world globe.

"I'm working with the Soviets, Shane. Have been for a long time. We're going to follow through and wipe those Nazi sonsofbitches off the face of the earth."

"Did you know that Salomé planned to sabotage this mission?"

"Of course. But obviously she failed."

"She wasn't able to sustain contact."

"She's probably dead. I'm surprised you aren't also."

"What?"

"Last I heard, the *Gestapo* was headed for the *Institut*. They learned what was going on."

"How did you get here?"

"The Soviets have had a mind control program going for a long time, more advanced than the Germans. Sergei Chekov was in charge. Thanks to me, Chekov's known about your plan for a long time, and has his own program to develop time travel. He realized that Sarah Stenstrom was the best person in the world to recruit for his project. That's why he was in Chicago."

In a flash it became clear to Shane. Sarah had innocently revealed to Chekov the technical key to generating telepathic connections to distant times. And Chekov had returned to Moscow just in time to send Carothers on his mission to 1939. What fools they had been to trust Chekov! And Carothers!

"You bastard!" Shane exclaimed. "You and that goddam Russian deserve each other!"

"Don't take it personally, Shane. This is business."

"What do you hope to accomplish, Nathan?"

"Isn't it obvious? We can't afford a disruption of the original time line. Everything is set in our own future for the Soviets and their allies to wipe out the Nazis."

"What do *you* get out of this, Nathan?"

"In return for the YLA's role in this takeover, I'll be appointed Governor of the Soviet United States. All except the western states, that is. They'll still be part of the Japanese Empire. All of the refugees will be allowed to return."

"My God, Nathan, don't you realize that a nuclear attack will destroy the country? Wipe out millions of Americans along with the Nazis?"

"They're not *my* 'Americans,' Shane. They're the remnants of the white elite that ran the country back in the 1930's and 40's. They don't want refugees back in their country any more than the Nazis do. They're the ones that made my people ride in the back of the bus, go to different schools, and sneak in and out the back door of the grocery store. We didn't have a vote, we couldn't find decent work, and we were more'n likely to be in jail! You think I have any sympathy for that contemptible overbearing shitty white class? You think I want your mission to succeed so we can turn the clock back to 1939? No fucking way!"

Stunned by Carothers' passionate outburst, Shane could think of no immediate response. But his mind churned furiously, trying to find a way out.

Finally, he asked, "Do you think you can get Rheingold to Berlin?"

"Shouldn't you be wondering what I'm going to do with you?"

"I think I know," Shane responded. "But you can't solve anything by killing Kreutzwil. He's just my host."

"Hah! I always said you were too smart, Shane."

"So, what's your plan?"

"Much better than your miserable ideas."

An icy chill gripped Shane as he realized suddenly that Carothers was not only aware of the identity-switch plan but also the genetic engineering strategy he had shared with Rheingold.

As if he had read Shane's mind, Carothers said, "You know that I will have to eliminate Kreutzwil, don't you? But, you, Shane, will be dealt with in real-time...in our future time line. The *Gestapo* will eliminate you while your mind is here. Very shortly Harri Kreutzwil's mind will be freed...and you will be stone cold dead in future time."

Shane's immediate impulse was to let go of Kreutzwil's mind now and return to his own future time. He could then arouse himself and fend off his attackers.

But Shane quickly realized that would only feed into Carothers' plan. Shane's departure would allow Carothers to carry out unobserved some unknown plan for getting Rheingold to Berlin. It would be impossible to develop a new intervention strategy.

But Carothers' last statement about the *Gestapo* threat had given Shane an idea.

Instantly, Shane reached a decision. He would not stay here with Carothers...but he would not return to the *Institut* either.

There was a chance—one chance—that Shane could yet save his mission. But he had to act quickly.

*   *   *   *

Shane had posed only one more provocative question, and Carothers had launched into yet another long spiel defending his alliance with the Soviets. Shane had not waited for the punch line. He hoped that Carothers would not notice immediately that he had released his hold on Kreutzwil's mind. Shane didn't need much time to execute his desperate improvised plan...if it worked!

He glanced casually at the world globe next to him on the desktop. Shane noted the latitude and longitude coordinates that he would need...and hoped he could remember those antiquated integer formulas his dad had used so many years ago during the crude pioneering telepathic time travel experiments at Wisconsin.

*   *   *   *

The new body in which Shane found himself was much older, but physically strong. And the mind was keen and sharp. It took Shane only moments to surmise that he had taken over the mind of Sergei Chekov and discovered himself in the middle of Chekov's large Neural Research Lab at the University of Moscow. A rapid scan of recent memories explained the sight of a supine unconscious Nathan Carothers on the examining table, surrounded by monitoring equipment similar to what had been used at the *Heisenberg Institut* in Chicago. One very prominent exception was the absence of a cable connection to microprobe brain implants. Shane could only assume that the Russians had perfected microchip implants that could be pre-programmed or controlled by wireless communications.

Chekov's memory verified that he had very recently sent Carothers on a telepathic mission to connect with Rheingold in 1939.

The one disturbing element was that two military guards stood near the examining table. Each was armed with a side arm and an assault rifle.

Without hesitation, Shane moved quickly toward Carothers. Surprise would be on Shane's side, he hoped, as he moved past one of the guards. He knew that the guards would observe only that it was Chekov examining his patient.

Suddenly, Shane whirled around behind one of the guards, reaching around, grabbing the assault weapon, and directing it at the other guard. The startled man in Shane's grasp could not react before a short violent burst caused the other guard to crumple to the floor.

Before the commandeered assault rifle could be re-directed at Carothers, as was Shane's plan, the guard had reacted to Shane's hold and whirled around in an attempt to shake him off. But Shane had anticipated this maneuver and had successfully extracted the automatic side arm from its holster. Before the guard could turn his rifle on Shane, the .45 caliber handgun dispatched two rounds into his head.

Turning around to take aim at Carothers, Shane was shocked to find that Carothers had awakened, had slid off the table, and had picked up the assault rifle dropped by the other guard. Before Carothers could aim the weapon, Shane was able to fire off another round, piercing Carothers' shoulder and thrusting him back into one of the electronics racks.

But Carothers did not let go of the rifle. With a painful grimace he twisted the rifle in Shane's direction and shouted, "Fuck you, Shane!" as he sent off a wild burst that scattered above Shane's head.

With both hands gripping the handgun, Shane squeezed the trigger, sending two quick rounds into Carothers' chest. He watched as Carothers dropped the rifle and fell back heavily against the electronics rack.

Striding quickly to Carothers' side, Shane kicked the assault rifle away and stood over the large mortally wounded black man.

"I'm sorry, Nathan," he said. "There just wasn't any other way."

"You sonofabitch!" Carothers croaked. "How…how did you do it?"

"I was always able to return to present time, Nathan. But I used my own mental computations to over-ride the specific location and concentrated on linking up with Chekov in Moscow. Fortunately, we were compatible and he was a good receptor. So, here I am.

"But what I'm wondering, Nathan, is how *you* figured I would come back here? I didn't expect to see you return."

"As soon as I…realized you…released Kreutzwil," Carothers mumbled, "I realized I…I made a mistake…mistake telling you…about Chekov. I…I had to…get back."

"I'm sorry it had to end this way, Nathan."

"Me...too...Tony," Carothers murmured as his eyes slowly closed and his head slumped forward.

Shane's feelings at that moment were a mixture of relief and profound sadness. He couldn't believe that he had just killed three men. His years as a terrorist had taught him about weapons. But he had never used one to injure another human being.

*   *   *   *

Suddenly, a sharp jolt seemed to rock the room for a millisecond, and Shane thought that Carothers' body had faded and disappeared briefly, only to re-appear an instant later as a ghostly image. Glancing around, Shane noticed that all his surroundings had become translucent. Carothers seemed to fall away from him as Shane drifted upwards. Then the walls around him began to shimmer and fade. He could now see both Chekov and Carothers below him. But then they also shimmered and faded, and Shane drifted further away, floating and disembodied in a dark void.

Shane realized then that something wonderful was happening.

His elimination of Carothers had removed *the final obstacle.*

In an instant Shane knew that Rheingold and Kreutzwil had indeed followed through in 1939. The time line was now changing to the new most probable future...a future of hope and promise.

An indescribable feeling of overwhelming joy filled Shane's soul. Against all odds, the many sacrifices—of his father, Fuller, Diana, Mironi, Sarah, and the others—would not have been in vain.

America would be liberated again!

The sensory transition seemed to unfold in slow motion, as Shane reflected on his own personal journey. Through the years of vengeful rebellion to the final sacrificial mission that would restore the land of liberty and freedom, Shane hoped he had buried deeply that cynical apathetic youth of 1985 whose father must have been so disappointed. Perhaps, finally, Shane would be redeemed.

As the void closed in, Shane's fading thoughts swirled chaotically as he agonized whether he might ever join the lovely Sarah on the other side of time.

Just as Shane expected the darkness to swallow him completely, draining his consciousness forever, an unexpected uniform glow grew out of the void—a gradual lightening that had no point of origin. The glow quickly filled the void, but there was nothing material that he could sense. He knew that he existed, but there was no impression of space or time—just being.

It was then that he understood. He was in *Einstein's Tunnel*—that dimension-less pathway connecting all of space-time. In a burst of insight he grasped that he had always been there—where all the infinite time lines intersected—the pathway connecting every Tony Shane *alter ego*.

But that realization lasted for only an instant—perhaps a second, a lifetime, or an eternity—as his consciousness began to merge into a higher plane where there was no past, no future, no present. There was only an all-encompassing awareness of essence, touching an infinite number of replicated beings with limited percep-tions of space and time.

In that last moment of awareness, before Shane's individuality was snuffed out by this higher essence, he experienced the ecstasy of becoming one with every *Tony Shane* that had ever been or would ever be.

EPILOGUE

PRINCETON—MAY 2001

Gen-Agra, the small genetic engineering company in Princeton, New Jersey, had been responsible for producing several varieties of genetically altered food products—including soybeans resistant to the San Joaquin white mold bacteria, Super-juicy™ tomatoes, and Gen-sweet™ corn. None of these products had yet been introduced to the market place, however, as a hysterical public outcry against "Frankenfoods" had halted the FDA approval process. It appeared that it would be several years before commercialization would be feasible.

Strapped financially, the founders of Gen-Agra had turned to a mysterious financier, who had asked them to conduct a secret—and illegal—developmental study. Surprisingly, one of their junior scientists, Andrea Martin, had arranged the connection with the financier. His name was Ahmed Sharif, an obscenely wealthy Arab-American.

Sharif had contacted Andrea after uncovering the classified seminal work that Joseph Rheingold had done years earlier at Lawrence Livermore National Laboratory. Sharif had learned that, before his death, Rheingold had established a trust and willed his personal papers to the granddaughter of his best friend, Harri Kreutzwil. That young lady was Andrea Martin.

Andrea had learned that Sharif was pursuing the trail of genetic evidence for mental telepathy. She was intrigued by what Sharif knew of Rheingold's classified work—including the fact that Rheingold's lab had secretly identified the human gene responsible for telepathic ability. When he had expressed a desire to fund research for genetic enhancement of human telepathic abilities, Andrea had seen an opportunity to achieve her own personal goal—which was just the opposite of Sharif's.

Today, as Sharif visited Gen-Agra for a progress report on the illicit project that was keeping them afloat financially, Andrea was frantically shredding papers that documented results of her personal studies. In the course of Sharif's project, she had isolated a quantity of the gene responsible for human telepathic ability and inserted it into common wheat cells. The resulting transgenic seed had produced wheat that appeared to have all the nutritional properties of the unaltered variety. But Andrea had obtained indirect evidence that brain cells of telepathic centers could be destroyed.

These results would not be presented to Sharif today—or ever. Although there was much more to be done, Andrea believed she had laid the groundwork for bringing the *Einstein Project* to a successful end.

But Andrea was concerned that there was much more to Sharif's agenda. She was puzzled that Sharif had required her to complete a graduate computer science program at Princeton. And she was yet to comprehend the significance of his frequent references to Professor Tony Shane's research at Daniels University.

What was most curious, however, was that Andrea had been drawn independently to Shane's work. Rheingold had revealed to her that Shane had been the messenger, from an alternate time line, that had inspired the search that was defining her life.

Despite these concerns, Andrea knew that her future would intertwine fatefully with those of both Ahmed Sharif and Tony Shane.

DANIELS UNIVERSITY, ROCKVILLE, ILLINOIS— JUNE 2001

Tony Shane, Professor of Computer Science at Daniels University, was frustrated—but hopeful. He had already interviewed three candidates in the past month for the postdoctoral associate position in his research group. Today's candidate, Sarah Stenstrom, was currently completing her Ph.D. in Neural Psychology at UCLA. Shane had not met the young lady previously, but her curriculum vitae was exceptionally strong. Her background in psychology, combined with thesis research in artificial neural networks, made her a perfect fit—on paper— with Shane's research program.

The U. S. Department of Energy was supporting Shane's research developing novel artificial intelligence software. This funding would support several graduate students and a postdoctoral associate, and Shane was looking for a postdoc with expertise in neural networks. What none of his research associates knew, however, was that Shane's DOE work was being shared with the CIA. Shane was a technical consultant for the CIA and was the lead investigator for them on the top secret *StarSight Project*. This project had the long-term goal of predicting terrorist strikes based on computerized interpretation of enormous quantities of seemingly unrelated data documenting global human activities.

As important as the *StarSight Project* seemed to Shane, he was disappointed that it had not received a very high priority within the CIA. If not for the efforts of Senator Gerald Moorhouse, Chair of the Senate Intelligence Committee, the project would not have taken shape at all. Moorhouse firmly believed that Osama bin Laden and al-Qa'eda were the greatest national security threats. He wanted to see the *StarSight Project* on a fast track, but had been frustrated by an administration that appeared to ignore the threat of terrorism. Nathan Carothers, the CIA assistant director in charge of the project had been told to focus on the Russians and Chinese. Nevertheless, through his other position on the Senate Energy Committee, Moorhouse had established a line item in the DOE budget that sustained Tony Shane's research crucial to the CIA.

Sitting in his office on the fourth floor of the Computer Science Building, Shane prepared himself for the two o'clock appointment with Sarah Stenstrom. He went over a mental checklist of questions he would ask, and took one last look at her curriculum vitae. She had already published four papers with her major professor as a graduate student—an exceptional achievement. And she was visiting Rockville today because she had presented a paper the previous day at the National Psychology Conference in Chicago. Today Ms. Stenstrom would give an informal talk to his research group regarding her research at UCLA.

"Dr. Shane, your two o'clock appointment is here," came the announcement from the doorway. It was Sandy Harris, Shane's secretary, sticking her head around the corner.

"Bring her in, Sandy," Shane responded, as he stood up.

Disappearing for a few seconds, the pretty little redhead in the pale blue shirtwaist dress returned leading a tall auburn-haired young lady in a dark pinstriped business suit, carrying a thin leather briefcase. "Dr. Shane, this is Sarah Stenstrom," Sandy said.

As Shane reached for Sarah's hand, Sandy quietly took her leave and closed the office door.

At first distracted by the striking wholesome beauty of the young lady that took a seat in his office, Shane soon forced himself to look past the sultry green eyes and the shapely legs and begin to probe her professional qualifications. It was nearly an hour before Shane reluctantly brought the interview to an end. As if on cue, Sandy knocked on the office door and opened it. Poking her head in, she announced that one of Shane's advanced grad students, Bill Campbell, was there to take Ms. Stenstrom on a tour of the facilities. Her talk was scheduled for four o'clock in the second floor conference room.

As Shane arose from his chair, and Sarah stood to leave, she reached out for Shane's hand and said, "Thank, you, Dr. Shane. Your research program sounds exciting. I'm looking forward to seeing your labs."

"I'm looking forward to hearing how our facilities compare to those in a psychology lab," Shane said. "Perhaps we'll be able to talk about the comparisons over dinner?"

"I'll be looking forward to it," Sarah replied with a sideways glance as she followed Sandy out the door, "very much."

*   *   *   *

As soon as Sarah Stenstrom had left with Sandy to meet Bill Campbell, Shane had closed his office door and phoned his best friend, history professor Harry Churchill. Not only was Harry an academic colleague at Daniels, but he and his wife Luci and their two children were Shane's neighbors. They all lived in the charming old faculty row neighborhood near the football stadium. Shane's bachelor pad was an old tree-shaded two-story frame bungalow standing next to Harry's nearly identical frame and brick structure.

Harry had been at Daniels a bit longer than Shane. A tall black former academic all-American basketball player from Penn State, Harry and his diminutive Vietnamese wife Luci had befriended and adopted Shane. Very few days passed when they did not share conversation and a glass or two of wine after work.

Politically astute, Harry had guided Shane through many bloody academic battlefields at Daniels. And both Harry and Luci had seen Shane through multiple disappointing love affairs. It was the latter aspect of their relationship that prompted Shane to call Harry this day.

"Harry," Shane was saying, "you and Luci have to join me for dinner tonight—my treat! You've got to meet this young lady from California who's interviewing for my postdoc position."

"What's the big deal?" Harry protested. "She win a Nobel Prize or something?"

"Don't be a jerk, Harry. I'm trying to impress her. I think she's the right one for this job, and I don't want her to go someplace else."

"Come on now, Shane," Harry laughed, "you think she's gonna be impressed by some old married history professor? I'm sure she'd rather spend the time with the university's most eligible bachelor."

"Listen to me, big guy," Shane insisted, "I want her to meet Luci...and listen to some of your tall tales. I want her to like this place...and decide to work with me."

"Hmmh," Harry remarked after a few seconds, "sounds serious. What's this gal look like? You got a thing for her, old buddy?"

Shane cleared his throat before replying. "Well, Harry, let's put it this way: I've never seen such a talented piece of merchandise presented in such an attractive package."

"Whew—" Harry whistled. "Now I get the picture." Then, after a silent moment he added, "Alright, Tony. We'll be there. And when it's all over, we'll do a post-mortem back at the house. Luci will give you her verdict."

"Thanks, big guy," Shane responded with a grin. "I owe you one."

After hanging up, Shane twirled around in his chair, stood up, and walked over to the back window overlooking the main quadrangle of the university. With a slight frown he thought *Who is this Sarah Stenstrom? And why am I so intrigued? She seems perfect for this job...but there's something else. I don't know what it is...but I really want to find out.* Then, shaking his head and breaking into a smile, he thought *The next couple years could be very interesting!*

*   *   *   *

Sarah followed her escort through one after the other of Tony Shane's well equipped research labs. But her mind was elsewhere, even as she was introduced over the next hour to a half-dozen of Shane's grad students. She couldn't shake this peculiar feeling of *déjà vu*.

Who was this Tony Shane? Why did he seem so familiar? Or so appealing? It wasn't like her to take to someone so quickly. She had never been comfortable meeting men. *Christ*, she thought, *I've only been intimate with two men in my life!*

But Shane was different. Whether it was his steel blue eyes, or his infectious smile, or his warm friendly style, she did not know. But she had sensed an instant attraction. She hoped it hadn't been obvious...but how could she have hidden the flush that she felt? Surely, Shane must have sensed something.

Did he feel something too, she wondered? Or was she reading too much into his enthusiasm? Perhaps his attention could be attributed to professional courtesy...nothing more, she worried.

But then, as her escort finally returned Sarah to Shane's office—and she enjoyed once again that crooked little-boy smile of welcome—she knew!

Sarah Stenstrom knew where she would be for the next very important chapter in her life.

AUTHOR'S NOTES

The framework for this fictional story is grounded in historical facts surrounding the outbreak and conduct of the Second World War. Many of these facts have been included in the story. The fictional portrayal of international conflicts and alliances that might have occurred during and after the war—given a successful German atomic bomb effort—are totally speculative, of course. Another author, given the same mix of known historical characters and conditions, could easily postulate a very different course of events. Hopefully, history buffs will find this author's hypotheses at least tolerable, and not be distracted from enjoying the fictional adventure that is the heart of the book.

Many individuals mentioned in this fictional story are real historical figures: Einstein, Szilard, Fermi, Roosevelt, Churchill, Heisenberg, Hitler, Himmler, Rommel, Stalin, Tojo, and others. Only Heisenberg, Hitler, and Einstein are portrayed as active characters in the story. Of these, I have taken the most liberties with Einstein's portrayal. I've simplified his theoretical concepts and put words in his mouth that he might never have uttered. But that is the license of historical fiction. Nevertheless, I have tried to portray a character consistent with a wealth of documented anecdotes. For those who admire and respect his heritage as I do, I hope you will find this treatment of Professor Einstein sympathetic.

Time travel fantasies have a way of introducing subtle paradoxes and inconsistencies if one digs too deeply. The reader should not let these concerns detract from enjoyment of the underlying human drama and the fanciful vision of alternative time lines that are the heart of this tale. Hopefully, the provocative political, historical and philosophical concepts will overshadow the science fiction devices used to present them.

There are several fictional technological devices used in the story: computer-enhanced telepathy, telepathic time travel, loyalty detector machines, genetic engineering, and others. Except for time travel, each of these is based loosely on imaginative projections of existing technology. The origins of telepathic time travel concepts can be found in the writings of numerous science fiction authors, particularly of Robert Heinlein, to whose inspiration this author is greatly indebted.

Readers of the previous books in this trilogy—*The StarSight Project* and *Crisis on Flight 101*—will appreciate that the time travel element introduced in the second adventure of the trilogy has allowed the construction of a circular story line. These readers will recognize that the ending of this book leaves the main characters roughly where they were at the beginning of *The StarSight Project*. Or does it? Intervention in past events has a way of messing with things in strange and remarkable ways. Stay tuned.

S. P. Perone
September, 2004

0-595-32682-X